COAL
RIVER

Books by Ellen Marie Wiseman

THE PLUM TREE

WHAT SHE LEFT BEHIND

COAL RIVER

Published by Kensington Publishing Corporation

COAL
RIVER

Ellen Marie Wiseman

KENSINGTON BOOKS
www.kensingtonbooks.com

KENSINGTON BOOKS are published by

Kensington Publishing Corp.
119 West 40th Street
New York, NY 10018

All Kensington titles, imprints, and distributed lines are available at special quantity discounts for bulk purchases for sales promotion, premiums, fund-raising, educational, or institutional use.

Special book excerpts or customized printings can also be created to fit specific needs. For details, write or phone the office of the Kensington Sales Manager: Kensington Publishing Corp., 119 West 40th Street, New York, NY 10018. Attn. Sales Department. Phone: 1-800-221-2647.

Kensington and the K logo Reg. U.S. Pat. & TM Off.

eISBN-13: 978-1-61773-448-9
eISBN-10: 1-61773-448-9
First Kensington Electronic Edition: December 2015

ISBN-13: 978-1-61773-447-2
ISBN-10: 1-61773-447-0
First Kensington Trade Paperback Printing: December 2015

10 9 8 7 6 5 4 3 2 1

Printed in the United States of America

For my darlings,
Rylee, Harper, and Lincoln—
I love you beyond words

In loving memory of our dear friend Billy

ACKNOWLEDGMENTS

Once again, it is with great joy that I express my appreciation for the people who helped, supported, and believed in me during the writing of this book.

To my readers, my online supporters, and the people who live in and around my community, thank you for your warm encouragement and continued enthusiasm. It truly means the world to me.

A thousand thanks to my friends and family for allowing me time to write and meet my deadlines, for celebrating my victories, and for always being there when I need to crawl out of the writer cave. Trust me when I say it is your friendship and steadfast love that make writing a novel possible.

To my mentor, William Kowalski, thank you for giving me the foundation I needed to continue down this path, and for always being in my head when I write. You have my deep, deep respect and gratitude always.

Thank you to my amazingly talented BP family for keeping me sane. We've been on quite a journey these last four years, and I thank my lucky stars that we continue to experience the highs and lows of this business together.

Heaps of love and appreciation go out to my friend and cosmic sister, Barbara Titterington, for reading an early draft of the manuscript and for understanding the way my brain works. Together, we feel the world.

Again, my sincere thanks go to my wonderful editor, John Scognamiglio, for your support and continued faith in me, and to everyone at Kensington for your hard work behind the scenes. I'm very fortunate to have such a fantastic team on my side.

I owe the genesis of this story to my agent and trusted friend, Michael Carr. Thank you for your brilliant advice, for working so hard to help make this novel stronger, and for continuing to be all I could ask for in an agent. To say I'm grateful for your wisdom and guidance would be an understatement.

As always, from the bottom of my heart, thank you to my beloved mother and father, Sigrid and Ted, for your unwavering love, support, and friendship, and to my husband, Bill, for your unfaltering belief in me. You are my best friend and my greatest champion. Finally, I want to express my infinite love and gratitude to my children, Ben, Jessica, Shanae, and Andrew, and my precious grandchildren, Rylee, Harper, and Lincoln. Thank you for loving and believing in me. You are my reason for being.

CHAPTER 1

Coal River
1912

On the last day in June, in the year when the rest of the world was reeling from the sinking of the *Titanic,* nineteen-year-old Emma Malloy was given two choices: get on the next train to Coal River, Pennsylvania, or be sent to a Brooklyn poorhouse. The doctor had released her from the Manhattan hospital, the Catholic church had donated a small suitcase with a few items of clothing—along with a proper mourning dress, undergarments, a hand brush, and a bar of soap—and her aunt and uncle had sent money for a ticket. After less than an hour to decide, she walked on shaky legs from the hospital to the station in what felt like a trance, said good-bye to the nurse, climbed the passenger car steps, and found her seat. The nurse had said Emma's escape from the deadly theater fire was a miracle, and she should be forever grateful for this second chance. The only thing Emma knew for sure was that she was an orphan now. It didn't matter what happened to her, or where she went. Just like her late brother, Albert, her mother and father would be with her everywhere. There was no escaping this wretched grief, this horrible, heavy pain in her chest.

Two days later, when the train exited the long tunnel beneath Ash Mountain and started across the timber trestle above Coal River, the tiny thorns of nerves prickled across Emma's skin. She had vowed never to return to the isolated mining town named after the black river that roiled through it, and yet here she was, barreling helplessly toward constant reminders of another day she'd give her life to forget.

Outside the train windows, the full weight of summer's heat bore down on Pennsylvania's interior, making it feel as if the world and everything in it were roasting inside a giant wood stove. Trees drooped beneath the blazing sun, their withered leaves already scorched yellow around the edges. It hadn't rained in over a month. Still, the black river beneath the train trestle was deep and swift, boiling along its rocky banks like poisoned pottage. Upstream, the shoreline was wild with trees and brambles, fit for neither man nor beast. In the distance, jagged mountains sloped down toward the riverbed, their steep cliffs cutting off the only other exit out of the valley.

Emma pictured the tiny vial of dark liquid in her drawstring purse, stolen from her hospital bedside when the nurse wasn't looking. She longed for the bitter taste of tranquility on her tongue. But only a few sips of the laudanum remained, and she didn't want to waste them. Lord knew she would need the medicine to get through the next few days. She dug her nails into the cloth armrest of her seat, counting the seconds until the passenger car was back on solid ground. *Maybe everything has changed,* she thought. *Maybe this time Uncle Otis will be different. Or maybe I'm just nervous because the train is high on a trestle, hundreds of feet in the air.* She wanted to believe those things. With all her heart. But she wasn't good at telling herself lies.

When the train finally reached the other side of the river, she ran a finger inside the high collar of her mourning dress, the bombazine like gravel against her sweltering skin. In the roasting passenger car, the heavy sleeves and tight neckline felt like a straitjacket or a suit of armor, despite the fact that the garment was several sizes too big. Certainly, some people still believed proper etiquette called for a grieving daughter to wear black for a full year, but why did "mourning costumes" have to be so stiff and restrictive? As if grief weren't cruel enough.

How she longed for her sailor dress with the loose waist, or a pair of summer trousers. If it were up to her, she would have removed her corset and the cotton slip beneath her skirt and tossed them out the train window within the first few minutes of the trip. She would have rolled up her sleeves, unpinned her hat, and taken off her stockings. But remembering the unsettled glances of the other passengers when she'd unpinned her weeping veil from her hat and stuffed it inside her handbag, she resisted.

Because Emma's childhood had been spent around people in show business—actors dressed as Vikings and pirates, ghosts and beggars, nuns and Egyptians—she never understood why some people judged others by what they were wearing. In the theater, no one gave it a second thought when she handed out playbills or ran around the neighborhood in sporting pants, newsboy caps, or boys' shirts. Granted, wearing flat shoes and knickers on her petite frame made her look more like an adolescent boy than a young woman on the verge of adulthood, and wearing her waist-length, nutmeg-colored hair in one long braid instead of rolled up in the latest styles made her look years younger. But bloomers and corsets made it hard to ride a bike through Central Park, and heels and skirts made it impossible to climb the theater catwalk to watch rehearsals. Her mother used to joke that she had two sons instead of one, and her father said she looked like a life-sized, porcelain doll, with tiny hands, a button nose, and Cupid's bow mouth. His little Lilliputian, he used to say. Her parents wouldn't have cared if she'd taken off the mourning dress and changed into her old clothes.

Then she remembered that the dress she was wearing, along with the broadcloth skirt, the shawl-collared blouse, and the muslin nightgown in her tattered suitcase, were the only clothes she owned. All the rest, including her sailor dress and her favorite pair of knickers, were gone. Burned to ashes in the fire.

The fire. The words felt like a knife in her heart.

Laughter and conversation faded in and out inside the passenger car, droning in her ears with the clack of iron wheels and the pounding of the locomotive. In a few minutes, when the train came to a stop, she would have to stand up and get out. That was it. There was no reason to think beyond that. Breathing was hard enough. Then the train braked and shuddered, turning a wide, slow curve as it approached the village station, and the valley opened up before her like a black and white sketch from a child's schoolbook.

Surrounded by peaks stripped nearly bare of trees and foliage, the village of Coal River sat huddled on the edge of Bleak Mountain, a sprawling congregation of wooden houses, shops, stone buildings, and saloons. Slag roads and dirt footpaths led through and around the community, then traveled out through the canyons and valleys, up into the miners' village and beyond, zigzagging across the earth like the dark legs of a giant spider.

Near the base of the center peak, the nine-story coal breaker of the Bleak Mountain Mining Company loomed above a church steeple, perched above the town like an enormous creature hunched over the earth, its black nostrils spewing streams of dark smoke. The breaker looked like a hodgepodge of different-sized structures piled on top of one another, as if new buildings were added every year with no mind to how each new addition would fit with the others. Rows of multipaned windows lined each story, and at the top was a curious little peak, like a miniature house added at the last minute. Leading up to the highest floor, a railroad trestle rose up from the ground, reminding Emma of the Switchback Railway ride on Coney Island, the one attraction she refused to step foot on because it was so high. Surrounding the breaker lay the rest of the colliery: smoke stacks, a labyrinth of buildings and sheds, railroad tracks and pipes, roadways and steam engines. Piles of mine waste smoldered around the outskirts of the mining site, emitting a thick, white smoke. At night, as a child, Emma used to imagine the red, blue, and orange glow coming from the burning culm banks were the fires of hell.

Farther up the mountain to the right, dirt paths and rows of miners' houses lined a vast hollow. Emma had never been up to the miners' village, but she used to envy the children living there, away from the pomp and rigidity of Coal River's upper class. She imagined them running in the grass and climbing trees, staying outside until dusk, sipping lemonade on the porch in their bare feet. Aunt

Ida would have scorched her ears if she had taken her shoes off outside or climbed a tree and stained her dress. Her aunt expected pinkies up at tea and made her walk with books on her head to improve her posture. Emma couldn't count the number of times she'd fantasized about running away with her brother and hiding in the miners' village until her parents came back from Manhattan. Maybe if she had, Albert would still be alive.

A flash of red caught her eye to the left, and when she glanced that way, she felt another jolt of dread. Near the north end of town, a three-story mansion stood on a hill surrounded by pine trees and manicured lawns, its red roof gleaming in the afternoon sun. It looked exactly the same, down to the marble fountain in the front yard. Her arms broke out in gooseflesh. Then the train depot blotted the mansion from view.

The train slowed, and the iron wheels caught and screeched, caught and screeched. The passengers stood and gathered their belongings, eager to exit after the long journey. Emma stayed in her seat and peered out the window at the station, a burning lump in her throat. The platform was crowded with people—men in waistcoats and straw hats, children in their summer whites, women in traveling dresses, cooling themselves with paper fans. A group of policemen in peaked caps and knee-length military jackets stood on the left side of the station, Winchesters held to their chests, blocking a mob of scowling miners in shabby coats, newsboy caps, and worn derbies. Everyone looked miserable and hot.

Emma considered staying on the train, continuing on to the next destination, or turning around and going back. But back where? Home? Her parents' tiny apartment above the theater was gone, destroyed in the fire along with everything in it. Besides, she didn't have another train ticket. The only thing in her handbag was the laudanum, an empty change purse, and her weeping veil.

She bit down on her lip and scanned the waiting crowd for Uncle Otis. Then she saw him standing opposite the police, talking to a young man in a morning suit and top hat. Her uncle was tall and wiry, the skin on his face and hands pulled tight over his bones, like a side of beef left out to dry in the sun. Streaks of gray lined his horseshoe mustache and mutton-chop sideburns. She thought how terribly old he looked, hard and ravaged by age and a love of whiskey.

If nothing else, the train ride had given her time to come up with a plan, one that might help her escape Coal River. If she played her cards right, it might seem like a good idea to Uncle Otis too. She hoped it would anyway. No, she prayed it would, even though she'd stopped praying after Albert died. If her plan failed, she didn't know what she would do. She couldn't spend the rest of her life in this place.

Outside on the platform, the man in the top hat nodded in response to Uncle Otis while searching the train windows, his narrow eyes scanning every car. His lanky, bowlegged frame looked familiar and strange at the same time, as if Emma had met him in another lifetime. Then she recognized the flat, pallid face, like a board with a nose and bulging eyes. It was her cousin, Percy, all grown up. She groaned inside. Percy was still here. Percy, who used to follow her around like a puppy, until she bloodied his lip and told him to leave her alone. Percy, who short-sheeted their beds, and led them down to the river the day Albert drowned.

Emma felt the blood drain from her face as a terrible image assaulted her mind—her eight-year-old brother in his red cap and winter boots, his eyes wide when the ice gave way, his bare hands clawing the slippery surface for something to grab hold. She could hear his screams, his terrified voice yelling her name. And then he was gone, washed away by the swift, cold current of Coal River. The look of horror and confusion in his eyes before he disappeared had burned itself into her memory, haunting every moment since.

She blinked against her tears, struggling to push away the thought of him trapped below the ice, his dark curls stirred by the current, his eyes empty and sightless. It was almost more than she could bear. *You were only ten. You warned him not to go out on the ice.* And then, in the next instant: *He was down by the river because of you.*

She touched the spot below her neck where her mother's silver locket had hung before it disappeared beneath the ice with Albert, and a sudden falling sensation swept over her. She grabbed the edge of her seat to stay upright. She had been prone to nervous spells since waking up in the hospital four days ago, but this particular bout swept over her with a savage wave that made her nauseous and dizzy. What was she doing, returning to Coal River? How could coming back to her aunt and uncle's house, where she and Albert had spent four miserable months while their parents looked for new jobs in Manhattan, possibly put right her ruined life? Then another thought came to her, a thought that made her stomach cramp.

Maybe I'm being punished.

The train shuddered one last time, jerked to a final stop, and let out a blast of steam, jolting the standing passengers back into their seats. Emma stood on shaking legs, ran her hands down the sides of her stiff dress, and picked up her suitcase. She waited until the last passenger had left the car, then lifted the heavy hem of her too-long dress and headed toward the exit, her heart slogging in her chest. She felt like she was watching herself from someplace else, in a dream or on a moving picture screen. Then she stepped off the train and covered her mouth, the sulfuric, rotten egg odor of burning culm confirming the awful truth. She had returned to Coal River.

After Albert died and her parents had taken her back home to Manhattan, she smelled the culm on her clothes for months, no matter how many times her mother washed them. For years, the stench of burning mine waste swirled through her nightmares, emanating from her pillowcase in the morning like a cloying, phantom perfume. Then one day it was gone, and she thought she'd never have to smell the wretched odor again.

Now, she tried not to gag, shaking her head when the baggage handler offered to take her suitcase. The other passengers milled about, carrying their luggage, waving and calling out to waiting friends and relatives. She stood on her tiptoes, trying to see over shoulders and backs, searching the crowd for Percy and Uncle Otis.

Two cars down, a group of men in worn jackets and work pants exited the train, their faces somber. The miners shouted at them to go back where they came from, and started throwing rocks and sticks in their direction. The police shoved the miners backward, yelling at them to simmer down. One of the miners broke through the line and started toward the train. Four police aimed their rifles at the rest of miners, while three others grabbed the escapee, pushed him to the ground, and wrestled his arms behind his back. Emma ducked and hurried toward the station, one hand on her hat, trying to remember where she saw her uncle. Suddenly, a strong hand closed over the handle of the suitcase and she turned, ready for a struggle. Percy smiled and pried the luggage from her grip. He tipped his top hat in her direction. His eyelashes were so light, they were nearly invisible, and his hair was such a bright shade of blond, it looked white.

"Hello, Emma," he said. "I'm sorry you've returned to Coal River under such sad circumstances, but it's so good to see you."

She nodded once. "Percy," she said.

Just then, a miner in a tattered coat broke through the police line and headed toward Uncle Otis, his face contorted with rage. A policeman caught him, wrapped an arm around his neck, and dragged him backward across the train platform. A second policeman hurried over to help, handcuffing the man's wrists behind his back.

"What in the world is going on?" Emma said.

"Everyone is restless these days," Percy said. "It's the heat."

"But why are the miners throwing rocks at those men?"

He glanced over his shoulder, as if noticing the disturbance for the first time. "Those men are new immigrants," he said. "The miners think they're here to take their jobs." He extended his elbow, asking permission to escort her through the crowd. "Shall we?"

She lifted the hem of her skirt and reluctantly took his arm. "I suppose."

"You look exactly the same," he said. "That is, I mean to say, you look wonderful."

She gave him a thin smile and searched the faces of those around her to avoid his probing eyes. No doubt he was surprised she was still so small in stature, despite the fact that nine years had passed since her last visit. She wondered how long it would be before he made fun of her for being so short. He ushered her through the crowd, using her suitcase to nudge people out of the way. Near the ticket window, Uncle Otis was talking with a policeman, his face red, his brow furrowed.

"Take down the names of anyone who gives you trouble!" he said.

"Yes, Mr. Shawcross," the policeman said.

"Father," Percy said. "Look who's arrived."

Uncle Otis smiled and opened his arms. "Welcome back, Emma," he said. "I'm sorry about your parents, but it's a pleasure to see you."

"Hello, Uncle," she said. She clenched her jaw and turned her cheek to let him hug her.

"My God, woman," he hissed in her ear. "Where is your mourning veil? Have you no decency?"

She drew away and gripped the edge of her handbag, twisting the drawstring between her fingers. "I removed my veil on the ride here," she said. "It was too cumbersome to wear the entire trip."

"Well, now that you've arrived," Uncle Otis said, forcing a smile, "you must put it back on before riding through town."

She shrugged. "I'm afraid that's impossible," she said. "The train was unearthly hot, and when I opened a window, the veil was sucked right out."

Uncle Otis frowned. "I don't have time for this right now," he said. "I've got my hands full with these miners. Take her up to the house, Percy, then come back for me. Tell your mother to get her settled in."

"Yes, sir," Percy said.

Uncle Otis started to move away, then stopped and turned to face Percy again. "Take the side roads," he said under his breath.

Behind him, a group of miners broke through the police line and rushed across the platform, shouting obscenities at the incoming immigrants. The police charged forward and pulled them back a second time. Uncle Otis stormed toward the commotion, arms flailing. A shot rang out and Percy grabbed Emma's arm, urging her through a door and across the station.

On the other side of the train depot, the dirt road was filled with horses, buggies, pedestrians, wagons, and bicycles. A yellow Tin Lizzie sat at the edge of a plank sidewalk, its high, white wheels stained gray, its gold head lanterns and low windshield coated with a fine, black powder. Like everything else—the surrounding buildings, the windows, the sidewalks, the store canopies, the telephone poles, the ground—the car was shrouded with coal dust. Percy opened the passenger door and helped Emma climb into the vehicle. She wrestled the black sea of her skirt into the car and settled it around her feet, then sat in the front seat and looked around.

A few yards away on the opposite side of the thoroughfare, a young boy in an oversized cap and frayed jacket sat slumped against a telephone pole covered with sooty flyers, his empty stare locked on the passing people and horse-drawn wagons. His face was puffy and pale, his sunken eyes the color of silver. His hair was dark and thick, like Albert's, and his left leg was withered and encased in a metal brace. His tattered boots and the ends of his crutches hung over the edge of the sidewalk, sticking out into the road.

Behind him, two older boys sat smoking cigarettes on a wooden box, their backs to the street. A policeman marched across the road and kicked the end of the boy's crutches, shouting and pointing at him to move back. The boy struggled to stand while the policeman waited for him to obey. Emma started to climb out of the car to go over and help, but before she could get out, the older boys pulled him to his feet, and the three of them wandered away.

Percy lifted her suitcase into the backseat, then climbed in the driver's side and started the engine. He took off his top hat, stretched a pair of goggles over his eyes, and put on a driving cap.

"Ready?"

She nodded, one fist over the knot in her stomach. Percy pulled the vehicle away from the sidewalk and steered it along the busy road, swerving around wheel ruts, honking at slow horses and wayward children. On the plank sidewalks, women stopped to watch them pass, whispering behind gloved hands. Policemen patrolled every other block, strolling the sidewalks and streets with rifles strapped to their shoulders. A few raised hands in greeting. Others walked with their heads down, spitting tobacco juice on the ground or smoking cigarettes.

Emma didn't recall the streets being filled with police the last time she was here. She thought about asking Percy why there were so many, but the engine was loud and she didn't feel like talking. As they drove through town, she was dismayed by how little things had changed. She felt like she'd gone backward in time and everything and everyone was still here, frozen and waiting for her return.

The two-story Company Store looked exactly the same, with brick chimneys, peeling red clapboards, and black shutters. A gathering of old codgers still sat in rocking chairs and stools on the slanted porch, whittling or playing checkers on overturned barrels. The burned-wood sign to the garbage dump was still nailed to the mule barn, and potholes still filled the narrow road leading past the village green.

Up ahead on the sidewalk, an old woman with white braids doddered toward them, hunched over as if she were about to pick something off the ground. Beside her, a young boy thumped along on wooden crutches, one empty trouser leg tied shut. Emma stiffened. The boy could have been Albert's twin. He had the same thick shock of black hair, the same sprinkling of brown freckles across his nose, the same buckteeth. As Percy drove past, she turned in her seat, unable to tear her eyes from the walking apparition. The boy stared back at her with solemn eyes, his head turning on his neck. Then he stopped and scowled as if he recognized her.

The icy fingers of fear clutched Emma's throat. Was it all just a horrible nightmare? Had Albert been alive all this time, trapped in Coal River and waiting for her to come back and rescue him? But why hadn't he aged? And what happened to his leg?

Then the boy turned and kept going, seemingly unfazed by the encounter. Emma faced forward, a hollow draft of grief passing through her chest. The falling sensation returned with such force that she had to resist the urge to grab Percy's arm to keep from swooning.

No, she thought. *Albert is dead. I saw his frozen body after it was pulled from an ice jam beneath the train trestle. I saw his small coffin lowered into the ground in Freedom Hill Cemetery on that bright winter day. I felt the bone-chilling wind shriek down from Bleak Mountain. I watched my mother sob in my father's arms. It can't be him.*

She took a deep breath and held it, trying not to panic. Was this how it was going to be? Was every little boy in Coal River going to remind her of Albert? Were they all injured or maimed? Or was she finally, once and for all, losing her mind?

Maybe she should have taken her chances in the Brooklyn poorhouse after all.

CHAPTER 2

Percy's Model T sputtered up the steep grade of Flint Hill, and the trees fell away on both sides of the road. On the right, Emma could look down on the center of town. On the left, the Flint Mansion overlooked all of Coal River. Perched high on a manicured lawn, the Italian-style manor was massive and rambling, with low roofs and wide eaves, a multilevel porch surrounding the two bottom stories, and cast-iron railings painted white to match the ornamental trim. At the house's highest peak, an oversized, octagon cupola sat above the red tile roof like a miniature lighthouse.

A chill passed through Emma. She shivered, staring up at the mansion and wondering if a house could put a curse on people. The scandal and death connected with the mansion occurred several years before her birth, but it had instantly become a tragic tale that would be ceremonially passed down from generation to generation.

The story of Hazard Flint and his wife, Viviane, was the closest thing Coal River had to a local legend. Viviane, the sole heir to the Bleak Mountain Mining Company, had married Hazard Flint in an arranged marriage when she was barely sixteen. Two months later, her parents died in a train wreck on their way to Chicago, and Hazard took over everything. According to the mansion help, he was mean-tempered and crass, controlling his pretty young wife along with the mining company. After their son, Levi, was born, Viviane insisted on separate bedrooms. Five years later, when she gave birth to a second boy, everyone wondered if Hazard had changed his ways, or if Viviane was having an affair. Then the nursemaid and the stable hand kidnapped the six-day-old infant and left a note in his cradle, demanding ten thousand dollars for his safe return. As instructed, Hazard left the ransom money in the alley behind the blacksmith shop, but the newborn was never seen again.

Rumor had it that Hazard was the one who found Viviane, hanging from the rafters in the cupola in the summer of 1889. On the cedar floor beneath her feet was a suicide note and a tear-stained letter saying she couldn't go on without her baby. From then on, the youth of Coal River had tortured themselves with stories of a female ghost standing at the copula windows, waiting for her son to come home. Over the years, many a local boy had been thrown off the property for climbing the trellis outside the nursery window, trying to look inside the baby's room, which was said to be untouched since the day he'd disappeared.

Emma could still picture the dark-paneled hallways, the Persian carpets and oversized furniture, the hand-painted portraits lining the walls. She could still smell the old wood and plaster, like sawdust and cold oatmeal in her mouth. Why hadn't she found another way out all those years ago? Maybe if she'd snuck out a side window or porch door, Albert would still be alive.

She thought back to that winter, when Percy and his friends dared Albert to break into the mansion. They had been teasing him for weeks, making fun of his city clothes and calling him "sissy boy" because of his thick curly hair. Then one day, on her way home from buying potatoes at the Company Store, she saw Percy and his friends peeking over the snow-covered hedgerow in front of Flint Mansion, snickering and taking wagers on whether or not the boy who went inside would get caught. When Percy told her they'd promised to stop calling Albert names if he stole something from the nursery to prove he'd been inside, she threw the sack of potatoes at him and ran up the sidewalk to rescue her brother.

She tiptoed across the garden porch, slipped in through a back door, and snuck through the summer kitchen into a back hallway. Midway down the corridor, a door stood partly open, and a soft, rhythmic voice drifted down the hall, as if someone were reading out loud. Keeping close to the wall, she edged forward and peeked around the doorframe, her legs vibrating. Inside the room, an older woman and a pale, dark-haired boy sat at a mahogany table, their heads bent over an open book. It was a tutor and Viviane's first son, Levi, who, according to Aunt Ida, was practically kept prisoner because Hazard Flint was terrified of losing him too. Emma crossed to the other side of the hall and hurried past, wondering how upset Mr. Flint would be if he knew how easy it was to sneak into his mansion.

She found Albert upstairs in the nursery, crying and shaking next to a cobweb-filled cradle, a dusty rattle in his hand, the front of his pants wet with urine. She pried the rattle from his grasp, tossed it back into the crib, and led him out of the room. On the way downstairs, Albert insisted over and over that Viviane's ghost had appeared in the nursery mirror, pointing a gnarled finger at him. She was wearing a white nightgown and a noose around her bruised neck. Her tongue was hanging from her mouth, black and swollen.

Trying to keep her brother quiet, Emma took the fastest way out of the mansion: through the main hallway and out the front door. Percy and his friends were waiting at the end of the sidewalk. They laughed and pointed at Albert's wet knickers, and mocked him when he swore he saw Viviane's ghost. When Percy pushed him to the ground, Emma punched Percy in the nose. Then she grabbed her brother by the coat, pulled him up, and turned to leave. But before they could get away, Percy caught her by the arm, yanked her mother's locket from her neck, and ran. She chased him and his friends down the road, Albert on her heels. Her brother begged her to stop and let them go, saying Percy would bring the locket home later. But she ignored him and kept running. The boys went down to the river, and she followed. When they stopped on the shoreline, Percy held the locket out of her reach, laughing. She kicked him in the crotch, and he dropped the locket in the snow. Then one of Percy's friends grabbed it and threw it out on the ice. And Albert went after it.

Emma struggled to push the memories away, blackness washing over her.

Percy noticed her looking up at the mansion and slowed the car. "Hazard Flint still lives there!" he shouted above the engine.

She fixed her eyes on the road, her mouth dry as dust.

"Levi too," Percy said. "He works for Mr. Flint. Only a matter of time before he inherits everything."

Emma said nothing. She felt like she was trapped inside a nightmare, and morning was never coming. Maybe she died in the fire after all, and this was hell. Percy pressed the gas pedal, wrenched the gear lever into low, and steered the vehicle up the steep hill toward his parents' house.

Uncle Otis and Aunt Ida lived in a yellow, three-story Queen Anne with a corner tower and gingerbread trim. The property was far enough from the mine to avoid the invisible rain of coal dust, and tall pines, mountain laurel, and lilac bushes surrounded the vast yard. Potted ferns and wicker furniture lined the round porches, and black-eyed Susans grew along the front fence. Percy parked the car in the driveway, helped Emma down from the vehicle, and pulled her suitcase from the backseat. Emma looked out at the view, which stretched for several miles in all directions.

The town of Coal River sprawled below, with Main Street and the village green centered in the middle of the valley. Houses and buildings gathered in haphazard groups, huddled between roadways and yellowed meadows. The red roof of Flint Mansion gleamed in the midday sun, like a basin of blood in a sea of brown. To the east, Coal River flowed beneath the train trestle, black and roiling, like a low band of thunderclouds wrapped around the earth. In the distance, the mountain ridges looked like waves of gray smoke in the sky.

Inside the house, they found Aunt Ida in the dining room, overseeing the setting of the dinner table. Like every other room in the three-story Victorian, the space was filled with oversized mahogany furniture, glass figurines, vases, oil paintings, rugs, and doilies. It seemed as though the decorations had doubled since Emma's last visit. Aunt Ida was wearing a layered violet dress and a cameo at her throat, almost certainly real ivory, surrounded by a band of gold so thin, it was nearly invisible. How many times had Emma seen that cameo in her nightmares, floating above her on the icy banks of Coal River? How many times above Albert's dead body? At the side of his grave?

At the table, a gray-haired woman in a maid's uniform folded peach-colored napkins, carefully placing them beneath the silverware. Arthritis gnarled her hands and distorted her knuckles. She dropped a spoon, and Aunt Ida snatched the napkins from the maid's hand, her lips puckered in irritation. Then Ida saw Percy and Emma coming through the doorway, and her features softened. She set the napkins on the table and moved toward them with outstretched arms.

"Emma," she said, her voice catching. Ida was Emma's maternal aunt, but you'd never tell by looking at her. While Emma's mother had been fair and willowy, Aunt Ida was short and round, her chestnut hair parted down the middle and pulled back, accentuating her moon-shaped face. "Come here and let me give you a hug, you poor dear!"

Emma wrapped her arms limply around her aunt. Aunt Ida pecked her cheek, then released her and stood back, tears wetting her fleshy cheeks.

"I can't believe my sister is gone," she said. "And under such horrible circumstances!" She pulled a handkerchief from her sleeve and dabbed her eyes. "God knows we had our differences over the years, but she was still my sister. I loved her."

Emma's chest tightened. "She loved you too."

Behind Aunt Ida, the gray-haired maid caught her shoe on the leg of a chair and dropped a tumbler onto the floor. The glass hit the thick rug with a muted thunk, then rolled toward the hem of Ida's skirt. In one quick movement, Emma stepped forward, picked up the glass, and handed it to the maid. The old woman nodded once, giving her a weak smile of gratitude.

"What in tarnation has gotten into you, Cook?" Aunt Ida said, her hands on her hips. "I swear you're getting clumsier by the day!"

"I'm sorry, ma'am," Cook said. "I'll try to be more careful from now on."

"You better," Aunt Ida said. "Now that my niece is here to help, you might just find yourself out of a job!"

"Yes, ma'am," Cook said. She set the tumbler on the table, folded the last napkin, and hobbled out of the room.

Aunt Ida stuffed her handkerchief back into her sleeve, then looked Emma up and down. "What in heaven's name are you wearing, child? That dress looks like something out of my grandmother's closet. Not to mention it's much too big!"

"I know it doesn't fit properly," Emma said. "But it's all I—"

"Maggie!" Ida shouted over her shoulder, making Emma jump. When Maggie didn't respond right away, Aunt Ida shook her head and frowned. "Maggie, come in here this instant!"

From the back of the house, footsteps rushed down a flight of wooden stairs. A few seconds later a young girl hurried into the dining room, her face flushed. "Yes, Mrs. Shawcross?"

"See to it we have enough material to make new dresses for my niece," she said. "She'll need one for everyday, one for housework, and two for going out."

"Yes, Mrs. Shawcross," Maggie said. "I'll run to the dress shop first thing in the morning."

Aunt Ida turned to face Maggie. "No. You'll run to the dress shop right now."

"Yes, Mrs. Shawcross." Maggie curtsied and hurried out of the room.

"Why don't you let Emma get settled before you try to fix something about her, Ma?" Percy said.

"It's fine, really," Emma said, forcing a smile. "But if you don't mind, nothing too fancy, please. I like to keep my clothes comfortable and simple."

Ida laughed. "Now, don't you fret none about that," she said. "We're not going to spend good money dressing you up like a little doll. These are hard times, Emma. It's enough that we've agreed to put a roof over your head, don't you think?"

Emma nodded, heat rising in her cheeks.

"Shall I show Emma to her living quarters so she can freshen up?" Percy said.

"No, no," Ida said. "I'll do it. Go and fetch your father. Dinner will be ready in a half hour."

"Yes, Ma," Percy said. He nodded once at Emma and left.

Aunt Ida hooked an arm through Emma's and led her out of the dining room into a hall, one pudgy hand patting her wrist. They crossed the hall and went through the sitting room, where Aunt Ida used to stand over Percy while he practiced the piano, swatting him upside the head when he hit the wrong key. No matter how hard he tried, Percy made mistakes during every song. Once, when no one was in the room, Emma lightly touched the keys, trying to play the song, "Oh My Darling, Clementine" by ear. But like a shot, Aunt Ida stormed in and nearly shut the cover on Emma's fingers, warning her never to touch the piano again. She never did.

When they entered the parlor, Emma's throat started to close. She knew seeing the room again would bring back painful memories, but she'd hoped it had been rearranged or redecorated in the past nine years. It looked unchanged. She could still picture Albert's small body, laid out for viewing beneath the brass chandelier. Black ribbons and violets had hung from every door, crepe had covered all the mirrors, and the hands on the clocks had been stilled. Emma had said nothing when her aunt insisted she pose next to her brother for a mourning portrait. Then she stayed in the darkened room, refusing to sleep, eat, or leave his side until her parents came back from Manhattan. Instead, she waited in a wingback chair in the corner, watching tiny droplets of river water fall from Albert's thawing body and darken the Persian rug beneath the bier.

When she finally saw her parents coming through the parlor door, she held her breath, unable to move, certain they would never speak to her again. Then they approached Albert, her mother with trembling fingers over her mouth, her father's face twisting in grief, and Emma finally stood.

"Mama," she said, and her legs collapsed beneath her.

Her mother ran across the parlor and caught her, dropping to her knees and hugging Emma to her chest. When Emma started to shake and howl, shedding tears for the first time since her brother drowned, her mother held on tight, telling her over and over that everything was going to be all right. Her father ran his hand over her cheeks, begging her to be strong, because they couldn't bear it if something happened to her too.

Emma had no idea it was possible to cry so hard you could barely breathe, your sobs bursting from your throat as if they were coming from the bottom of your soul. She remembered wondering briefly if it was possible to lose your mind at ten years old. Then her parents died in the fire and she'd fallen apart all over again, certain the sheer agony of losing them would kill her. That time, she'd been in a white hospital room with a stone-faced doctor and a glassy-eyed nurse standing at her bedside, with no one to hold her, no one to tell her everything would be all right, no one to kiss her sweaty brow. Thinking about it now, a fresh wave of grief nearly brought her to her knees.

"Emma?" Aunt Ida said, bringing her back to the here and now.

She blinked. "I'm sorry. What did you say?"

"I was wondering what you thought of the new drapes," Aunt Ida said proudly, as if she had made them herself. "The old ones were so old and faded, I just had to get rid of them!"

"They're very nice," Emma said, trying to sound like she cared. As far as she could tell, the curtains looked exactly the same as they did nine years ago.

Aunt Ida led her through the white-tiled kitchen toward the rear of the house, their footsteps echoing on the floorboards. They moved through a door into a short hall, then started up the steep, narrow stairway toward the servants' quarters.

"I do hope you'll forgive me," Aunt Ida said. "But the room you and . . ." She hesitated, pausing on the steps. "Oh, mercy me. I can barely say his name without feeling faint."

"Albert?"

"Yes, your poor brother, Albert. God rest his soul." She crossed herself and continued up the stairs. "Such a shame. And with his whole life ahead him. Now my poor sister is gone too." She shook her head, her face crumpling in on itself. "I'm sorry," she said. "It's just . . . It's all too painful for me. I never imagined my life would turn out so sad."

Emma gripped the banister tighter. "I know what you mean."

"There's just so much wretchedness in this world," Aunt Ida said, sniffing. "It can be terribly hard on a sensitive person like me. I wish I didn't have to see or hear about people suffering. That's why I try to focus on happy things, for my own sake."

If only it were that easy, Emma thought. Then she remembered the boy slumped next to the telephone pole, and Albert's twin with the missing leg. "Speaking of suffering," she said. "May I ask you something?"

"Of course, dear," Aunt Ida said. "Anything."

"On the way here, I saw two young boys in the village," she said. "One was missing a limb, and another had a leg brace. Do you know what happened to them?"

Aunt Ida stopped on the stairwell again. She put a hand over her brooch. "Oh dear," she said. "You mean those poor breaker boys?"

"Breaker boys? Who are they?"

Aunt Ida held up a finger, indicating that Emma should stop speaking. "Please," she said. "It's much too depressing for me to talk about right now. We've had enough sorrow for one day, don't you think?"

"Yes, ma'am," Emma said.

Her aunt continued climbing the stairwell, wheezing with the effort. Then she smiled, her mood suddenly turning. "As I was saying, the room where you and Albert stayed last time has been converted into a sewing room. And Maggie is the most fabulous seamstress. Wait until you see the beautiful dresses she makes for me! Anyway, there's no longer enough room for you in the main part of the house."

"That's fine," Emma said. "I don't need much."

In truth, Emma was relieved. The bedroom she had shared with Albert would be filled with memories of playing hide-and-seek in closets and beneath beds, peeking out the windows to spy on Percy when he was being tutored in the backyard, competing at Pick-Up Sticks and Twenty Questions when Uncle Otis locked them in their room during dinner parties. It would be too hard to stay in there.

At the top of the steps, Aunt Ida led her down a narrow, white-washed hall and stopped in front of a squat door. She paused, trying to catch her breath, then said, "Most of the help has been let go because we just can't find good people anymore." She pointed toward the end of the hall. "The water closet is down there. Now, mind you, you'll have to share it with Maggie and Cook, but it should be sufficient." She pulled a ring of keys from her apron pocket and unlocked the door. "I'm certain you'll have all the space you need right here."

Inside the narrow room, a single bed with an iron headboard sat pushed against one wall, the mattress covered with a brown wool blanket. Opposite the bed, a six-paned window overlooked the side yard. There was a wooden washstand, a blue dresser, a spindle-back chair, and a green threadbare rug covering half the plank floor. Yellow wallpaper with tiny roses covered the back wall. The other walls had been painted white.

Emma forced a smile. "It's perfect," she said.

"I'm delighted you think so," Aunt Ida said. "I was so afraid you'd be upset because you're not in the main house with us."

"Not at all. It's bigger than my bedroom was back in Manhattan." Emma set down her suitcase, unpinned her hat, and laid it and her purse on the bed. "But if you don't mind, the train ride was exhausting. I could use a little rest."

"Right now?" Aunt Ida said, wrinkling her nose as if she smelled something rotten. "But your uncle will be expecting you at dinner! You know how he gets when—"

"I'm sorry," Emma said. "You're right. I'll freshen up a bit, then I'll be right down."

Aunt Ida tented her hands beneath her chin as if praying, and shook them. "It's for the best," she said. "We have a lot to talk about, Emma. This is your home now, and your uncle has certain rules and expectations. You don't want to start off on the wrong foot."

"Of course not," Emma said. Nerves prickled the skin around her lips. She gripped the door handle and started closing the door, ushering Aunt Ida backward into the hall.

"Twenty minutes," Aunt Ida said. "No longer."

"Yes, ma'am."

"Remember what your uncle always says," Aunt Ida said. "Clocks were made for a reason!"

"Yes, Aunt Ida. I remember."

The door clicked shut, and Emma took a step back, staring at the white knob, trying to keep her wits about her. It was no use. Panic clawed at her insides like a cat inside a sack. With shaking hands, she tore open her drawstring purse, yanked out the mourning veil, and grabbed the glass vial. She pulled out the stopper and took a tiny swallow of the bitter liquid inside. Then she took off her shoes and collapsed on the bed. Closing her eyes, she put her hands over her face, homesickness and grief washing over her in torrential waves.

After a few long, unbearable minutes, she felt the laudanum slithering through her veins and muscles, loosening the crush of anguish inside her chest. When she thought she could trust herself to sit up without feeling dizzy, she swung her legs over the bed and stood. She unbuttoned the long sleeves and high collar of the mourning dress, undid the waistband, and slipped the garment over her head. The skirt's underwire caught in her hair, and for a minute she was stuck. Finally she ripped the heavy garment over her head, tearing out a small clump of hair. Tears of pain sprang up in her eyes, and she blinked against a new flood of despair. She removed her petticoat, untied her corset, and took off her stockings.

Finally able to breath, she opened her suitcase and retrieved the copy of the *New York Times* from the inside pocket—given to her by a nurse before she left the hospital. She sat down on the bed, turned to the page featuring the list of theater employees who had died in the fire, and read her parents' names for the hundredth time.

Back in Manhattan, when she and her father used to walk past the offices of the *New York Times* at One Times Square, he always joked that the only time he'd get his name in the paper was after he was dead. When that day came, he used to say, he wanted her to remember that he had lived the life he wanted, and that he loved her more than anything on Earth. No matter how much she missed him after he was gone, he wanted her to look forward, toward the rest of her life, and make the choice to be happy.

The black and white print blurred on the page, and Emma tried to make the choice to be happy. It didn't work. She returned the newspaper to the suitcase and slipped off her chemise.

At the nightstand, a thin towel hung from a wrought-iron hook, and a bar of lavender soap sat on top of a folded washcloth. She lifted the pitcher and was relieved to find it full of water. She filled the washbasin and rinsed her face, then used the washcloth and soap to clean her arms, hands, and neck, scrubbing three days' worth of grime and sweat from her skin. How she longed to soak in a tub of hot, soapy water, to wash her dirty hair and relax her tired muscles. But there wasn't time.

She finished washing, unpinned her hair, brushed the snarls out of it, and worked it into one long braid, leaving it free to hang down her back. She put on her petticoat and the broadcloth skirt, unbuckled the belt and tied it around her waist to keep the skirt from falling off, then put on the baggy, shawl-collared blouse and her only pair of shoes—lace-up boots with heels and pointed toes. Then she took a deep breath, opened the bedroom door, and went downstairs.

CHAPTER 3

They sat beneath a gas chandelier in the dining room, tiny, flickering flames reflected in the walnut-paneled ceiling. Uncle Otis was at the head of the table, Aunt Ida to his left and Percy to his right, wine bottle in hand, studying its label. Aunt Ida had insisted that Emma be seated next to Percy to avoid having to shout along the length of the outlandishly long piece of furniture. Behind Aunt Ida, platters of roasted beef filled the sideboard, along with bowls of green beans and pickled beets, and a basket of fresh-out-of-the-oven tea rolls. Nearly nauseated by the thought of eating, Emma would have been happy with a glass of cool water. The only beverages on the table were wine, coffee, and hot tea. To her dismay, the small sip of laudanum was already beginning to wear off, leaving her with the heightened sense of feeling trapped. She thought about having a glass of wine, but was afraid she wouldn't stop drinking once she started. All she could smell was warm dust drifting up from the Persian carpet. She wanted to ask if she could open one of the three tall windows, but thought better of it.

The dark wood walls and an enormous canvas painting above the stone fireplace heightened the feeling of suffocation. The portrait showed the Shawcross family, Uncle Otis in a black suit and plaid tie, sitting in a ladder-back chair, looking bored. Aunt Ida stood beside him in a red gauze dress, her bosom corseted nearly up to her double chin, one hand on Uncle Otis's shoulder. A young Percy stood in the center, wearing a white sailor suit with a blue collar, his chubby legs like sausages stuffed inside navy leggings, his face pale as a ghoul's.

Emma thought back to the day her parents left her and Albert in Coal River while they went back to Manhattan to look for new jobs. On the wagon ride back to her uncle's after dropping them off at the train station, she held her mother's locket so hard, the edges nearly cut her fingers. Then, later, at this very dinner table, Uncle Otis informed her and Albert that from that day on, they would be expected to earn their keep. After all, he had taken them in after their parents lost their jobs in New York, and they'd already stayed twice as long as planned. The next morning, Albert polished shoes while Emma scrubbed the bathroom floor on her hands and knees, Aunt Ida standing over her to make sure she rinsed twice. Every day after that, Emma polished the silver, folded the linens, swept the rooms, and pressed the clothes while Albert slopped the hogs, split and hauled wood, and cleaned and filled the oil lamps.

Once, during a winter thaw, Uncle Otis sent Emma up a ladder to wash the outside of the second-story windows. She begged him not to make her do it, and Albert even offered to do the job in her place. But Uncle Otis refused his offer, insisting Emma face her fears. When she froze at the top of the ladder and couldn't climb back down, he sent the stable hand up to rescue her. As punishment, he withheld her supper for the next two days, accusing her of weaseling her way out of the job. A week later, when Albert forgot to lock the hog pen, Uncle Otis forced him to kneel on a corncob in the mudroom for three hours, then told him to "buck up" when he limped into the kitchen with red and swollen knees.

Now Emma had to face Uncle Otis alone, without Albert to make faces behind his back during his nightly lectures and angry rants. How would she get through this without her brother?

"While she's living in this house," Uncle Otis said, "she must wear the proper mourning clothes!"

"Her mourning dress is too big," Aunt Ida said. "Even the outfit she's wearing now is too loose. I don't think her parents made enough money to buy proper attire for the poor thing. God rest their souls."

Emma opened her mouth to respond, but Uncle Otis interrupted.

"Then have a new one made for her! It's bad enough she's sitting at my table with no respect for her dead parents. I won't tolerate it in public." He yanked his napkin from beneath his silverware, wiped his brow with it, then stuffed it into his vest like a bib.

"The rules are changing, Uncle," Emma said, her fists in her lap. "In the city, women are turning away from wearing black during mourning. Now, it's gray or purple, or even mauve. My mother only wore a mourning dress for a week after my brother died. Albert knew she loved him, so it didn't matter what she wore."

"Maybe it's that way in the city," Uncle Otis said. "But this is Coal River, and I won't have you bringing disgrace to our family."

"Of course she won't, dear," Aunt Ida said, patting the tablecloth beside her husband's plate. "I'll make sure she has a proper mourning dress for going out. If you really think that's the right thing to do."

Uncle Otis scowled as if tasting spoiled meat. "Have you lost your mind?" he said. "Of course it's the right thing to do."

"I'm not so sure about that," Aunt Ida said. "I'm starting to think it might be a bad idea for Emma to go waltzing around town in her funeral garb."

"Horseshit!" Uncle Otis said. "I won't listen to such talk!"

Aunt Ida pursed her lips. "Please," she said. "There's no need for foul language."

Uncle Otis sighed heavily. His shoulders dropped, and he gazed at his wife, his eyes suddenly soft. "I'm sorry, my pet," he said. "You know I trust your opinion, but this time you're wrong. You can see that, can't you?"

"Just hear me out before you say another word," Aunt Ida said. "You know how miners are. They're a superstitious lot. And there's already been gossip at the Saturday ladies' luncheon that Emma might be bringing bad luck to Coal River."

Emma winced as though struck. "Me?" she said. "But why?"

Uncle Otis rolled his eyes. "You've got to stop listening to those old hens," he said to his wife. "They haven't got anything better to do than tittle-tattle and peck at one another."

Aunt Ida shook her head. "No, no," she said. "It's not just the ladies over at church. Mary Fergus said she heard Asa Clark talking to the fire boss over at the post office. Seems he's worried about checking the mines before the workers come in. Everyone thinks Emma is cursed, on account of her brother drowning in the river and her parents dying in that horrible fire. They're worried she's bringing it with her to town."

Emma swallowed and looked down at her plate. Pinpricks of light from the chandelier reflected off the silverware and china. It was hard enough being forced to come back to this place, hard enough struggling to get through every minute. Now the whole town was turned against her?

"Albert wasn't the first person to drown in Coal River," she said.

"True enough," Aunt Ida said. "But he was the most recent. And now your parents are dead too, and they died in such an awful way. . . . Well, it seems you've been labeled something of a bad omen."

"But that's absurd," Emma said. "I—"

"Mother is right," Percy said. "Miners are suspicious. They sit in the same spot every day to eat lunch, or with the same friends in the same seat on the cars going into the mines. They refuse to move or start a new shaft on Fridays. Some think it's bad luck for a woman to enter a mine because she might put a curse on it. They say it's bad enough to work so close to Satan's domain without a possible witch practicing black magic on them. Some even think it's bad luck to meet a woman on their way to work in the morning. They'll turn around, go back home, and start over."

"Surely you don't believe all that," Emma said.

"What does it matter if I believe it?" Percy said. "The miners do. Those men hear sounds in the mines and immediately think they're hearing ghosts."

"It might sound like a lot of poppycock," Otis said, "but don't dismiss the miners so quickly. They have their wisdom. Even about rats."

"What about rats?" Emma said.

"Miners never kill a rat in a mine because they can hear the sound of splintering timber and cracking rock before humans can. If the men see rats panicking and heading up the slopes, they follow. Rats will always abandon a mine if a cave-in is about to happen or poisonous gases are present."

"Same with mules," Percy said.

"Right," Otis said, nodding. "Mules have an instinct for impending disaster. Many a mule has lead a miner to safety just in time."

"I don't know about the miners," Aunt Ida said. "But you brought Emma here the same day the new immigrants arrived. Some of the foremen and their wives are starting to wonder if you've got the mine's best interest at heart. We need everyone to see Emma as the innocent girl she is, a victim of life's circumstances. She should pretty herself up a bit and dress in light, carefree materials, like a young woman on the cusp of a new life."

Uncle Otis tapped his fingers on the table, thinking. "But everyone knows she's in mourning," he said. "What would we tell them?"

Aunt Ida reached for her wineglass, smiling like a fox. "We'll tell them Emma's parents were stars of the stage. We'll say they went to all the big city fashion shows and were on top of the latest styles. You heard Emma. People in the city don't dress in black these days. No one around these parts will admit they're not up-to-date on those things. You leave everything up to me. I'll get everyone to come around."

Uncle Otis shrugged. "All right, dear," he said. "I'll let you handle this."

"That's right," Aunt Ida said. "Sometimes I wonder what you would do without me." She smiled and tapped her cheek, indicating Otis should give her a kiss. He stood, leaned over the table, and did as he was told.

Percy glanced at Emma, embarrassed by his parents' display of affection. His ears turned red around the edges.

Uncle Otis directed his attention back to Emma. "On account of the rules changing, you have my permission to stop wearing black."

Emma nodded, her nails digging into her palms. She had

planned on waiting a few days before attempting the plan she had come up with on the train, but maybe this was the perfect time.

"I feel horrible causing so much trouble for all of you," she said. "But I might have a solution if you're willing to listen."

Uncle Otis raised his eyebrows. "This ought to be good," he said. He took a sip of wine and set down his glass, looking at her expectantly.

"What is it, Emma?" Aunt Ida said. "Have you come up with a way to help everyone take a liking to you?"

Emma cleared her throat, ignoring her aunt's remark. "Back in Manhattan, I was working in the theater box office and attending classes part-time to become a teacher. I really don't want to be more of a burden to you than I already am, so I thought, if I could get a little help . . . to go away to normal school—"

Aunt Ida coughed, as if choking. "You want to go away to school?" she said, eyes wide. "Do you have any idea how much that costs?"

"Yes," Emma said. "But you're already spending so much money by taking me in and putting a roof over my head. You're having clothes made for me, and sharing your food. I'm certain there's a normal school here in Pennsylvania. It might be cheaper to send me there than to—"

Aunt Ida leaned back in her chair and laughed, a small bitter sound, like a baby pig caught in the mud. "Well, don't you worry about that," she said. "You're going to help out around here. You didn't think we were going to house you and feed you for free, did you? How are you going to earn your keep if we send you off to school?"

"I could pay you back when I'm finished," Emma said, struggling to keep her voice even. "After I got a teaching job. I could—"

"Maybe she brought a suitcase full of cash with her on the train," Uncle Otis said, laughing.

"Or maybe, because we live in a real house and have nice things, she thinks we're made of money," Aunt Ida said.

"Of course she does," Uncle Otis said. He eyed Emma. "Just like her parents thought we were made of money when they left her and her brother here for four months while they had a high time of it in Manhattan."

Aunt Ida's face fell. A hot coil of anger twisted beneath Emma's rib cage. She started to respond, but her aunt interrupted.

"Oh no," Aunt Ida said, wagging a finger at her husband. "You leave my sister out of this. I won't stand for you speaking ill of the dead in my house."

"Your house?" Uncle Otis said. "Last I checked, I was the one going to the mines six days a week!"

"Here we go," Percy said, rolling his eyes. He finished the wine in his glass.

"Now, you listen here, Otis Shawcross," Aunt Ida said. She leaned toward him, practically coming out of her chair. "You might go to the mines every day, but while you're gone, I'm here running this household and making sure you have clean clothes on your back and warm food in your belly. So don't you sit there and act like I'm eating bonbons all day while you—"

"Enough!" Emma shouted, slapping both hands on the table. Uncle Otis and Aunt Ida stopped short, their shocked faces snapping toward her. "Please! I'm sorry I brought it up!"

Aunt Ida settled back into her chair. "Well, I'm sorry you brought it up too," she said. "It's just a ridiculous notion. From now on, think before you speak."

"Your aunt is right," Uncle Otis said. "You can put going to school right out of your head, young lady."

Emma chewed on the inside of her cheek, blinking back tears. Maybe she should ask for a train ticket back to New York. Maybe she could find a job there as a maid or a waitress, and look for a roommate to share a cheap room. She berated herself for not doing that in the first place, before ever stepping foot on the train. Then she remembered waking up in the hospital, learning her parents were dead, and being given a choice between the poorhouse and Coal River. She had been in shock, indifferent to what happened next. Besides, the doctor wouldn't have released her to wander the streets alone. And no one would have hired a penniless girl wearing a donated, oversized dress, let alone paid her enough to rent a decent room. She had seen the seven-cent lodging house on Manhattan's Lower East Side. She had seen the back alleys of the tenement houses, and the beggars outside the pauper barracks. Surely, she would have ended up in one of those places, or worse. She had come back to Coal River because there was no other choice.

Aunt Ida sighed. "Now that we've gotten through all that unpleasantness," she said, "let's eat, shall we? Heaven knows I took a lot of time and trouble to plan this nice meal to welcome you, Emma. The least you can do is let us enjoy it in peace."

Uncle Otis patted his wife's hand and exhaled, blowing out his breath with more force than necessary. With a nod from his mother, Percy muttered a short grace. Silence followed as Cook went around with the beef, stooping over at each place, scraping the serving fork across the china platter.

"Any more trouble with the new immigrants?" Percy asked his father.

Uncle Otis finished his wine, then twirled the stem of the crystal goblet between his boney fingers. "The Irish are settled in the kettle," he said. "And the Germans and the Italians are in the boarding house for now. The Coal and Iron Police warned the miners to leave them be. But we'll bring in more police if we have to."

"Do you think they'll strike?"

"Probably not until the end of summer, when the weather turns and people need coal to heat their homes through winter."

"What about Clayton Nash?" Percy said. "He still up to no good?"

"Can't be sure," Uncle Otis said. "Word has it he's trying to arrange secret meetings with the rest of the miners. Can't have more than four nonfamily members gathered at a time or he's breaking the law."

Emma looked at her uncle, confused. When did it become illegal to hold a meeting of four or more people in the United States of America? The idea that everything and everyone in Coal River was frozen in time returned. Or maybe they were just backward.

"Nash doesn't care about the rules," Uncle Otis added.

"Do you think he's trying to reorganize the union?" Percy said.

"You can bet he's trying," Uncle Otis said. "But if any of them start that kind of trouble, they'll be out of a job and run out of town so fast, it will make their heads spin. A hundred men are ready to take their places at any time. I just got word that two hundred Germans are in Scranton, waiting for work. And those immigrants are willing to do just about anything for a job, no matter how dangerous."

"But if they go on strike and scabs break the line, all hell will break loose," Percy said.

"You just go to work and let me worry about that," Uncle Otis said. "It's not going to have any effect on your job."

"But it does have an effect," Percy said. "If the miners aren't getting paid, they won't have money to spend in the Company Store."

"That's right," Aunt Ida said. "And if production drops, what's going to happen to us? I've got five reams of satin and a half a cow coming next month. How are we going to pay for everything if there's a strike and you get laid off?"

Uncle Otis threw his hands in the air. "Jesus, Mary, and Joseph!" he said. "Before you send yourself into a conniption fit, try to remember I'm the mine supervisor!"

Aunt Ida frowned, furrows of disapproval lining her forehead. "Otis," she said, her tone firm. "How many times do I have to remind you to watch your language?"

Uncle Otis ignored his wife's remark. "You stay out of it and let me worry about the miners. I'll let you know if and when we need to worry about anything!" He got up, went over to the sideboard, filled a tumbler with whiskey, and drank it down in three noisy swallows. Then he refilled the glass, brought it back to the table, and sat down, his face tight with anger.

"I'm sorry, dear," Aunt Ida said. "You're right. Now, please, calm down and eat your dinner before you give yourself indigestion." She glanced at Emma. "Speaking of jobs, I have a list of chores for you."

"Yes, ma'am," Emma said. She took the saltshaker from Percy, wishing her aunt and uncle owned dogs so she could slip her food beneath the table.

"Percy could use help at the store," Uncle Otis said.

Emma's eyes darted to her uncle, her spirits lifting a tiny bit.

The last thing she wanted to do was work with Percy, but maybe, if she had a paying job, she could save enough money to go back to New York and start over.

"That's true," Percy said, chewing. He wiped his napkin across his mouth, then returned it to his lap. "But I need a man who can work hard, not a woman."

"And I need help here," Aunt Ida said. "Around the house."

"What do you mean you need someone who can work hard?" Uncle Otis said to Percy. "How difficult can it be to push numbers on a cash register?" He shoved a forkful of meat into his mouth, breathing hard as he chewed.

"Percy does more than run the cash register," Aunt Ida said. "And you know it. He works hard at that store. And for not much pay, I might add!"

"I'd be happy to work at the store," Emma said.

"I need someone strong enough to unload stock," Percy said to his father. "It's hard stocking shelves, doing orders and paperwork, and trying to wait on everyone. More than once the deliveryman got tired of waiting and left me without mattress ticking for nearly two weeks. Another time it was lantern oil. I'm the one who has to listen to everyone moan and groan when we don't have what they want."

Otis ignored him and addressed his wife. "What in blue blazes does Percy need more money for? It's not like he's got a house and a family to take care of. He's not even courting anyone. Last I looked, I was the one taking care of him!" He directed his scorching gaze at Percy. "And you listen here, boy. Coal mining is hard work. Don't you ever try telling me about hard work."

"You know Percy can't tolerate the wet conditions and all that dust," Aunt Ida said. "The doctor said—"

"I know what the doctor said!" Uncle Otis shouted. "You've been telling me for the past six years what the doctor said. But there are men working in those mines every day with the same problems Percy has. Difference is, they don't have a choice. The boy is twenty years old, but you treat him like a child, keeping him at home, making sure he doesn't bend a fingernail. Now let's talk about something else. I'm not going to sit here listening to my wife and excuse-for-a-son tell me about hard work. I'm the only one in this family who under-stands hard work!"

Aunt Ida swallowed, her face growing crimson. She put her hands on the tablecloth on either side of her plate, taking slow, deep breaths. After a minute, she cleared her throat and looked at Emma. "Perhaps you can work around the house a few days a week," she said. "Then help Percy at the store on the other days. And it only makes sense that your paycheck goes into the household funds. You have to earn your room and board, just like Percy does."

Emma's heart dropped. "Yes, ma'am," she said.

"Does that seem fair to you, dear?" Aunt Ida asked her husband.

Uncle Otis bit into a buttered tea roll and wagged a finger at Percy. "You let Emma run the cash register while you unload and put up stock," he said. "It won't kill you to do the heavy lifting."

"Have you ever run a register, Emma?" Aunt Ida said.

"Just the one in the box office," she said. "But I'm a quick learner. And I can help stock shelves. I'm not afraid of hard work." If nothing else, at least working in the store would get her out of the house.

"That's good, darlin'," Aunt Ida said.

Uncle Otis snorted. "Maybe if your father hadn't been afraid of hard work, your parents would still be alive."

Emma went rigid, breaking out in an instant sweat.

"Not now, dear," Aunt Ida said. "My nerves are already fixing to give out."

"Just think," Uncle Otis said. "If Emma's father had taken me up on my offer to work in the mines, they wouldn't have died in that fire. They could be sitting here right now, having dinner with us."

"Please," Aunt Ida said. "What's done is done, and there's no going back. We did our best to get them to stay in Coal River. They made their own choices. And now we're all left behind to . . ." She lowered her head, pushing her napkin into the corners of her eyes.

Emma held Uncle Otis's gaze. "My father was a hard worker," she said, struggling to keep her voice even. "And so was my mother. They were artists, painting scenes and making costumes for the the-ater. They loved their jobs, and they were putting every spare penny into my education. They wanted to live in Manhattan because there were more opportunities. . . ." Her throat closed and she dropped her eyes, blinking back tears. Then she swallowed and found her voice again. "Just because my father didn't want to spend his life in a hole in the ground making someone else rich, doesn't make him lazy. If anything, it makes him smart."

Uncle Otis's mouth fell open, anger darkening his brow.

"I'm sure that's not what your uncle meant," Aunt Ida said quickly. "It's just . . . well . . . it always seemed like what we had to offer was never good enough, even though we had more than your parents ever dreamed of. And now. Let's just say we must all remember to bow down before the Lord and be grateful for what we've been blessed with instead of looking elsewhere for satisfaction. Otherwise . . ." Aunt Ida shook her head.

Emma pushed back her chair and stood. "May I be excused?" she said. "I'm not feeling well."

"What is it?" Aunt Ida said. "You're not taking sick, are you?"

Percy leaned away from Emma, his napkin over his nose and mouth. "She did just come out of a hospital," he said. "You don't suppose you caught something, do you?"

Emma shook her head. "No," she said. "It's nothing like that. It's probably just the heat. Or maybe it's the small-minded people in this room." She wrapped her arms around herself and headed toward the door. Behind her, Aunt Ida started crying.

"I told you it wasn't a good idea to bring her here," Uncle Otis said. His tone was withering, and there was no doubt it was directed at Emma. She walked out, feeling his burning eyes on the back of her head.

CHAPTER 4

The day after Emma's arrival in Coal River was payday for the miners, and the Company Store stayed open later than usual. After supper, when most of the miners' wives would be finished shopping, Aunt Ida took Emma down in the wagon to get the weekly supplies—flour and sugar, lantern oil and lye soap, buckwheat and salt. She had a list, and Emma was to learn it by heart.

The evening sun was hard and bright, baking the earth and turning the already brown grass brittle. The motionless air smelled of warm wood, burning culm, and horse manure. Emma's acorn-colored skirt soaked up the heat, roasting her inside.

Last night, Aunt Ida's seamstress, Maggie, had taken apart and reconstructed Emma's secondhand clothes, shortening the hem of the broadcloth skirt and taking in the bodice of the shawl-collared blouse. Today Maggie was making her some new outfits, including an everyday housedress, a visiting costume, and a flowing pink tea dress. On one hand, Emma didn't want the new clothes, knowing everything she took from her aunt and uncle would need to be re-paid with interest, one way or another. If she could get by without eating, she would. On the other hand, she looked forward to having something cooler to wear.

Since this morning, she had pinned three loads of clothes to the line, snapped green beans on the back steps, patched and ironed trousers, and mopped the summer kitchen floor after Cook tracked in mud from the chicken coop. Aunt Ida supervised her every move, giving her instructions on how to work faster and more efficiently. On the ride into town, her aunt delivered a sternly worded lecture after Emma left her gloves at home, snapping the horse with a whip when she wanted to stress a point.

"Gloves are to be worn at all times on the street, at church, and at other formal occasions," she said. "Unless one is eating or drinking."

"My mother never made me wear gloves," Emma said.

"Well, you're my responsibility now that your mother is—"

"Don't," Emma said.

"Don't what?"

"Don't ever speak of my mother again."

"Oh, for heaven's sake," Aunt Ida said. "How many times do I have to tell you your uncle is sorry for last night? He didn't mean to upset you. You know how he gets sometimes. And it's even worse when the miners are restless."

"And you?" Emma said. She unbuttoned her collar and rolled up her sleeves, ignoring her aunt's disapproving glances. The horse was moving at a good clip, and she wanted to take advantage of the breeze. "Are you sorry for what you said?"

Aunt Ida pulled back on the reins and brought the wagon to an abrupt halt. Emma had to grab the edge of the seat to keep from falling out.

"Me?" Aunt Ida said, her voice high. "What have I done? I only want what's best for you, can't you see that?"

"It seems to me like you only want free help," Emma said before she could stop herself.

Aunt Ida gasped. She dropped the reins in her lap and fished a white handkerchief out of her sleeve, her eyes filling. "Lord almighty," she said. "I've never been treated so poorly for trying to help someone in my entire life. Don't you know you're like a daughter to me? The daughter I never had?"

Emma sighed. There was no point in telling Aunt Ida anything. She was too busy seeing the splinter in everyone else's eyes while being blind to the beam in her own. Emma tried to swallow her anger, but it got stuck in her throat. "I'm sorry," she said, forcing the words out. "Please, just forget I said anything."

Aunt Ida wiped her nose, sniffling. "I know we've got some adjusting to do," she said. "So I'll accept your apology. But please, consider others' feelings before you speak. And button your collar and roll down your sleeves before someone sees you."

Emma ignored the request. Instead she picked up the reins and flicked them lightly, clucking her tongue to get the horse moving again. "I thought you were going to teach me how to drive?"

Aunt Ida took the reins. "Not yet," she said. "When you start working at the store, you can walk and Percy will bring you home, along with any items on my list. I need this wagon at my disposal at all times. I never know when I might need to run into town."

When they reached the Company Store, Aunt Ida stopped the wagon on the edge of the dusty road, then waited for Emma to tie the horse to a hitching post. When she had finished, Emma helped her aunt down from the seat and followed her along the plank sidewalk toward the entrance. Two women came out of the store, talking and laughing. The younger one carried a wicker basket covered in a red-checkered cloth, and the older woman held a brown paper package beneath one arm. There was no mistaking they were mother and daughter, with matching upturned noses and rainwater blue eyes. The daughter wore her blond hair in long ringlets that spilled over her shoulders like a yellow mane. The mother wore her mouse-colored hair in a Gibson girl bun, gray streaks running up from her temples and the middle of her forehead. They both wore pastel-colored dresses, the mother in baby blue, the daughter in lavender.

"Good evening," Aunt Ida said.

The women began to respond, then gaped at Emma as if noticing her for the first time. They looked her up and down as if a girl with an open collar and bare forearms were someone to fear. After a short, awkward silence, they came to their senses and said hello.

"Emma," Aunt Ida said, smiling a little too hard. "You remember Sally and Charlotte Gable, don't you? Sally is a dear, dear friend of mine from way back. Her husband, Grover, is the inside boss over at the mine. And pretty Miss Charlotte was one of Percy's childhood playmates."

Emma didn't remember either of them. The last time she was here, she was only ten, and back then the only thing she cared about was when her parents were coming back to get her and Albert. *Not to mention the fact that most of my memories are buried beneath the horrible specter of my brother's death,* she thought. But nothing good would come from contradicting her aunt. "Nice to see you again," she said, extending her hand.

Charlotte took a step back, and Sally gripped her package tighter, her face going dark. They stared at Emma's bare, outstretched hand as if it were a poisonous snake.

"Oh," Sally said. "You're the one who . . ."

Emma withdrew her hand. So it was true. The whole town was talking about her.

"You know," Charlotte said. She leaned toward her mother and lowered her voice. "There was another accident up in the breaker yesterday."

"Oh my," Aunt Ida said, anxiously fingering her cameo brooch. "I heard. Isn't it the most dreadful thing?"

"Ripped a boy's arm and leg clean off," Charlotte whispered. "Bled to death before anyone could get help."

Emma's stomach turned over. *What was a boy doing inside the breaker? Is that what Aunt Ida meant when she said the breaker boys?* She opened her mouth to ask, but Sally interrupted.

"Hush, Charlotte," Sally said, a flash of warning in her eyes. She looked at Emma, her face a mask of feigned pity. "We're terribly sorry about your parents. What a horrible way to—"

"I think the breaker accident happened at the same time Emma's train pulled into the station," Charlotte interrupted.

"Enough!" Sally snapped. "You're tempting fate by talking like that!"

Emma bit down on her tongue. *Are they blaming me for the boy's death?*

"That's nonsense," Aunt Ida said, chuckling nervously. "It was a coincidence, nothing more. My niece has had a streak of bad luck, that's all. But now that she's here with us, I finally have the chance to lead her down the right path. Everything is going to be fine from here on out. Isn't that right, Emma?"

So this was how it was going to be. Everyone was going to act like she had typhoid or yellow fever. She forced a smile and gave Charlotte's wrist a friendly squeeze, pressing her fingers into the exposed skin between her sleeve and white glove. The blood drained from Charlotte's cheeks, and Sally made a small gasping sound, like a dying mouse.

"It was lovely to see you again," Emma said. "Perhaps we can get together for tea and girl talk soon. You too, Mrs. Gable." She let go and went around them, brushing a hand along Sally's arm as she passed. Then she hurried through the store entrance, humiliation burning like a fever in her cheeks.

The bell over the door jingled, and the screen slammed shut behind her. She stood on the other side of the threshold for a moment to let her eyes adjust to the murky interior. The dark-chocolate aroma of coffee mixed with the underlying tang of aged cheese and old wood reminded her of the corner bakery in Manhattan where she and her father used to buy bread every Saturday morning. Along with the bread, her father always bought two petits fours, one for her and one for her mother, a special treat for the women he loved. Thinking about it now, a gnawing ache filled Emma's chest. She thought about turning around and waiting in the wagon, but she'd have to pass those dim-witted women. Besides, Aunt Ida had brought her here to help.

Percy looked up from behind the cash register on the far side of the store. He wore a white apron over a dark suit and a sleeve garter on his right bicep, like the barber who used to cut Emma's father's hair. A spindle of twine hung from the ceiling above his head, and a stack of wrapping paper sat beside the register, along with a wheel of cheese under a glass lid, and a coffee mill. On this side of the counter, a woman stood with her back to Emma, a mewling baby on one hip, a little girl with bare feet and dirty legs at her side. The hem of the woman's floor-length skirt was threadbare and worn, her mutton-sleeved blouse stained and wrinkled. Her short hair was dirty and matted, making it hard to discern the color. The girl turned to look at Emma, her wide eyes like miniature oceans in her pale face, her blond hair stringy beneath a muslin bonnet turned gray with age. Her dress was two sizes too big, its waist held up by a soiled rope. Just looking at her, Emma could feel the girl's misery—year after year of doing without, month after month spent shivering in the winter cold, night after night of trying to sleep with a stomach filled with nothing but hunger pains.

On the other side of the room, three boys in patched knickers and dog-eared caps stood in front of the candy counter, counting their coins and eyeing the glass jars filled with horehound drops, licorice, peppermint sticks, and Necco Wafers. Soot blacked their faces, and their hands were the color of mottled stone. The oldest boy looked to be seven or eight. He reached over to remove one of the candy jar lids.

"You boys, wait until I'm finished here!" Percy shouted.

The boy replaced the lid and turned his back to the register, putting his hands in his pockets and mumbling to his friends. He scuffed his boot on the floor and eyed Percy over his shoulder.

Emma wandered down the first aisle, the oiled floor groaning and creaking with every step. She remembered coming here as a girl and wishing for more time to look at the plethora of goods, but her aunt had always warned her not to dawdle. Now it seemed as though the store's inventory had doubled.

General merchandise and household goods filled this side of the room: clothespins, floor wax, buckets, brooms, ironing boards, mixing bowls, wooden spoons, coffee mills. The other side held groceries: bins of flour, sugar, salt, dried beans, spices, and canned goods. The center of the store was lined with counters and racks of men's work shirts and trousers, women's stockings and blouses, children's jumpers and underwear. Near the back was a wall of draperies and bed linens, a corner section of soaps and lotions, and another corner for sewing notions like pins, thread, and material. Teakettles and dishpans, pots and iron skillets, funnels and hurricane lanterns, coffeepots and buckets, washtubs and washboards, pitchers and baskets hung from the ceiling. A potbellied stove sat in the middle of it all, surrounded by chairs, spittoons, and wooden barrels filled with pickles, salt herring, various seeds, and potatoes.

Emma made her way to the back room and saw it was filled with hardware, farm and garden tools, kegs of nails, horse collars, horseshoes, harnesses, ax handles, shovels, stovepipe, wire fencing, and a kerosene tank with a hand pump. Another room held chickens, chicken feed, bags of fertilizer, egg crates, and coils of rope, along with an assortment of machine and carriage bolts, wood screws, garden plows, stoneware crocks, and cases of Ball canning jars. Mining supplies filled a fourth room—augers, blasting powder, squibs, shovels, picks, kerosene, and oil. Even in Manhattan, Emma had never seen a store with such a wide variety of goods.

After exploring a bit, she headed toward the front counter, past shelves filled with bread and rolls.

"I'm sorry," Percy said to the woman at the register. "You're still short ten cents."

The woman bounced the baby on her hip, trying to stop him from fussing. "Can't you carry it over 'til next week? It's not that much."

Percy shook his head. "Your deductions are already more than your husband's paycheck. And you still owe money from last week."

"But I've got a passel of hungry mouths to feed," the woman said, "including three more at home."

"Sorry," Percy said. "But that's not my problem." He wiped the top of the register with a cleaning rag, avoiding the woman's eyes. To Emma's surprise, he looked pained.

Emma edged closer, trying to see what the woman wanted to buy. A loaf of bread and bottle of milk sat on the counter.

"How about takin' a few cents off the bread?" the woman said. "I swear I'll pay the difference next time."

Percy shook his head again. "If you still owe at the end of the week, I can't start a new bill until the old one is paid in full. Sorry, but that's the way it works."

The woman rocked back and forth, digging at the nape of her neck with dirty fingernails, as if trying to puzzle out a solution to her problem. "Can I do something to change your mind?" she said. "Maybe I can come down after closin' and—"

"No!" Percy said, cutting her off. He glanced nervously at Emma. "Now, either pay up or leave."

The woman stopped rocking. "Well, I hope you can sleep while my babies cry themselves to sleep tonight 'cause of their empty stomachs!"

Percy's features softened. "You know I don't make the rules."

The woman turned to leave, urging her daughter forward by the shoulder. The baby started wailing, his face purple. The woman saw Emma and stopped, her eyes blazing. "If your husband don't work for the mining company and you can buy your goods elsewhere, you better do it!" she said. "They don't call this the pluck me store for nothing!"

Behind Emma, the boys tore the lids from the candy jars, grabbed handfuls of licorice and lemon drops, then bolted out the side door. Percy raced around the counter and chased them outside. The woman watched him leave, then considered Emma with narrow eyes. She hesitated for just a moment, then grabbed the bread and milk, put it in a cloth bag hanging from her forearm, and hurried out of the store. Less than a minute later, Percy stormed back inside, red-faced and panting.

"Those good-for-nothing scoundrels!" he said.

Aunt Ida came in through the main entrance, her forehead lined with concern. "Heavens to Betsy!" she said, fanning herself with a paisley fan. "What's all the commotion?"

"Those damn breaker boys!" Percy said. "Every payday they come in here and cause trouble."

"Well, why do you let them get away with it?" Aunt Ida said. "You're in charge, remember?"

"I try not to, Ma," Percy said. "But I don't have eyes in the back of my head. That's the other reason I need help. I can't watch everybody!"

"When Emma is done learning what I need her to do at the house," Aunt Ida said, "I'll send her over to help you out."

"The sooner the better," Percy said. He stomped around the counter, stopped at the register, and noticed the bread and milk were gone. "Shit!"

Aunt Ida's eyes went wide. "What now?" she said.

Percy shook his head, the veins in his forehead bulging. "Nothing," he said. "I just remembered something I forgot to do. Do you need anything special today?"

"I was hoping you could show Emma where everything is so she can find things on her own next time," Aunt Ida said.

"Not today," Percy said. "I've got work to do."

"Now you listen here, Percy Francis Shawcross," Aunt Ida said. "One minute you're cussing for no good reason, the next you're saying no to your mother. What would your father think? One hand wipes the other, remember? You want me to make sure Emma can help you out, then you best help me out when I ask."

"Yes, Ma," Percy said. He made his way back around the counter, his face long.

Aunt Ida handed Emma the list. "I'll be outside, finishing my visit with Sally Gable," she said. She headed toward the door. "Seems her son married a nice girl over in Wilkes-Barre, and they're already expecting." Before disappearing into the thinning light outside, she called over her shoulder, "Nothing makes a mother prouder than seeing her son marry a nice girl!"

Percy watched her leave, his hands on his hips. "Son of a bitch," he said under his breath.

"What is it?" Emma said, pretending she didn't know why he was upset.

"That damn woman stole the bread and milk she was trying to buy," he said.

"No, she didn't," Emma said. "I figured I might as well start making myself useful, so I put the bread back on the shelf and the milk back in the icebox."

Percy sighed heavily, relieved. Then, as if coming to his senses, he squared his shoulders. "Listen," he said. "Don't touch anything else around here unless I tell you to."

"I thought you wanted my help."

He snatched the list from her hand and headed toward the rear of the store. "I do. But you don't work here yet, do you?"

"No," she said, staying put. "I don't. And I'm fairly certain I can figure out a way to make sure I never do."

He stopped and turned to face her, throwing his hands in the air. "Jesus," he said. "I'm sorry. It's just . . . this job isn't as easy as my father thinks. And now, seeing you after all these years . . ."

"Do you think any of this is easy for me?" she said.

"No," he said. "I can't imagine it is. I didn't mean to—"

"Listen," she said. "We're going to have to figure out a way to get along. At least until I can figure out how to get out of here. So, please, don't do it again."

He moved forward and put a hand on her shoulder. "I want you to know how sorry I am about what happened with your brother last time you were here. I should have apologized back then, but I didn't know what to say."

She brushed his hand away and made her way down the aisle. "There's no point in talking about that now," she said. "All the apologies in the world won't change what happened."

"I know," Percy said. "I just want you to—"

She turned to face him. "Can we please talk about something else?"

He shrugged and went to the end of the aisle to start gathering the items on his mother's list. "Like what?"

She followed him. "What did that woman mean when she said I should shop somewhere else if my husband doesn't work for the mining company?"

He took a tin of lantern oil from the shelf and headed toward the register. "Miners and their families have to shop here."

"Why?"

"The mining company owns the store." He grabbed a basket and moved down the center aisle.

She went with him. "So?"

He looked at her as if she thought the world was flat. "The miners would be out of a job if they shopped anyplace else."

"Why?" she said. Then the answer came to her, and she made a face. "You mean they're forced to shop here? I've never heard of such nonsense!"

"It's always been that way."

"I only lived here for a few months, remember? And I was ten. I didn't pay attention to things like that."

Percy pulled two bags of dried beans from a shelf. "Then you've got a lot to learn about this place," he said. "And I'm not just talking about this store."

"What can you tell me about the breaker boys?" she said. "Aunt Ida won't tell me who they are."

He frowned, took the basket to the front of the store, and set it on the counter. "The breaker boys work in the breaker."

"Doing what?" she said. "Some of them can't be any more than six or seven years old!"

"Sorting coal."

"Every day?"

"Of course every day," he said. "Every day except Sunday. That's the only day the colliery isn't running."

"I heard there was an accident, and a boy was killed. Is their job dangerous?"

"It can be."

"Is it legal?"

"The Bleak Mountain Mining Company isn't doing anything different than the rest of the collieries in this state," he said.

"What about school?"

He shot her that look again, as if she'd just fallen off a turnip truck. "There's no school for miners' children in Coal River."

She gaped at him, trying to recall if she'd seen miners' children wandering around in the middle of the day the last time she was here. She couldn't remember. "Why not?" she said. "Aren't there state laws requiring all children to get an education?"

He looked troubled. "I don't know," he said. "It's been the same around here for as long as I can remember. Half of them barely know English, let alone how to read and write. How would anyone teach them anything?"

She shook her head, unable to believe what she was hearing. What kind of people put young boys to work in a coal mine instead of sending them to school? Some way, some how, she had to find a way out of this Godforsaken place. Then she had another thought. *Maybe, if I'm able to get out from under Aunt Ida's thumb for a bit, I can find a way to teach the miners' children something, even if it's just how to write their names.*

A little while later, she helped Percy carry Aunt Ida's purchases out to the horse-drawn wagon. The sun was hanging just above the horizon, casting long shadows across the road. When they had loaded and covered the bags and parcels in the back of the wagon,

Emma grabbed the wooden armrest and hoisted herself into the bench seat. On the driver's side, Aunt Ida rearranged the thick folds of her skirt and picked up the reins.

Percy squinted up at them. "Go straight home, now," he said.

"Yes, sir," Aunt Ida said, her words tinged with sarcasm.

"Why didn't the driver bring you?" Percy said.

"You know I like driving the wagon," Aunt Ida said. "Besides, the driver was busy helping Cook make sausage in the summer kitchen."

"But everyone knows who you are," he said. "And with everything that's going on—"

"Don't worry about me." Aunt Ida patted her skirt. "I can handle myself."

Until now, Emma hadn't noticed the slight bulge beneath one side of her aunt's dress.

Percy's brows shot up. "That better not be what I think it is."

Aunt Ida grinned. "Your daddy's pistol?" she said. "Darn tootin' it is. And don't you be telling him I've got it either. If something happens, you'll both be glad I didn't listen." She sat up straight and flicked the reins. The horse flinched and started moving, its sides and hindquarters covered in dried sweat. Percy shook his head in frustration, then waved and watched the women make their way down the dusty road.

Emma gave Percy a quick wave, then turned forward. "What do you mean if something happens?" she said. "What could happen?"

Aunt Ida made a pshaw motion with one hand. "It's nothing for you to worry about," she said. "You heard your uncle and Percy talking. There's a lot of unrest with the miners these days. As usual, they blame everyone in charge."

"But they wouldn't," Emma said. "I mean . . . they wouldn't actually hurt someone, would they?"

Just then, a group of shouting boys ran across the road in front of the wagon, their worn knickers and scuffed shoes making them look like a band of orphans. One of the boys was using crutches and hopping along on one foot, the empty leg of his trousers tied closed. In what seemed like slow motion, he turned his head toward Aunt Ida and Emma. It was the boy from yesterday, Albert's twin. Up close, he looked ravaged and childish at the same time, like an ancient, tortured soul trapped inside a young body. He hesitated in the middle of the road and fixed his eyes on Emma. *You let your brother die.*

Despite the heat, Emma shivered, unable to pull her eyes from his. *How does he know?*

Aunt Ida yanked back on the reins, jerking the horse to a stop. "You good-for-nothin' boys, watch where you're going!"

Albert's twin dropped his eyes and made his way across the road. Emma slumped in her seat as if released from a trance. She shook her head to clear it. *I must be imagining things,* she thought. *That boy doesn't know anything about me. It's just a coincidence that he looks like Albert, nothing more. I need to get ahold of myself before I drive myself mad!*

Aunt Ida snorted in disgust and got the horse moving again, her lips twisted in an angry pucker. Then another boy ran across the road, jumping out of the way at the last second. He laughed and stuck out his tongue, then turned and caught up to his friends.

"Are they breaker boys?" Emma said.

"I'm afraid so," Aunt Ida said.

"Percy told me what they do and how dangerous it is. Can't' Uncle Otis do something to help them?"

A dark look passed over Aunt Ida's face, but she kept her eyes on the road. "I told you before, I don't want to talk about it."

"Not talking about something doesn't make it go away."

"Please!" Aunt Ida said. "Stop asking me about them. That's your last warning!"

"But it isn't right!"

Aunt Ida ignored her and snapped the reins harder. Emma turned in her seat to watch the breaker boys join a gang of older boys in a dusty alley between the tobacco shop and a saloon, flocking around them like playful puppies. The older boys held out cigarettes and chewing tobacco while the younger ones reached into their pockets for change, pushing and shoving to be first in line. After paying the older boys, the younger boys—some as young as six—lit cigarettes and corncob pipes, or shoved chewing tobacco between their gums and cheeks.

"Am I seeing what I think I'm seeing?" Emma said. Suddenly it seemed hard to breath.

Aunt Ida clucked her tongue. "It's a shame those miners don't have better control over their children. They're like a pack of wild animals if you ask me! But some people are just not meant to be civilized." She picked up a whip and lashed the horse's rear end, forcing the already overheated animal to trot faster.

CHAPTER 5

Following a century-old Coal River tradition, the Fourth of July festivities were held in the village green near the center of town, where Main Street split off Railroad Avenue and Murphy Lane. American flags and colored bunting festooned the Pennsylvania Boarding House and Hotel, Herrick's Apothecary, Judd's Blacksmith shop, Abe's Livery, and the United States Post Office; the red, white, and blue swags like billowing sheets hung from every roof and window. More flags hung from the streetlamps and surrounded the village gazebo, where a twenty-piece band played patriotic tunes beneath streamers and banners. After the one-o'clock parade, the villagers would meet for a picnic in the park, and later that evening a dance would be held in the hall next to the pavilion.

By one thirty, the sun was a blazing fireball in the sky, the afternoon temperature climbing to even greater heights than the previous few days. Hundreds of people swarmed the grounds—men in morning jackets and afternoon suits, women in pastel-colored gowns, boys in fancy trousers and shiny shoes, girls in white pantaloons and sailor dresses. The smell of sausage, beer, and roasted peanuts filled the air, along with the snap of firecrackers and the sounds of several foreign languages. Members of the Coal and Iron Police roamed the crowd, truncheons and revolvers on their belts.

A few carried rifles strapped to their shoulders. In sharp contrast to the fancy clothes worn by the upper class, clusters of single men, bands of boys, and mining families wandered through the gathering in patched trousers, worn dresses, and tattered shoes. The youngest children were in bare feet.

Emma had tried to get out of attending the celebration by claiming the heat was making her stomach queasy, but Aunt Ida was having none of it. If Emma was going to live with the Shawcross family and be treated to all the rewards of being kin, the least she could do was accompany them to the festivities. Besides, it was imperative to make an appearance so the townsfolk could see she was a normal young woman. If she stayed hidden at home, it would only fuel the spreading rumors. The last thing the family needed was for anyone to think she was someone to be avoided and feared.

Now, Emma strolled beside her aunt through the village green, a white parasol balanced on one shoulder. Aunt Ida had chosen every aspect of Emma's outfit—from the ivory tea dress with a lace collar to the white, patent leather Mary Janes. After all, it was important for Emma to look like a civilized young lady on her first family outing, not a cursed girl who brought bad luck, or a hooligan who grew up passing out theater programs on the streets of Manhattan. Uncle Otis was the mine supervisor, and the Shawcross family had a reputation to uphold. But Emma had refused to pin up her hair, insisting it was too hot to wear a heavy roll of curls sitting on the nape of her neck. She could still hear Aunt Ida tsk-tsking when she had appeared on the front veranda with a long braid down her back. Of course, Aunt Ida was dressed to the nines in a yellow tea gown with a white sash, jeweled galloons, and a wide-brimmed hat festooned with peacock feathers. And Uncle Otis and Percy were wearing their best suits.

Emma wondered what the townsfolk would think if they saw Uncle Otis huffing and puffing at the dinner table every night, worrying that the fires in the culm banks would spread to the breaker and complaining that the miners and mules were more cantankerous than normal. What would they say if they saw him at the end of the meal, slumped in his seat like a hot, sweaty child, letting his wife mollycoddle and wait on him? Every evening it was the same—

Aunt Ida took his whiskey glass, unbuttoned his collar, wiped his face with a wet napkin, and had Percy help take him up to bed.

Between Uncle Otis's drinking problem and what happened earlier that day, Emma had enough information to ruin the Shawcross reputation in five minutes flat. All the peacock feathers and pinstripe vests in the world wouldn't change the truth once it came out. Then again, no one in Coal River seemed to care about the boys getting hurt and killed inside the breaker. Why would they care what happened to her? She put a hand to her sore cheek, wondering if it was still red, and thought back to when they left the house that morning. Aunt Ida had insisted they take a family portrait, goading Uncle Otis until he went back inside to get his Folding Pocket Kodak. They could stand on the porch steps, her aunt said, and get a nice picture with the house in the background.

"We're all dressed up," she said. "And the light is just right. Let's take the picture before you and Percy get to rabble-rousing and mess up your fine clothes."

"It's too hot," Percy said with a groan.

"And I'd have to go back inside and all the way upstairs to get the camera," Uncle Otis said. "Just get in the Lizzie so we can be on our way." He flicked his hand, as if dismissing a servant.

"Now you listen here, Otis Shawcross," Aunt Ida said, putting her fists on her hips. "You insisted on spending all that money to buy that fancy new camera, and now you never use it. It's been sitting in the bedroom closet for the better part of a year collecting dust! What on God's green earth are you saving it for?"

Uncle Otis shrugged.

"Well, go inside and dig it out so Emma can take our picture!"

Uncle Otis did as he was told, but not without cursing under his breath. He emerged a few minutes later with a camera and a roll of film, his face red and his hair disheveled, as if he'd been digging through linens and hanging clothes. Aunt Ida directed Percy onto the steps and stood beside him, waiting while Uncle Otis loaded the film, pulled out the lens panel, and showed Emma how to take a picture.

"Hold it steady like this," he said, demonstrating. "Then look through here and push this exposure level."

"All right," Emma said, moving to take the camera.

He pulled it out of her reach. "And whatever you do, don't break it," he said. "It was expensive."

"I won't," she said.

Reluctantly, Uncle Otis gave her the camera. Then he climbed the steps, stood beside his wife, and raked his fingers through his thinning hair. Percy stood on the other side of his mother. Just then, Cook came around the side of the house, a crate of canning jars in her arms. She set down the crate and hobbled over to Emma.

"Let me take the picture," she said. "You get on up there and stand beside your kin."

"That's not necessary," Uncle Otis barked. "Just push the button and get it over with, Emma."

"I can do it," Cook said. "So Emma can be in the picture too."

"We're taking a family portrait," Aunt Ida said. "She can pose for her own afterward, if she'd like."

Cook gave Emma a weak, wavering smile that was both kind and sad.

"It's all right," Emma said. "They're not my real family." She reached out to touch Cook's arm and thank her for her kindness, and somehow the camera slipped from her grasp. In what seemed like slow motion, it fell through the air, then hit the dirt with a solid thump. Emma's stomach dropped. Before she could retrieve the camera, Uncle Otis flew down the steps, his eyes wild, and shoved her out of the way. He picked up the camera. Then there was a loud crack, and Emma was on the ground, not at all sure how she'd gotten there. She tasted blood and looked up to see her uncle standing over her, his arm raised. He blinked and lowered his hand. Percy hurried down the steps.

"Are you all right?" he said. He helped her up.

She touched her burning cheek, her chin trembling, and nodded.

Percy gazed at his father, contempt flashing in his eyes. "It's just a camera," he said.

Uncle Otis ignored him. "I told you to be careful!" he snarled at Emma. "Now go wait in the car! And for Christ's sake, don't touch anything! Just get in and sit still!" He handed the camera to Cook, then stomped back up the steps. Cook took the picture, gave the camera back, picked up the crate, and disappeared around the side of the house. Otis took the camera inside, and Percy and Aunt Ida climbed into the Tin Lizzie.

"I don't know what it is with your father and that camera," Aunt Ida said to Percy. "I swear one of these days I'm going to sell it and buy myself something useful, like a bolt of satin or a new brooch."

"I heard he won it playing poker down at the Pennsylvania Hotel," Percy said. "Sally Gable's husband, Grover, had to ante it up when he ran out of cash."

"That wouldn't surprise me," Aunt Ida said. "Those two always had an old rivalry. Never understood that either."

"They say it's because Grover proposed to Sally before Pa had the chance," Percy said.

Quicker than a whip, Aunt Ida spun around and slapped Percy across the face. "Don't you ever talk about your father like that!" she shouted. "He wouldn't be caught dead with that whore. And he never proposed to anybody but me!"

"Sorry, Ma," Percy said, rubbing his cheek.

Now, up ahead on the village green, Uncle Otis waded through the crowd, waving and nodding as if he were royalty surrounded by his loyal subjects. Percy walked beside him, carrying picnic baskets filled with fried chicken, potato salad, deviled eggs, and Aunt Ida's famous angel food cake with strawberries. Cook had made all the food, but Aunt Ida had instructed Emma ahead of time that if anyone asked, she'd been slaving over a hot stove since five that morning.

As they headed toward the pavilion, Emma searched the gathering for familiar faces, hoping the boys who'd tormented her brother all those years ago had moved away. She couldn't remember their names, but she could still see their curled lips and spiteful grins when they taunted Albert. She could still see their blanched cheeks and frightened eyes when he fell through the ice. Did any of them regret what they'd done? Did they ever give Albert a second thought? Or did they just go on with their lives, forgetting the innocent boy they killed? Over the years she'd pictured different reckonings for each bully. One grew up to be a sweaty drunk, living out his days in a saloon. One was a criminal, in jail for robbing a bank. A third was a panhandler living out on the streets, everything he owned lost in poker games. The worst scenario belonged to the boy who threw the locket out on the ice. She pictured him locked away in a state asylum, driven mad by nightmares and guilt.

But now that she had seen Percy face-to-face and knew firsthand that there had been no repercussions for what he'd done, the thought of seeing his friends at the Fourth of July celebration filled her stomach with dread. She couldn't bear the thought of seeing the boys responsible for Albert's death playing croquet in cuffed trousers and panama hats. She didn't want to see them escorting wives or girlfriends toward the picnic pavilion, or holding their children up so they could see the band in the gazebo. Albert never had the chance to do any of those things. And he never would. How in God's universe would it be fair for the boys responsible for his death to be happily living out their lives? How would it be just that they never had to pay? She took a deep breath and pushed the thought away, wishing she'd brought the vial of laudanum with her instead of leaving it hidden beneath her bedroom mattress.

They passed an open expanse of grass, where groups of breaker boys were playing football and tag. Other boys sat on the sidelines, cheering on the teams. Briefly, Emma wondered if the boy who looked like Albert's twin was over there, observing her, hidden among the others. Then she noticed that the majority of the boys on the sidelines were either missing entire limbs, a hand, or part of an arm. A young boy with no legs and a scarred cheek sat on a wooden crate, watching the others run and play. His face was filled with misery. A lump formed in Emma's throat, and she looked away. *There are so many.* Maybe, when it came to innocents dying and suffering, there was no such thing as fair or just.

Blinking back tears, she followed her aunt past a group of children having a sack race, then tried to keep up as they made their way around a gathering of men holding a weight-lifting contest.

The ground near the men was soft and wet underfoot, soggy with tobacco juice and spilled beer. Lifting her skirt to keep the hem from getting soiled, Emma stepped around beer bottles and empty peanut bags. In the center of the circle of men, a bearded man in a gray shirt and red suspenders lifted a huge barbell over his head, his face dripping with sweat. The other men erupted in cheers, their fists in the air. Emma flinched, startled by the sudden commotion. She walked faster.

She was nearly past the group of men when a beer bottle dropped at her feet, gurgling dark stout into the grass. A man stepped out of the crowd and bent over to pick it up, blocking her way. He snatched up the bottle before all the beer ran out, then straightened to his full height and turned to face her. He was big as a draft horse, his grimy jersey and bib overalls stretching over his chest as if they were two sizes too small. He grinned at her, revealing crooked, tobacco-stained teeth, then took off his wool cap and ran plank-thick fingers through his stringy hair. His hairline was stained black with coal dust.

"Excuse me, miss," he said in a thick Irish brogue. "Sorry for blocking yer way."

Emma nodded and lowered her eyes, making a move to skirt around him. He grabbed her arm with a beefy hand.

"What's the matter?" he said. "Ye too fancy to talk to a poor bloke like me?"

Emma's heartbeat quickened. She shook her head. "No," she said, pulling her arm from his grasp. "I'm just trying to keep up with my aunt." She searched the crowd for peacock feathers.

"Yer aunt?" he said. "Shouldn't a pretty lass like you be with a handsome fella at a nice party like this?"

Several of the other men turned around to watch the exchange. One of them called out, "She wouldn't ride ye to battle, ye big dolt!" Everyone laughed.

"If you'll excuse me," Emma said. "I must be on my way."

The giant Irishman took a long swig of stout, grimaced, and wiped his chin with the back of his wrist. "Ye know," he said. "The higher a monkey climbs a tree, the further up its arse ye see."

"I'm sorry?" she said.

"Ye think you're too good for me. With your fancy clothes and all your money."

Emma started to turn away when someone called out, "Leave her alone, Nally!"

A tall young man pushed his way toward them through the gathering of onlookers. The Irishman squared his shoulders and lifted his chin, ready for a fight. But when he saw who had spoken, he relaxed and grinned.

"We were just having a wee chin-wag, Mr. Nash," he said. "It's all in good fun."

"Better let the young lady be on her way," the man said, stopping beside them. "We don't need any trouble." He looked to be in his early twenties, with a straight nose and pale green eyes, a full mustache and dark beard the color of blackstrap molasses. His shirtsleeves were rolled up, showing his muscular forearms. He stood with one hand in his pocket and his sturdy legs rooted to the ground as if he belonged to this place. As much as the roiling river belonged, the low, sooty clouds, and the coyotes in the hills. Despite the fact that his clothes had seen better days, he was handsome and rugged-looking, a miner dressed in his Sunday best, all cleaned up for the celebration. He took Emma's breath away.

Nash, she thought. The name sounded familiar. Then she remembered Percy and Uncle Otis talking about a man named Clayton Nash. *A troublemaker,* they'd said.

A member of the Coal and Iron Police appeared, one hand on his truncheon. He was broad-shouldered, with a ginger mustache and dark rings under his eyes. A gold badge on his cap read: CAPTAIN.

"What's going on here?" he said.

"Nothing at all, officer," Clayton said.

Nally raised his hands in concession.

"You better be telling the truth," the captain said. "We don't want any trouble today now, do we?"

"No, we don't," Clayton said. "Least of all from you." He glanced at Emma and nodded once. "Good day, miss." Then he strolled away, signaling Nally to follow him.

The giant Irishman did as he was told. "Cheers," he said, grinning at her as he moved away.

"Are you all right, Emma?" the captain said.

Emma nodded and started walking again, her heart still racing. The last thing she needed was another enemy, or to draw attention to herself in public again. Sally and Charlotte Gable had certainly already started gossiping about her, spreading the details of their encounter among the upper class of Coal River, talking in hushed voices about how she touched Charlotte's arm to hex her with a curse. Emma didn't need the miners against her too. She just wanted to be left alone until she could find a way out of this place. Thank God Clayton Nash had come over to interrupt the exchange.

Then Clayton's handsome face flashed in her mind, and she wondered if her pounding heart was caused by fear, or something else. Certainly, she had seen other fine-looking men, but there was something about Clayton that made him especially attractive. She couldn't quite put her finger on it—a mysterious, dangerous air perhaps, or the way he projected confidence with just the lift of his chin. Right or wrong, he was the sort who knew what he believed in. And somehow, in those few short moments she had spent with him, she felt like he was a man who could have ruled nations. Maybe that was why Uncle Otis saw him as a threat.

"Are you here with your aunt and uncle?" the captain said, following her.

"Excuse me?" she said, coming out of her trance.

He grinned. "I asked if you were with your aunt and uncle."

"Oh yes," she said. "And Percy."

"How is good old Percy?" the captain said. "Still as prissy as ever?"

Emma stopped and looked up at him, suddenly realizing he had called her by name. "Do I know you?" she said.

He squared his shoulders and put his hands behind his back. "Of course you do," he said. "I'm Frank. Frank Bannister. Captain Bannister now. Don't you remember? I spent time with you and Albert the last time you were here. I'm very sorry to hear about your parents."

She tensed. Was he one of the boys responsible for her brother's death? She looked at the policeman's face, searching his eyes for something familiar. Then an image came to her: Percy and the other boys laughing and pointing at Albert's urine-stained pants. A thin, ginger-haired boy pushing Albert down in the snow, his lips curled in anger and disgust. It was Frank Bannister.

Bile rose in her mouth, and she nearly choked. "I'm sorry," she said. "I have to go." She started walking again, as fast as she could without running. How she longed for a sip of laudanum.

He followed. "It's all right if you don't remember me," he said. "It was a long time ago. Just let me give you a little friendly advice. Stay away from Clayton Nash. He's a liar and a thief, possibly worse."

Then the two of you should get along well, she thought.

She was getting ready to tell him to stop following her when Aunt Ida appeared, wheezing and fanning her sweaty face. "There you are!" her aunt said. "Is it too much to ask for you to keep up? I didn't come here to spend the day looking after you!" She grabbed Emma's wrist and pulled her along. "Now, stay with us, will you, please?"

"Yes," Emma said. "I'm sorry. It's just—"

"Save your excuses," Aunt Ida said. Then she stopped and looked back at the police captain, as if noticing him for the first time. "Oh! Good day, Captain Bannister! Be sure and tell your mother I said hello, will you?"

Frank tipped his cap in her direction. "Will do, Mrs. Shawcross. Perhaps I can stop by to call on Emma sometime soon? With your permission, of course."

"Of course," Aunt Ida said with a laugh. She hooked her arm through Emma's and started away, calling over her shoulder. "You can come by anytime you'd like!"

When they had left him behind, Emma said, "Why would you say that?"

Aunt Ida scanned the crowd as if searching for someone, a forced smile on her face. "Oh, for heaven's sake," she said. "Stop acting like a scared little girl. If Captain Bannister comes to call, you'll visit with him in the parlor. After that, you can get to know each other at church suppers and holiday dances. Of course, if you were to marry, you'd continue to work for us until you repaid your debt."

A knot of anger twisted below Emma's rib cage. "I won't see him if he comes to call!"

"I understand you don't know him very well," she said. "But he was Percy's best childhood friend. And in your situation, dear, it doesn't matter if you know a potential suitor or not. As long as a man has the means to put a roof over your head and food in your mouth, you'll take what you get and be grateful for it. Most girls would feel lucky to be wooed by Captain Bannister."

"But I *do* know him," Emma said. "He was with Percy the day Albert drowned."

Aunt Ida shook her head, clucking her tongue. "We're not going to talk about unhappy things today," she said. "Now wipe that frown off your face and smile. People are watching."

Later, in the dance hall, Emma sat in a folding chair beside Percy at a linen-covered table decorated with American flags and red bunting. Aunt Ida and Uncle Otis were dancing to "Everybody Two-Step." Despite the open windows and double doors, the lumber-walled building was stifling hot and airless. Every table and seat was taken, every wall and leaning spot filled with miners and single men. The band was from Wilkes-Barre, and the townspeople took every opportunity to dance to the latest songs. Men in expensive suits and women in flowing tea gowns two-stepped beside miners in patched trousers and worn shirts, their wives in faded cotton dresses and scuffed shoes. A group of miners, including Nally the giant Irishman, stood near the main entrance, swigging beer from tin growlers, spitting tobacco juice through the windows, and watching the young women.

Emma scanned the gathering for Clayton Nash but didn't see him. Maybe troublemakers didn't have time for something as frivolous as a dance. She plucked a red carnation from the vase in the middle of the table and leaned back, twirling the wet stem between her fingers and thinking about her parents. They loved to dance. After every Saturday night show, the stage manager would play the phonograph while everyone cleaned up. When they finished, her parents would waltz, fox-trot, and tango across the empty stage, much to the delight of the rest of the workers. Everyone said they could have been ballroom champions, if only they'd grown up under better circumstances. Emma's eyes filled. Maybe the townspeople were right. Maybe she was cursed. Everyone she loved was gone.

"Are you feeling all right?" Percy said, pulling her from her thoughts.

She blinked back her tears and sat up. "Yes," she said. "I'm fine."

"Would you like to dance?"

"No, thank you."

"Are you sure?" he said. "I don't usually dance at these things, but it can't be much fun for you just sitting here."

"I'm sure," she said. "You don't want to be seen dancing with me anyway. I'm cursed, remember?"

"That's nonsense, and you know it. Besides, I'm not everyone's favorite person around here either. I don't care what they think, and neither should you."

"You're not? How come?"

"Isn't it obvious?" he said. "The regular miners hate me because I work at the Company Store, and the higher-ups think I'm spoiled."

She shrugged. "Well, you kind of are."

"Thanks," he said. His lip twitched, and he dropped his eyes to the floor. "It's my mother's fault."

Suddenly, she had an idea. Maybe Percy was her way out of Coal River. Maybe the two of them could go back to New York. "Did you ever think of doing something about it?" she said. "Why don't you leave? You've been working at the store a long time. You must have some money stashed away."

He looked at her and gave a cynical laugh. "My mother gives me a weekly allowance and puts the rest of my paycheck in the bank under her name. Besides, it would break her heart if I left home."

Emma rolled her eyes and shook her head. There was no doubt about it; Percy was a momma's boy. He'd never leave unless something drastic happened. Or he fell in love. She could only imagine Aunt Ida's reaction if Percy started caring about someone more than her, especially if she didn't like the poor girl. Emma stuck the carnation back in the vase and glanced around the hall, searching for someone to dance with him. Maybe the person to help Percy gain his independence was in this very room. Across the way, a young woman in a red dress sat sandwiched between her father and mother, looking bored.

"Why don't you ask her to dance?" she said. "She was eyeing you earlier."

"No, she wasn't," Percy said.

"Yes, she was. What are you afraid of? Go ask her to dance!" She looked over at the young woman again and saw Frank standing next to the wall. He was staring back at her. She lowered her eyes, then checked again. He was squeezing around a table, threading his way across the room and making his way toward her. She stood and grabbed Percy's hand.

"You're right," she said. "If you're not going to ask someone else to dance, we might as well make the best of it." She pulled him onto the dance floor just as the two-step ended and the first strains of a waltz began. Percy let go of her hand and froze, color rising in his pale features. Out of the corner of her eye, she saw Frank drawing closer.

Despite her reluctance to get close to Percy, she put his arm behind her back and lifted his other hand in the air. But Percy stood immobile, his feet stuck to the floor. "What is it?" she said. "I thought you wanted to dance?"

"I-I do," he said, stuttering. "It's just . . . I've never waltzed with anyone but Mother."

"You're pulling my leg, right?" she said. "Well, don't you think it's high time you danced with someone your own age, even if I am your cousin?" She started to sway back and forth, practically pushing him across the floor. Once he gave in, she did her best to move them toward the middle of the room, away from Frank.

At first, Percy stomped in circles like a marionette, his arms and legs stiff, his lips moving as he counted steps. Then he loosened up, and they were whirling around the floor, the other dancers a blur beside them. Frank disappeared into the crowd, and Emma breathed a sigh of relief.

Just as she was beginning to think she had avoided a second run-in with Frank, she and Percy bumped into another couple and lost the tempo. Percy stopped dead on the floor and released her hands, stepping backward. Out of nowhere, Clayton Nash appeared beside them. The rumored troublemaker stood six inches taller than Percy, which meant he towered above Emma. If they stood face-to-face, the top of her head wouldn't touch the bottom of his chin.

"May I cut in?" he said.

Emma gasped and took a step back. Despite the fact that she found him striking, a jolt of apprehension quickened her heart. Everyone had warned her that he was dangerous—even Percy—and she could tell he was the type of man who didn't give up on what he wanted. And right now he wanted to dance with her.

Percy frowned. "I don't think that's a good idea," he said. "My parents . . ."

Ignoring him, Clayton stepped in to take Percy's place. "Don't worry," he said. "There's no harm in us taking a turn on the dance floor. If your uncle doesn't like it, he can take it up with me." He put a hand on Emma's lower back, ready to usher her away. Despite her hesitation, a warm quiver ran up her spine.

"No," Percy said, grabbing Emma's wrist. "Step away from her, Clayton."

Beside them, the couple they had bumped into stopped dancing and turned to face them. The man was good-looking, with a square jaw, a pencil-thin mustache, and auburn hair parted on the side. He wore a three-piece suit of the highest quality, with a high white collar and satin ascot. A pretty, rosy-cheeked woman linked her arm through his, smiling and batting her eyelashes. She looked to be about Emma's age.

"What seems to be the problem here?" the man said.

Percy blanched. "Mr. Flint!" he said. "Excuse us, sir. Please forgive us for bumping into you!" At first Emma was confused. Surely, this handsome young man couldn't be Hazard Flint. Then she remembered the dark-haired boy she'd seen when she went inside the mansion to rescue Albert. This was Mr. Flint's son, Levi, all grown up. Regardless of Percy's astonishment, he held fast to Emma's arm. Clayton released her but kept one hand on her lower back, burning the skin beneath her dress.

"Percy!" Levi said. "How many times do I have to tell you to call me Levi?" He gripped Percy's thin shoulder, shaking him back and forth like a long-lost friend. "How are things at the Company Store?"

"Fine," Percy said, nodding. "Everything's just fine, Mr. Flint."

Levi directed his attention toward Emma, and noticed Percy's grip on her wrist and Clayton's hand on her back. "Is this man bothering you, miss?" he said. He gestured toward Clayton, then raised his arm above his head to motion someone over.

"No, not at all," she said. "We were just heading back to our table. I think Aunt Ida is looking for me."

Levi's face lit up. "Why you sly dog, Percy," he said. "Is this lovely young woman your cousin, the infamous Emma Malloy?"

Heat crawled up Emma's cheeks. Even Levi Flint was talking about her.

"Yes, sir," Percy said, nodding eagerly. "Emma, this is Levi Flint. Remember I told you—"

She nodded once, ignoring Levi's outstretched hand. "Good day, Mr. Flint," she said. "I'm sorry, but I really must be going."

"Please," Levi said. "Call me by my first name. Any friend of Percy's is a friend of mine."

The rosy-cheeked woman gripped Levi's arm tighter, as if afraid he would get away. "I'm Beulah," she said, beaming and reaching for Percy's hand. Her delicate fingers were bejeweled with rubies and emeralds.

"Pleased to meet you," Percy said.

Beulah grinned and nodded once at Emma.

Just then, Frank appeared and stopped beside Levi. He stood with his legs apart, his thumb hooked over his belt near his truncheon. An older man with a white beard limped up beside him, scowling and leaning on a gold-headed cane. Like Levi, he wore an expensive suit, with pinstripe pants, an ascot tie, and shiny leather shoes. Despite one crusty eyelid and liver-colored lips, the rem-

nants of a younger, handsomer man lingered in his high cheekbones and dishwater blue eyes.

"Everything all right, Mr. Flint?" Frank said.

"What's going on?" the older man said. He eyed Clayton, then
addressed Levi. "Is Mr. Nash causing trouble again?"

"I'm not entirely sure," Levi said.

"Is there a law against dancing now?" Clayton said.

"Not yet," the older man said. "But maybe we should start ban-
ning miners and their families from the village celebrations. Half
the time they're nothing but a bunch of drunks causing trouble for
nice folk like Percy and his lady friend here."

"I'm not Percy's lady friend," Emma said. "I'm his cousin. And
Mr. Nash is not causing any . . ."

Clayton patted her back, and she fell silent. "Nice to see you as
always, Mr. Flint," he said. Then he saluted the older man with two
fingers and walked away.

The older man laughed as he watched Clayton walk away. "Corner a rat and they always run," he said.

"Emma Malloy," Levi said. "This is my father, Hazard Flint."
He gestured toward the old man with an upturned hand, then did
the same to Emma. "Father, this is Otis Shawcross's niece."

Mr. Flint gazed at her, but made no move to shake hands. "I'll
ignore what just happened because you're new in town," he said.
"But from now on you might want to think about who you're keeping company with."

"Mr. Flint is right," Frank said. "I warned you about Clayton.
He's nothing but trouble."

"We're only looking out for you, that's all," Levi said with a
smile.

"She wasn't encouraging him," Percy said. His voice was anxious.

"I can assure you," Emma said. "I'm perfectly capable of looking out for myself."

"Emma is helping out down at the Company Store," Percy said.
"If that's all right with the two of you, of course."

Mr. Flint considered Emma, his white, bushy eyebrows knitted together. "But isn't this the young gal who's bringing the curse of death to Coal River? You don't suppose she'll scare off the customers, do you?" He laughed grimly, the hairs of his mustache curling around his lips.

"Of course she won't," Levi said. "Please, excuse my father, Emma. He's only joking."

A fine sheen of perspiration broke out on her forehead. "I won't scare the customers off," she said. "But from what I've heard, you fire people who shop elsewhere. So what choice do your customers have whether they're scared of me or not?" The words were out before she could stop them.

Percy's face went ashen. He latched onto her arm, his fingers digging into her flesh. "Please, forgive my cousin, Mr. Flint. She's been through a lot and sometimes speaks without thinking. My apologies for disturbing your celebration."

"You don't need to apologize for me, Percy," Emma said.

Mr. Flint scowled. "Maybe your cousin is bringing bad luck to Coal River after all. For some people anyway. Try to remember I'm the man who puts food on your uncle's table, young lady."

Levi shook his head as if embarrassed by his father's behavior. Beside him, the rosy-cheeked woman held a pale hand to her lips, concealing a smirk. Emma turned and stormed across the dance floor, her hands in fists, her face on fire. Who did Hazard Flint think he was, making fun of her and telling her what to do? Was this a mining town or a dictatorship? She fought the urge to go back, to tell Mr. Flint to apologize, to make him understand that her entire family was dead and her heart had been shattered into a million pieces. The last thing she needed was an entire town against her, or someone else running her life. Then she remembered he was the man who made it nearly impossible for the miners to feed their children while they risked their lives making him rich. He was the man who allowed young boys to get hurt and killed in the breaker. It wouldn't do any good to explain anything to someone like him.

Fuming, she fought her way through the crowd and looked for Clayton, squeezing between steaming bodies, getting knocked about by drunken men and laughing women. She didn't see him anywhere.

Maybe she was wrong about him. Maybe he didn't believe in anything. Why else would he let Mr. Flint tell him what to do? Why else would he just walk away?

Desperate to escape the noise and chaos, she lurched through a side door to get some fresh air. Once outside, she closed the door and leaned against it. The yard was empty and quiet except for the muffled thumping of music coming out of the dance hall. Several feet away, a row of evergreens lined the grass, their narrow tops like black arrows against the cobalt sky. A full moon lit up the lawn and gave the night a bluish glow. She took a deep breath and let it out, trying to slow her thundering heart. Then, somewhere to her left, a man laughed.

Toward the rear of the building, two dark figures—a man and a woman—tried to hide in the shadows. The woman leaned back on the wall while the man pressed himself against her, one hand inside her blouse. She lifted her chin and he kissed her neck, his mouth working toward her cleavage. Then she laughed and turned her head in Emma's direction, her red lips parted. Moonlight washed across her ivory face. It was Charlotte Gable, the young woman whose wrist Emma had squeezed outside the Company Store. When she saw Emma, her eyes went wide. She pushed the man away and pulled her blouse closed.

"Get away from me!" she said, fumbling with her buttons.

The man stumbled backward, then laughed and lunged for her cleavage again.

"Stop it!" Charlotte said, pushing him away. "I told you a hundred times, you're too old for me!"

"Oh, I get it," the man said. "Playing hard to get tonight, is that it?"

Charlotte shook her head and jerked her chin in Emma's direction, her face contorted with shame and fear. The man turned to look. It was Uncle Otis.

"Shit," he said.

Emma yanked opened the door and hurried back inside, her skin crawling with disgust. How dare Uncle Otis take advantage of a girl young enough to be his daughter? Not only was he an alcoholic tyrant, he was an adulterer, and a dirty old man. And why would someone as youthful and pretty as Charlotte behave like that with him? Emma couldn't imagine kissing Otis's wrinkled lips, smelling his whiskey-soured breath and rotting teeth, feeling his bone-dry hands on her body. It made her sick.

At their table, Aunt Ida and Frank Bannister were standing behind the chairs, deep in conversation. When Aunt Ida saw Emma, her face lit up.

"Oh, here she is now!" she said. "Emma, Captain Bannister would like to dance with you. He's been waiting patiently and I've given him permission to . . ."

She walked past the table. "I'm leaving," she said.

"Leaving?" her aunt said. "And going where?"

"Back to the house."

"But it's dark outside!" Aunt Ida said. "You can't walk the streets alone at night. It's not safe. Or proper!"

Emma ignored her and kept going.

"I'll escort you!" Frank called out, following her.

The band finished the last note of a song just as Aunt Ida shouted, "Emma Malloy! You turn around and come back here this very instant!"

All eyes turned toward Emma, staring as she marched toward the main exit. Women whispered behind their hands. Men grinned and swigged their beers, eager to see what would happen next. When she reached the open main door, Clayton Nash stepped in front of her and blocked her way.

"You should probably do what they say," he said. "It's not safe out there."

"Please, just let me pass," she said, avoiding his eyes. "I can take care of myself."

"Trust me on this," he said. "You shouldn't go out there alone. And they won't let me go with you." He leaned in and added in a low voice, meant only for her ears. "Don't run away with your tail between your legs. It'll only give them more to gossip about."

She looked at him then. His eyes were filled with kindness, his forehead lined with concern. At that moment, she felt like she finally had someone on her side. But how could she know if he was sincere?

Then Frank appeared beside her, breathing hard. "Stay out of this, Nash."

Clayton lifted his hands in concession. "I'm only telling her to be safe, to let you escort her home."

Behind Clayton, a towheaded boy in patched knickers wandered out of a group of miners, studying the exchange with wide brown eyes. He looked to be about four years old. His face was thin, his cheeks hollow. Another, older boy came up behind him and rested his hands on his shoulders. The older boy's expression looked pinched, as if he had seen and experienced things too horrible to talk about. His eyes were the color of smoke, his hair the color of a tarnished penny. Briefly, Emma wondered why the boys were watching Clayton so intently. Were they his brothers? His children? They didn't look anything like him.

"This doesn't have anything to do with you," Frank said to Clayton. "Now, move out of the way."

Emma glared up at Frank, her eyes on fire. "It doesn't have anything to do with you either." She gathered her skirt and moved to squeeze past Clayton.

"Wait," Frank said. He grabbed her arm.

She shook it off. "Don't touch me!"

Clayton stepped between them, squaring his shoulders. "Leave her alone."

"I'm the law here," Frank said. "Don't you forget that."

Percy and Uncle Otis appeared beside him. Percy was pale and fidgety, while Uncle Otis was sputtering and cursing under his breath, his thin hair sticking up in gray clumps.

"Break it up, boys," Uncle Otis said. "This isn't the time or the place."

"You're nothing but a yellow-bellied dog," Clayton said to Frank, jutting out his chin. "Kicking the working man when he's down."

With that, Frank threw a punch at Clayton. Clayton ducked and Frank fell forward, landing on his knees. Percy gasped and scurried out of the way. Nally and half a dozen miners stormed toward them, ready to fight. Emma backed away from the men, keeping her eyes on Clayton.

"Stop!" she shouted. "Please! Stop!" No one listened.

Frank found his footing and lunged at Clayton, but before he reached him, Nally grabbed him by the collar and punched him in the face. Frank fell backward into Uncle Otis, then scrambled to his feet again and tackled Clayton, blood gushing from his nostrils. Another miner grabbed Frank's shoulders and jerked him backward. A second policeman appeared and tried breaking up the fight. Two miners wrestled him to the ground. From all over the dance hall, police and miners hurried toward the commotion.

A strong hand pulled Emma out of the way. It was Levi.

"Please step back, Miss Malloy," he said, worry written on his face. "I wouldn't want you to get hurt." Beside him, Beulah gripped his jacket sleeve and chewed nervously on her lip.

On the outskirts of the brawl, one of the policemen drew his pistol. "Break it up!" he shouted. The men kept fighting. "I said break it up!" He pointed the gun in the air, and Emma put her fingers in her ears. He fired two shots, startling everyone. The bullets sliced a string of overhead banners in half and put holes in the ceiling. The banners silently floated down and landed on the gathering of onlookers. The miners and policemen stopped struggling, pulling apart to separate into their respective groups. They straightened their jackets and hats and hair, many with bruised and bloody faces.

"Are you all right?" Levi asked Emma.

She ran her hands along her skirt to brush away invisible debris. "I'm fine."

How is it possible that Levi is Mr. Flint's son? she wondered. He seemed gentle, kind, soft-spoken even. Then she remembered he worked for his father. He had to know about the store policies and the breaker boys, didn't he? While Mr. Flint was clearly an ogre, Levi might very well be a wolf in sheep's clothing.

Aunt Ida stormed over to Emma, trembling and out of breath. "Now look what you've done. What on earth are people going to think?"

"What I've done?" Emma said. "Frank was the one who—"

Mr. Flint started shouting orders at Frank and the rest of the policemen. "Arrest Clayton Nash! And anyone else who was in on this mess!"

Clayton and Nally made a dash for the door, but the police cut them off. Three men wrestled Nally to the ground and wrenched his arms behind his back while a fourth beat him about the shoulders and neck with a truncheon. Clayton lifted his hands in surrender, knowing he was outnumbered. When Frank and another policeman cuffed Clayton's hands behind his back, the towheaded boy burst out of the crowd, crying and shaking his head. He wrapped his arms around Clayton's leg. The older boy followed and pulled him off, telling him to let go. The younger boy did as he was told, then crumpled to his knees, his shoulders convulsing.

"Everything will be all right," Clayton said to the boy. "Don't worry. I'll be back."

With blood still dripping from his nose, Frank yanked Clayton toward the exit and snarled an order for him to move.

"Behave yourself now," Clayton called over his shoulder to the boy. "Mind Sawyer. He'll take care of you."

Emma went over to the towheaded boy and knelt on the floor beside him. "It's okay," she said, rubbing his small back "Don't cry. Can you tell me your name?"

Tears dripped from his nose. "Jack," he said in a tiny voice.

"Is Clayton your father?"

He shook his head. Emma looked at the older boy, a question on her face.

"His father is dead," the older boy said. "Killed in a cave-in last year. Clayton looks after him now."

"Are you Sawyer?" she said.

"Yes, ma'am."

"Where is Jack's mother?"

"Dead too," Sawyer said. "From the fever, six months ago."

Sadness tightened Emma's chest. Jack was an orphan, just like her. "What will happen to him now that Clayton has been arrested? Where will he go?" She stood and turned to Aunt Ida, wringing her hands. "We have to help this poor boy!"

Aunt Ida shook her head. "Maybe from now on you'll listen to me and stay out of trouble! Now come along. It's not our place to get involved in such things. I'll have Percy take you back to the house. You've caused enough problems for one day." She reached for Emma's wrist, but Emma ripped it away.

"You might be able to ignore this," Emma said. "But I can't." She pointed at Jack, who was still crying on the floor, his head in his hands. "He's just a baby! Who's going to take care of him?"

A woman in a faded paisley dress stepped forward. She was rail thin, with high cheekbones and haunted eyes. "Don't you worry none about that," she said. "We take care of our own. Always have, always will."

Otis and Percy took Emma by the arm and pulled her away. Her eyes filled as she looked over her shoulder at the boys. Sawyer helped Jack to his feet, and they disappeared into the crowd.

CHAPTER 6

After the dance hall brawl, Uncle Otis warned Emma never to talk to Clayton again or he'd send her to the nearest poorhouse. He refused to tell her how long Clayton would be in jail, but Percy later admitted it would likely be for only one night. The fear was that if Clayton didn't show up for work the next morning, some of the miners would sabotage the colliery. Disgruntled miners could cause all sorts of mischief, Percy said—obstruct loaded coal cars, misplace switches, plunder the warehouse—and there was little chance they'd get caught doing anything. No one knew for sure who Clayton's followers were, but Hazard Flint was determined to find out.

The next evening, Emma walked to the Company Store so Percy could teach her how to run the register and show her the stock room. On her way down the hill, she passed simple, clapboard homes set in openings in the woods, their neat gardens and fenced-in yards like rooms in a house. Women worked among the vegetable gardens, pulling weeds or watering seedlings, while others hung freshly washed clothes on a line. According to Percy, the homes belonged to workers higher up the chain than the rest of the miners, men like the fire boss, the inside boss, and the members of the first-aid and rescue corps.

When she reached the store, Percy showed Emma the customer

ledger and explained how to keep track of the miners' purchases, how much their wages were, and how much they owed. A quick glance through the ledger showed that many of the miners spent nearly their entire salary in the store week in and week out, and occasionally even exceeded it.

"What happens when they owe more than they make?" she said.

Percy shrugged. "It depends," he said. "If someone does it on occasion, the balance is carried over to the next payday. If they do it more than two weeks in a row, I can't allow it to continue. And it won't be long before that miner is looking for a new job."

"But you get the money eventually, don't you? Why would you let someone get fired for trying to provide for his family?"

Percy's eyes raked the store, looking to see if anyone was listening. Two women were examining the brooms and wire-bristle brushes, while a third held up a pair of red long johns to check the buttons and seams.

He kept his voice low. "Not all miners have families, and even if they do, not all of them worry about their wives and children first. Some drink their wages away at the pub before their wives get a hold of their paychecks. It's not my job to worry about how a miner spends his money. And I don't make the rules."

"But when a woman comes in here with two hungry children, how can you turn her away? And the prices." She snatched a loaf of bread from the shelf and shook it at him. "A loaf of bread didn't cost this much back in Manhattan!"

He shot her a wide-eyed look, warning her to keep her voice down. "The prices aren't up to me," he said. "And Mr. Flint checks the books once a month. If I lower the prices or let miners' bills go unpaid, I'll be out of a job along with the miners. And I'd get my father in trouble too."

"Maybe Mr. Flint should pay the miners enough to make a decent living, then he wouldn't have to worry about them not having enough to pay their bills!"

"I said be quiet!" Percy took her by the elbow and herded her inside his office, a worried look on his face. "Will you please watch what you say? This is not fun and games!"

"I agree," she said. "This is not fun and games. And I'm sure you don't have to tell that to the miners' children who go to bed hungry every night."

"Just go outside and wait for me. I'll be closing up in a few minutes."

"With pleasure," she said, and marched out of the store.

But instead of waiting on the porch or climbing into the passenger seat of the Tin Lizzie, Emma started walking. She lifted her chin and pushed stray strands of hair out of her face, letting the breeze caress her hot skin. The sun was starting to sink below the ridgelines, and the mountains stood gray in the gathering dusk. She could almost smell the coming night.

With no particular destination in mind, Emma wandered through town, past the weathered storefronts and the post office, past a hog pit and Abe's livery stable. Men tipped their hats as she walked by, while the women stopped and stared. Either they were shocked that a young woman would be out alone at this hour, or they knew she was the cursed girl who put a pox on Charlotte Gable and started the fight at the dance hall.

In Manhattan, her parents had allowed her to wander the streets as long as she stayed in their neighborhood. It was ridiculous that Aunt Ida, or anyone else, thought it improper or unsafe for her to walk unaccompanied in this small mountain town. Even when she was with someone, there was an expected way of doing things. She could hear her aunt now, warning her to adhere to a modest and measured gait, instructing her to keep her eyes straight ahead and not turn her head to one side.

She turned right onto Sullivan Lane with the intention of following it toward the Pennsylvania Hotel, then stopped, surprised to find herself on an empty street in front of the town jail. She recalled passing the massive stone structure once or twice the last time she was here, but had forgotten where it was until now. The square, two-story jailhouse was built on higher ground and surrounded by a retaining wall. It loomed above the surrounding buildings like a medieval fortress. A watchtower sat on top of the flat roof, and the tall, narrow windows were covered with black bars. For some reason, the jail made her uneasy. It was as if the pain and misery suffered within emanated through the gray stones and penetrated her skin, like heat from a rock on a sunny day. She couldn't imagine Clayton in one of the cells, sitting on a hard cot and worrying about Jack. She hoped Percy was right, and Clayton had been released.

She thought about going over and pounding on the massive front door, to see if they would let her in or tell her if Clayton was still there. But before she could make a decision, a flock of grackles appeared in the graying sky and landed on the jail roof, crowding the stone cornices, jostling for space and filling the air with raucous natter. Then, one by one, they grew quiet, and it seemed as if they were looking down on her with their beady black eyes. In the near silence, a soft, rhythmic thump echoed along the sidewalk off to her right. It got closer and closer. At first she thought it was the thud of her heart getting louder and louder, but then she felt it, a slight vibration in the planks beneath her feet. Out of the corner of her eye, she caught sight of a boy, his pale face floating above black clothes as he made his way toward her. She turned to look, knowing full well it was Albert's twin, the breaker boy with the missing leg. He stopped beside her, leaning on wooden crutches stained black by coal dust. She forced a smile, fighting the urge to run.

"Hello," she said. "My name's Emma. What's yours?"

The boy said nothing. He just stood there, staring up at her, his face grave.

"Can I help you with something?" she said.

"He is here," the boy said. His voice was raspy and hoarse, as if it took all of his effort to speak.

"Who is here?" she said. She looked toward the jailhouse. "Are you talking about Clayton? Is he still locked up?"

The boy shook his head.

She glanced up and down the sidewalk. They were alone. "Who are you talking about then?"

"Albert."

She flinched as if slapped. "Albert?" she said. Alarm rushed through her like a jolt of electricity. At the same time, gooseflesh rose on her arms. "How do you know..."

"You have to help," he said.

"Help who? Albert?"

The sky and sidewalk seemed to tilt around her, and her legs nearly gave out. Again, the notion that Albert was alive filled her head. *Could he be trapped somewhere in Coal River, waiting for me to find him?* Then, for the thousandth time, she pictured his coffin being lowered into the cold ground. *No, that's impossible. He's gone and he's never coming back.*

"Why are you just standing there, doing nothing?" the boy croaked.

Briefly, she wondered if the laudanum could leave lingering effects that caused hallucinations. Or maybe this was a nightmare, brought about by being back in this dreadful place. She bit down on the inside of her cheek until the coppery taste of blood slid over her tongue. No, she was awake. How in the world did this strange boy know Albert? How did he know she had stood by and done nothing while her brother drowned? And what did he want? Then she remembered that the entire town was talking about her. This was nothing more than a cruel joke.

"Who put you up to this?" she said, trying to keep her voice even.

He stared at her for a long time, the center of his eyes as black as washed chalkboards. She could almost see little white reflections of herself in his irises. Something cold and hard flashed behind those eyes. Then he turned and went the other way, his crutches thumping on the sidewalk as he disappeared. Emma wrapped her arms around herself and hurried across the street, her eyes filling. *What in the world is going on?* she thought. *Why he is tormenting me like this?*

The sidewalk became a blur, and she nearly bumped into a priest from the nearby parish. It was Father Delaney, the priest who'd given the eulogy at Albert's funeral. Back then he was white-haired and wrinkled, but now he looked like a man on the verge of death. A handful of silver hairs sprouted from his age-spotted head, and deep, zigzagging cracks lined his sunken face.

She swallowed hard. "I'm so sorry, Father. Please, excuse me."

"Are you all right, miss?" Father Delaney said. "Do you need help?" The sharp aroma of alcohol wafted from his wet lips like a fine mist, and his rheumy eyes were bloodshot.

"No, thank you," she said. "I . . . I just need to pay more attention to where I'm going."

"Go in peace, my child," he said. He held up a withered hand and watched her hurry on, blessing her from afar.

I'll never find peace in this place, she thought. She ran two more blocks, then stopped to catch her breath. For the life of her, she couldn't understand why she kept seeing that boy, or why he would say something about Albert. Someone had to be playing a trick on her. It was the only thing that made sense. Maybe they were so afraid of her "curse" that they were trying to scare her into leaving. Maybe Charlotte Gable wanted her to think she was imagining things so she wouldn't tell on her and Uncle Otis. Or maybe Frank wanted revenge because she didn't want anything to do with him. And yet, from the very first moment she saw the boy, something about him made her uncomfortable. And then there was the fact that she hadn't told anyone about seeing him. It had to be more than a prank or a coincidence. She glanced over her shoulder, suddenly worried he was following her. The sidewalk and street were empty. She raked her hair away from her face and kept walking.

Three blocks over, she passed McDuff's Ole Alehouse, a two-story saloon with a timber veranda and curtained windows. Ragtime music floated out from the glowing interior. A group of older boys sat on the porch, playing cards and drinking beer from tin growlers. On the dusty lawn, men and boys gathered in a circle, yelling and swearing at two roosters fighting in a wire pen. A woman came out of the swinging doors and sauntered over to a young man on a bench, her hair loose on her bare shoulders, her lips red as blood. She bent over to show off her cleavage, smiling and running her fingers through the young man's hair. He grinned and pulled her close to grab her breasts.

Uneasy, Emma picked up her pace and moved to the other side of the road, sidestepping wheel ruts and horse manure as she crossed. Some of the boys outside the saloon looked only about thirteen or fourteen, while others looked younger still. Aunt Ida had said that the miners didn't have control over their children, but letting them go to a tavern? It was carelessness and downright neglect. Where were their mothers? Then she had another thought, one that made her skin turn cold. Maybe they were all orphans, let loose to do as they pleased. Maybe the people who took them in didn't have the time or resources to do anything more than put a roof over their heads and give them something to eat. Maybe the boys were risking their lives in the breaker every day to pay for beer, cigarettes, cockfights, and prostitutes.

A few minutes later, she passed two buildings with broken windows and missing shingles, and wished she'd gone a different way. Gruff voices emerged from the dark alley between the buildings. She couldn't make out every word or see anyone in the shadows, but she could tell it was two men, arguing and threatening each other. She slowed, wondering if she should turn around. Then a man shouted, and the alleyway filled with the sounds of fighting—heavy breathing, fists meeting muscle and bone. Then the metallic rasp of a knife being pulled from a sheath, a grunt, and a man's strangled groan. Terrified, Emma raced to the other side of the road, turned down a side street, and hurried toward home.

When she reached her aunt and uncle's, Percy was in the driveway, leaning against the Tin Lizzie, his arms crossed over his chest.

"Where have you been?" he said. "I told you to wait outside the store."

"I wanted to walk home," she said.

"All right," he said. "But do you know what would have happened if I had gone in the house without you?"

"I'm sorry."

"That's it? That's all you're going to say?"

"What do you want me to say? I'll say it."

He shook his head in disgust, uncrossed his arms, and moved away from the car. "I don't want you to *say* anything," he said. "I just want you to remember that my parents expect me to keep an eye on you when you're working at the store. If you get in trouble, we'll both pay." He headed toward the house.

"Wait!"

He stopped and turned to face her, scowling. "What?"

"Do you know a young boy with black hair, freckles, and a missing a leg? He uses wooden crutches and—"

"A lot of boys around here use crutches."

"I know," she said. "But this one is different. He looks. . . ." She hesitated, unsure how to describe him without using the words haunted and old. Then she remembered something. "The first time I saw him, he was with an elderly woman with white braids. She walked with her back hunched, like she was about to bend over."

"Oh, you mean Michael Carrion," he said. "His grandmother Tala is Indian. She's worn her hair in braids for as long as I can remember. Although I don't see her around as much as I used to."

"How did he lose his leg?"

"The same way all the boys around here lose their limbs. In the breaker. Why are you asking about him?"

She shook her head, unable to meet his gaze. If she told him the truth—that either someone paid Michael to tease her, or he could read her mind—Percy would think she was crazy. And if he told Uncle Otis and Aunt Ida, they'd have reason to get rid of her once and for all. She'd heard stories of women being sent away to public asylums for lesser things. Like the wife of one of the theater owners, who was sent to Willard State for kissing another man and never returned. Emma wanted to get out of Coal River, but not like that.

"It's not important," she said. "I just ran into him on my way home, and he said something I didn't understand."

"What do you mean?"

"He was saying things that didn't make sense."

"But that's impossible," he said. "Michael can't talk."

"Because of his accident in the breaker?"

Percy shook his head. "No, because he hasn't spoken a word since he was born."

A chill crawled up Emma's back, raising tiny bumps of flesh on her neck. "Are you sure?"

"I'm sure. Michael was born a deaf-mute."

The early morning air was thick with humidity when Emma left her uncle's and made her way down the steep hill into town, the soles of her shoes crunching on the gravel road. Katydids and crickets clicked and buzzed among the poison ivy and long grass, and mosquitoes buzzed around her ears. Robins and sparrows flitted through the blue sky like black arrows. For the hundredth time she wondered why God filled the Earth with so many beautiful things, only to let them die so soon and unexpectedly. It didn't make sense.

Every time she saw a bird or other small creature—a squirrel, a chipmunk, a rabbit—her first thought was how, despite being beautiful and perfectly designed to live in this world, despite being born with the instinct to do what was necessary to survive, their life spans were incredibly short, their tiny bones and fragile skulls easily crushed by a wagon wheel, their tender flesh torn from their skeletons by bigger animals. She wondered if the field mouse, as it gathered seeds and nuts for the coming winter, realized a fox or eagle could snatch it from the grass without warning. If the eagle soaring above the fields knew a hunter could shoot it down. If the squirrel crossing the road knew an automobile could run it over. Or did the birds and animals go about their lives happy and carefree, unaware they could end at any second?

High on the mountain, the rising sun slowly lit up row after row of windows on the breaker as the wide shadow of Ash Mountain retreated from the mine entrance like a creeping veil. The coal train pounded in the distance, echoing in the valley like a giant beating heart. Even from here, Emma could hear the inner workings of the breaker droning on and on, the constant strain and screech of gears and belts. The crunch and splinter of coal being dumped into the crusher reminded her of breaking bones.

She walked slowly but steadily, trying to brace herself for what lay ahead. It was Saturday, her first day of work at the Company Store, and it was payday for the miners. Percy had warned her it would be busy. How was she going to look in those poor mothers' eyes and tell them they owed money, or that they couldn't buy milk and bread for their hungry children?

Thinking about the children reminded her of Michael. She bunched her hands into fists, her chest constricting. He was a deafmute who had never spoken a word. How and why, all of a sudden, was he speaking to her? Was it a miracle? Should she find his parents to tell them he had spoken at long last? No. It didn't feel like a miracle. It felt like something else entirely, something dark and threatening. Perhaps it was a warning, an omen, a message only she would understand. Except she didn't understand it. At all. And why in the world did he mention Albert? How did he even know his name? Then another thought crossed her mind. What if Percy was lying about Michael, or had him confused with someone else? Or what if she had imagined the entire thing?

She walked faster, tears of frustration misting her eyes. Last night, after learning Michael was a deaf-mute, and afraid she was having hallucinations, she had dumped the rest of the laudanum down the toilet. There had only been a few sips left in the bottle, but if the medicine was having that kind of effect on her, she was never going to touch it again. She was trying to move on with her life and needed a clear head. Taking medicine would only make it harder to think straight. Except now, in the light of day, she no longer believed the laudanum had anything to do with it. What happened with Michael felt real.

Outside the Company Store, women with goat-drawn wagons and hand-pulled carts filled the street. Emma kept her eyes on the sidewalk, worried that Michael would be among the crowd. She took a deep breath and let it out slowly, trying to push all thoughts from her mind so she could concentrate on the task at hand. She couldn't afford to make mistakes on her first day at work.

Inside the store, a line of miners' wives stood at the register, wicker baskets and canvas bags slung over their arms, children with dirty faces clinging to their frayed skirts. Percy worked at the register, running a finger down a page of the customer ledger, his brow furrowed in concentration.

Emma went into the office, grabbed a white apron, and hurried back out and behind the counter.

"What do you need me to do?" she said, slipping the apron over her head and tying it behind her back.

Percy kept his finger on the open book. "Here," he said. "I'll run the register while you check to see if they owe anything from last week. See this? Mrs. Anderson still owes twenty-six cents. I'll add it to what she's buying now, and you can mark it paid. If any purchases need to be wrapped, you can do that while I take their money."

"All right," she said. She smiled at the woman in line to show her she was on her side. Mrs. Anderson stared back at her, her face dour. Percy rang up her purchases: a bag of flour, a tin of lard, three boxes of matches, and a bar of lye soap. Then he added twenty-six cents and announced the total.

Mrs. Anderson reached into a drawstring pouch tied to her waist, counted out the coins, and gave them to Percy. He handed Emma a rubber stamp and told her to mark the woman's total PAID. Emma did as she was told and, without a word, Mrs. Anderson gathered her groceries, put them in a hand-pulled cart, and exited the store. The next woman waddled up to the counter, one hand on her huge belly. She looked like she was about to give birth any second. She said her name, and Emma looked it up.

"She owes one dollar," Emma said. She gave the woman a weak smile, hoping she would see that she sympathized with her dilemma.

The woman scowled. "Are you sure?" she said. "Check it again."

"William and Meredith Trent?" Emma said, raising her eyebrows. The woman nodded, resting her knuckles on the counter and leaning to one side as if nursing a sore leg. Emma ran her finger beneath the woman's name to follow the pencil line to this week's total. "Yes. It says right here." She turned the ledger around so Mrs. Trent could read it herself, but Percy grabbed her wrist to stop her.

"We don't show anyone the ledger," he said, his voice firm.

Emma turned the book around and shrugged. Percy finished ringing up Mrs. Trent's purchases, added the dollar, and waited patiently while she dug in her apron pocket for more change. With tears in her eyes, Mrs. Trent handed him what she owed, leaving two nickels in her hand. Unable to meet her gaze, Emma marked her total PAID.

For the next few hours, Percy and Emma worked at the register, slowly making their way through the line. Every time Percy told one of the miners' wives to put their purchases back on the shelves because their husband's paychecks weren't enough to cover them,

Emma blinked back the moisture in her eyes and tried not to look at the children's dirty, desperate faces. Some of women swore at her and Percy before stomping out of the store, while others quietly wiped their cheeks, trying to put on brave faces.

Shortly before noon, a high-pitched whistle suddenly pierced the air, shrieking through the screen door like a banshee. The women gasped and froze, staring at one another with wide, frightened eyes. Then, in a frantic mob, they stampeded out of the store, dragging their children behind them.

"What's going on?" Emma asked Percy.

Percy's features sagged. "When the breaker whistle goes off at an odd hour, it means only one thing . . . disaster at the mine."

"Oh no," she said. "But where are they all going? I thought—"

"They're going up to the colliery to find out if anyone was hurt or killed. But the mine bosses won't tell them anything. And unless it's a huge accident with a lot of miners involved, everyone has to keep working."

She gasped. "Keep working? That's ridiculous!"

He picked up the ledger and the PAID stamp. "Being injured or killed is the worst offense a miner can make against the coal company," he said. "So why would the bosses stop production?" He shrugged and started toward his office.

She shook her head, unable to believe what she was hearing. "No wonder the miners want to go on strike," she said under her breath.

He stopped and turned to face her. "What did you just say?"

"Nothing."

Six hours later it was closing time, and Percy agreed to let her walk partway home, as long as she promised to wait for him near the deserted woodshed at the bottom of the hill leading up to his parents' house. The woodshed sat just inside the edge of the forest, and she could hide behind it if she heard anyone other than him and the Tin Lizzie coming up the road. He wouldn't be long, and it was important for them to return home together.

She left the store while Percy finished locking up, her mind spinning and her feet aching. The light in the sky was just starting to thin, and the dark shadow of Ash Mountain was draping itself over the coal breaker. She thought it bizarre that the breaker had always reminded her of an enormous creature looming over the town. Now she knew the truth, and it was more awful than she could have imagined. The breaker *was* a creature. It was a monster that ate little boys. How was it possible that the citizens of Coal River were having parties and celebrations, cooking dinner and tucking their children into bed in the shadow of such a horrible place? Were they blinded by greed, or was it something else?

As she made her way along Main Street, she thought about Uncle Otis criticizing her father for not taking a job in the mines. How could anyone think it was a good idea, especially if a man has another choice? She couldn't picture her father in the mines, or Albert in the breaker. She couldn't imagine her mother shopping in the store, being told where she could buy her food and clothing, being turned away for not having enough to pay for an overpriced bag of sugar. In Manhattan her mother used to haggle with the greengrocer and baker, offering to mend aprons or shirts in return for a bag of potatoes or a loaf of bread. Everyone in the neighborhood bartered and worked together, willing to help one another out during hard times. Seeing how things were done in Coal River felt like visiting another country, where she didn't speak the language or understand the culture. And this country was savage and cold.

When she reached the turnoff leading up to the miners' village, a covered wagon pulled by a team of massive, sweaty mules rattled past her and made its way up the hill. A black box with the first-aid symbol painted on both sides enclosed the back of the wagon. A group of women and children in worn clothing hurried after it.

"What's going on?" Emma asked a girl carrying a toddler on her hip.

"It's the Black Maria," the girl said, her face grim.

"The Black Maria?"

"Don't you know?" the girl said. "It's the hearse!" She hitched the toddler higher on her waist and ran to catch up to the others.

Emma stood on the side of the road and tried to decide what to do. If she wasn't waiting for Percy at the bottom of the hill when he came through, he'd never let her walk home again. Then again, it would only take a few minutes to go up to the miners' village and find out what was going on. If she hurried, she could make it up and back before Percy even finished sweeping the floor and latching the shutters. If they met on the road before she made it to the woodshed, he wouldn't have any idea she had taken a detour. She'd just say she was walking slowly and enjoying the cooler air. He couldn't fault her for that.

Her mind made up, she trudged up the hill behind the Black Maria. The slag road grew steeper and steeper. Out of breath from exertion and fear, the women begged the driver to tell them who was in the back of the hearse.

The driver shook his head and said, "Next of kin, only."

Some women dropped their shoulders in relief, while others remained panic-stricken, no doubt worried the driver couldn't know everyone.

A few minutes later, the miners' village came into view, and Emma slowed, trying to comprehend what she was looking at. She knew the miners were poor, but seeing where they lived made her shake with shock and sadness. It was nothing like she had imagined as a little girl.

The village was made up of row after row of shanties sitting back to back, their shallow front yards separated by ragged dirt paths, their small backyards surrounded by misshapen fences made of splintered planks and twisted metal. Several of the houses sat on or between old culm banks, the loose piles of refuse from the breaker. One house had fallen into a huge, jagged hole, its corner sticking out of the collapsed ground.

From down in town, the houses looked square and true, lined up in neat columns like the outlying neighborhoods of a large city. Up close, they were nothing but shacks and shanties, cobbled together with raw scraps of lumber and rusted tin, with porches and railings and steps that looked ready to collapse. Thin, grimy curtains hung in open windows with broken or wood-covered panes. Gray smoke rose from crumbling, soot-covered chimneys to mix with the acidic smell of burning culm and the sour tang of human waste. A string of outhouses ran up the center of each row of shanties, the ground around them black and moist. At the far end of the outhouses, a rusty water pump stood surrounded by mud.

Chickens, pigs, goats, and the occasional dog ran loose in the roads and yards, their faces and feet stained black. Children in torn, dirty clothing played on lawns filled with washtubs, broken bicycles, struggling gardens, and sparse grass. An elderly woman sat in a rocker, a naked infant on one knee, silently watching the Black Maria pass. Some porches held twenty people or more: elderly men and women, adolescent girls, weary mothers, and children of all ages. Coal dust covered everything—the walls and roofs and gardens, the steps, the fences—even the leaves on the trees.

Emma blinked back tears and, at the same time, felt anger burning in her feet, as if it came from the very earth she was walking on. It rose through her legs and torso, traveled up to her neck and to her head where it burned like fire. She pictured Hazard Flint in his expensive clothes, counting his money at a rolltop desk inside the Flint Mansion, while up in the miners' village, children cried with hunger and babies shivered beneath threadbare blankets. She thought about Uncle Otis and Aunt Ida, their fancy clothes and china-filled cabinets, their sideboard piled high with shepherd's pie and beef stew, lamb chops and deviled eggs, bread pudding and cherry tarts, tea rolls and scones with orange marmalade. How could they live with themselves, knowing they were living high on the hog while the families of the men who dug the coal from the earth lived in poverty? Then her stomach turned over and she nearly gagged, realizing she'd been wearing the same clothes and eating the same lavish cuisine, bought with money made off the backs of miners who could barely afford to feed their own children.

Michael's words rang in her ears: *You have to help.* Was that what Michael was trying to tell her? That she had to help the miners and their children? But how? What in the world could she do? And what did Albert have to do with any of this?

Trying to shake the sensation that dark shadows were brushing up against her, even in the light of the day, Emma followed the hearse as it passed Scotch Road, Dago Street, and Welsh Hill, then turned into a narrow dirt path called Murphy's Patch. The wagon mules were foaming at the mouth, their hooves kicking up clouds of black dust.

Someone shouted, "It's the Black Maria!" and women erupted from their shanties to stand on their front stoops. They wrung their hands and clutched their stained aprons, waiting to see where the hearse would stop. Young children appeared beside their mothers' long skirts and looked toward the road with curious eyes. One by one, as the death wagon passed each house, the women bowed their heads in relief, as if saying a silent prayer of thanks that their husbands or sons hadn't been killed that day.

Finally, the driver of the Black Maria pulled back on the reins and stopped at the second-to-last shack at the end of the lane. The woman on the porch went white and fell to her knees. Then she started screaming. Two young children ran out the door and clutched the splintered porch railings with dirty hands, staring at their mother, their faces filled with terror. The rest of the women moved down their steps and silently walked toward the new widow's house. The driver and his helper climbed down from the Black Maria, pulled a covered body from the wagon bed, and carried the stretcher toward the shanty, only stopping long enough to replace a dangling foot beneath the bloodstained sheet. A neighbor woman helped the new widow to her feet, then moved her and her children out of the way so the men could take the body inside.

A big-bosomed blonde left her porch and strode toward Emma, her long, faded skirt twisting around her legs as she marched in her direction. Emma recognized the woman from the store. Her name was Fern, and she'd been charged for two pair of long johns she claimed she didn't buy. Percy had warned the woman to be quiet and pay or else her husband would be looking for another job. Emma remembered feeling frightened when Fern glared at them for a full minute before leaving the store. Now Emma clenched her teeth, hoping Fern didn't recognize her.

"You best be going back down to the rich folk where you belong!" Fern shouted before she reached her. "The likes of you aren't welcome here. Especially since you're working at the pluck me store."

"I only wanted to see—"

"See what?" Fern said. She stopped and stood, her fists on her hips, scowling. "Some poor miner's dead body? His crying widow? His hungry children?"

"No," Emma said. "I . . . Is there anything I can do to help?"

"There's nothing you can do 'cept go back where you came from. Now git!"

"I wish I could," she said, not knowing what else to say. "I don't want to be here any more than you do."

The woman crossed her arms. Her elbows and lower arms were scaly and red. "Now, what's that supposed to mean?"

"I'm here in Coal River because my parents died in a fire," Emma said. She directed her attention back to the new widow's shanty, hoping Fern would take pity on her and leave her alone.

Fern harrumphed, and Emma turned to look at her, surprised to see that her features had gone soft, the hostility gone. The woman was shaking her head, her eyes sad.

"I'm only working at the Company Store because my aunt and uncle expect me to earn my keep," Emma added. "I'm not getting paid."

Fresh sympathy crossed Fern's face. "When I was a little girl," she began, "we used to wait on the front porch for Pa to come home. When we saw him walking up the dirt path, his hands and face black with coal, we'd all run into him, never mind that we'd get dirty when he picked us up to hug him. We were just happy to see him come home alive, his hands and feet and arms and legs all still attached. He was one of the lucky ones who died of old age. Can't imagine what it felt like to lose your ma and pa at the same time. Sorry I was so hard on you."

Emma nodded once to show she'd accepted Fern's apology. "What's going to happen to the new widow and her children?"

"Hard to say," Fern said. "Company might send her to Widow's Row, where she'll earn rent by taking in new immigrants and single miners. Supposin' there's room, that is."

"And if there's not?"

"She'll be evicted."

Emma shook her head, unable to find words.

"You seem like a nice girl," Fern said. "Why don't you take my advice and go on back home? There's nothing you can do here."

She patted Emma's arm, then made her way to the new widow's house with the rest of the women. Emma's eyes filled as she looked around at the thin children on the porches and in the yards. Maybe Fern was right. How in the world could anyone stand up to the Bleak Mountain Mining Company and put a stop to Hazard Flint? How could anyone put an end to this tragedy, least of all, someone like her? When Michael said she should help, he must have been talking about something else.

She searched the young faces for Jack, hoping she could figure out where Clayton Nash lived, but she didn't see the boy anywhere. She looked for Michael's grandmother, thinking a woman with long white braids would be easy to spot. Maybe Tala would understand how and why Michael had spoken to her, and how he knew about Albert.

Just then, a group of miners appeared at the end of the dirt lane, their clothes and hats and gumshoes covered in coal dust, their sleeves and pants heavy and wet. Their canteens and dinner pails clanged together as they walked, echoing like cowbells in the hollow. They carried metal bars, shovels, picks, tamping rods, safety lamps, and cans of blasting powder. Their faces were black beneath caps with attached oil wick lanterns, their swollen, bloodshot eyes like bleeding holes in their heads.

Emma scanned the crowd for Clayton but couldn't see him. Except for Nally, who was heads and shoulders above the others, it was impossible to tell one coal-covered face from another. Every brow was furrowed, every mouth in a thin, hard line. Nally and several others broke away and headed toward the next row of shanties. She turned her attention back to the new widow's house. A few seconds later, someone tapped her on the shoulder. It was Clayton, his dust-caked lips clamped around the end of a clay pipe. With a black hand, he took the pipe out of his mouth.

"What are you doing up here?" he said.

"I followed the Black Maria. Do you know what happened?"

"Cave-in."

"Does that happen often?"

He sniffed as if it were the most ridiculous question he'd ever heard. "It's a coal mine," he said. "We work hundreds of feet underground. What do you think?"

She stiffened, surprised by his hostile demeanor. Was he blaming her for getting him arrested? "How would I know?" she said. "I didn't grow up in a mining town. I spent a few months here when I was ten, that's all. And it was a long time ago."

"Lucky you," he said.

"Yeah, lucky me."

"It's worse when there's an explosion," he said. "Then we have to pick up the pieces, an arm here, a leg there, a man with no head, his brains splashed against the walls, mules blown to bits. Can't even eat after that."

"Please," she said. She put a hand over her stomach. "Why do you insist on torturing me with such horrible stories?"

"I want you to see," he said. "I want you to see that your uncle and the man he works for need to change the way this colliery is run before disaster strikes. Simple decency is all we ask. Emergency exits, proper ventilation. Better pumps to keep it dry and safe. The richest vein lies right next to the riverbed. Part of that could cave in at any second and drown us all. Instead Hazard Flint cuts corners and takes risks, digging columns too narrow, going back into partially collapsed shafts because there's too much coal to ignore."

"What does that have to do with me?" she said. "The last time I checked, you worked for Hazard Flint too!"

He said nothing for a long moment, then met her gaze. "Fair enough. But are you sure it doesn't have anything to do with you? Who's paying for those fancy clothes you're wearing? And I suppose you're growing your own food, milking your own cow, butchering your own pig?" He took off his hat, revealing a white forehead smudged with coal dust. "I'm sorry. I just found out you're working at the Company Store. And I get angry when a good man gets killed."

Behind him, a group of policemen crested the hill on horseback, their rifles resting on their thighs, a cloud of dust rising up behind them.

"You better leave," Clayton said. He put his cap back on and sprinted, his head down, to catch up with the other miners.

The women and children went back inside their shanties, and Emma started toward home, her eyes on the road, her head swimming. No wonder the miners were talking about a strike. If they refused to dig coal from the earth, Mr. Flint would have to listen to them, wouldn't he? What were they waiting for? The herd of horses trotted past, their hooves throwing dirt and slag in the air. A horse stopped beside her and snorted, its brown hide covered in foamy sweat. She looked up at the rider. It was the police captain, Frank Bannister.

"What are you doing up here?" he said.

"Nothing," she said, continuing on.

He turned his horse and followed her. "Who were you talking to?" he said. "Was that Clayton Nash?"

She stopped and glared up at him. "Who I talk to is none of your business."

"I'm trying to protect you, Emma," he said. "Can't you see that?"

"I don't need anyone to protect me, least of all you."

"Let me give you a lift back to town. The other men can handle this."

"Why are you even here?" she said. "These people don't need the police. Someone's already been killed. They need food and clothing and fair wages."

Frank scowled. "Well, I guess I've got my answer. Sounds like you've been talking to Nash after all."

"I'm not a fool," she said, "I don't need anyone to tell me that these people aren't being treated fairly. All I have to do is look around. So unless you're here to help them, we don't have anything to discuss."

"I'm here on official business."

She looked back at the miners' village. The rest of the policemen were making their way toward a two-story shanty with boarded-up windows. Three of them stopped and waited on horseback near the front porch while two others dismounted and climbed the steps, rifles in hand. One knocked on the door while the other stood off to the side, waiting. A pregnant woman opened the door. She wore a thin housedress with a fraying hem, and held a toddler in her arms. The first policeman showed her a piece of paper and pointed toward the road. The woman blanched and clutched her throat, her face contorted with fear and anguish. She pleaded with the officers.

The bitter tang of contempt filled Emma's mouth. She stared angrily up at Frank. "Are you throwing her out of her house?" she said.

His face hardened. "It's not hers," he said. "Hazard Flint owns it. He owns all these shacks."

"But why are you evicting her?" she said. "What did she do?"

"Your cousin, Percy, says they haven't paid their bill at the Company Store in a month," he said. "And her husband just got injured and can't work. Right now he's down at the saloon, drinking the last of his money."

"But they have a toddler and a baby on the way! Can't you let them stay until her husband goes back to work?"

"We're just doing what Mr. Flint pays us to do." He reached down for her. "Give me your hand. I'll pull you up."

"No," she said. "Please. Just leave me alone."

CHAPTER 7

At half past midnight, when she was certain everyone was asleep, Emma got dressed, grabbed her suitcase, and snuck downstairs. She crept through hallways filled with grainy shadows, then slipped through the door into the kitchen. A bluish, otherworldly glow bathed the white-tiled kitchen, and the coal stove ticked in the quiet room. Moonlight reflected off the glass-front cupboards, making the panes look like squares of ice. She tiptoed across the floor and into the pantry, freezing with every creak and wooden groan. Moving as quickly as possible, she filled her suitcase with canned goods, taking one jar each of beans, carrots, beets, tomatoes, corn, and peas. She prayed Cook wouldn't notice anything missing. When she was finished in the pantry, she shoved two loaves of bread into a cloth sack, stole a half a wedge of cheese, and took a tin of milk from the icebox.

Then she left the kitchen and crossed the dining room, her shoulders hunched, trying to ignore the feeling that her aunt and uncle were watching from the portrait above the fireplace mantel, their dark eyes following her every move. A high-pitched ringing filled her ears, along with the sound of her blood rushing through her veins. She went to the cherry sideboard, wrapped three scones inside a cloth napkin, and put them in the sack. Then she reached for a jar of marmalade, and froze. Someone was behind her, breathing hard and fast. Fear clutched her throat. She'd been caught. Trying not to panic, she tried to come up with a lie that would sound believable. Nothing came to her.

Then a darker thought came to her mind, and the hairs on her arms stood up. It was Michael. He had broken in because he had another message for her. She spun around to face him, certain he would be standing there, staring at her with black eyes.

There was no one there.

A window was open on the far side of the dining room. A tree branch was brushing back and forth over the sill, rustling across the wood with a rhythmic swish-swish. Emma's shoulders dropped, and she let out a sigh of relief, her thundering heart starting to slow.

She made a move to go over and close the window, then decided it might make too much noise. Instead she grabbed the marmalade and hurried into the hall. Once there, she paused, waited for her eyes to adjust to the gloom, and made her way through the living room toward the back veranda.

Holding her breath and saying a silent prayer that the porch door would be unlocked, she gripped the glass doorknob and turned it. The latch clicked and the door slipped loose of the frame, squeaking softly. She slipped outside, carefully closed the door behind her, lifted the suitcase and sack of food over the veranda railing, and set them in Aunt Ida's flower bed, trying not to disturb the prized roses. Then she straddled the railing, climbed over, and crossed the moonlight lawn. She stole a final glance over her shoulder to make sure she'd escaped undiscovered.

Uncle Otis and Aunt Ida's bedroom curtains were open. And their light was on.

She ducked and sprinted toward the side yard, staying low until she reached a line of eastern hemlock and leafy dogwood on the far end of the lawn. There she hid in the shadows and looked back at the house again, nervous sweat breaking out on her forehead. Then she shook her head, a shaky laugh erupting from her lips. The bedroom curtains were closed, but the material was so sheer, it gave the illusion of them being open. No one was pulling the curtains back, watching her sneak across the yard. No one was opening the sash to yell after her into the night. She said a silent thank-you, then climbed over the wrought-iron fence at the rear of the yard and made her way down the hill toward town.

The moon was high, and a million stars shimmered in the night sky above the mountains, like ice chips in a coal dust blanket. Praying everyone was in bed, she followed the residential streets of the village, avoiding the roads that ran beside saloons, hotels, and taverns. When she reached the village green, she started across the shadowy grass, hoping to take a shortcut across the lawn toward the road leading up to the colliery. Then she caught a glimpse of movement, and froze. A gathering of silhouettes lurked around the bandstand, the orange tips of cigars and cigarettes glowing in the dark. Drunken laughter and loud voices traveled across the green through the humid night air. Unless she wanted to take the chance of being harassed by a band of drunks, she would have to take the long way around. So she turned and went the other way, hardly daring to breath until she was safe from view.

Keeping close to buildings and hurrying from one house to the next, she finally reached the road leading up the mountain. She trudged up the steep hill, her hand aching from the suitcase handle digging into her fingers. Black branches and leaves seemed to make shapes like faces and reaching hands. All of a sudden she stopped and drew in a dry breath. What if Michael was here, waiting for her on this dark road? What if she didn't see him until the last minute?

That's enough, she told herself. *There is no reason to be afraid. Michael is just a boy. He has no reason to harm me. If anything, I should be worried about running into more drunks.* She exhaled and continued on her way, trying to devise a plan for what she was about to do.

When she reached the miners' village, she hid beneath a lone high-skirted spruce and set down the suitcase, checking to make sure the coast was clear. Other than a few open windows yellowed by flickering lantern light, the houses were dark, the roads empty. She picked up the suitcase and moved along the far edges of the main thoroughfare. Slag crunched beneath her shoes, and an owl hooted in the distance. At the end of Welsh Hill, a coonhound jumped off a porch and barked at her, making her jump. She scurried away and entered the dirt path that led into Murphy's Patch. Behind her, the dog howled into the night, a long, sorrowful moan that echoed through the quiet hollow.

With her heart in her throat, she continued along the lane until she reached the shanty of the new widow. The windows were dark, and black ribbons hung from the front door. Emma went around the side of the leaning front porch, knelt in the damp grass, opened the suitcase, and removed three jars of vegetables. She crept up the porch steps, careful not to trip on the broken treads, and set the jars of vegetables on the threshold, along with the cloth sack filled with a loaf of bread, the cheese, and the tin of milk. Then she pounded hard on the door, scrambled down the steps, picked up her suitcase, and ran. She sprinted across the dirt path and hid behind an outhouse, where she waited, hardly daring to move. When she peeked around the corner, the sour tang of human waste wafting from the outhouse door hit her and she clamped a hand over her nose and mouth, swearing under her breath. She wanted to move to a better spot, but worried the widow would come out and see her.

A few seconds later, a lantern flickered behind a front window, and the door opened. The widow searched the empty porch, looking left and right, her weary face etched with confusion. When she didn't see anyone, she stepped back and started to close the door. Then she noticed the jars of vegetables on the threshold. She knelt and peered inside the cloth bag. Her mouth fell open. She picked up the bag and grabbed the jars, clutching them to her chest with one wiry arm, then raised her face to the sky and crossed herself before closing the door.

When she thought it was safe again, Emma stepped out from behind the outhouse and moved away from the shack, a surge of elation loosening the tightness in her neck and shoulders. For the first time in what seemed like forever, she felt a weight being lifted, as if she were crawling out from beneath a boulder, or being let out of prison. It felt as though she were taking her first deep breath since coming to Coal River. Maybe this was what Michael meant. Maybe this was what she was supposed to do.

Still, there were so many unanswered questions. How did Michael know this was what she needed? And why was he able to speak to her if he was a deaf-mute? More importantly, why did he say Albert's name? She had to find answers.

On her way out of Murphy's Patch, she left the rest of the vegetables and bread on random porches, wishing she knew if the evicted pregnant woman still lived somewhere in the village, so she could leave food on her doorstep too. When all the food was gone, she made her way back down the hill, her spirit soaring with something that felt like an exhilarating mixture of love and triumph. It was like nothing she had ever experienced before, and it was completely unexpected. Her insides felt full of light, her mind full of possibilities. She remembered reading a quote by Booker T. Washington a few years ago that said, "Those who are happiest are those who do the most for others." Now, for the first time, she understood it completely. She couldn't explain it, but she felt intoxicated, drunk on life and love for her fellow human beings. Tomorrow morning this elation would be gone, buried beneath the returned weight of crushing sorrow. But for now she would savor the reprieve. And in the days to come, maybe helping the miners would lessen the wretched grief she carried inside her heart. She could hope anyway.

CHAPTER 8

The morning after the cave-in, and Emma's nighttime excursion into the miners' village, the sky was low and threatening, as if the endless smoke from the culm banks had gathered below the clouds, obscuring everything like a giant shroud of churning grief. It was a Sunday, and Emma was free to do as she pleased as long as she made it to church on time. She left her uncle's house early, before everyone was awake. The world was gray and silent, except for the distant, snarling roar of Coal River.

The previous night, she had gone to bed filled with hope and purpose, certain she was doing the right thing by leaving food on the widow's doorstep. She had vowed then and there to take food up to the miners as often as she could without getting caught, hoping she had found a way to stay sane in Coal River. But then, after tossing and turning half the night, trying to figure out more ways to help the mining families, and wrestling with the fact that she was counting on her uncle to provide food and shelter with money earned off the miners' backs, the weight of heartache and anger returned. Leaving food for the miners wasn't enough. She had to do more. What, exactly, she wasn't sure. But if she was going to start over, if she was going to help anyone, there was something else she had to do first.

She made her way down the steep hill and around the edge of the village, following the road behind Flint Mansion and Susquehanna Avenue. She walked past the train depot, then took a narrow lane toward the river. She passed the coal pit used as a stoking point for the trains that ran through the switching yards, then she plodded down a steep, dirt path, her arms swinging in rhythm with her steps, trying not to think until she reached her destination. Locusts whirred in the river birch, and a cardinal called from the pines. Fir trees and honeysuckle bordered one side of the trail, and a tangle of grapevines and poison sumac lined the other. Nine years ago, when she'd chased Percy and his friends down this path, the trees had been mere saplings, the bushes an overgrown patch of chickweed and witchgrass. Still, she remembered the twists and turns, sidestepped the rocky sections, and slowed on the hairpin curves that edged foliage-camouflaged cliffs as if she'd run down it yesterday.

"I'll just walk on and on," she said to anything or anyone that might be listening. Maybe the path turned into a foot trail along the riverbanks and followed the waterway right out of Coal River. If only she had dressed for hiking and brought provisions. If only the surrounding mountains weren't endless and steep and the woods weren't filled with wild animals. If only she had someplace to go. *Remember what you came here for,* she reminded herself.

When she came to the third fork in the path and turned down it, her throat grew tighter and tighter. Just then, a flock of crows exploded from the branches of a tall maple, making her jump. She stopped and held a hand over her racing heart, trying to catch her breath. The crows screeched and beat their mighty black wings, scolding her for disturbing them. Then they were gone as quickly as they had appeared, and she was alone again. She kept walking, trying to ignore the sense of dread that crept up her spine, the light chill caressing the nape of her neck. She held her breath around every corner, certain Michael would be standing in the path, waiting. While she was grateful that he had led her toward the decision to help the miners, and felt that his intentions were good, he was still a deaf-mute who had never spoken a word to anyone except her. His face showed no emotion, and his dark eyes seemed to look into her soul. It was eerie. What would he say this time?

She steeled herself and kept going. If Michael had something else to tell her, she would listen. Especially if it had something to do with Albert. Finally the ground leveled out, and she crossed a narrow clearing between birch and fir trees. Stepping through a wide swatch of grass, she came to a gray mosaic of flat rocks near the shoreline. The river looked brown and cold, and the smell of muddy water hung in the air, equal parts iron, coal dust, sulfur, and wet rock. As always, the waves were high and churning, the rocky banks stained yellow from mine runoff. The thunderous roar of rapids filled the air, a constant whooshing that some might have considered peaceful, but set Emma's nerves on edge. The snarl of water reminded her of the uncontrollable power of the river, and the speed at which a life could be carried away.

She stared at the dark water for a long time, then went back to the grassy clearing and faced east, toward the train trestle in the distance. This was where she needed to be, not where her brother was buried in the cold, hard ground, but where his soul had left his body. This was where she'd been standing nine years ago, feet rooted to the icy ground, doing nothing while he drowned. She closed her eyes and pictured his small face, his brown eyes and freckled nose, his toothy grin. She thought of all the things he'd missed out on—growing taller and falling in love, family dinners and snowy Christmases, their mother's famous chocolate birthday cakes. He would have loved the growing number of automobiles in Manhattan, and the feature-length films at the theater.

Her heart ached, thinking how much she missed and needed him now that their parents were dead. Before returning to Coal River, it had been so long since she'd seen and talked to him that it almost felt like he was someone she had known in a dream, or loved in another lifetime. Only one thing remained constant over the last nine years—the profound weight of her guilt. Here, in Coal River, that burden was multiplied tenfold. In this isolated mining town, he was everywhere, like the coal dust that covered the mountains, the buildings and the roads, the leaves and the bark of the trees, the dirty faces of the boys and young men. Now she felt like she was being punished for forgetting about him, for not keeping him first and foremost in her mind, for going on with her life when he no longer could.

If only she hadn't chased Percy and his friends down to the river that day. If only she hadn't stood there, frozen, watching her little brother fall through the ice. She should have saved him. She should have grabbed a branch or a stick, something for him to hold on to until help came. But it happened so fast. So fast.

"I'm sorry!" she cried above the rush of water. "I was scared. I was only thinking about myself! It was selfish and unforgivable, and I'm a horrible sister!" She hung her head, tears dripping from her nose. "Please, please, Albert. Forgive me if you can."

She knelt in the grass and buried her face in her hands, dark thoughts erupting in her mind. *Maybe everyone is right,* she thought. *Maybe I am cursed. Maybe I should walk into the river and let the rapids pull me under, away from this anguish. Maybe I should walk out on the train trestle and throw myself off.* She imagined the fall from the high bridge, the wind whipping through her hair, the hard impact of the water, and then . . . peace. She raked her hands through her hair. *No. I can't do it. I'm too scared. Besides, I finally have a chance to make up for what I've done. And I'm not willing to go down without a fight.*

Just then, a sharp crack pierced the air, a quick, loud bang above the roar of the river. A gunshot. Emma flinched, the shock of sudden fear tingling through her body. It sounded close. Another shot rang out. She ran for cover behind a giant oak, unsure where the shots were coming from. A third shot sounded, a muted pop in the distance. After a few minutes of silence, she inched out from behind the tree and made her way toward the shoreline, staying close to the bushes. Maybe someone was hunting. The gunshots sounded like they were coming from upstream, in the opposite direction of the train trestle.

When she stepped out onto the flat rocks, her skin went cold. A man floated down the river just inches from the shoreline, his face covered in blood, his arms and legs undulating on the waves. Her breakfast rose in the back of her throat, and she clasped a hand over her mouth to keep it down. Before the body passed, she recovered and dropped to her knees to try to reach the man before he was washed away. But again the river was faster than she was. The rapids swiftly carried the body downstream, the man's pale hands appearing and disappearing like white fish just below the riled surface. She swore and pounded her fist on her leg, then looked up-river, toward the direction the body had come from. A group of men stood on an outcropping of rock. Her breath caught, but they hadn't noticed her.

One of the men was Hazard Flint, looking on while a man in a deerskin jacket with an oversized cross engraved on the back held a revolver to a kneeling man's head. A fourth man, this one wearing a police uniform, stood next to the kneeling man, his back to Emma. She couldn't be certain, but it looked like Frank Bannister. Then Mr. Flint nodded, Frank stepped back, and the man in the deerskin jacket pulled the trigger. The kneeling man slumped forward, and Frank pushed him over the rocky bank with one foot. The man in the deerskin threw the gun into the river, watching it splash into the water about halfway across. Then he looked in her direction.

For a fraction of a second, Emma froze, unsure if he could see her. Then he pointed at her, and she bolted into the brush, her head down, ignoring thorns and the slap of branches on her face and arms. She took a shortcut toward the path, slamming through bushes and brambles. Finally the path opened up just ahead, and she nearly fell when she burst out of the underbrush. Behind her, to her right, she heard the crackle and crash of someone running through the woods. Whoever it was, they were headed in her direction. She turned and raced up the hill, breathing hard and pushing herself to get to the top before her pursuer could cut her off.

Halfway up, she stumbled and fell. Pain flared briefly in her ankle, rocks and sticks stabbing the skin on her palms. She pushed herself upright and hobbled a few steps before finding her stride again. Ignoring the ache in her leg, she sprinted on and up, no sound but her own labored breathing in her ears. Then, behind her, someone crashed out of the woods and shouted. She kept going, the slippery soles of her shoes kicking up sand and gravel. If she could make it to the top of the path, she could run to the train depot, or hide in one of the storage buildings next to the gravel pit.

Then someone grabbed her by the arm and spun her around. It was Frank.

"Emma!" he said, his sweat-rimmed eyes wide.

She yanked herself from his grasp and started running again. He caught up and captured her, his strong fingers digging into her upper arms.

She kicked his shins. "Let me go!" It was no use. He tightened his hold.

"What are you doing down here?" he said.

"I was just . . ." she said.

"What did you see?" he said, shaking her.

"Nothing!" she said, her voice trembling. "I didn't see anything!"

"Why were you running then?"

Her mind raced as she tried to come up with a believable excuse. "I thought I saw . . . a body," she said. "In the river. It scared the hell out of me!"

"That's it?"

She nodded.

"You're lying," he said. Just then, Mr. Flint and the man in the deerskin jacket rounded a bend a few hundred yards down the hill, moving fast. Frank glanced over his shoulder, then directed his attention to her again. "Keep your mouth shut about this," he said under his breath. "Or you'll be sorry. Now hit me! Hard!"

She shook her head, confused. "What are you—"

"Hit me!" he said through clenched teeth, his eyes wild with an odd mixture of power and fear. "Unless you want to join your brother in that river, do it now!"

She clawed his face and hit him hard with both fists, releasing fury and fear with every blow. He howled and let go, bending over in pain. "Go on," he hissed. "Run."

She turned and ran up the hill, faster than she had run in her entire life.

After seeing the men murdered down by the river, Emma raced home, convinced that she had to flee Coal River. If she hurried, she could leave before her aunt and uncle came home from church. But by the time she reached the house, she remembered that nothing had changed since she'd first arrived. She still had no money and nowhere to go. And even if she had somewhere to go, Aunt Ida and Uncle Otis would never buy her a train ticket. After all, she was bringing in extra income and working around the house for free. Why would they pay good money to get rid of a slave?

Besides, what was she going to do, tell them she needed to leave because she saw Hazard Flint order someone killed? That he and Frank Bannister were murderers? They'd never believe her. Or maybe they already knew. After all, they were part of the problem, letting Mr. Flint run this town. And even if something happened to her, would her aunt and uncle even care? She collapsed on the bed, tears of frustration burning her eyes.

Frank had warned her to keep her mouth shut, and she would do just that. For now, at least. Who would she tell anyway? The only person she remotely trusted was Clayton Nash. And she barely knew him. Besides, what could he do? If he tried anything, Mr. Flint would get rid of him too. For now she would play innocent. She would pray Mr. Flint didn't recognize her down by the river, and Frank didn't turn her in. Because what choice did she really have?

The next morning, on her way to the Company Store, she hurried down the steep hill, constantly glancing over her shoulder and into the woods, worried Mr. Flint's henchman would burst out of nowhere and take her down to the river, where he would shut her up for good. Everything around her seemed to move in slow motion, while her own movements felt sped up and jittery, as if her limbs were shaking out of control. Worrying about seeing Michael was one thing, like being afraid of ghosts or bad dreams, something that felt like it could hurt you but really couldn't. Worrying about Hazard Flint and his henchman was another thing entirely. She felt like a rabbit being chased by a fox, or a soldier hiding from battle.

Halfway into town, she met a group of people making their way toward Freedom Hill. She slowed, unsure at first what she was seeing. Six teenage boys in dark jackets carried a small pine coffin up the gravel road, followed by a sobbing woman and a somber-faced man. The man was wearing black trousers and scuffed leather boots. He carried a toddler on his hip and was trying to hold the woman up with his free arm, urging her to keep walking. The woman stumbled beside him, her shoulders convulsing, her face twisted in agony. A few yards behind them, a gathering of miners' wives and children plodded wearily along the road, their faces long. At the rear of the procession, a ragtag troupe of boys in short jackets and patched knickers trudged together in an uneven cluster, their hands in their pockets, their heads low. They looked between the ages of six and twelve, with the younger boys outnumbering the older ones three to one. A few glanced at Emma with haunted eyes, their lips pressed together. Most were trying not to cry. Some walked on crutches, missing half a leg, one foot, an arm. Two boys were missing hands, and one had a black patch over his eye.

Is it ever going to end? she thought. *The death, the maiming, the terrible toll the mine is taking on this town, its families, its children?*

She stepped aside to let the funeral procession pass, but could not draw her eyes away from the coffin. Somewhere, she had heard it was bad luck to meet a funeral cortege. If you met one, you were supposed to turn around and go the other way. If it was unavoidable and you couldn't change directions, you were supposed to hold a button in your hand. She had never believed in such nonsense, but Coal River had a way of making one suspicious. Besides, she'd had enough bad luck to last a lifetime. A burning lump formed in her throat. She pinched a button on her blouse, squeezing so hard, her fingers went numb.

It's such a small coffin, she thought, her eyes flooding. *Did one of the miners' children get sick? Did they go hungry for too long and die of starvation?*

She swallowed a sob and wiped her cheeks with her free hand. A minute ago she had been afraid for her life; now she would have almost welcomed the freedom from this horrible, unrelenting grief. How was it possible that this world was filled with so much suffering? How was it all right for humans to be given the ability to love if their loved ones were only going to be taken away? How could it possibly be God's plan to rip children away from their parents, shattering their hearts and souls forever? For the life of her, she'd never understand it.

A boy on crutches stopped in the middle of the road and turned to look at her. The rest of the boys streamed around him, too lost in their misery to care what he was doing. For some reason, Emma's eyes were drawn to him and she felt rooted to the ground. It was Michael. He moved toward her, hopping on his crutches, then stopped a few feet away. She waited, her hands clammy, her breath coming shallow and quick. Briefly, she thought about asking him why he had spoken to her, then decided to see if he would do it again.

"Will you help?" he croaked.

Emma swallowed. Suddenly, everything except Michael—the funeral procession, the hill, the sky, the trees—seemed covered in a fine haze, like paper-thin ice after a spring thaw. It felt like they were inside a distorted glass ball where no one else could see them.

"What do you want from me?" she said.

Michael looked over his shoulder at the breaker boys following the coffin up the hill. He watched them for a long moment, then gazed up at her again, his eyes wet.

"Are you asking me to help the breaker boys?" she said.

He nodded.

"But how?" she said. "What am I supposed to do? And what does my brother have to do with this?"

Then the haze disappeared and, without another word, Michael turned away, moving fast on his crutches to catch up to the funeral procession.

She watched him leave, fighting the urge to chase after him and force him to answer her questions. It was one thing to take food to the miners' village, but how was she supposed to help the breaker boys? And why her? Because she was new in Coal River? Because she was the supervisor's niece? Because he could tell she was sympathetic to their plight? It didn't make sense. Her stomach filled with a heavy mass of nausea and confusion.

Twenty minutes later, when she entered the Company Store, her eyes were still swollen and red. Between seeing the funeral procession and talking to Michael again, it had taken forever for her tears to stop. Percy was in the far aisle along the opposite wall, piling bags of flour on a bottom shelf.

"Do you know anything about the funeral being held today?" she asked him.

He grunted and lifted a flour sack over one shoulder, his forehead and lashes covered with white powder. "Was there a group of young boys following the casket?" he said. He put the bag on the shelf and straightened, wiping flour from his sleeves.

She nodded.

"Then it was for a breaker boy. I heard one of them fell in a coal chute the other day and smothered to death. They didn't know he was in there until yesterday because they were busy with the cave-in."

She gasped. "But the coffin was so small! How old was he?"

"I believe he was six," Percy said, his voice detached, as if she had inquired about the price of flour.

"I thought the breaker boys were older!"

"They're different ages," he said with a shrug. He headed toward the stock room.

"Wait," she said. "What else can you tell me about Michael Carrion?"

"Not much. I used to see him and his grandmother shopping in the store. But that was before his parents died. Haven't seen either of them in here for months."

"Why not?" she said.

"No money, I suppose," he said. "Rumor has it she makes potions and tinctures out of herbs to trade with the miners' wives for food and goods. And he hunts rabbit and sells the pelts. But I also heard they're living with some old miner. Hard to know what's true." Then his eyes went wide. "Why? Did he talk to you again?"

"No," she said. She had decided not to say anything to anyone until she found out more.

"You must have him confused with someone else," Percy said. "Everyone knows he can't talk."

"I'm surprised the breaker boys were allowed to go to the funeral," she said, trying to change the subject.

"Mr. Flint's not heartless. He gave some of the boys a few hours off."

She scowled, a jolt of anger making her head hurt. "Not heartless? He puts six-year-olds to work in the breaker! And have you been up to the miners' village? Those people are living in poverty while he sits in that mansion like a king!"

The bell over the door jingled before Percy could respond. Sally Gable entered the store, a wicker basket hooked over one arm. Percy shot Emma a scorching look, warning her to be quiet, then moved toward Sally. Emma followed.

"Good morning, Mrs. Gable," Percy said. "Is there anything I can help you find today?"

"No, thank you," Sally said in a high, singsong voice. "I'm just here to pick up my usual things." She went down the first aisle, toward the middle of the store.

Percy checked to see if Sally was within earshot, then looked at Emma. "You'd better be careful," he said under his breath. "If someone hears you talking like that, they might get the idea you're spending time with the wrong people. You think my parents are hard on you now? If they find out you've been talking to Clayton Nash again—"

"The wrong people?" Emma interrupted, not caring who heard. "This entire town is filled with the wrong people!"

Sally raised her chin and looked over the dried goods at Percy and Emma, her eyes wide and bright, like a hunting dog smelling the air. She made her way toward them and stopped by the sewing supplies, picking up spools of thread. Emma knew she was only pretending to browse so she could eavesdrop. Percy started toward the back room, and Emma busied herself by straightening the canned goods.

"I don't know what it is with my daughter," Sally chirped. "No matter how many times I mend her things, she keeps coming home with her dresses ripped. I guess she still has a little bit of a tomboy in her, despite all my schooling on how to be a young lady." She smiled at Emma. "You're about Charlotte's age. What on earth could she be doing that causes her to have such trouble keeping her clothes in good repair? Climbing trees? Hiking?"

Emma bit down on the inside of her cheek, fighting the urge to tell Sally Gable that her daughter's clothes were probably being ripped off by a dirty old man named Otis Shawcross. "I have no idea," she said. "Perhaps a suitor is being a little too rough?"

With that, Sally went white and dropped the spool of thread. Her lips puckered as if she were sucking on a lemon. "Well, I never. You wait until I talk to your aunt Ida. I can see now she was right all along. You, young lady, have no respect for your elders!" Then she stomped out of the store, huffing and puffing.

Percy stormed toward Emma. "What is wrong with you?" he said. "I don't need this aggravation! If you hate it here so much, why don't you leave? You know what? I'm starting to think my father was right. You're just like your parents, thinking you're too good for us. So go ahead. Pack your suitcase and take the next train out of here!"

She glared at him. "Trust me. I would if I could."

"Well, in the meantime," he said, jerking his chin toward the office door. "Grab a broom and make yourself useful instead of standing there, fuming about something you can't change!"

She did as she was told, knowing there was no point in arguing. For the rest of the day, she couldn't get Michael and the image of the small coffin out of her mind. She could still picture the young boys following the grieving family up the hill, their sad, dirty faces and glassy eyes. The thought of a little boy smothering to death in a coal chute made her think of Albert, trapped below the ice, thrashing in the water, unable to breathe. She imagined his last moment, when he could no longer hold his breath, one final, powerful gasp pulling water into his lungs. Was that what it was like to smother inside a coal chute? Did the six-year-old boy's lungs fill with coal dust? The thought nearly brought her to her knees.

She had little knowledge about the workings of a colliery, but how did someone fall into a coal chute anyway? Wasn't there a gate or barrier to keep that from happening? And where were the coal chutes located: in the mine, or in the breaker? Didn't Percy say the boys sorted coal inside the breaker? Was the boy somewhere he wasn't supposed to be? Or did young boys work inside the mine too?

Then she had an idea. Today her shift was scheduled to end a few minutes before the mine whistle blew to signal the end of the miners' day. When she got out of work, she would hike up to the mine to see for herself. Maybe, when the boys came out of the breaker, she could ask them about their job and find out why so many were getting hurt. She couldn't help anyone if she didn't know what was going on.

And then, after she went to the colliery, she would go over to the miners' village and look for Michael and his grandmother Tala.

CHAPTER 9

Up on the mountain, near the main shaft of the Bleak Mountain Colliery, Emma hid behind a timber shed, waiting for the miners to get off work. She held a cotton bandanna over her mouth and nose, her eyes burning from the breaker smoke and smoldering culm. Blackened tree stumps surrounded the area, and any remaining vegetation looked dark and strangled. The breaker loomed above her against the sky, an enormous wooden structure with whirring gears and machinery flashing behind row after row of grimy windows. At the top of a long track leading up to the highest peak of the breaker, miners tipped coal into the shaker machine. The black lumps tumbled out of the coal cars into iron chutes, toward their journey down through the giant building.

Now that she was closer to the mine, Emma's image of the breaker as a hideous monster grew more vivid. She imagined the great teeth of the crusher on revolving cylinders, chewing the coal into smaller and smaller chunks, the breaker grinding its mammoth jaws and belching out smoke with a ravenous roar, waiting for boys to fall in.

The mine whistle blew, signaling the end of the shift, and she jumped at its piercing shriek. A few minutes later, the monotone growl of the breaker slowed and ground to halt. Then there was near silence, as if the colliery had been working on its own, with no help from human hands, a great beast of machinery that lived and breathed and slept on the side of the mountain. The only noises were the thump of her heartbeat in her ears, and a series of strange metallic bangs and hollow thumps coming from deep inside the earth. There were no birds singing, no leaves rustling in the afternoon breeze, no insects buzzing in the grass. Then, after what seemed like forever, voices floated out of the mineshaft, along with the rattle of chains, and the screech of metal wheels.

Finally, miners trudged out of the black mouth of the shaft, their gumboots grinding on the gravel, their canteens and dinner pails hanging from their belts and filthy hands. Most of the men were on foot, while others rode slope cars pulled by heavy spreader chains. As soon as the slope car cleared the mine entrance, the men stood and jumped off without waiting for the car to stop. The miners coughed and spit on the ground, took off their hats and scratched their heads and necks, raked their hands over red, blinking eyes.

Emma craned her neck to search for Mr. Flint or Uncle Otis, ready to slip behind the shed if she saw either one. Behind the slope cars, a group of black-faced boys with snake whips hanging around their necks led mud-covered mules out of the shaft by their bridles. Some of the boys looked no more than eight or nine years old. Something cold and hard twisted beneath Emma's ribs. So there *were* young boys working inside the mines, not just inside the breaker. Behind the mules, two miners came out of the shaft, their arms around the waist of a limping teenage boy, his leg bound and bleeding. They helped him over to a flatbed car and laid him on it, then went on their way.

Off to the left, young boys filed out of the breaker, running down the wooden stairway that ran along the outside of the building like ants abandoning an anthill. Soot blackened their caps and faces, overcoats and pants, hands and boots, making them look like little men made out of mud. When they reached the ground, they spit out wet wads of chewing tobacco, then wiped their chins on their dirty sleeves or the scarves tied around their necks. Some of the boys plodded toward the main shaft, where they waited for friends and uncles and fathers to come out of the mine, while others headed in Emma's direction, toward the slag road that would lead them home.

A number of boys thumped along on crutches, their legs or feet missing. Some had one crutch; others had two. Even with missing limbs and eyes, they still worked in the breaker. Emma blinked back tears and scanned the faces for Michael. But it was impossible to tell one boy from another at this distance, they were so filthy.

As the swarm of breaker boys grew closer, talking, cussing, laughing, shouting, and coughing, she shrunk back, not knowing what their reaction would be if they saw her. One of them snatched a filthy cap off the boy next to him, revealing the boy's pale forehead. The snatcher started running, three boys chasing after him. The cap-less boy gave chase too, swearing and calling the other boy names. How did they have enough energy to walk home after a ten-hour shift, let alone act like they'd been let out of school for recess?

Before Emma knew it, the breaker boys were nearly on top of her. When one of them saw her standing next to the shed, he dropped his eyes and moved to the other side of the road. Another eyed her and scowled, as if fighting the urge to swear at her or tell her to go home. A third boy spit in the dirt a few yards from where she stood, demonstrating his disapproval.

On the other side of the road, a thin woman in a brown dress appeared, her arms wrapped around herself as if she were freezing, her hair wild, her bloodshot eyes searching every soot-covered face.

"Where's my Chippy?" she asked the boys as they passed. "Have you seen him?"

Emma's breath hitched in her chest, her throat suddenly aching. It was the woman from the funeral procession. Her boy had been put in the ground that very morning, and yet she was here, looking for him. Unless she had another son. No. There had been no other boy at her side, only her husband and baby. The river of breaker boys moved away from the grief-stricken mother in waves, taking a wide berth as if she were infected with disease.

"I can't find my Chippy," the woman cried. "Do you know where he is?"

"He's dead, you barmy fool!" one of the boys shouted.

Emma put a hand to her trembling mouth, wondering if she should help the confused woman find her way back home. Then she noticed some of the breaker boys had tears streaming down their filthy cheeks. Several wept openly while others tried not to cry out loud and attract attention. When Emma saw the reason for their distress, she gasped. Their fingers were swollen and black, their fingertips cracked and bleeding. She moved toward one of the crying boys, no longer caring who saw her.

"What happened to you?" she said. He looked to be about five years old and was leaning against an older boy who had his arm around him and was telling him to stop crying.

"Mind your own business," the older boy said.

"Why are his fingers bleeding?" she said. "Did someone do this to him?"

"He's a red tip," a voice behind her said.

She turned to see who had spoken. It was the boy from the Fourth of July dance, the one Clayton said would take care of Jack. What was his name? *Sawyer. Yes, that's it.* "A red tip?" she said. "What's that?"

"It's what we call the new boys," Sawyer said. "Today was his first day. Everyone's fingers bleed the first few weeks on the job."

"That's horrible!" she said. "What on Earth has he been doing?" Shock and fury churned inside her head, nearly making her dizzy.

"Picking slate and rocks out of the coal," Sawyer said, "sending them down the chutes to the culm banks. The sulfur burns your skin. Makes your fingers swell and crack open. And slate can be sharp. But don't worry. His fingers will toughen up." He held up one hand. His fingers were black with soot, but there was no blood or cracked skin. They looked hard and calloused. "Then they'll only bleed if he don't watch what he's doing."

The other boys skirted around Emma and Sawyer, watching with curious eyes. Some looked at them blankly while others scowled with disapproval.

"Why don't you wear gloves?" Emma said.

"You have to feel the culm to work fast," Sawyer said. "Gloves slow you down. If the boss caught us wearing them, we'd get our knuckles rapped, or worse."

"Your boss hits you?" she said, trying to control her emotions. Was there no end to the nightmare these poor boys suffered?

He shrugged. "Sometimes," he said. "If we ain't doing our job." Just then, a taller, huskier boy bumped into Sawyer's shoulder and nearly knocked him off his feet. Sawyer dropped his dinner pail but held his footing. He turned to see who had bumped into him, his shoulders tense, ready to scrap.

"Who's your girlfriend, patsy?" the husky boy said. "She's a little old for you, don't you think?" He laughed, and his friends joined in.

Sawyer ignored him and turned back to Emma, his face pinched. "I better go. It'd probably be best all around if you went back home, ma'am."

"Do you know if Mr. Flint is here?" she said.

The boy shook his head. "He don't come around much, unless there's trouble."

"What about the supervisor?" she said. "Do you know where he is right now?"

He gazed at her for a moment, then dropped his eyes and made a move to go around her. "I better get home."

She caught him by the shoulder with a gentle hand. He shrugged away from her and frowned. "Sorry, ma'am," he said. "You seem real nice, but I don't want no trouble. If you want to talk to somebody, go on ahead and look for them. But I'm warning you, they ain't going to be happy about seeing you up here."

"Can you just tell me where Otis Shawcross might be?" she said. "There are so many buildings, it would take me forever to find him."

Sawyer hesitated for a moment, then jerked his chin toward the opening of the shaft. "He's right there. Good day, ma'am." He put his cap back on and hurried off.

Emma looked toward the mine. Next to a gray building with a sign that read: Engine Room, Uncle Otis was watching their exchange, his hands on his hips, his eyes narrowed. He looked cleaner than the other miners, his face only lightly coated with coal dust, his jacket and pants dry. Emma took a deep breath and started toward him. When he saw her coming, he spit on the ground and stormed in her direction, waving his arm in the air and yelling at her to go away. The other miners stopped to watch.

For a split second, Emma thought about fleeing, heading down the mountain and going home. *No,* she thought, *I've come this far. I'm not going to turn back now.*

When he reached her, Uncle Otis yelled, "What in blue blazes are you doing here? Go on! Get the hell home!" His face was red, his eyes wild with anger.

"I heard a young boy died up here, and you didn't even know because of the cave-in," she said. "Did he work in the breaker?"

"That's none of your concern. Now turn yourself around and get off this mountain!"

"You tell her, boss!" one of the miners shouted. The miners started talking amongst themselves, shaking their heads or nodding. Some smiled in amusement while others frowned in anger. A few dozen moved toward Uncle Otis, advancing forward and forming a line, as if to keep Emma from getting any closer to the mine.

"Get her out of here!" a man shouted.

One of the miners picked up a rock and held it in his hand. Several more followed suit. Fear and anger tightened Emma's chest. Would these men really hurt her? Were they afraid of her because she was a woman? Or was it something else? Percy had warned her that the miners were suspicious and she was treading on dangerous ground, but this was ridiculous. Then again, if they were anything like Hazard Flint, willing to let young boys die for the sake of getting coal out of the ground, maybe she should be afraid.

Uncle Otis grabbed her by the arm and yanked her away from the mine, his boney fingers like pokers in her skin. She struggled to break free.

"Get your hands off me!" she said. "I just want to know what's going on. Why are children doing such dangerous work?"

Uncle Otis dragged her down the slag road, nearly running past the breaker boys. When they were out of earshot, he pushed her roughly down the hill. She tripped and caught herself, then turned to face him, breathing hard.

"Get the hell out of here!" he yelled. "And don't ever come back!"

"I'm turning you in to the police!" she said. "Little boys are getting injured and killed, and you're letting it happen! There must be some kind of law to protect them, and you're breaking it!"

A spiteful grin split his face. "Go ahead and turn me in. And while you're at it, you can turn in Hazard Flint and every other mine owner, foreman, and mining boss in this state. See how far that gets you." Then he wiped a hand over his sweaty forehead, leaving a black streak of coal dust, and his face went dark. "I know one thing for sure. You're going to be sorry you came up here." He turned to go back up the hill. She followed.

"How can you live with yourself?" she yelled. "You have a big fancy house, buy your wife whatever she wants, and stuff yourself with fancy food and whiskey while young boys are dying to make you rich!"

With that, he spun around to face her, his jaw jutted out, his hands in fists. "Why, you ungrateful little wench," he said. "You're just like your parents. You don't care where the money comes from as long as you've got a warm bed and food in your belly. Before they left to go have a good time in Manhattan, your parents stayed with us for two months. Bet you don't remember that, do you? Oh, they had a high time of it, drinking my whiskey and eating my food, sleeping all morning, lazing around the sun porch while your aunt Ida waited on them hand and foot."

"I remember it," she said. "I remember my father fixing the roof for our keep, and I remember my mother washing the floors. But what I remember most is my mother comforting Aunt Ida while you were out carousing every night."

"Bullshit!" he said. "You have no idea how the real world works. Now get the hell out of here!"

"I won't sit by while you and Hazard Flint put children in danger."

"Now you listen here," he said, his nostrils flaring. "You're going to march yourself right back down that hill and go home. And from now on, you're going to mind your own business. Because if you don't, I'll find a way to put you out on the street so fast, it will make your head spin!"

"You can't do that," she said, her voice tinged with sarcasm.

"What would people think if you threw out your poor, orphaned niece?"

A crazy-sounding chuckle escaped his lips. "After this little stunt, they won't care. But don't worry. I'll be sure to put in a good word for you with Miss Sylvia down at the Lehigh Hotel. She knows how to help women with nowhere to go. I'm sure she'd be happy to take in a fresh young thing like you."

Emma dug her fingernails into her palms. "Aunt Ida won't let you kick me out," she said. "She wants my help, and my income from the Company Store."

"I don't care what she wants. I'm the man of the house and what I say goes!"

"I wonder if you'll still be the man of the house after I tell her about that young girl I saw you groping behind the dance hall on the Fourth of July? What was her name again? Charlotte Gable? Isn't her father a friend of yours?"

He cast a murderous look at her. "Why you conniving little . . ." he hissed. "Tell your aunt whatever you want. She knows you're nothing but a liar. She always knew you weren't telling the truth about what happened with your brother, trying to blame Percy the whole time. It's your fault Albert is dead, and we all know it. Ida won't believe a thing you say. If you try to tell her anything, it will only prove you're more trouble than you're worth."

Emma went rigid. A memory flashed in her mind—her aunt on the icy riverbank, hugging a sobbing Percy to her bosom, wagging a finger at Emma. When Emma said Albert fell through the ice because Percy took her locket, her aunt slapped her across the face. After all, she pointed out, Percy had run to get help while Emma sat on the riverbank doing nothing. Her aunt warned her to never say anything of the sort, ever again, and she never did. Uncle Otis was right. No matter what, Aunt Ida would always side with her husband and son. If Emma tried to tell her about Charlotte, once she found out Emma had gone up to the mine, she'd just accuse her of starting trouble. And that would be reason enough to send her to the poorhouse. Or worse, to an asylum.

"I'm not a liar," Emma said, nearly choking on her anger. "And someday, somehow, the truth will come out. About my brother, about this mine, and about you!"

Before her uncle could respond, she stormed away, her body trembling with fury. The miners cheered behind her. To her surprise, when the breaker boys saw her leave, they joined in.

"I'm warning you," her uncle yelled after her. "Mind your own business and stay away from the mine, or you'll be out on the street!"

Maybe she was fooling herself, thinking anyone in Coal River would want her help. Who did she think she was anyway? And what made her think Michael wanted her to be the breaker boys' savior? Maybe guilt was making her imagine things.

Instead of going up the miners' village to look for Michael and Tala, she headed home, her legs like stone. Suddenly, she was exhausted and wanted nothing more than to crawl under her bedcovers and go to sleep.

CHAPTER 10

The morning after her confrontation with Uncle Otis at the mine, Emma hurried into Percy's office, glancing over her shoulder to make sure no customers were coming into the store. Percy was out back, unloading a delivery wagon full of mops, washtubs, irons, and brooms. The door between the main floor and the stock room was open, and Percy's conversation with the driver drifted in from outside, along with the thump of boxes and other goods being stacked on the wooden floor.

With her heart in her throat, she went to Percy's desk and opened the bottom left-hand drawer. She pulled out the store ledger, clasped it to her chest, and returned to the office door, checking again to make sure no one was coming. Then she darted back into the office and searched the drawers for the PAID stamp. When she finally found it, wedged between a roll of twine and a box of paper clips, she opened the ledger to a bookmarked page and scanned the names, trying to remember who had young children and needed the most help.

The bell over the front door chimed. Emma's stomach flip-flopped. She paused for a second, then took a deep breath and marked a miner's bill PAID. She skipped a page, marked two more paid, then skipped two pages and marked three more. After eight names she stopped, afraid that if she marked too many, it would look suspicious. Out in the store, Aunt Ida called for Percy. Emma shoved the stamp and the ledger back into the desk and straightened, running her shaky hands over her skirt and apron. She blew out a long breath and hurried to the office door.

"He's out back," she told her aunt. "Unloading stock."

"What were you doing in the office?" Aunt Ida said. "You're supposed to be watching the store."

Emma tried to keep her voice even. "I was looking for a clean apron."

Aunt Ida looked her up and down, her nose wrinkled. "Your apron looks fine. Now do your job. You've caused enough trouble around here."

Emma made her way over to the cash register and forced a smile. "Is there anything I can help you with?" she said.

Aunt Ida rummaged through her handbag, pulled out a slip of paper, and handed it to Emma. "I'm having a birthday dinner for your uncle this weekend," she said. "I need you to gather everything on this list. The poor man has been under an awful lot of strain lately, so I'm not sparing any expense. And after what you pulled yesterday, I figured the least you can do is help prepare for the party. Just add everything to our weekly bill and bring it home when you get out of work. Percy can put it on our monthly tab. And don't go anywhere but home and work. If I hear about you strolling around town or going anyplace else you're not supposed to go, I'll lock you in your room until you've learned your lesson! Do you understand?"

"Yes, ma'am."

Aunt Ida opened the paper fan hanging from her wrist and waved it in front of her red face, her lips set in a firm and self-righteous line. "You're lucky I didn't let your uncle after you last night, young lady. He was fit to be tied! I haven't seen him that angry in a long, long time. I hate to think what he might have done. But you better understand one thing. The only reason I'm protecting you is because you're my sister's daughter. I can't promise that'll work all the time, so you better straighten up."

"Yes, ma'am," Emma said again.

Emma had forced herself to sound more meek than she felt, and as soon as her aunt left, she hooked a wicker basket over her arm and moved through the store, gathering the items on Aunt Ida's list: canned peas, two pounds of butter, a side of bacon, a tin of cinnamon, dried beans, five pounds of sugar. For nearly every item on the list, she took one extra, except for the larger things like the smoked ham and the ten-pound bag of potatoes. When she was finished, she added the food to Aunt Ida's bill and packed it in paper bags.

When she got home that evening, she put the food from the list away in the kitchen and pantry, but hid the extras behind tins of flour and oatmeal, or inside clean kettles and pots. Cook had finished preparing meals for the day, so there was little chance of anyone finding it. But even if the woman found the extra food, Emma would just say she was daydreaming and somehow put things away in the wrong spot. Cook knew better than to question Aunt Ida's decisions if she thought there were too many provisions for the party, and she would never tell anyone about Emma's mistake.

Later that evening, when it came time for Aunt Ida to do the nightly Bible readings with Otis and Percy in the dining room, Emma said she was tired and wanted to retire early. Then she snuck the extra food up to her room. After midnight, when everyone was asleep, she crept out of the house and went up to the miners' village, where she left the groceries on the doorsteps of the poorest-looking shacks.

CHAPTER 11

The red, yellow, and blue posters for Professor Sid Roscoe's Traveling Carnival and Freak Show appeared either very late Saturday night or early Sunday morning, while most of the village was asleep. Someone had pasted the advertisements from the north end of Main Street to the far end of Railroad Avenue. They were on the soot-stained clapboards of the Pennsylvania Boarding House and Hotel, Herrick's Apothecary, Abe's Livery, the post office, the Company Store, and every other weathered utility pole, dotting the dust-covered town with bright blocks of color.

Despite the sudden appearance of a much-needed rain, young and old gathered around the vivid posters, oohing and ahhing beneath their umbrellas at images of Ferris wheels and merry-go-rounds. They stared, slack-jawed, at pictures of the bearded lady, the two-headed man, and the lion-faced boy. The breaker boys ran from one advertisement to the next, pushing and shoving to get a closer look, their wide-eyed faces speckled with raindrops and left-over coal dust. At the Pennsylvania Boarding House and Hotel, the proprietor shooed a group of boys off the porch when they collected beneath the roof to smoke cigarettes and examine the poster of a mermaid lady.

The rain had not stopped by the time church ended, but it was slackening. It tapped on Emma's umbrella, and she was grateful for the coolness it brought to the air as it washed coal dust from windows and sidewalks and store canopies. Thankfully, Uncle Otis and Aunt Ida were attending a fellowship luncheon at Sally Gable's house, which gave her and Percy a little over an hour of freedom. To her surprise, she was allowed to walk home, as long as she promised to be there when her aunt and uncle returned.

Stopping to examine a poster on the side of the livery, she wondered if the breaker boys would be allowed to attend the carnival. It was only scheduled to be in town on Friday and Saturday, both days when the colliery was normally running. She couldn't imagine Mr. Flint stopping production so his employees could have a little fun, but she wondered if the carnival owners could be persuaded to stay open one more day.

She smiled thinly, remembering the first fair her parents took her to in Central Park. The sun had been shining in a cobalt blue sky, and her parents bought her a strawberry ice cream cone. She was too afraid to go on the Ferris wheel or inside the house of mirrors, but she loved the carousel and the games of chance. She remembered feeling happier than she had in a long time. The only thing missing was Albert.

But a poster farther down Main Street wrecked the enjoyment of her memories. When she saw it, she gasped. Staring back at her from the brown and red placard on a utility pole was Lionel, the Camel-Legged Boy. He looked about four years old, and was wearing nothing but a pair of undershorts. His belly protruded more than normal, and his big, brown eyes were filled with misery. His knees were bent backward, opposite of how they were supposed to go, which made his legs look like those of a camel. Emma gathered her collar beneath her chin and hurried along the sidewalk, struggling to push a new image from her mind—a young breaker boy on a freak show poster, his skin black, his fingers raw and bleeding, his legs gone. The agony on his face was almost more than she could take.

On the morning of the opening day for Professor Sid Roscoe's Traveling Carnival and Freak Show, Aunt Ida urged Emma to hurry up and finish her chores so they could go into town. Percy had been instructed to give Emma the day off from the store so she could accompany her aunt to the carnival. Not only did Aunt Ida refuse to attend the festivities alone, she had also decided it was an opportunity for Emma to make up for the trouble she'd caused at the mine. After that fiasco, the townsfolk needed to see that Emma had been reined in and properly reprimanded. From now on she would be quiet and demure, and she would behave like a proper young lady. Emma would have preferred to work at the Company Store.

But shortly before seven, just as Emma and Ida were preparing to eat breakfast, Uncle Otis returned to the house in a fury, slamming the back door and stomping into the dining room.

"What are you doing here?" Aunt Ida said. "Is something wrong?

"We had to shut down and send everyone home!" Uncle Otis said. He threw his dirty gloves on the floor, then went to the sideboard and filled a tumbler with whiskey.

"What happened?" Aunt Ida said.

Uncle Otis slugged down the whiskey in four noisy gulps. When it was gone, he wiped his mouth, refilled the glass, and looked at his wife with angry eyes. "They sabotaged the breaker!"

"Who did?" Aunt Ida said.

"Those goddamned breaker boys!"

"Why on Earth would they do that?" Aunt Ida said.

"Why the hell do you think? So they can go to the carnival!" Uncle Otis shook his head and glared at his wife. "I swear, sometimes you don't have a brain in your head!"

Emma dropped her eyes to the napkin in her lap, worried her aunt and uncle would see the pleased look on her face.

"Don't you talk to me like that, Otis Walter Shawcross!" Aunt Ida said. "I know you're upset, but there's no need to be short!"

Uncle Otis pinched the bridge of his nose between his fingers, squeezing his eyes shut with a grimace. After a long moment, he let go and straightened. "You don't understand," he said, his voice tight. "We can't afford to lose production time right now."

"I'm sorry, dear," Aunt Ida said. She went around the table and put a hand on her husband's arm. "I know it's frustrating. But I, for one, am delighted you had to shut down for the day. I don't get to see nearly enough of you." She pulled out his chair and led him to it. "Now, sit down, have some breakfast, and you'll feel better. After that, you can take me down to the carnival and buy me a candy apple. We can ride the Ferris wheel, just like we did on our first date. You remember our first date, don't you, sweetheart?"

Uncle Otis slumped into his chair. He took a gulp of whiskey and put the tumbler on the table. Aunt Ida called for Cook to bring more coffee, sat back down, and slid the platter of sausage and corn muffins in her husband's direction.

Despite her dislike of Aunt Ida, Emma couldn't help thinking how pathetic she was. Did she coddle her tyrant husband because she truly loved him, or was it all an act because his money supported her lavish lifestyle? Either way, it was sad. And Emma would never understand it.

Emma took a muffin from the plate and stood. "If you'll excuse me, I'm going to get washed up and head into town. I want to see what the carnival is all about."

"You can't go alone," her aunt said. "It's not proper!"

"I'm sure I'll find someone to befriend," Emma said. "Captain Bannister will probably be lurking around. Or maybe I'll run into Charlotte Gable." She looked at Uncle Otis, hoping to get a reaction. It didn't work. He was someplace else, his face dark and angry.

"Oh, what a lovely idea!" Aunt Ida said. "Charlotte would be a perfect friend for you. She is a real lady!"

"I'll be sure to ask her for guidance," Emma said, and left the room.

The village green was filled with white tents, carnival rides, balloon-carrying clowns, and strings of triangular blue, orange, and yellow flags. The townspeople meandered along the midway, crowding the concession stands and games of chance, stopping to hear a carnival barker hawk the wonders inside the freak show tents.

Grateful to be on her own for the day, Emma strolled through the excited throng, watching the rich of Coal River buy balloons and cotton candy for their children, making her way around rowdy clusters of breaker boys who were waiting in line to ride the Ferris wheel and merry-go-round. The air was filled with calliope music, laughter, raised voices, clapping, and the smell of roasted peanuts and candy apples. Beneath a yellow and white awning, a group of breaker boys shared a box of popcorn, passing the container back and forth. Beside them, two other breaker boys sat at a battered table sharing a scoop of ice cream in a hand-rolled cone. The older boy gripped the cone with both hands, his soot-stained fingers covered with sticky white drips, while the younger one watched with eager eyes. His hands were wrapped in bloodstained gauze. The older boy took a few licks of the ice cream, then held it out for the younger boy to take a turn.

On the west side of the village green, a parade of canvas tents lined the grass opposite the rides and games of chance, the entire row fronted by oversized banners painted with colorful images of the marvels waiting inside—the Giant Rat, the Living Mermaid, the Three-legged Boy, the Viking Giant. A man in a white top hat stood on a wooden stage at the center of the tents, shouting above the gathering crowd.

"That's right, folks!" he barked. "We're going to have a free show here! A free show! Gather around, ladies and gentlemen, and see what we're going to do! This is the one your neighbors have been talking about! We're going to bring out the fire-eater, the snake girl, the midgets! Watch the doorway—here they come! Keep your eyes wide open! You don't want to miss any of it!"

Emma stopped to watch, twisting her drawstring purse between her fingers, a strange mixture of curiosity and fear swirling beneath her rib cage. On one hand, she wanted to see if there really was such a thing as a mermaid or a giant rat. On the other, she worried the sight of a three-legged boy or a snake girl would give her nightmares. There was enough heartbreak and sadness in Coal River to last a lifetime; she certainly didn't need to seek out more.

"I'm going to wake up the sweet little fat lady from Fort Lauderdale!" the man said. "My God, is she ever fat! It takes four men to hug her and a boxcar to lug her! She's going to do a little dance for you, and once she does, the whole tent shakes!" He spread out his arms, looking back and forth down the row of tents, first to one side and then the other. "To my left and right, you'll see the freaks and the strange people inside these tents, all alive, all able to talk and answer your questions! This is not an illusion, folks! But you've got to see it to believe it! I want you to see the magician, the electric girl, and all the other action!" Then he stopped and put his hands in the air, waving them back and forth and shaking his head as if suddenly changing his mind. "No, no," he said. "I know how hard you work for your money! So I'll tell you what. Today we're going to do something special! Our ticket taker is setting a timer for three minutes, and we're going to let all of you in! All of you nice people who are standing here listening to me, we're going to let you in to see the show at half price! We have wonders and curiosities suitable for all sensibilities. So step right up before time runs out!"

Emma breathed a sigh of relief, realizing the man wasn't going to bring out the freaks after all. He was just trying to pull the crowd closer, to pique their curiosity. She stepped backward as the onlookers surged forward, like cattle on their way to feed. When she turned to make her way toward the concession stands, someone gently squeezed her elbow. She spun around, hoping it wasn't Frank Bannister.

It was Clayton Nash.

Remembering their last exchange up at the miners' village, her shoulders tensed. At the same time, she couldn't ignore the fact that she was happy to see him.

"Fancy meeting you here," he said with a grin. Thankfully, the flash of anger she'd seen in his eyes the other day was gone. "Where is your chaperone, young lady?"

Her cheeks grew warm. "I must have lost her."

He gestured toward the freak show tents, bowing slightly. "May I accompany you inside?"

"Oh no," she said, shaking her head. "I'd rather not.

"Are you sure? It's quite a spectacle!"

She shook her head again and started walking, her eyes on the ground.

He followed. "May I walk with you?"

She nodded, and clasped her purse in front of her. Then she let go of her purse and clasped it again, suddenly unsure what to do with her hands and arms. She didn't want to brush against Clayton's hand accidentally, or make him think she was waiting for him to take her arm. "So you've been inside the freak show?" she said at last.

"It was a long time ago. The last time the carnival was here, I was eleven."

"Did you see the mermaid?"

He laughed. "I don't think they had a mermaid back then."

"What about the others?" she said. "The three-legged boy? The giant?"

He stopped and pointed back at the tent. "Are you sure you don't want to see for yourself? My treat?"

"No, no," she said. "I was just curious. I mean, I was wondering if they were real."

He shrugged and started walking again. "Well, the people I saw were real, all right. But I don't know if some of the sights inside the tents were a trick of the eye or what. Last time, I saw a two-headed man, and I'll never forget it. I even remember what he was wearing. A white shirt, a blue bow tie, pinstripe trousers, and a shiny red vest. He was sitting in a wingback chair, smoking a cigar and looking back at people. He moved the cigar from one mouth to the other, drawing on it with one set of lips and blowing smoke out with the other. And all of his eyes moved left or right, or up and down, at the same time. It gave me nightmares for weeks."

She shivered. "Don't tell me any more. I don't want to know."

"I'm sorry," he said. "Shall we do something fun to take your mind off it? Maybe we should ride the Ferris wheel."

Just then, Jack and Sawyer—the orphan and the breaker boy who were watching Clayton when he was arrested at the dance hall—came running toward them. They were laughing and excited, their smiling faces sticky with cotton candy.

"Can I have a nickel to go to the freak show?" Jack said.

"Did you spend your money already?" Clayton said.

Jack dropped his chin, shoved his hands into his pockets, and scuffed his shoe in the dirt. "Yes."

"Well then," Clayton said. "You know the answer. I told you not to spend it so fast."

"I know," Jack cried. "But I wanted to—"

"No more bellyaching," Clayton said. "There are plenty of other things to see that don't cost a penny. Now run along and stay out of trouble."

Sawyer tugged on Jack's shirt sleeve, and the two boys ran off toward the red and white awning of the fry tent, where other children were gathered around a clown.

Clayton grinned at Emma. "Sorry about that."

"I don't mind," she said. "I know how rambunctious young boys can be." They continued on, strolling toward the midway. "Sawyer told me about Jack. It's wonderful that you've taken him in."

Clayton's brow darkened, and he scanned the horizon, as if looking for something that wasn't there. For what seemed like forever, he said nothing. She was about to ask if she'd said something wrong, when he spoke.

"Do you have children?" he said.

"Me?" she said. "Lord, no." She fingered the lace cuff of her sleeve, surprised by her desire to open up to him about Albert. "I had a little brother once, but he's gone now. He was eight when he drowned, right here in Coal River."

"Oh no," Clayton said. "I'm so sorry." He touched her hand, his fingers like sunbaked stones on her skin. She'd never felt a hand so warm. "Please, forgive me for prying. I hope I didn't upset you."

"I'm surprised you didn't know. It seems to be the talk of the town."

"I don't pay much attention to gossip," he said.

She chewed on her lip, wondering if she should ask him if he knew Michael. Percy had been no help. Maybe Clayton knew where the boy lived, or whether what Percy said was true. Maybe the story about Michael being a deaf-mute was nothing but more gossip. And yet, in her heart, she knew it was true. There was something about Michael and the way he spoke to her that was strange. Just thinking about it gave her chills. "Can I ask you something?" she said.

"Sure."

"Do you know a boy named Michael Carrion? Or his grandmother Tala? She has white braids and—"

Clayton shook his head. "The name sounds familiar. But I can't place it."

She started to say more, then stopped. She didn't want him to think she was foolish, or worse, crazy. "That's all right. It's not important."

"I've got my hands full with so many things, I barely know my own name sometimes," he said.

"Like what?" she said. If he couldn't tell her anything more about Michael, maybe he would tell her more about himself, and what, if anything, he was going to do about the mining company and Hazard Flint.

"Today is not the day to talk about unpleasant things," he said. "Look around." He smiled and swept a hand through the air, like a magician presenting a trick. "We're supposed to be having fun! Now how about that Ferris wheel ride?"

"I'm afraid I didn't bring any money with me," she said, hoping he wouldn't see through her lie. She didn't want to tell him that she didn't have a red cent to her name because Aunt Ida had decided the money she earned at the Company Store should go straight into the household funds. And she'd be damned if she'd grovel for a single penny from her aunt and uncle. For now she'd have to be content with the sights and sounds of the carnival. "Maybe another time."

"Another time?" he said. "Didn't you hear me say how long it's been since the carnival came to Coal River? Come on. It's my treat."

"I can't. Really. The Ferris wheel is not my cup of tea."

"Why not?" he said. Then he tilted his head and grinned at her. "You're not afraid of heights, are you?"

She shrugged and said nothing, but he knew.

All of a sudden, a wave of breaker boys shoved around and past them, laughing and yelling at one another to hurry up. She watched them run away, trying to see where they were headed. Why were they so excited?

Up ahead, the crowd parted to let someone through. It was a man in a chalk-stripe suit and black top hat, making his way along the midway. Breaker boys surrounded him on all sides, walking beside and in front of him, vying for his attention like chickens around a farmer scattering corn. He was reaching into a leather pouch and handing out coins to the boys, smiling and telling them there was enough for everyone.

It was Levi Flint.

Emma and Clayton fell silent, stepping aside to watch him pass. Emma searched the surrounding faces for Mr. Flint, but didn't see him.

"I can't believe what I'm seeing," she said.

"Me either," said Clayton.

"Do you think Mr. Flint knows?"

Clayton shook his head. "He must be away on business or something. I admire Levi's nerve."

A few yards behind Levi and the swarm of breaker boys, Frank was striding toward her and Clayton, his face hard. Without thinking, Emma grabbed Clayton's hand and yanked him sideways into a cluster of people gathered around a man guessing people's height and weight.

"The Ferris wheel is the other way," Clayton said.

Emma ignored him and pulled him through the crowd, hurrying around baby prams and laughing children. She crossed the stream of people on the midway, then turned and went in the other direction, where they passed the shooting gallery and the ringtoss. When they reached the other side of the carnival, Emma stopped and faced him, breathing hard. She let go of his hand.

"I'm sorry," she said, heat rising in her cheeks. "But I—"

"It's all right. I saw Frank Bannister coming toward us. You don't want him to see us together."

"It's not that . . ." she said. For a second she considered telling him about Frank and Mr. Flint murdering someone down by the river. Maybe she should warn him. Then she changed her mind. She still didn't know him that well. And if he told anyone, it could put them both in more danger. "Let's just say I've known Frank a long time, and I'd just as soon never talk to him again."

"People find Frank intimidating because he's Mr. Flint's right-hand man," he said. "And he's not the smartest bloke to walk the streets of Coal River." Clayton moved closer and took her hands in his. "But you're shaking." His hands were wide and rough, the kind of hands that would catch you if you fell, or pull you quickly out of the path of an oncoming wagon. The kind of hands that made you feel safe. Emma pulled free of his grasp, afraid she would throw herself into his arms and sob.

He searched her face, as if trying to uncover the secrets behind her eyes. Then he straightened and grinned mischievously, offering his arm. "I shall protect you from harm, my fair lady," he said in a fake English accent. "Now, please, if you don't mind. May we continue on with today's merriment?"

Emma drew in a deep breath and regained her bearings. She took his arm and let him direct her toward the midway. He was right. Carnivals were for having fun. She would think about Michael and Frank and Mr. Flint tomorrow. Of course, if Uncle Otis and Aunt Ida saw her with Clayton, there would be hell to pay. But for now she was going to make the best of the day. Besides, her aunt and uncle were probably hoping to marry her off; why would they care who her suitor was as long as she was out of their house? When she was someone's spouse, she would no longer be their concern. Why would it matter to them if she married a poor miner, a rich banker, or a boorish policeman?

She drew closer to Clayton, brushing her shoulder lightly across his arm. He smelled of wood smoke, pine, and shaving soap, like a strong, capable man who would know how to protect the woman he loved. Emma shook her head to clear it. What was she doing, thinking of Clayton as a potential husband? She barely knew him! And besides, she didn't want anyone, or anything, tying her to Coal River.

Lost in her thoughts, she hadn't noticed where Clayton was taking her. When they reached the Ferris wheel, he stopped. The carnival workers were loading the ride, and there was only one other couple in line. "Shall we?" Clayton said.

She smiled, her face uncertain. "I'm not sure."

"There's nothing to be afraid of, I promise," he said, leading her toward the queue. "Come on. It's fun. See those cars up there?" He pointed at the Ferris wheel seats. "It's like sitting on your grandmother's davenport."

"Maybe we could play a game of chance instead," she said. "Or ride the carousal?"

"The carousal is for children!" he said, laughing.

She looked at the Ferris wheel, trying to decide. Maybe it wasn't as scary as it looked. At the top of the loading ramp, a carnival worker held open the safety bar of an empty car, beckoning them toward it. Emma glanced behind her to see if they were holding up any other riders. There was no one else in line. But then she gasped. Uncle Otis and Aunt Ida were making their way arm in arm through the crowd, and they were heading straight for them. Aunt Ida was eating a candy apple while Uncle Otis kissed her cheek. His face was sweaty and flushed, as if he were boiling hot or drunk. Emma looked back at the loading ramp. It was either the Ferris wheel, or her aunt and uncle. The carnival worker was gesturing with some irritation, telling her and Clayton to hurry up and get on. She grabbed Clayton's hand, ducked, and climbed into a red metal car with blue stars on the sides.

The carnival worker pushed the safety bar closed, let go of the car, and told them to hold on. The car rocked back and forth, metal squeaking against metal, and Emma's stomach went up and down. Just as she was about to say she'd made a mistake and had to get off, the car lurched backward and up, flying toward the top of the giant metal wheel as if pulled by a rope. She gripped the safety bar, her knuckles turning white. Loose strands of her hair flew in her face. She squeezed her eyes shut, held on for dear life, and tried not to scream.

"Open your eyes!" Clayton shouted above the whoosh of air and rattle of metal.

She shook her head, certain she was about to throw up or die. "There's no reason to be afraid!" he said. "Just enjoy the view. That's half the fun!" Then, to her surprise, he put his arm around her and pulled her close. "I promise, I won't let anything happen to you."

She tried to breathe normally, taking slow, deep breaths and letting them out slowly. Despite her terror, she was aware of the close proximity of Clayton's jawline, the clean, piney smell of his thick neck. On one hand, it felt inappropriate to be this close to him, to let him put his arm around her. On the other, it felt comfortable and safe, as if this was where she belonged, and nothing could ever happen to her as long as she was with him. She opened one eye and then the other, her heart pounding in her chest, and tried to shake the dizzy feeling that threatened to send her reeling over the side of the car, where she would fall like a rock to the ground. Frozen, she stared straight ahead, not daring to turn left or right.

Rooftops appeared before her like a river of brown waves, followed by the leafy tops of trees, the peaks of canvas tents, the sea of carnival goers. And then she and Clayton were soaring backward and up again, floating toward the top of the wheel, where the mountains loomed over the village, over the rooftops, over the roads, over the people, over everything. Her legs and arms were trembling, but she couldn't resist looking down on the people below. From the top of the ride, hats and heads looked like the beads of a multicolored necklace scattered on the ground—red, green, white, purple, gray, black.

Just as she was beginning to think she might not be sick or die after all, there was a loud crack, like the sound of metal breaking in two. The Ferris wheel jerked and shuddered to a screeching stop. Emma and Clayton's car came to an abrupt halt at the top of the ride, where it swung wildly back and forth. Terrified, she tried not to scream. Maybe she wasn't as brave as she thought.

"What happened?" she cried.

Clayton tightened his grip on her shoulder. "We're all right," he said. He reached out and grabbed the metal frame of the Ferris wheel with his free hand, holding the thick bar to steady their car.

"Why did it stop?"

"Don't worry," he said. "This happens all the time. I was watching them test the rides last night, and they told me this engine breaks down at least once a day. We're perfectly safe up here while they see to it."

"But how will we get down?"

"We'll wait until they fix it, then they'll let us off."

"You mean we have to stay up here until they get it started again?" she said. "But what if—"

"Shhh," he said, pulling her closer. "Calm down. It's all right. We're going to be fine, I promise. We'll be back on the ground in a few minutes, you wait and see."

"I never should have let you talk me into this," she said.

"Pretend you're on a porch swing," he said. "Close your eyes if you want, but you'd better calm down before you send yourself into a fit."

"I'm not going to have a fit," she said. "I'm just scared!"

He laughed. At first she thought he was laughing at her. But then he said, "I can see your aunt and uncle. They're looking up here, trying to figure out what's going on. Everyone is watching and pointing. I could drop a hunk of coal in their mouths if I had one."

"Can my aunt and uncle see us?"

"No, they can't tell who we are from down there."

"Are you sure?"

"I'm sure."

"I hope they're gone when we get off."

"Is that why you changed your mind about getting on? Because you didn't want them to see us together?"

"You don't know my uncle," she said.

"Oh, I know your uncle."

"How?" she said, doing her best to concentrate on the conversation and ignore the fact that she was hanging high in the air.

"I've been working under him for years. My father always said you could judge a man by how he treats those below him. Using that measuring stick alone, I can tell what kind of man your uncle is. Besides, he doesn't like me, and he has no qualms about showing it."

"Why doesn't he like you?"

"My father used to work under your uncle too."

"Used to?"

"My father died when I was five."

"What happened to him?"

He sighed and shifted in his seat, rocking the car. She tried to pretend she was on a porch swing, and that helped a little.

"He was working in a section of the mine that they were getting ready to close off, when a roof collapsed. Otis refused to shut down production and send in a rescue team, so my uncle stopped working and went in to get my father out. He had to scrape my father's body off the floor with a shovel because he'd been pulverized by falling rock. Afterward, Otis docked my uncle's pay for the day. When my uncle found out, he hunted Otis down in a saloon and punched him in the face. It was a long time ago, but there's been bad blood between our families ever since. I don't care if your uncle likes me or not. He's a no-good, rotten son of a bitch."

She swallowed. "I'm so sorry."

He looked out over the town, toward the mine, his thoughts somewhere else. "I'm sorry too. I shouldn't have said all that. Otis is still your uncle."

"I wish he weren't. And we're only related by marriage. I'm just sorry he treated your family so poorly. It's inexcusable."

"I saw you arguing with him up at the mine," he said. "Caused quite a ruckus from what I could tell. What were you doing up there? Everyone's talking about it, trying to figure out what you were up to."

She wondered how much she should say. If she told him the truth, that she was up there because she wanted to help the breaker boys, he might laugh. Or maybe he'd be angry that she thought she could change things. "I wasn't up to anything," she said. "I was just trying to find out more about the breaker boys."

"What about them?"

She searched his face, wondering if his belief that "you could judge a man by how he treated those below him" extended to getting little boys out of the mines, or if that was a step too far. If he said it was all right to put the breaker boys in danger because "that's how it's always been done" she wasn't sure what she would do. One thing was certain, if he used that excuse, it would be easier to stay away from him. He held her gaze, his eyes as green and still as a millpond. "I wanted to find out how dangerous their job was," she said.

"It's extremely dangerous. Everyone knows that."

"I didn't know it," she said. "I'd never heard of the breaker boys until I came back here. And then I saw boys with missing limbs and bleeding fingers, and the other day there was a funeral...." Her throat closed, and she hesitated, trying to find her voice. "Shouldn't there be a law to protect them, especially the little ones?"

"There is," he said, his voice grim. "Pennsylvania state law says no boys younger than twelve can work in the mines."

Her breath caught. She couldn't believe what she was hearing. "Then Mr. Flint is breaking the law."

"Yes," he said. "A lot of mining companies are."

"That's what everyone keeps telling me, but that doesn't make it right. Someone needs to turn in Mr. Flint and protect those boys."

He shifted in his seat again, rocking the car. "You're right. But it's not as easy as you think...."

"I don't care if it's not easy," she said. "Why haven't you tried?"

He took his arm from around her. "How do you know I haven't?"

Heat crawled up her neck. "I don't. But—"

"You should think before you talk about something you don't understand."

"I'm sorry," she said. "It's just ... I want to help. Mr. Flint needs to be stopped."

"And you think you can do something," he said. "You think you can take on the Bleak Mountain Mining Company and save the breaker boys."

Save. Yes, Emma wanted to save the breaker boys. She had done nothing to save Albert. Michael's words rang in her ears again. *Why are you just standing there, doing nothing?* She nodded, and her eyes flooded despite her determination not to cry. Suddenly the world blurred around her, and she forgot all about being stuck on a Ferris wheel. "It's not right," she said, her voice catching.

"I agree." He pulled a handkerchief from his pocket and handed it to her. "Did anyone tell you about the fire in the breaker ten years ago?"

She shook her head, wiping her tears with his handkerchief.

"My brother and I were working in the breaker when it happened," he said. His face was set in the long lines of a man traveling a hated road. "One morning the furnace draft ignited the timbers separating the flue from the carriage way. The flames leapt to the breaker, and it started to collapse over the main shaft. Thirteen boys, including my brother, died. If Hazard Flint hadn't sold off all the firefighting equipment, they might have been saved."

She gasped. "How old was your brother?"

"I was ten. My brother was twelve," he said. "He broke a window, lifted me through it, and shoved me out of the breaker right before the inside stairway gave way."

"Oh my God. I'm so sorry."

"I couldn't work for a while after that," he said. "And my father was dead, so Mr. Flint evicted my mother and me because we couldn't pay rent. We moved into another widow's shack with ten other people until I was old enough to earn a man's pay."

She gaped at him, shocked. "Why on Earth are you still working for Mr. Flint? How can you?"

"Right now I don't have a choice. Mining is all I've ever known. And I can't just walk away from this place."

"Because you want to make things better," she said. "You want to force Mr. Flint to change the way he treats the miners."

"If only I had that kind of power."

"But Percy and Otis said you're setting up secret meetings. That you're trying to organize a union!"

He stared at her hard, then looked away. "I don't know what you're talking about."

"Is there going to be a strike?"

"I don't know."

"Are you going to help the breaker boys too?"

"Why are you asking me all these questions?" he said, impatience creeping into his voice.

She sighed, wondering how she could get him to trust her. She thought about telling him she'd been leaving food on miners' doorsteps and marking their bills paid, but it was too soon. Besides, he might think she was foolish and tell her to stop. "I told you," she said. "I want to help the breaker boys."

"Well, you're barking up the wrong tree," he said. "And if I were you, I'd stop asking so many questions. You're just asking for trouble."

"But if everyone stood together," she said. "If all the miners went on strike . . ."

Clayton gestured toward the mine with his chin. "You see those wooden sheds overlooking the colliery? And that other one over there, near the courthouse?"

She nodded.

"Members of the Coal and Iron Police stand guard in those sheds," he said, "with Gatling guns. And they'll shoot anyone not in accord with the way Hazard Flint wants things done. A miner was shot just last week coming out of the mine at the end of his shift because he'd been mouthing off down at McDuff's Ole Alehouse."

"Are you telling me you're not even allowed to complain?"

Just then, the Ferris wheel engine finally shuttered to life. Their car jerked forward a few inches, swinging wildly again. She grimaced and hunched her shoulders, gripping the safety bar. Then the car started moving again, making its way forward and down.

When she'd gotten ahold of herself, she said, "How can I help?"

"There's nothing you can do."

"Think of something."

"I told you," he said. "I'm keeping my head down and minding my own business."

"I don't believe you."

Before Clayton could respond, the car slowed to a stop on top of the loading ramp. A carnival worker grabbed the backrest to stop it from swinging. He unlocked the safety bar and pulled it back, one greasy boot on the footrest. Clayton stepped out of the car, then turned to help Emma get out. She lifted the hem of her skirt and took his hand, then straightened and stood on trembling legs. He hooked his arm through hers, and they made their way down the ramp. She was so relieved to be on solid ground that, at first, she didn't notice Uncle Otis and Aunt Ida standing side by side in the center of the crowd, their withering stares locked on her and Clayton.

CHAPTER 12

Four days after the carnival left town, Emma crept around the end of a wooden outbuilding up in the miners' village, then followed a worn footpath along the back of a henhouse made of tin and lumber scraps. Nighttime dew soaked her shoes and the hem of her long skirt. A slight breeze rustled through the pines, and coyotes howled in the hills, crying like a pack of lost children. It was well before dawn, and she could only see as far as the yellow circle of light surrounding her oil lantern. Three hours earlier, long before her uncle and aunt would shut off their alarm and shuffle to the bathroom in their nightclothes—Ida in a cotton nightgown, Otis in a pair of red long johns—she'd gotten dressed and snuck out of the house.

After Clayton told her that Mr. Flint was indeed breaking the law, she was certain she could find a way to help the breaker boys. Unfortunately, at the moment, providing food and talking to their families was her only plan. But she had to believe another solution would present itself if she kept her eyes and ears open. For now, she would wait until the miners and breaker boys left for work, then talk to some of the boys' mothers.

In a gunnysack hanging from a rope on her shoulder, she carried gifts to smooth the way: tins of black tea, jars of honey, bars of

Cashmere Bouquet and Ivory soap. She'd found the tea hidden among the kitchen supplies in the back of Aunt Ida's pantry, stolen the honey from the Company Store, and taken the soap from the never-ending supply in the wicker basket inside the linen closet, certain no one would notice a few bars missing.

In another lifetime, in another place, she would have thought stealing was wrong. Not in Coal River. Here, they treated boys like men, deaf-mutes could speak, and stealing felt right. No, it felt more than right. It felt like precisely what she was meant to do.

Over the past two weeks, she'd taken canned goods from Aunt Ida's pantry, hunks of cheese from the icebox, potatoes from the root cellar, and sugar and flour from the Hoosier cabinet. Every time she worked at the Company Store, she marked at least two of the miners' bills paid, grateful and relieved that the miners' wives never questioned the ledger. When they came to the counter and she said their bill was paid, she always looked them in the eyes, hoping they would understand and play along. She lied to Percy, saying his mother had instructed her to pick up a few things, then filled a shopping basket with jam and bread, ham hocks and dried beans, and the occasional bag of peppermint sticks and lemon drops. Then, on her way home, she hid the food in the woods between her uncle's house and the neighbor's, keeping it safe from animals inside a battered metal container she'd found in the woodshed. After everyone was asleep, she snuck out, retrieved the food, trekked up to the miners' village, and left it on the steps of different shacks. On her way home, she felt satisfied and powerful because she was undermining Mr. Flint. And, for a little while, she was free from her aunt and uncle's control. But stealing food and sneaking out of the house was almost too easy, and she knew it was only a matter of time before she got caught. In the meantime, she'd never felt more alive. Except it wasn't enough. She needed to do more.

She could still picture Uncle Otis and Aunt Ida waiting for her when she got off the Ferris wheel, their eyes furious, their mouths twisted in anger. Uncle Otis had grabbed her by the arm and yanked her through the crowd toward his car, too livid for words. Aunt Ida followed, stammering and sputtering about how disappointed she was that any niece of hers would keep such dreadful company. Clayton tried to stop Otis, but Emma begged him to let her go before things got out of hand. She didn't want him to be arrested and taken from Jack again, and she assured him she would be all right. Luckily, he listened.

When they reached the house, Uncle Otis locked Emma in her bedroom, telling her to think long and hard about her actions, and whether she wanted to continue to receive their help. He confined her for the next three days, while Aunt Ida brought in eggs and soup, and let her out to use the bathroom. Her aunt only spoke to her once, on the first day of her incarceration.

"Being seen with that hooligan was a slap in your uncle's face!" she said. "Between that and going up to the mine to question him, you've hurt his feelings deeply. I'm not sure he'll get over it until you can be more grateful for everything we've done for you."

Now, Emma blew out her lantern and hid behind a smoke-house, watching the silhouettes of wives and mothers in backlit doorways saying good-bye to the men and boys as they left in the darkness of early morning. One by one, the miners filed out of their shanties and walked in silence through pools of water and black slag, each seemingly lost in his own thoughts, their bodies still warm from sleep and a kitchen fire, their bellies filled with chicory and fried eggs. Breaker boys plodded silently beside their elders, yawning or looking at the ground, a solemn procession of small men in ragged clothing, small men who should be sleeping and dreaming about baseball and fishing.

Moving in a dark, ragged group, the workers converged on the main road and trudged up the mountain toward the shaft, the only sounds the clink of dinner pails, the crunch of slag beneath hundreds of feet, and the miners' short, hacking coughs. The women watched until the men and boys were out of view, no doubt thinking about their daily chores—making beds and pressing Sunday suits, mopping floors and washing dishes, stretching last night's leftovers into one more meal. After the last man was over the hill, the women turned and went back into their homes—no doubt praying that the mine whistle wouldn't blow until quitting time— and dozens of doors slowly closed in unison.

Emma rounded the smokehouse and moved toward the first row

of shanties. She passed the first two shacks and climbed the steps of the third, her insides fluttery with nerves. On the porch, an old rocking chair sat gray and splintered in one corner like a dried-out skeleton. Switchgrass and nimblewill grew through missing planks in the floor. She set down her lantern, smoothed her dress, and knocked. Behind the door a baby cried, and a mother softly sang a lullaby. Then there was the sound of footsteps padding across a wooden floor, and the door opened. A thin woman in bare feet and a loose cotton dress stood there with a baby boy in her arms, blinking at Emma in surprise. Her limp, brown hair hung loose and oily around her pale face, and she had bags under her eyes.

"Help you?" she said, her voice flat.

Emma cleared her throat. "Hello," she said. "I'm Emma Malloy. I was wondering if I could talk to you for a few minutes."

"'Bout what?" the woman said.

"May I come in?"

The woman continued to stare, her mouth in a hard line. Emma took a deep breath and forced a smile.

"I'm . . ." She paused, not sure how to begin. "I work at the Company Store."

"I know. I seen you down there."

"I'm sorry," Emma said. "I've forgotten my manners. What's your name?"

"Pearl," the woman said.

"Nice to meet you, Pearl," Emma said, extending her hand. The woman shook it halfheartedly. Emma took the bag from her shoulder, rummaged around inside and produced a bar of Cashmere Bouquet soap. She held it out to Pearl.

"I brought this for you," she said. "It's my favorite."

Pearl stepped backward, and a little girl appeared, about two years old, chewing on her finger, drool shining on her chin. Wearing nothing but a pair of yellowed underwear fashioned out of a flour sack, she stared up at Emma with wide, wet eyes.

"Come on in," Pearl said.

Emma stepped over the threshold, wishing she'd brought something for the little girl, and entered the main room. It was both kitchen and living room at the same time, with two roughhewn doors on the back partition. The outer walls of the shack were bare wood, with no inner plaster, and the floor was made of lumber planks. The smell of fried eggs and burning coal hung in the air, along with the heavy, wet-coal odor of mud-soaked clothes. Two pairs of long johns hung over a line strung along the back wall, together with a pullover shirt and a pair of work overalls, the legs and knees stained black. A small coal stove sat at the back of the kitchen area, its flue leaking. An assortment of cast-iron pans and kettles hung from hooks in the ceiling, and a round, galvanized tub sat on the floor next to the coal stove. The floorboards around the tub were stained black by sooty water. On the wall above the chipped sink, a crude wooden shelf held scratched cups, cloudy glasses, and stacks of mismatched plates and mixing bowls. A battered kitchen table sat surrounded by chairs that looked like they'd fall apart if you touched them. On the far end of the room, a mouse skittered along the baseboard, disappearing through a hole beneath the sink. The woman didn't seem to notice it.

The little girl toddled over to a corner of the living room on little bowlegs and pulled a cloth doll from a homemade cradle. She lifted the doll and hugged it beneath her chin, then carried it over to Emma and held it up to show her. Emma knelt down and touched the doll's face with gentle fingers.

"Is this your baby doll?"

The little girl nodded enthusiastically, her eyes shining.

"Are you taking good care of her?" Emma said.

The little girl nodded again, then went back across the room to return the doll to the cradle. Emma straightened and smiled at Pearl, who was bouncing the baby on her hip.

"I'd offer you a cup of coffee," Pearl said. "But we're out."

"That's all right." Emma rummaged around inside her bag again. "I brought some tea. Do you like tea?"

Pearl narrowed her eyes. "What'd you come here for?" she said. "You need something?"

Emma cleared her throat and smiled again, hoping she looked friendly. "Well," she began, "you know those canned goods you been finding on your doorstep? I'm the one who's been leaving them."

Pearl stopped bouncing the baby and searched Emma's face. "How come?" she said.

"I know it's a struggle," Emma said. "I know the mining company doesn't pay enough. And I know the Company Store charges too much for the things you need for your family."

"I don't got the money to pay you for that food," Pearl said. "I didn't ask you for nothing."

"No, no," Emma said. "That's not what I mean. I don't want your money."

With a doubtful look on her face, Pearl took a seat in a kitchen chair, lifted the baby to her shoulder, and patted his back. Her hands were chapped and calloused, her fingernails ragged and dirty. "Ain't nobody does something for nothing," she said. "So what do you want?"

"I want to help," Emma said.

Pearl let out a bitter laugh. "Well then, you better get on back where you came from. You ain't got any idea what you're talking about."

"I know," Emma said. "But I'm hoping you can explain it to me." She pulled out a chair and sat at the table. "I saw two boys leave here this morning. So you have two other sons?"

Pearl stopped patting the baby's back. "What do my boys got to do with this? They do something wrong?"

"No, it's nothing like that. If you don't mind me asking, how old are they?"

"Tanner is eight," Pearl said. "He'll be nine in three weeks. Jasper is ten."

"And they work for the mining company?"

Pearl frowned. "I don't see how—"

"Do your sons work in the breaker?"

"Tanner does. But Jasper is a spragger."

"What's a spragger?" Emma said.

"Only the fastest boys can be spraggers," Pearl said. A flicker of pride lit up her tired face. "They're the ones who control the speed of coal cars as they roll down the slope."

"How do they do that?"

"With long pieces of wood they jab into the wheels," Pearl said. She made stabbing motions with one hand. "The wood locks the wheels and slows the cars."

"Sounds dangerous."

"I s'pose it is. Mining is a dangerous job."

"Did you know Hazard Flint is breaking state law by letting your boys work in the mines?"

Pearl took the baby from her shoulder and stood. "I'm done talking."

"Oh no," Emma said. "Please. You're misunderstanding me. I'm not trying to get you in trouble."

"Get me in trouble?" Pearl said. "I already got enough trouble, trying to keep these little ones fed."

"I can see that," Emma said. "That's why I left food on your porch. That's why I'm up here talking to you today. I want to help you and your family. I want to help all the miners and their families."

"I don't see how talking is going to help," Pearl said. She sat back down again, setting the baby in her lap. "My pa started out as a breaker boy, then worked in the mines for years. When he got too old to dig coal, he went back to work in the breaker as a boss. Before he died of the black lung, Doc said he got so much of that old black coal dust in his lungs, it turned them like concrete. If we could of taken a hammer to them, it would of been like breaking a dish. I sat by my pa for three weeks and watched him die. Reckon my husband and sons will die of the same thing. They start out in the breaker and end up there. Twice as a boy and once as a man, that's the poor miners' lot. It's just the way it is."

"How long have your sons been working?"

Pearl shrugged. "Three, four years."

"Did the mining company ask for their birth certificates before they hired them?"

Pearl dropped her eyes.

"Did they?" Emma said. "Did they know your boys were so young?"

Pearl lifted her gaze and glared at Emma, her eyes glassy. "You see this house?" she said. "You see that barrel of potatoes over there, that tin of flour? My boys have to work in those mines, or else we wouldn't have enough food. We wouldn't have the money to pay our rent, and the mining company would turn us out!"

"I understand that," Emma said. "But don't you worry about your boys getting hurt or killed? A breaker boy died just the other day and—"

Pearl jumped up from her seat, put the baby on her hip, marched across the room, and yanked open the front door. "You've outstayed your welcome. Best be on your way."

Emma stood, her mind racing. She had to prove to Pearl that she was on her side. "What about school?" she said. "Who is teaching your boys to read and write?"

"Ain't no need to read and write to dig coal from the earth."

"But don't you want more for your children?" Emma said. "Don't you want them to have a choice about what they do for a living?"

"Miners' children don't go to school," Pearl said. "Been that way for as long as I can remember."

"What if I could teach your children to read and write? Would you like that? I could come in the evenings, a few nights a week."

Pearl shook her head. "My boys are too tired for schooling by the time they get home. After they get cleaned up and have a little something to eat, they usually go to bed."

"But don't you see?" Emma said. "They deserve more. If you and the other mothers stood together and refused to let your boys work under such dangerous conditions—"

"You know what happened to the last person who stood up to Hazard Flint?" Pearl said. "He got thrown in jail. His wife and three kids was put out of their house! Last I heard, the mother and youngest died of pneumonia, and the rest of the kids was sent off to an orphanage. Now you tell me if that's any better than what I got right here."

"But if you all stick together. If you all . . ."

Pearl jerked her chin toward the porch. "I got work to do," she said.

Emma put her bag over her shoulder and went to the door. "I'm sorry you feel that way," she said. "And I'm sorry if I upset you.

That wasn't my intention. If you change your mind, you know where to find me."

"Reckon I won't," Pearl said.

Emma stepped across the threshold and turned to face her. "Can I just ask you one more thing?"

"What?"

"Do you know Michael Carrion and his grandmother Tala?"

"Never heard of them," Pearl said. She started to close the door, but Emma put out a hand to stop it.

"If you tell me your husband's name," she said, keeping her voice low, "I'll be sure to mark your store bill paid this week as a way of thanking you for your time."

Pearl stared at her, as if trying to decide what to do. Deep lines creased her forehead. After a long moment, she started to close the door again, her expression softening. The baby started to wail. "Roy Sinclair," she said in a weary voice, and shut the door in Emma's face.

By eight o'clock, Emma had spoken to a dozen or more women. Most were too afraid to stand up to the mining company or worried about losing the extra income from their sons, while others were downright hostile, telling her to get out of their house and never come back. In some sections of the village, they spoke German, Polish, or Italian, and she couldn't make herself understood. At every new door, she held her breath when she knocked, wondering if she would find Jack, and Clayton's home, on the other side. Then again, maybe Jack spent the day at someone else's house while Clayton worked. She thought about asking someone where Clayton lived, but changed her mind. Knocking on his door by accident would be one thing. Looking for him would be quite another.

She did ask where Michael and Tala lived, but no one seemed to know for sure. One woman said they were on Widow's Row but had been recently evicted. Another said Tala was shacked up with an old widower, but she didn't know which one. The most common story was that Michael and Tala lived in a makeshift shed in the woods, moving from one section of the forest to the other, only coming into the village to trade potions, tinctures, and animal hides for food. The one thing everyone agreed on was that Michael was indeed a deaf-mute.

To Emma's dismay, each shanty was more desperate and sparse than the last, filled with dirty children in worn clothing, gaunt wives and mothers with calloused hands and weary eyes. Some shanties housed ten to twenty people—widows, young children, orphans, old ladies, and sick and crippled men. Everyone agreed that things were not good, but they weren't sure what to do about any of it. A few brave women hoped aloud that there would be a strike, and mentioned Clayton as a possible leader.

On the porch of the last shanty on Scotch Road, a rail-thin woman with matted hair snatched a tin of tea and a jar of honey from Emma's hands, then hurried back inside without closing the door. Emma hesitated on the threshold, unsure of what to do, then followed her in, closing the door behind her. The woman scurried over to the coal-fired stove and, with quick birdlike movements, pried open the tin of tea, poured hot water from an iron kettle into a milky white cup, then added some tea leaves and a spoonful of honey. After that, she poured hot water over a rag in a bucket, handed the bucket to Emma, and led her toward the back of the shanty. All the while she was talking fast, with a thick Italian accent. Her name was Francesca, she recognized Emma from the Company Store and thought she was pretty, and she'd been living in Coal River for five years.

In a narrow back room, a willowy boy lay covered with a thin sheet on a wooden cot, his chest rattling as he struggled to breathe. His corn silk hair lay tousled on the stained pillow beneath his head, and his skin was a deathly shade of ash. A dog-eared Bible sat between a water-filled basin and an earthen crock on a bedside table, along with a set of rosary beads and a grainy photo of a handsome man in an oval frame. Moving slowly now, Francesca set the mug of tea on a table, took the bucket of hot water from Emma, and set it beside the cot. She gently wiped the boy's brow with a cloth, rewetting it in the basin of cool water.

"*Questo è Nicolas,*" she whispered. "We are fearing the black lung. He has breathing problems since he came into this world, but nothing like this." She helped Nicolas sit up, propping more pillows beneath his head, then sat on the edge of the bed and offered him a spoonful of tea. "He worked so hard the last four years, just like his father. But last week he . . ." She paused, her chin trembling. "He *crollato,* collapsed."

Emma stood watching, not knowing what to do or say. How she wished she had those last few drops of laudanum now, to ease the poor boy's suffering. Francesca spooned the tea between his pale lips, catching any drips with gentle fingers. After the fourth mouthful, Nicolas coughed and shook his head, whispering that he was too tired to stay awake. Francesca set the tea down and wiped damp strands of hair from his forehead. With shaking hands, she pulled the sheet down from his bare torso, exposing ribs that stuck out beneath his white skin every time he drew in a breath. She opened the earthen crock and applied a poultice of elderberries, dandelion leaves, slippery elm bark, and yarrow to his chest. Then she wrung the hot water out of the rag in the bucket, laid it over the poultice, and drew the sheet back up beneath his chin. She stood and kissed him on the forehead.

"He must rest," she said. She led Emma back to the kitchen and offered her a chair. "*Grazie* for the tea and honey. It will surely help."

"You're welcome," Emma said. "I'm so sorry your son is ill."

"*Grazie,*" Francesca said again. "We pray for a miracle, but I . . ." She shook her head, her lips quivering.

Emma took a deep breath, wondering if she should leave the poor woman alone. "Do you have any other children?"

Francesca smiled thinly and held up two fingers. "Twins."

"How old?"

"Seven," Francesca said. "I had another. He was two, blond like his brothers, just learning to speak."

Emma steeled herself for more terrible news. "Where is he now?"

Francesca crossed herself. "With our Father in Heaven," she said. "He had . . . How do you say it?" She patted her chest with an open hand.

"Pneumonia?"

"Yes," Francesca said. "Last winter."

"I'm so sorry," Emma said. "And the twins? Where are they?"

Francesca eyes filled, and the corners of her mouth pulled down. "They are working," she said in a quiet voice.

"In the breaker?"

Francesca nodded.

Emma decided not to say anything about Hazard Flint breaking the child labor law. Poor Francesca already had enough troubles, grieving for her two-year-old and caring for Nicolas. Surely, she wasn't up to staging a rebellion. Then Emma had another thought. "If you don't mind my asking, did you make the poultice for Nicolas?"

"No," Francesca said. "I would not know how. I traded our last loaf of bread for it."

"Traded? With who?"

"She was a . . . How do you say, Indian?"

"An older woman?" Emma made a pulling motion beneath her ears, indicating hair. "With white braids?"

"Yes."

"Do you know where she lives? Or how I can find her?"

"No," Francesca said. "But her granddaughter lives across the way, near the far end of the next lane."

"Does her grandson live there too?"

Francesca shook her head. "No," she said. "He is with the grandmother in the woods. Some people are afraid. They make it too hard for him to stay."

"Afraid of who? The grandson?"

Francesca nodded.

Emma leaned forward. "Why?"

"They say he is not right in the head."

"In what way?"

"It's just what I heard." Francesca shrugged. "My husband is not happy about me trading with the Indian woman, but I have to do something. We are trying to save money to buy real medicine for Nicolas, but we have no rain for the garden and must buy food. Nothing will grow this summer. I don't know what else to do." She wrung her calloused hands.

Emma swallowed hard, trying to get rid of the burning lump in her throat. In her mind's eye, she did a quick inventory of the knickknacks and decorations in her uncle and aunt's house, wondering if there was anything she could sell to buy medicine for Nicolas—the porcelain ballerina statue on the fireplace mantel, the Italian vase in the dining room, the silver candelabra in the parlor, Aunt Ida's ivory brooch. Then her heart dropped. It would never work. Aunt Ida might not notice food missing from the pantry, but she would certainly notice if any of her prized possessions disappeared. And where would Emma sell a ballerina statue anyway? Maybe she could steal a dollar or two from the store till. Only to buy medicine, to save a life. No, that was too risky. Percy counted the cash register every day without fail. Then she remembered walking past Percy's bedroom on her way to the linen closet. Once, he'd left his door open partway, and she could see his dressing table. On the dressing table, a silver platter lined with red felt held his wallet, his pocket watch, a handful of shiny change, and a stack of bills held together with a gold clip.

"How much money do you need?" Emma asked Francesca.

A few minutes later, Emma left Francesca's shanty and made her way toward the next lane. If she couldn't find Michael and Tala, maybe she could get answers from Tala's granddaughter. At the first house, a woman with ruddy cheeks stood on the sparse grass of the front yard, using a pair of rusty scissors and a broken comb to cut a boy's hair. Her hands were red and chapped, as if they'd spent too much time in hot water. Emma recognized her from the store. The boy, aged seven or eight, was sitting on a peeling blue stool in short pants and bare feet. Both his arms were missing past the elbow. Two toddlers played on the porch with sticks and a grime-covered ball, and a baby napped in a wooden cradle. A young girl, about ten, sat on the porch steps looking down at a book in her hands. Surprised, Emma stopped in her tracks.

"Nice day," she said to the girl's mother.

The woman nodded and kept trimming the back of the boy's hair. The boy tried to look up at Emma while keeping his chin down.

"Is that your daughter on the steps?" Emma said.

The woman glanced over her shoulder at the girl and said, "Yes."

"Does she know how to read?"

"No, she just looks at the pictures."

"What if I could teach her? I could teach your boy too, if you'd like."

The woman stopped cutting and straightened, eyeing her suspiciously. "What for?"

The girl got up from the steps and came over to stand by the woman's side. She smiled shyly at Emma, the book held to her chest. On the cover was a lion with a red mane and green glasses. It was *The Wonderful Wizard of Oz*.

"Just because," Emma said. She looked down at the girl. "Would you like to be able to read your book?"

The girl nodded, her hazel eyes sparkling.

"I can't pay you," the woman said.

"You don't have to pay me anything," Emma said. "I'll do it for free, if that's all right. I enjoy teaching children to read."

The woman lowered her brow, thinking. Then she said, "I s'pose that'd be all right."

"Can I come in the evenings then, sometime after supper?"

"I don't see why not." For the first time, the woman smiled.

Emma thanked the woman, said good-bye, and kept walking. Finally she was getting somewhere. Between the girl with the book and her brother, two other girls, and Francesca's twins, she had six students. Maybe when the rest of the mothers heard that other children were learning to read and write, they would come around. Despite Emma's heavy heart, she looked forward to the first lesson. She couldn't wait to see the children's eyes light up when she read to them. Right now she only had two appropriate books from Aunt Ida's library: *Anne of Green Gables* and *The Wind in the Willows*, but they were a start. Maybe, like the hazel-eyed girl, some of the other children had books at home. And it would be easy to steal pencils and paper from the Company Store to teach them to write. She could start the lessons tomorrow, after she finished helping Cook clean up after dinner. The one good thing that had come out of upsetting her aunt and uncle by going up to the mine and being seen with Clayton was that they no longer cared, or noticed, when she went to bed extra early. It would be easy to sneak out and go up to the miners' village without them knowing.

Lost in her thoughts, it took a moment for Emma to notice the old woman. When she did, she stopped short, her breath catching in her chest. It was Tala, sitting at a spinning wheel in a front yard, her bare feet going up and down on the treadle, her white hair pulled back in one long braid. Emma tried to remember if she had left food at that particular house, but couldn't recall. So many of the shanties looked the same. She stood on the path, the gunnysack twisted in her fingers, wondering if she should tell Tala that Michael had spoken to her. Surely, the boy's family would want to know. Maybe they could try to get him to speak more. Or maybe they already knew he could talk. Then she remembered Francesca's words. *They say he is not right in the head.*

Was it possible that Michael was insane? Maybe that's why he said things that didn't make sense. Maybe she had read something into his words that wasn't there. Still, that didn't explain why he had mentioned Albert. There was only one way to find out. She took a deep breath, forced a smile, and proceeded across the path toward Tala.

"Good morning," she said hesitantly.

Tala glanced up with rheumy brown eyes, nodded once, and went back to her spinning. With gnarled fingers, she pulled gray fibers from a mass of wool, her feet pumping up and down, and fed them into the spindle. Up close, her skin was dark and lined with deep creases and folds, as if she were carved out of wood. The nubs of two yellow teeth hung between her thin lips.

"I'm sorry to bother you," Emma said. "But I was wondering if I could ask you about your grandson, Michael."

Tala kept spinning, her face set in concentration. Emma squatted next to the wheel.

"Is it true that he can't speak?" she said.

Tala nodded in rhythm with her foot.

Emma tried to breath normally. All the lines she had prepared to say flew from her head like pigeons from a coop. "I thought you would want to know that he spoke to me."

Tala stopped spinning and fixed her gaze on Emma, her eyes

suddenly hard and clear. She set down the ball of wool and struggled to push herself up from her stool. Emma straightened, nervous sweat breaking out on her forehead. She made a move to help
Tala stand, but stopped short, unsure if her assistance would be
welcomed. Was Tala angry or shocked? It was impossible to tell.
Just then, a young, dark-haired woman hurried out of the shanty,
concern lining her brow. She wiped her hands on her apron, came
down the steps, and helped Tala to her feet.

"What is it, Grandmother?" the woman said. "Are you all
right?"

Emma recognized her from the store. She was always alone.
"I'm sorry," Emma said. "I'm afraid I've upset her."

"How?" the woman said. "What did you do?"

Uncertainty clawed at Emma's throat. Was this Michael's sister?
Would she be upset too? Would she accuse Emma of lying and tell
her to go away? Briefly, she wondered if she should leave the
women in peace. It was clear they were struggling, and taking care
of Michael couldn't be easy. But she needed to know why he had
said her brother's name. And they would want to know Michael
could speak, wouldn't they? Choosing her words carefully and
leaving out the part about Albert because it was too much information all at once, Emma told the younger woman her story, then
waited for a response. The woman searched her face, as if trying to
decide if she was telling the truth.

"I'm sorry for upsetting your grandmother," Emma said. "But I
thought she would want to know. If you're a relative of his, maybe
you can work with him, try to get him to talk more."

"I'm Michael's sister, Simone," the woman said. "And I'm sorry,
but you must be confusing him with someone else." She turned
away to help Tala toward the porch steps.

"Please," Emma called after them. "He knew my dead brother's
name!"

Simone stopped and turned to face her. "I'm sorry about your
brother, but Michael is *my* brother, and I need to protect him. He's
been through enough."

"I understand," Emma said. "And I promise I don't want to
hurt him, or you. I'm just trying to figure out why he spoke to me

and how he knew my brother's name. Please, it's my fault Albert is dead." Her voice cracked on the last words.

Simone gazed at her for a long moment. Then, finally, she said, "Come inside."

Emma and Simone sat at her kitchen table while Tala listened intently from a rocking chair. Simone explained that her grandmother was there to use the spinning wheel while Michael was working. In the spring, summer, and fall, her grandmother and Michael lived in a makeshift shanty in the woods. In the winter, they stayed with her sometimes, but only when the snow got too deep and the temperatures went below freezing. Simone wanted them to stay with her year-round, but they refused, insisting they could take care of themselves. Thankfully, Michael was good at setting traps for game, and Tala knew how to identify edible mushrooms, roots, leaves, and berries. She traded herbs for food, and the small amount of money Michael earned in the breaker bought other things they needed to survive. Simone did their shopping because they tried to avoid going into town. The self-imposed exile came about two years ago, after her and Michael's parents were killed in a carriage accident.

"Michael tried to run away after they died," Simone said. "So our grandmother took him into the woods." She rested her chin on her hand. "And they've been there ever since."

"Why did he try to run away?"

"He was scared."

"Of what?"

"A lot of people were cruel to him, yelling and throwing rocks, calling him names. He didn't understand what was going on."

Emma's face grew warm with shame, remembering how goose bumps crawled across her skin when she thought about Michael. "He's just a boy," she said. "Why would they do that?"

"People are afraid of things they don't understand," Simone said. "The only reason everyone leaves him alone while he's working in the breaker is because Mr. Flint told them to."

Emma's eyebrows shot up. "Mr. Flint protects Michael?"

Simone shrugged. "He needs Michael to sort coal. And my

brother doesn't get distracted like the other boys because he can't hear and doesn't speak. He's a good worker."

Emma nodded. *Of course. What other reason would Mr. Flint have?* "But why are people afraid of Michael?"

Simone sat back in her chair, one thumb rubbing her knuckles. "It's a long story. Are you sure you want to hear it?"

Emma nodded.

"All right," Simone said. She leaned forward. "Our maternal grandfather was from France. He was well known there because he had a gift. Some respected him while others scorned him. They thought his abilities came from the devil."

"What kind of gift?" Emma said.

"Some call it mediumship. Others call it possession. Our grandfather called it channeling."

The hairs on the back of Emma's neck stood up. "Do you mean speaking to the dead?"

She had heard stories about this in New York. Once, a stagehand had told her about visiting a medium to connect with her dead son. The medium had said she could channel loved ones who had passed on to the other side, and the stagehand's son would be able to speak through her. But the stagehand's late husband came through instead, an overbearing man who used the session to tell her to cut her hair and stop wasting money on fresh flowers. Afterward, the medium explained she couldn't always control who came through. She said the dead longed to be heard and would use any means possible to do so.

Simone nodded. "Our mother inherited those abilities, but she didn't want to admit it. And we were never allowed to talk about it because our grandfather disowned her when she married our father, who was half Indian, and went back to America with him."

"I don't understand. What does this have to do with Michael?"

"We think Michael inherited the gift from our mother. He's only used it once that we know of, but everybody heard about it when it happened. That's why he tried to run away."

"When *what* happened?" Emma said, her skin tingling in anticipation.

Simone took a deep breath and closed her eyes, as if building up the courage to continue. When she opened her eyes again, they were glassy. "The day our parents were killed, someone overheard Michael tell the carriage driver to check the axle before they left."

"So they heard him speak?"

Simone nodded. "Yes."

"For the first time?"

"Yes. The only time."

"And that made everyone afraid?"

"No," Simone said. "They were afraid because Michael obviously knew what was going to happen. The axle broke, the carriage went over a cliff, and our parents died. After that, rumors started spreading that Michael was channeling our late grandfather. Or he was possessed by him. And that's why he could speak."

Emma gasped, wondering if what Simone said could possibly be true. After Albert died, she used to talk to him all the time, begging him to give her a sign that he was all right. But he never did. And after a few years with no response, she stopped trying. Could Albert finally be speaking to her through Michael? Could her brother be the one asking her to help the breaker boys?

No, she thought. *That can't be it. There has to be another solution.* Aunt Ida said everyone in Coal River was gossiping about her brother's early death. Maybe Michael had overheard someone talking about it. Maybe he had overheard Simone and Tala discussing it. Maybe mentioning Albert's name was his way of letting her know he meant no harm. Of course. That had to be it. He could have heard about Albert anywhere. The idea that her brother was communicating from beyond the grave through Michael was foolishness. Wasn't it?

CHAPTER 13

Two hours after church on a Sunday afternoon, Emma sat up in bed, her back propped against a pillow, trying to read while Percy fumbled through *Fur Elise* on the piano in the parlor below and rain swept across her bedroom window. Over the past week, she had claimed she was tired after dinner every other night, then snuck out the back door up to the miners' village to teach her new students. Luckily, her aunt and uncle were still so angry with her, they'd barely meet her gaze at the dinner table, let alone care if she disappeared into her room after helping Cook clean up. If Emma had known she was going to be ignored for going up to the mine and being seen with Clayton, she would have done it sooner. Things were certainly easier that way.

Class was held in the living room of the girl with *The Wizard of Oz* book, who was picking up words faster than Emma thought possible. Using papers and pencils stolen from the Company Store, Emma had started teaching the children to write, beginning with the first few letters of the alphabet. After writing lessons, she read from *The Wind in the Willows,* and the children were spellbound. Even the twins, who sometimes complained that they were too tired to learn, sat silently listening to the story. By Emma's third visit, three more women had brought their children to the house for instruction, for a total of nine students. It wasn't much, but it was a start. Along with teaching the children to read and write, Emma wanted to gain the trust of their parents. If they knew she had their children's best interest at heart, maybe, when the time came to protect the breaker boys, they would stand beside her. So far, the women said, their husbands had either been out, too preoccupied to question what was going on, or were grateful that their children had an opportunity to learn.

Then, two nights ago, as she was leaving a shanty on Hazel Patch Road, she saw Jack, the orphan who lived with Clayton. He was playing on a porch four doors down, spinning a wooden yo-yo over the railing. Briefly, she thought about going over to say hello. But she wanted to talk to Clayton first because she was afraid he wouldn't approve of her impromptu school. She wanted the chance to convince him that Jack deserved some education too, before he made up his mind based on gossip and hearsay.

Whether Michael was trying to help her, or, by some miracle, Albert was guiding her, she had no idea. But she felt like she was on the right path. She thought about asking Simone to arrange a meeting with Michael, then decided that if Albert were really trying to communicate with her, he would find a way. And if Michael had more to say, she would run into him sooner or later. So far, things had happened naturally. It seemed like a mistake to force it. For now, teaching the children was the right thing to do, and it felt like another step closer to finding a way to stop Mr. Flint. If she had to bide her time until then, that's what she would do.

But then, last night, after stealing bills one by one from Percy's dressing table over the last several days—a feeling of dread building up in her chest because she was certain she'd get caught sooner or later—she had finally taken the money up to Francesca, only to learn that Nicolas had died the previous evening. When she arrived at their house, she found Francesca in the back room, curled up in a fetal position on the cot next to her dead son, delirious and inconsolable. Nicolas looked like he was sleeping, his eyes closed, the white skin of his hollow cheeks smooth as silk. His struggling, short breaths were stilled, the pain on his face erased. Someone had crossed his thin hands over his chest, and laced a rosary and a tiny bouquet of wildflowers between his fingers. The twins were at the kitchen table, staring silently into bowls of thin soup. Even in their grief they were beautiful, with flaxen hair and cornflower blue eyes. Emma left the money with Francesca's husband, who was smoking on the back stoop, staring out into the night. Without a word, he took the bills, nodded, and turned toward the dark again.

Now, desperate to stop the miserable thoughts inside her head, Emma tried reading one of Aunt Ida's books. It didn't work. She couldn't get past the first page, her mind constantly drawn to the heartbreaking image of Francesca and Nicolas lying side by side, each as bone thin and white as the other. Finally it was raining, the rain Francesca had prayed for so her garden would grow. But it had come too late.

Sitting in her room, listening through the floorboards to Percy playing the piano, the thought of that beautiful boy being buried in the cold, hard ground was almost more than Emma could take. Along with grief, burning anger at Mr. Flint and God and the entire world churned in her stomach like a bowl of hot tar. She fought the urge to throw the book across the room, or storm downstairs and smash Aunt Ida's piano with her bare fists. But getting mad wasn't going to do any good. The only thing that would help was putting an end to child labor in Coal River. Maybe, if she got all the mothers to refuse to let their boys work, someone would take notice. Maybe if Clayton could organize a strike, things would change. Maybe . . . maybe . . . maybe it was too late for all of them.

Emma put the book down and buried her face in her hands, hope collapsing inside her. Then the doorbell rang downstairs, and Percy stopped playing. A minute later, hurried footsteps sounded along the narrow corridor leading to the bottom of the servant quarter stairs.

"Emma!" Aunt Ida shouted up the stairwell. "Come down here this instant!"

Emma sat up and swung her legs over the edge of the bed, wondering why her aunt sounded irritated. She thought about ignoring the request and making her aunt come up to get her, then wiped her eyes, pushed her feet into her shoes, and went into the hallway. Aunt Ida was at the bottom of the steps, her lips pursed.

"What is it?" Emma said.

"There's someone at the door to see you."

"Me? Who is it?"

"Come see for yourself," her aunt said. "I, for one, can't wait to see what this is all about." She turned and went down the hallway, the back of her hair flat from napping on the parlor lounge.

Emma hurried down the staircase, trying to imagine who it could be. If it were Frank, Aunt Ida would have been happy. If it were Clayton, she would have ordered him off her property. Maybe it was one of the miners' wives. Maybe it was Pearl or Francesca. Maybe someone needed her help.

Or maybe it was Michael.

No, it couldn't be. If Aunt Ida saw a one-legged breaker boy on her porch, she would have shooed him away without even asking what he wanted. Besides, Michael had no idea where she lived, did he? And how could he have asked for her, unless he was with his sister?

Aunt Ida was waiting in the kitchen, her arms crossed.

"Who is it?" Emma asked again.

Aunt Ida lifted her chin, sniffing in disapproval, and led her through the dining room toward the front entrance. Male voices floated in from the foyer. One was Percy's, but Emma didn't recognize the other. Her aunt entered the foyer and stepped aside, watching Emma's face as she revealed who was at the door. Emma stopped in her tracks, confused.

It was Frank Bannister.

"Good day, Miss Malloy," Frank said, his tone serious. He stood in one spot, his police hat under his arm, his face void of emotion. Percy stood opposite him, his eyes worried, his lips pressed together in a hard line. This wasn't a social call.

"What can I do for you?" Emma said, her heartbeat picking up speed. Had Frank told Mr. Flint that she was the woman who saw them murder those men? Was he going to take her to the mansion and let Mr. Flint's henchman shoot her? Carry her body down to the river and toss it in?

"We're missing about ten breaker boys," Frank said. "Their

mothers seem to think you've been filling their heads with nonsense, and now they've run off."

Aunt Ida gasped.

"I can assure you," Emma said, "if those boys have run off, it didn't have anything to do with me."

"Are you sure about that?" Frank said. "Some of the women say you've been nosing around, asking a lot of questions."

"I've talked to women at the store," she said. "And I've talked to the children too. Is there a law against being friendly?"

"Emma!" Aunt Ida said. "Watch your tongue, young lady. Captain Bannister works for Mr. Flint, and he is a guest in my home. I won't have you disrespecting him. Now apologize!"

"No harm done, Mrs. Shawcross," Frank said. "But if it's all the same, I'm in a bit of a hurry. Mr. Flint sent me to fetch your niece. He has a few questions he'd like answered."

Emma's blood ran cold. *What did Mr. Flint want with her?* "This is ridiculous!" she said, trying to sound annoyed instead of scared. "Those boys have minds of their own. If they left, it was of their own accord. Nothing I could say would make them leave their families and everything they've ever known. Maybe they're just hoping for a better life than the one they have. Did Hazard Flint ever think of that?"

Aunt Ida rolled her eyes to the ceiling, her face red with anger and shame. "Lord in heaven what a mouth she has. I'm so sorry, Captain Bannister. Emma will be more than happy to cooperate."

"Do you really think it's necessary to take her in?" Percy said. "I mean—"

"You hush, Percy Shawcross!" Aunt Ida said, wagging a finger at him. "If Mr. Flint wants to see Emma, she's going to go see him. If she's done something wrong and they need to take her down to the jailhouse to teach her a lesson, they're welcome to do that too! Lord knows, I'm not getting anywhere with her."

Sweat broke out on Emma's forehead. "You can't expect me to go with Frank alone," she said. "What would people say? Besides, do you want the whole town to see him take me away?"

"She's right," Percy said. "We can't let her go alone. I'll go with her."

"That's not how it's going to work," Frank said. "Mr. Flint wants to talk to Emma alone."

"Why?" Percy said. "Because she's been talking to the miners' families? I don't understand how that—"

"Stay out of it, Percy," Aunt Ida said. "We know Captain Bannister and Mr. Flint personally, and that's all that matters. Emma will be fine." She went to the hall closet, got out a coat and umbrella, and handed them to Emma. "You're lucky your uncle had business to attend to this afternoon and isn't here to see this." She spit out the words as if they tasted bad.

Emma took the coat, trying to keep her hands from shaking. At first she wasn't going to take the umbrella, but she changed her mind. If Frank tried anything, she could use it to defend herself. Frank pushed his hat back on his head and opened the front door. She shoved her arms into the coat, pulled the collar up around her neck, and stepped out onto the front porch. He ran ahead, hurrying down the front steps toward a touring car with enclosed windows, a hand on his hat to keep it from blowing off. Emma followed, the driving rain like tiny bullets on her skin. Frank opened the rear passenger door of the vehicle, waited for her to climb in, then jumped in and started the engine. Raindrops dripped from her lashes and drizzled down the collar of her coat, making her shiver. She tried to relax, hoping she looked more angry than terrified. Then the car lurched forward and bumped along the road, bouncing her around on the seat.

"What's going on?" she said. "Why does Mr. Flint want to see me?"

Frank kept his eyes on the road and said nothing. The rain drummed on the windshield and roof, filling the silence inside the vehicle.

Ten minutes later, the clouds had burned black, and a thunderstorm was creeping out of the Northeast, turning the sky the color of coal. When Flint Mansion came into view, Emma swallowed the sour taste of fear in the back of her throat. Frank drove across the front of the building, then pulled around the back and parked the car beneath a stone archway. From this side, the mansion looked even bigger, with half a dozen balconies, two oversized wings, and a double staircase leading up to the back door. The cupola looked enormous, about the size of Aunt Ida's dining room, and electric lights shone behind the tall windows.

When Frank opened the rear passenger door, Emma climbed out and glanced down the long brick driveway, wondering if she should make a run for it. Then she remembered that Frank had a pistol. If they were going to kill her, they didn't need to wait until she was inside. The umbrella lay on the backseat of the car. Maybe she could knock him out with it. But before she could grab it, he closed the door.

Frank hurried up the marble staircase, opened one of the double doors, and waited for her to enter, his expression unreadable. Inside, they crossed a large room with high ceilings and brass chandeliers. To Emma's surprise, nothing looked familiar. Then she remembered that the first time she was inside the mansion, she'd snuck into the servants' entrance on the other end of the house. It would have taken her all day to see the entire place.

But then they went into a wood-paneled hallway, through what felt like the center of the house, and it all came back to her—the smell of old wood and cold plaster, the dusty rugs and hand-painted portraits. Now, moving through the mansion felt like reliving a nightmare. This was the hallway she had tiptoed down all those years ago, past the dining room and library, toward the staircase that led up to the nursery. The walls started closing in. It was all she could do not to turn around and run. Then the final turn of the banister came into view, the carved wooden knob, the iron spindles. Goose bumps prickled on her skin.

Suddenly it was nine years ago, and she could feel Albert's small hand in hers. They moved together in slow motion, gliding toward the last few minutes of his life, before he chased her and the boys down to the river. Then Frank took her past the staircase and kept going. Albert let go of her hand. The sensation of reliving a nightmare broke.

Glancing up the stairs, Emma half expected to see Albert and Mr. Flint's late wife, Viviane, at the top steps, staring down at her with haunted eyes. She wasn't sure what she would do if she saw her dead brother's ghost, and right now she didn't want to find out.

Would his face be black and bloated, his tangled hair dripping with icy water? Or would he look more like she remembered, with rosy cheeks and a mischievous grin? She knew some people wanted to see spirits, and sought them out by holding séances and visiting graveyards, but she wasn't one of them. Maybe she was still too fragile from the loss of her parents and the recent hard-to-believe discovery that Albert could be trying to communicate with her, but seeing her brother's ghost felt like the very thing that would do her in. To her relief, the top of the staircase was empty. She let out a dry breath and concentrated on putting one foot in front of the other.

Then Frank stopped in front of a set of double doors and knocked. A low rumbling voice instructed them to enter. Frank pushed open the pocket doors, slid them into the wall, and stood back, motioning for her to go through first.

Inside the tall-ceilinged room, Mr. Flint sat behind a wagon-sized mahogany desk, smoking a cigar. He stood when they entered, and offered Emma a seat in one of the padded chairs. Frank took a spot next to a row of high bookcases, his feet apart and his arms crossed. Framed photographs covered every inch of the peach-colored walls—trains, coal cars, breakers, mules, miners, and men in suits shaking hands.

"How are you enjoying Coal River, Miss Malloy?" Mr. Flint said.

She clasped her hands on her lap to keep them from shaking. "I'm not here on holiday, Mr. Flint."

"Of course not," he said. "I was just wondering if you'd come to appreciate all your uncle and aunt have done for you. Sometimes you have to make the best of a less than ideal situation."

"I'm well aware of that," she said.

"Did you enjoy the carnival?" he said.

"Is that why you wanted to see me?" she said. "To ask if I like living in Coal River and if I enjoyed the carnival? I thought this was about the breaker boys?"

He grinned. "Touché," he said. "I can see nothing gets by you, Miss Malloy. So let's get down to business. I'm sure Captain Bannister has told you that ten breaker boys have run away with the carnival. Their mothers are upset, and some are blaming you for filling their heads with ideas. But that is neither here nor there. What's done is done."

"Then why did you bring me here?" she said. "What do you want?"

"If you don't mind, I'll ask the questions." Mr. Flint leaned back in his seat, holding his cane across his thighs, one age-spotted hand gripping the gold head. "How well do you know Clayton Nash?"

Emma's heart skipped a beat. "Why are you asking?"

Mr. Flint sat forward, banging the end of his cane on the floor. "Clayton Nash," he said. "Tell me what you know about him." Despite trying to hide it, he was clearly angry now. She had the feeling he was a man who hadn't had to conceal his emotions in a very long time.

She shook her head, trying to hide the tempest of thoughts whirling inside her mind. "Nothing," she said. "I mean . . . I just met him. We've barely said two words to each other." Thunder crashed outside, rumbling like a train above the mansion.

"Do you have a habit of riding the Ferris wheel with men you hardly know?" he said. Then he winked, one crusty eyelid lowering. His swift change of mood was bewildering, and she wondered if it was intentional. She wanted to grab his cane and knock the self-satisfied grin off his face.

"You must be confusing me with someone else," she said. "I can't ride the Ferris wheel. I'm afraid of heights."

"Lying won't help your situation."

"My situation?" she said. "Excuse me for asking, but what exactly is my situation? And why would I have any reason to lie?"

"That's what I'm trying to figure out."

"I'm sorry," she said. "But I'm afraid you're wasting your—"

"There's unrest in this town, and it's not a waste of time to warn newcomers to watch themselves. I'm a family man, and my workers are part of that family. So I'm especially concerned when a member of my supervisor's family gets involved with the wrong man."

"I'm not involved with anyone," she said. "So as you can see, you are, indeed, wasting your time. And I don't see how the unrest in Coal River has anything to do with me." Outside, the storm rumbled and crashed, lighting up the rain-streaked windows.

172 • *Ellen Marie Wiseman*

"Clayton Nash is a dangerous man. And we have reason to believe he might be bringing in members of a fraternal organization called the Ancient Order of Hibernians, which is a cover for the cutthroat gang, the Molly Maguires."

"Like I said, you're wasting your time. I have no idea what you're talking about."

"Forgive me," he said, forcing a smile. "Perhaps I'm getting ahead of myself. Let me ask you this. Did Captain Bannister tell you what's been happening in Coal River since you arrived?"

She shook her head.

Just then, someone knocked on the door behind her.

"Enter!" Mr. Flint shouted, making her jump.

The doors slid open and Mr. Flint's son, Levi, came into the room. "Excuse me for interrupting," he said. "But I'm afraid we've got a problem over at the—" Then he saw Emma and stopped short, his forehead furrowed in confusion. "Oh, I'm sorry. I didn't know you had company. Hello, Miss Malloy. It's nice to see you again."

She nodded once to acknowledge him, wondering briefly if he could help her.

"What is it?" Mr. Flint said, irritated.

"There's a problem with one of the engines in pump house number nine," Levi said.

"I'm aware of it," Mr. Flint said.

"So it's been taken care of?"

"No," Mr. Flint said. "I told you yesterday, we'll run her until she shuts down."

"I know what you said, but the engine house foreman is worried."

"Do you have any idea how much it costs to replace a pump house engine?"

"Yes," Levi said. "But if we don't, someone could get injured or killed."

"If there's anything I understand," Mr. Flint said, "it's the machinery in the colliery. That old girl has a lot of life left in her, and I plan on getting every penny's worth." He shook his head. "As usual, you're just like your mother, thinking with your heart, not your head. Now stick to the payroll and selling our coal, and let me take care of the rest."

"Yes, Father," Levi said. "Good day, Miss Malloy." He nodded once at Frank, then left the room.

Again, Emma wondered how Levi could be Mr. Flint's son. From everything she had heard and seen—his polite demeanor at the Fourth of July dance, his apology for his father's behavior, his generosity at the carnival—it was hard to believe they were related, let alone father and son. Briefly, she thought about Mr. Flint's second boy, the newborn who had been kidnapped. If he was still alive, had he grown up to be more like Hazard, or like Viviane? And if he hadn't been taken all those years ago, would he be here now, helping run the mines? Would he have tried to change things, or would Levi have been outnumbered? Maybe if he hadn't been kidnapped, Mr. Flint would have stepped down and she wouldn't be sitting here.

With Levi gone from the room, Mr. Flint directed his attention back to her. "As I was saying," he said. "In a span of three days, one of my mine bosses was found in the woods with his throat cut, a missing miner was found dead in an abandoned mine shaft, and another man, a good man, was found shot to death behind a saloon. In the last two weeks, two more men have come up missing."

Goose bumps rose along Emma's arms. She wasn't sure how to react. Was this a confession or a threat? And what was going on in this town?

She glanced at Frank. "It sounds to me like your police force is not doing a very good job."

Frank uncrossed his arms and moved toward her, his face contorted with anger. "Clayton and his gang are a bunch of sneaky—"

Mr. Flint put up a hand to silence him. Frank returned to his place by the bookcase, blotches of color still blooming in his cheeks. Outside, the storm rumbled in the distance, finally moving over the mountains.

"We think Clayton Nash and the Molly Maguires had something to do with the murders," Mr. Flint said. "The Mollies are a secret society of miners who use violence to undermine coal companies. We haven't had trouble with them in a number of years, but they're making a comeback. In other mining towns, they've been arrested and hanged for murder, arson, and kidnapping."

Emma felt something shift inside her head, as if she'd found a piece of a puzzle she didn't know was missing. Could she have been wrong about Clayton? Was that why he wouldn't admit he was holding secret meetings? Being a miner didn't automatically make him innocent of wrongdoing, but was he desperate enough to resort to violence? Granted, Mr. Flint was underhanded and vile, but two wrongs don't make a right. *No,* she thought. *I saw Hazard Flint and his henchmen murder those men. I can't trust anything he says.*

"I still don't understand why you're telling me any of this," she said.

"We think Clayton is planning something," he said. "And if that happens, there could be more bloodshed. We have to stop it before it starts. But we need help. We need someone to get close to him."

Emma's eyes went wide. "And you want me to . . . ?"

Mr. Flint nodded.

"No," she said, shaking her head. "I won't do it."

"I'll pay you. Bring me word of any upcoming meetings or strikes, and I'll give you fifty dollars. A hundred more after the ringleaders are arrested."

Emma drew in a sharp breath. With that much money, she could get away from her aunt and uncle. She could go back to New York, find an apartment and look for a job, or go back to school to become a teacher. She could escape Coal River forever. Then she remembered her students, the way their faces lit up when they wrote their names for the very first time. She remembered the breaker boys, and how she had vowed to help them. She remembered poor Nicolas, and his grieving family. She remembered Clayton and Jack and Sawyer. If she turned her back on them for money, she'd be just as guilty as Hazard Flint.

"No," she said again. "Absolutely not. I don't care how much you would pay me. I'm not involved in any of this, and I don't want to be."

A baleful smile touched Mr. Flint's lips. "But you're already involved. You're gaining the trust of the miners' families, and you're friendly with Clayton Nash. If you're not on my side, I'll consider you on theirs."

She went quiet. Did he know she had been sneaking up to the miners' village, asking questions and teaching the children to read? If so, why hadn't he said something about it? Maybe he enjoyed making her squirm. Resolve solidified inside her. Somehow she had to stop this man. She leaned forward and looked him in the eyes.

"Maybe you can explain something to me," she said. "Why are there sides in the first place? Why does it have to be you against them?" She was trying to sound tough, but it wasn't a tough voice. It was an angry, frightened voice, cracking on every other word. "You're all working on the same side, taking coal out of the earth to make money. The miners just want to survive, to be able to feed and clothe their families. But you're making it nearly impossible for them. No wonder there's unrest in Coal River. The only problem I see is you. You want it all for yourself."

With that, his face went dark. He fixed intimidating eyes on her. "The Bleak Mountain Mining Company has been in my late wife's family for nearly a century, long before any of those miners were here," he said. "And it will be here long after they're gone. Those men came to me, looking for jobs. If they're not happy, they're free to leave at any time. Immigrants pour into this country every day, and they'll work for less than my miners are getting paid now."

"And the little boys?" she said. "The boys who risk life and limb working in the breaker? Are they replaceable as well?"

"Of course they are. Miners multiply like rabbits."

She stood, shaking with rage. In that moment, she finally understood the depth of her hatred for Hazard Flint.

Mr. Flint tapped his cane on the edge of the desk. "Your uncle is replaceable too. Keep that in mind while making your decision."

"Do whatever you want with my uncle," she said. "He's of little concern to me. And I won't be living in Coal River much longer, so I can't help you with anything. Now, if you'll excuse me, I'm leaving." She started toward the door, but Frank grabbed her arm.

"It's all right," Mr. Flint said. "Let her go. We know where to find her."

Frank did as he was told and followed her out of the room, closing the doors behind him. "I'll take you home," he said.

She kept walking. "No. I know my way."

"You'll get drenched."

"I don't care."

He grabbed her by the shoulders. "I know you've been going up to the miners' village."

"Oh," she spat. "So it's your fault I'm here." She struggled to get away. He held her tighter.

"I didn't tell Mr. Flint that," he said. "I just said you were talking to the boys at the store."

"But you told him I rode the Ferris wheel with Clayton."

He nodded.

"Why?"

"Because you need to see what you're getting yourself into!"

"What I'm getting myself into?" A crazy sounding chuckle escaped her lips. "Mr. Flint is a bigger threat to me now than Clayton will ever be, thanks to you."

He squeezed her shoulders, his face twisting in frustration, as if fighting the urge to shake her. "I'm not like him," he said. "Haven't I proved that to you? I can protect you from all of them."

She gaped up at him, unable to believe what she was hearing. "Did you forget the other day? What I saw you do?"

"I wasn't the one who pulled the trigger."

"Oh my God. You don't understand anything, do you?" She broke free and hurried away.

"But I let you go," he said, still following. "I could have taken you back down to them. I could have—"

Emma spun around to face him, her eyes on fire. "You could have what? Thrown me in the river to drown?"

"No!" he shouted. He glanced over his shoulder and lowered his voice. "I could have let them get rid of you. Mr. Flint has no idea it was you down by the river. I said I didn't recognize you. And if he finds out the truth, we'll both pay for that lie."

She turned away, heading for the front entry. "It's about time you paid for something."

"What's that supposed to mean?"

Without answering, Emma yanked open the door, darted across the veranda, and raced to the bottom of the steps. It was pouring now, the rain coming down in heavy sheets. She ran along the sidewalk and headed home, glancing over her shoulder to make sure Frank wasn't behind her. After a few minutes she slowed, trudging through deep puddles and wet gravel, her hair soaked and the bottom of her skirt growing heavier with every step. Now what was she supposed to do?

CHAPTER 14

Later that night, after everyone was asleep, Emma snuck up to the miners' village with a tin of raisins and two slices of lemon pound cake wrapped in parchment paper tucked beneath her overcoat to keep them dry. The rain had let up, but every now and then the skies opened up again to release a quick, cold drizzle. By the time she reached her destination, her hair and the bottom of her skirt were soaked through. She shivered, unsure if it was from rainwater dripping down the back of her neck, or nerves. Standing in the middle of the dirt road, she hoped she was at the right place.

The windows of the shanty were dark, the porch empty. She took a deep breath, crept up the steps, and knocked on the door. No sound came from inside, no footsteps across the floor, no voices asking who was there. She knocked harder. Finally the handle turned and the door inched open. Halfway down the frame, a wedge of cheek became visible, and an eye peeked out through a dark crack.

It was Jack.

"Hello," she said. "Remember me?"

He nodded.

"Is this Clayton Nash's house?"

Jack opened the door farther, one hand on the handle. He was barefoot and wearing a threadbare nightshirt with faded red stripes. He nodded and blinked, looking up at her with sleepy eyes. "Yes," he said in a small voice.

"Is he awake?"

Jack shook his head.

Retrieving the food from beneath her overcoat, she knelt and unwrapped the pound cake. The sweet, buttery smell of lemon and sugar wafted into the damp night. She smiled and held out a piece. "Would you wake Clayton up for me?" she said. "I'd like to talk to him."

Jack grabbed the piece of pound cake and took a bite. A look of rapture passed over his features, and then he disappeared into the house, letting the door swing slowly open.

Emma stood rooted to the porch for a moment, unsure if she should enter. Then, deciding not to let in the damp air, she stepped into the dark house and closed the door behind her, but stayed near the threshold. Jack's footsteps thumped across the room. He knocked on a door. The door opened and closed. She blinked, hoping her eyes would adjust to the gloom. But the room was too dark to see anything other than the vague shapes of furniture. Jack's high, muffled voice came through the wall from somewhere in the back of the house, like an excited pixie talking underwater. Another, deeper voice followed, rumbling and surprised. For a second she thought about leaving. Maybe it was a mistake to come. Then something moved on the other side of the dark room, a rustle and a soft thump, like a body shifting in bed. She froze. She wasn't alone. Someone coughed and she spun around, groping blindly for the doorknob.

Then something banged near the back of the house, and footsteps sounded on the floorboards. She glanced over her shoulder. A door opened, and a yellow glow filled the doorframe. Body-shaped shadows flickered on the walls of another room. She let go of the doorknob and turned. Jack appeared, and then Clayton's confused face above a hurricane lamp, his skin yellowed by the light, his dark hair sticking up in all directions. He wore a sleeveless undershirt and brown trousers, his suspenders hanging loose from his waist. Lantern light filled the room, and Emma looked around.

Another boy and three girls slept on cots and a threadbare davenport, thin sheets and lumpy pillows bundled beneath their heads and bodies. Emma recognized the two older girls from the store, and the other boy was Sawyer. She gaped at Clayton, her mind racing with questions. Who were these children, and what were they doing here? She knew he was taking care of Jack, but what about the others? And why didn't he tell her about Sawyer? What else was he hiding? A wife? A radical mine striker? A penchant for murder?

Clayton whispered in Jack's ear, then motioned for Emma to follow him toward the back of the shanty. Jack returned to his makeshift bed. Emma followed Clayton down a short hallway into a back room lined with canning jars and wooden barrels, trying not to stare at his bare arms and shoulders. Growing up in the theater, she'd seen plenty of male actors in their undergarments in dressing rooms, but they were either pale and slender, or overweight. Clayton's chest and arms were corded with muscle, like iron bulging beneath his skin. The sheer size of his back reminded her of a workhorse. He turned to face her, and her cheeks flushed.

"You have a family," she whispered.

"You might say that." He turned down the lantern and set it on a shelf.

"And your wife?" she said. "Is she sleeping? Maybe I shouldn't have come. . . ." She turned to leave.

He caught her by the elbow and shook his head. "My wife . . ." He paused, as if searching for the right words. "Jennie died during the yellow fever outbreak last year."

She swallowed. "I'm so sorry. That must have been extremely difficult."

"If it weren't for those kids in the other room, I'm not sure what I would have done. She did her best to hold on, but . . ." He scrubbed his fingers across his mouth and looked away, pain passing like a shadow over his face.

For a moment, Emma couldn't speak. She wasn't sure why, but seeing Clayton so distraught over the loss of his wife unsettled her in ways she didn't understand. Yet she was determined to control her emotions, so she ignored the burning lump in her throat and went on. "It must be hard taking care of all those children alone."

"It can be."

Then she had another thought and furrowed her brow, unsure if she should broach the subject, yet knowing she must. "But Sawyer works in the breaker," she said. "Aren't you afraid something will happen to him?"

Clayton leaned against the wall. Weariness seemed to weigh him down like a sodden overcoat. "What choice do I have? I can't let those kids starve to death. I work extra shifts when I can, but I still have a hard time keeping them fed."

"I'm sorry," she said. "It's really none of my business. They're your family after all, and I—"

"They're orphans."

Emma stared at him, wide-eyed. "All of them?"

He nodded. "Sawyer and Jack are brothers."

"But when Sawyer told me about Jack's mother and father, he acted so . . . so . . . matter-of-fact. I never would have guessed he was talking about his own parents."

"Sawyer is strong," Clayton said. "Too strong sometimes."

"But why are they all living with you?"

"My wife and I took in Violet, Sadie, and Edith shortly before she passed. After she was gone, I added Jack and Sawyer to the herd."

In that instant, Emma knew Mr. Flint and Frank were wrong about Clayton. He had a rough exterior, but inside, he was a good man who, despite his own suffering, wanted to make life better for those around him. She believed it with all her heart, and now, finally, she knew she could trust him. She just needed to convince him that she was on his side. If he would just give her a chance, whatever he wanted or needed her to do, she would do it. And she would be safe with him. She was sure of it. Suddenly the storage room felt like the inside of a coal stove. She longed to tell him what she was feeling, but had no idea what to say or where to begin. Or if she even should. And words wouldn't do justice to the jumble of feelings rushing through her head. She wanted to wrap her arms around him, to kiss his lips and ease his pain, to let him know he was no longer alone. Blinking back the moisture in her eyes, she said, "What happened to their parents?"

"Mining accidents, illness, disappearances."

She shook her head, speechless.

"What are you doing here, Emma?" he said.

She hesitated, trying to find the words to explain. "I came to warn you that Hazard Flint thinks you're up to something. He wants me to spy on you. He offered me money."

He straightened, his face filled with alarm. "When did he say that? And why were you talking to him?"

"Frank Bannister forced me to go with him to the mansion. He said Mr. Flint wanted to interrogate me about the breaker boys who ran away."

"Why would he question *you* about that?"

"Probably because I've been sneaking up here, bringing food and teaching some of the children to read and write. Someone found out."

"So you were the one leaving food on our porch! I knew it!"

Her mouth fell open. "You did?"

"I know a fighter when I see one, and you told me you wanted to help. It was pretty easy to figure out."

"If I'd known you had all those children living here," she said, "I'd have left more for you. But I wasn't even sure this was your house."

"It was enough. The kids thought it was Christmas every time they found something outside the door. Thank you." He smiled at her, his green eyes shimmering in the lantern light. It was all she could do not to move closer.

"You're welcome. I'm glad to help."

Then his face went dark. "Now, tell me about Mr. Flint. What did he want?"

"He said the boys' mothers accused me of filling their sons' heads with ideas, but he really wanted to ask me about you. He says you're involved with the Molly Maguires, a secret society of miners who use violence to get what they want."

"I know who they are."

"He thinks you're planning something big, something that will cause a lot of bloodshed."

Anger hardened his features. "That's not true. I'm trying to help the miners stand up for their rights. Get what they deserve. But we're peaceful, not violent agitators. If there's bloodshed, it will be Hazard Flint's fault, not mine."

"I want to help," she said. "I'm doing all I can right now, but I need..."

Clayton moved toward her, and she felt herself go weak, ready to be taken into his arms. Instead he grabbed her by the shoulders. "No," he said. "It's too risky. You need to be extra careful now that Mr. Flint is watching you. He's dangerous, and he'll stop at nothing to get rid of any opposition."

"I know. I saw him murder two men."

"What? When?"

"A little over a week ago, when I was down by the river. Mr. Flint was there, with Frank Bannister and some man I've never seen before. I didn't see them kill the first one, only the body floating down the river, but they shot a second man and shoved him into the water."

"Shit." Clayton moved away from her, his hands in fists. "Did they see you?"

"I'm not sure about Mr. Flint and the other man," she said. "But Frank did. He told me to keep my mouth shut."

His head snapped in her direction. "He didn't turn you in?"

She shook her head. "No. We knew each other as children and..." She shrugged.

"So you're friends with the police captain?"

"No," she protested. "He wants to be friends, but...he's the reason Mr. Flint wanted to talk to me. Frank wants me to think he can protect me. He wants—"

"Did you recognize either of the men they killed?"

For a second, she was hurt by his lack of interest in her relationship with Frank. But that was childish. There were more important things to worry about. "I don't know the miners," she said, "only some of the wives."

"They were probably single men or immigrants," he said. "Someone who wouldn't go along with something Mr. Flint wanted them to do." He paced the room, silently stewing. Then he stopped and turned to her. "Maybe you should play along with Mr. Flint."

"No, I won't. I said I hardly knew you."

"Well, if he tries anything else, tell him what I just said, that I'm trying to organize peaceful opposition."

"What does that mean?"

"A strike."

She gaped at him. "You want me to tell him you're planning a strike?"

"Yes," he said. "If he asks again, tell him I'm trying to plan a strike but no one wants to cooperate because they're scared of him."

"Is that the truth?"

"Maybe," he said. "Maybe not. But what you don't know can't hurt you. And that might just buy me some time. Now you'd better go. And be careful no one sees you."

CHAPTER 15

A week later, during the first days of August, a group of coffins and mourners traveled up Freedom Hill Road in a long, jagged line, twisting out of sight around the last bend before turning into the cemetery. Hazard and Levi Flint followed the mourners and their families in their touring car, its engine growling and spitting black smoke into the morning air. Behind them, the entire regiment of the Coal River Coal and Iron Police—forty men—rode on horseback, rifles slung across their backs. The rest of the villagers followed on foot, except Uncle Otis, Aunt Ida, Percy, and Emma, who were in the Tin Lizzie.

Two days earlier, a sixth-level section of the breaker had collapsed right before the midday break, sending massive beams, heavy machinery, and one end of the still-rotating crusher crashing through three floors. Four breaker boys were killed instantly, and two more died within minutes of being pulled from the wreckage. Several others suffered serious injuries, including broken bones, crushed limbs, and deep lacerations.

Emma had no idea which boys were killed because the mine was shut down for two days, leaving her trapped at home while Uncle Otis stayed up half the night, drinking and tooling around the house at odd hours. She was afraid he would catch her if she snuck out to go up to the miners' village. Even the Company Store was closed, giving her no excuse to leave the house. The only thing she could do was pray that Sawyer was all right and that Clayton didn't think she had abandoned them. Other than the time spent waiting for her parents to return to Coal River after Albert drowned, and the day she woke up in the hospital after the fire, the last two days felt like the longest of her life.

Luckily, her aunt believed her story about what happened at the Flint Mansion. When Emma returned, she claimed she and Mr. Flint had determined that the breaker boys had run away with the carnival. It didn't have a thing to do with her. If anything, Emma suggested, Mr. Flint was a caring man who seemed thankful that she was developing a friendly relationship with the miners' families. He hoped it would bridge the misunderstandings between the miners and the better sorts of townspeople during the recent discord. While Aunt Ida seemed relieved that Mr. Flint hadn't found Emma guilty of any wrongdoing, she still kept a close eye on her niece. She also decided it would be best not to tell Uncle Otis about Frank Bannister coming to fetch Emma. He had enough on his mind.

Now, Uncle Otis drove the Tin Lizzie through the iron gates of the cemetery, braking and swearing under his breath every time the procession slowed. In the backseat with Percy, Emma dabbed her swollen eyes with a handkerchief, watching the tombstones roll past the car windows. She hoped they wouldn't go near Albert's grave, which was in a separate section near the back of the grounds. Maybe it was selfish and wrong, but she hadn't visited his grave since her return, and had no intention of going there anytime soon. Besides the fact that he was buried in Uncle Otis's family plot, the thought of him lying beneath the earth, his small body in a wooden box—cold, still, and alone—cut into her heart like shards of glass.

Uncle Otis parked the car, came around, and held Aunt Ida's hand to help her step off the fender. Percy got out and opened Emma's door, offering his arm, his face solemn. Emma refused, then hunched her shoulders, pulling down the edge of her hat in the hopes that Clayton and the miners' wives wouldn't see her. On shaking legs, she followed Percy and his parents toward the gravesites. Emma had tried to leave earlier that morning by saying she wanted to walk to the cemetery alone. In truth, she'd wanted to arrive before her aunt and uncle did so she wouldn't have to stand beside them during the services. But as usual, Aunt Ida insisted they attend the funeral as a family, to show a united front to the community and Hazard Flint.

The six burial plots had been dug earlier that morning, and the mounded clods of raw earth sat like miniature culm piles beside the dark holes. Father Delaney waited by the open graves with a book in his hands, his gnarled fingers resting on the first page of the children's burial service.

Emma stopped behind her aunt in the second row on one end of the loose horseshoe of mourners grouped around the burial site. She steeled herself and desperately searched the front row for Clayton, for Jack and Sadie and Edith and Violet. If she saw Clayton in the front row without Sawyer, it would mean her worst fears had come true. Her heart skipped a beat, then thudded hard, preparing for the shock. What would she do if she saw Clayton over there, shoulders slumped and crying? Would she be able to stop herself from running over to him, to comfort him and the surviving children? Would she collapse in a sobbing heap on the ground?

But thankfully, Clayton wasn't in the front row. Emma dropped her shoulders in relief, then scanned the other faces, praying she wouldn't recognize any of the dead boys' parents.

The pallbearers—uncles, friends, older brothers of the deceased—lowered the coffins into the ground. One by one, Father Delaney sprinkled holy water on the coffins to sanctify them for all time. The mothers of the deceased, wearing worn church dresses and hats with makeshift veils, their faces the color of watered-down milk, stood swaying and clinging to their husbands' protective arms, as if they were rafts in a stormy sea. The fathers looked around with shocked eyes, as if to verify they weren't dreaming.

One of the mothers began to sob hoarsely, a white handkerchief pressed to her mouth. Her husband held her up with one arm, a baby cradled in the other. Beside him stood an older boy and a little girl with a baby doll clutched beneath her chin. Emma's heart dropped, and a fresh flood of tears stung her eyes.

The woman was Pearl.

Poor Pearl, whose fear was disguised by pride. Poor Pearl, who put on a brave face no matter what. Her words rang in Emma's ears: *Twice as a boy and once as a man, that's the poor miners' lot.* Now one of Pearl's sons had been robbed of his chance to be a man. Emma drew in a shaky breath and looked at the rest of the mothers, hoping she wouldn't know anyone else. Then her breath clogged, and the world began to spin. She had to fight the urge to grab Percy's arm. Six people down from Pearl, Francesca leaned against her husband's shoulder, her eyes closed, her arms limp at her sides. She was thin as a skeleton, white as a bone. How was she staying upright? How was her broken heart still beating?

Emma bit down on her trembling lip, swallowing her sobs. Panic scratched at the edges of her mind. If she started weeping, she wouldn't be able to stop. She'd fall apart, like she did when Albert and her parents died. Then she noticed Mr. Flint and Levi a few feet away from Francesca, and a jolt of rage shot through her. Levi was staring at the graves with glassy eyes, his face somber, while Mr. Flint leaned on his cane and checked his pocket watch. She fought the urge to march over and ask him what he was doing there, if this was enough proof that boys shouldn't be working for the mining company. She wanted to ask him how he was going to help the grieving families. How he could sleep at night knowing parents' hearts were shattered and children were dead because of him. Grief and anger twisted like acid through her body, threatening to burn a hole through her chest. Her limbs trembled with the effort of remaining in control. How could these poor people tolerate having the man responsible for their children's deaths at this funeral? Was she the only one filled with revulsion and hate, or was everyone else too scared and grief-stricken to send him away?

"Let us pray," Father Delaney said in a raspy voice. The mourners bowed their heads. "Lord God, through your mercy, let those who have lived in faith find eternal peace. Bless these graves and send your angels to watch over them. As we bury the bodies of these young boys, welcome them into your presence, and with your saints, let them rejoice in you forever. We ask it through Christ, our Lord. Amen."

"Amen," the congregation muttered.

During the rest of the service, the Catholics muttered their answers, "Lord, hear our prayer" while the rest of the group stood in silence, their heads bowed reverently. While everyone prayed, Emma searched the crowd for Clayton and Michael, but didn't see them. There were too many lowered heads, too many drooping shoulders. Robins and redwing blackbirds flitted above, chirping and shooting through the indifferent sky.

"Our Father, who art in Heaven," Father Delaney began, and other voices joined him in reciting the Lord's Prayer, their words swept away by the wind.

Francesca had begun to rock back and forth, moaning.

"Amen," the congregation muttered.

Francesca began to weep loudly. She staggered forward in spite of her husband trying to hold her back, her ravaged face streaming with tears. She weaved to the right, toward the end of an open grave, and for a brief, panic-filled second, Emma feared she was going to throw herself in. Hands reached out to stay her, and she took a few more steps, then fell to her knees at Mr. Flint's feet. She grasped his trousers with thin hands.

"Give me back my twins," she screamed. "Please, there's been a mistake! My boys are still alive! You have to keep looking!"

"Oh my," Aunt Ida said, pressing a silk handkerchief to her lips.

Emma reeled in horror, suddenly dizzy and nauseous. *My God. Both* twins had been taken.

Mr. Flint grimaced in disgust, as if fighting the urge to kick Francesca away. Her husband hurried to her rescue, his face falling in on itself.

"Please!" Francesca wailed. "They're all I had left in this world!"

While the rest of the mourners watched with shock and sadness, Levi helped Francesca's husband lift her to her feet and return her to her spot. Then Levi hugged her, put a comforting hand on the grieving man's shoulder, and went back to stand beside his father. Mr. Flint shook his head, as if ashamed by his son's public display of emotion.

Lowering her chin, Emma ground her teeth so hard, they would surely crack. She felt cold all the way down to her bones. Percy took his mother's arm and drew her close, while Uncle Otis stood stiff and unyielding.

"Lord," Father Delaney said, finishing the service, "comfort these men and women in their sorrow. You cleansed their children in the waters of baptism and gave them new life. May we one day join them and share Heaven's joys forever. We ask this in Jesus's name, amen."

When Emma raised her head, she saw that Francesca had fainted.

CHAPTER 16

At two a.m. on Sunday morning, four days after the breaker boys' funeral, the white-paneled ballroom on the top floor of the Pennsylvania Boarding House and Hotel was dark, save for four flickering oil lamps on two wooden tables. Wool blankets had been nailed over the closed windows, and the air in the room was stagnant, thick with tobacco smoke and the sour odor of human sweat, nervous excitement, and fear. Four dozen glum-faced miners and breaker boys sat on stools and wooden chairs, or leaned against walls festooned with red, white, and blue bunting. All eyes were locked on Clayton Nash, standing at the center of the middle table. On either side of Clayton, six immigrant miners sat in wooden chairs, including Nally, the giant Irishman.

In a back corner, Emma slumped in a chair, avoiding eye contact with those around her. Despite the heat, she fought the urge to wipe the sweat from her brow and neck. She kept her arms crossed, her fists hidden beneath her elbows to hide her hands. Earlier, she'd cut her fingernails to the quick and rubbed her hands with road slag to make them look worn. Still, she worried someone might notice that her pale, delicate fingers were those of a woman. The trousers and shirt she was wearing belonged to Sawyer, and her hair was pinned in a tight bun beneath one of Clayton's mining caps. Luckily, her feet fit into a boy-sized pair of gumboots, and, with a little help from a chunk of soft coal, she had darkened her brows and given the illusion of faint stubble on her upper lip. She wouldn't pass for an adult male, but in the dim light, it would be easy to mistake her for an older boy, maybe around the age of twelve or thirteen. Even so, her heartbeat roared in her ears. After seeing how angry the miners got when they saw her at the mine, she was terrified of being discovered.

Clayton had warned her that the miners would be uneasy, worried Hazard Flint and his men might break down the doors and arrest everyone in attendance. If that happened, she would be in all sorts of trouble. But hopefully, in the meantime, it meant less attention paid to her.

For two days she'd begged Clayton to let her attend the meeting, arguing that she couldn't figure out a way to help if she didn't understand what was going on. Right now it was all too confusing. Between the immigrants and the miners, the mine owner and the Coal and Iron Police, she couldn't keep things straight in her head. The fact that the police couldn't be trusted went against everything she'd grown up believing. And listening to Percy and Uncle Otis, she thought the English-speaking miners were worried the immigrants would take their jobs. But somehow Clayton had gotten some of the native-born Americans and the immigrants to come together, to see they were on the same side. Now he just needed the rest to agree.

At first, he'd been adamant she stay away. But then she threatened to come regardless, reminding him she had gone up to the mine and confronted Otis despite knowing her uncle and the miners would be upset. Eventually Clayton gave in. He told her it was only the second meeting in six months because it had taken that long to spread the word and get everyone to agree to come. At the first meeting, held back in February, four months before Emma had arrived in Coal River, there had been only twenty in attendance. Now it seemed the breaker accident had brought everyone together. There were over twice as many miners in the room. Clayton cleared his throat and addressed the crowd.

"Before we begin," he said. "I want everyone to take mind of the windows back here." He pointed at the wall behind him, drawing the audience's attention to four tall windows beside a brick fireplace. "If Mr. Flint's henchmen show up, we're going to hurry out those windows. Outside, there are ladders leading down to the back porch roof, and two more from that roof to the ground. But some of you might have to jump from there. After that, scatter. Understood?"

The miners and breaker boys nodded.

"Good," Clayton said. He looked around the room, his face serious. "This is the day that marks the beginning of an uprising against Hazard Flint and the Bleak Mountain Mining Company. We're going to stand up for what is right, throw down our tools, and march against oppression. We're going to come together to fight for our rights and the rights of our children, and our children's children."

A number of miners sat forward, listening intently. Emma sat rapt, goose bumps rising on her arms. She was right. Clayton was a born leader. And he was on the right side of truth and justice.

"You see these men?" Clayton pointed at the new immigrants. "They don't want to steal your jobs. They're just men, workers, like you. And right now they're slaves to the mining company too. Hazard Flint takes money from their wages to pay their room and board. He supplies them with clothes and powder, then takes that out of their pay too. If they get hurt or sick, he takes two dollars out of their pay so they can see a doctor. He even took the price of their train tickets to get here out of their pay! It's not us against them! It's all of us, together, against the company! And if we stick together, if we all walk out at the same time, Hazard Flint won't be getting his coal out of the earth. The coal we dig is not German coal or Polish coal or Irish coal. It is just coal."

The miners mumbled amongst themselves. Some nodded in agreement, while others crossed their arms and scowled, as if not convinced.

"This man, Nally," Clayton said, "arrived here at the end of June with the rest of the immigrants. Seven months ago he led a successful strike against the mine owners at Cabin Creek. Now he's offered to help us."

Nally stood, his face grave. "Look at those grand mansions in the hills," he said. "The supervisors' wives dress with the blood of yer young lads. Mr. Flint makes ye load coal for any price he chooses. Up there on Paint Creek and Cabin Creek, we obeyed the laws. Then we went on strike and got twice what we used to get for loading coal. We reduced our hours to nine a shift. I will be with ye, and the Coal and Iron Police, those bloody bastards, will go!"

"How many miners died during the strike at Cabin Creek?" a miner called out. "How many were shot down by the Coal and Iron Police?"

"What about Eagle Hill?" someone else shouted. "Them miners were carrying nothing but the American flag, and the deputies and sheriff met them with rifles. How many miners died that day? Twenty? Thirty? We want that happening here?"

"I'd be a right fool to say there weren't clashes between strikers and police," Nally said. "But the police were hired to protect the mines, just like they are here! If ye lads aren't willing to sacrifice to fight for your rights, maybe ye don't belong at this meeting. Let me tell you what I saw in '02, the big strike in the Pennsylvania coalfields. Better than a hundred thousand men and boys dropped their tools, and it didn't matter what, if they starved or lost their jobs, nobody backed down. A few good men lost their lives, but that's a whole lot less than would have died in the mines if they'd kept going that way. From what I heard, mining accidents here in Coal River are even more common than in other mines, where they're bad enough."

"We hardly know you from Adam!" another man shouted. "How do we know we can trust you?"

"Ye don't," Nally said. "But right now you're trusting your livelihood, nay, yer very lives, to a criminal."

"Clayton," the first man said. "You gathered us here. I've known you since you were cutting teeth. Most of us here worked with your father. You should be the one doing the talking, not this stranger."

The majority of the miners nodded, muttering, "That's right," and "We agree."

Nally threw up his hands and sat down.

"All right," Clayton said. "Simmer down. But Nally's right. They did a lot in '02, but it didn't solve our problems. They cheat us on the scales, and underpay us for the coal we dig. When we finally got them to set a price for a full coal car, Hazard Flint bought bigger cars. Then he hiked up the price of goods at the Company Store. How are we supposed to live like that?"

"The state don't care," a deep voice called out. "The country don't care. The government don't even care!"

"That's not true," Clayton said. "The mine laws are on our side. No breaker closer than two hundred feet from the mouth of the shaft, every mine with an emergency escape in case there's an accident in the main shaft. Good ventilation. Plus rules on storing blasting powder in the mine, proper working of the breaker, even the kind of lamp oil they give us so we don't blow ourselves up!" He was worked up now, talking fast. "Got to have proper stretchers, ambulances, the works. There are laws! Hazard Flint just breaks them all!"

Clayton's anger seemed to energize others in the room. An old man stood in the back row. He wore an eye patch and leaned to one side, as if nursing a sore hip.

"I been working in the mines my whole life," the old man said. "And I haven't a whole bone in my body. My skull was fractured, my eye was put out, and one leg feels like it's made of wood. Last time I was injured, I couldn't work for six days. On the last day, I got an eviction notice because I was behind on my rent. I asked for one more day because my wife had fallen ill. The police said I couldn't stay another five minutes. They took me, my sick wife, and my blind mother-in-law down the road, and we took up with a widow and her five boys. It was raining, and the cold worsened my wife's condition. I didn't have money to pay for a doctor. A few days later, she died." He hung his head and sighed, then looked up again. "Clayton is right. It's time for us to stand up to Hazard Flint."

A few seats away from Emma, a thin boy of about twelve stood, wringing his cap in his coal-stained hands. "After my pa got sick and died," he said, "I moved into Widow's Row and went to work in the breaker. Supposed to get sixty-five cents a day. But they gave me a rent due notice instead, saying I owed nearly a hundred dollars for back rent my father never paid. I'm still workin' to pay it off."

This brought grumbles and angry shouts from the miners. Emma could hardly believe what she was hearing. Things were worse than she thought.

Then another man stood. "I don't know if you all know me, but I been married to the local midwife going on some twenty years now. My wife has held young'uns in her arms and seen them die from tuberculosis, pellagra, and the bloody flux. I saw my own sister's baby starve for milk while the mine owners were riding around in their fine cars, their wives and children dressed in diamonds and silk, all paid for by the blood, sweat, and tears of the coal miners. I hear the hungry children crying in my dreams. It ain't right!"

The miners started talking all at once, some shifting in their seats, some standing and shaking their fists. Clayton raised his hand to quiet them.

"I appreciate your stories," he said. "Our suffering is even more important than the laws." He glanced at Emma, then looked away. "And that reminds me. We have another fight on our hands. Child labor was outlawed by the anthracite commission, but these boys have got to keep working the mines and the breaker as long as their parents need wages and the coal companies need their labor. Take a look around. Has to be one mine worker in four a boy under the age of sixteen. Plenty of them are seven, eight years old. Here in Coal River, all our boys work in the colliery. I've seen boys as young as five in the breaker. If the funeral last week didn't convince you to put a stop to that, I'm not sure what will. You need to talk to your neighbors and friends, tell them what you've heard here tonight. Tell them the only way we can change things is if we stick together. Tell them we'll be having another meeting, and I want to see them all here. Are you willing to do that much for yourselves?"

The miners and boys nodded in agreement.

"Now go back to work on Monday morning," Clayton said. "Be good men. I want you to deal fair with every man. There are some good operators, some good bosses, but their hands are tied. We can't blame them. Let Hazard Flint see you are law-abiding. I have a plan in place, and if we all stick together, Hazard Flint will be forced to do right by us. But you must have patience, my friends, and you must trust me. Now go back, like men, and go to work when you should."

"Easy for you to tell us to be patient," one of the miners said. "Last month, I buried my youngest child, and on the day of the funeral there was not one scrap of food in the house with six children to feed."

"Listen," Clayton said. "This fight is going on, but not today. And not tomorrow. We've got work to do first. Go home, all of you, peaceable, law-abiding. Take a drink—I know you need it. But I may have to call on you again inside of two weeks to make another move."

Then, just as he was about to remind everyone to spread the word, the thunder of hooves pounded along the dirt road outside and came to a stop in front of the hotel. Moving fast, he and Nally blew out all but one lantern. Everyone stood, careful not to scrape chairs across the floor. Outside, boots stomped across the front porch of the hotel, rattling the windows of the ballroom. Clayton darted to one of the escape windows and pushed it open. Nally and two others opened the other three. Emma made her way toward Clayton, her heart booming in her chest. She moved quickly but quietly among the miners and boys, keeping her chin down. Everyone scrambled out the windows without a word. The wooden ladders thumped against the clapboard siding. When Emma made it to the window, Clayton glanced her way but said nothing. For a split second she froze, her hands on the window casing.

"Move!" Clayton demanded under his breath.

Emma eased over the sill, trying not to think about the fact that the ballroom was four stories up from the ground. Two men were climbing down the ladder, disappearing into blackness. She couldn't see the porch roof. To her surprise, not being able to see the distance between the window and the roof made her less afraid. That, and knowing if she were caught, she'd be thrown in jail, after which Uncle Otis would either lock her up forever or send her to the poorhouse. Clenching her jaw, she swung herself over the window edge and followed the miners into the darkness. At the bottom of the ladder, she stepped onto the porch roof and moved to one side, her hands against the wall. From there, she could make out the backyard, the flagstone sidewalk, and the circular flower beds filled with struggling roses. Some of the miners and boys were jumping off the roof, landing on their feet, rolling forward or falling backward. She went to the top of a ladder and waited her turn. There was no way she could jump.

Finally she climbed onto the second ladder and scurried down. On the ground, the rest of the miners scattered, disappearing into back alleys and the open windows of nearby buildings. She hurried toward the back fence, stopped, and crouched in the shadows, wondering if she should wait for Clayton. No. The risk of being caught was too great. She followed a group of miners toward a short passageway, then ducked into an alley between the post office and the apothecary. On the other end, she ran along a side road, staying close to buildings and glancing over her shoulder to make sure she wasn't being followed. It was only when she got home and crawled into bed that she started shaking.

CHAPTER 17

The morning after the secret meeting, Emma stood in front of the mirror above her washstand, brushing the snarls out of her hair and trying to figure out what she'd tell Aunt Ida if she noticed the scratches on her hands. She could say she fell in the road, or got scraped by something at work. Luckily, the coal on her face had washed off. Then again, her aunt probably wouldn't notice anyway. Today, following church, Aunt Ida was going to another fellowship luncheon. She'd be too busy preening and memorizing the latest gossip to notice anything amiss.

Emma set down the brush and started braiding her hair, then stopped, listening. Downstairs, anguished wails echoed through the hallways. It was Aunt Ida. An image flashed in Emma's mind—the Black Maria outside their door, stopping to deliver Uncle Otis's body. But it was Sunday. The mine was closed. Uncle Otis was downstairs, probably drinking coffee to relieve his headache from too much alcohol the night before. She opened the bedroom door and stuck out her head. On the first floor, a door slammed, and then another. She finished braiding her hair, got dressed, and hurried down the steps.

In the dining room, the curtains were drawn and Aunt Ida was sitting at the table, red-faced and weeping. Uncle Otis was pacing the floor, the veins in his forehead engorged and pulsing. Percy sat perched near the fireplace on the edge of a settee, his face whiter than usual. On the dining room table, three sheets of paper lay crumpled and torn around the edges.

"What's going on?" Emma said.

"This has nothing to do with you," Uncle Otis said. He went to the sideboard and poured a glass of whiskey.

Emma pulled out a chair, sat beside Aunt Ida, and rested a gentle hand on her arm. "What happened?" she said. "Are you all right?"

Aunt Ida wailed and put her face in her hands, her shoulders convulsing. Percy stood and pulled aside one of the red velvet curtains. He looked out, toward the driveway, then let the curtain drop and turned back into the room.

Aunt Ida looked up. "Is anyone out there?" she said. Her voice trembled.

Percy shook his head.

"They won't come in the middle of the day," Uncle Otis said. He emptied his glass in four noisy gulps and refilled it. "If anything, they'll ambush us in the middle of the night."

"Oh my lord!" Aunt Ida cried. "My nerves can't take it!"

"I told you to pack your bags and go to Scranton 'til this is over," Uncle Otis said. "I've got enough to worry about without a hysterical wife on my hands."

"And then what?" Aunt Ida said. "I come home and find you and Percy dead? We should all pack our bags and leave!"

Uncle Otis slammed his glass on the sideboard. Whiskey sloshed over his fingers. "I'm not putting my tail between my legs and running away like some yellow-bellied coward!" he said. "I've worked too long and hard to give in to their demands! If those miners want a fight, we'll give them a fight!"

Emma stiffened. *A fight? But Clayton said the miners weren't ready to make a move yet. It was too soon.* "Will someone please tell me what's going on?"

"Have a look at those," Percy said, pointing at the papers on the table.

Aunt Ida sniffed and blew her nose into an embroidered handkerchief.

Emma pulled the crumpled papers across the table and smoothed the wrinkles with her fingers. They were handwritten signs with drawings of coffins, pistols, skulls, and crossbones surrounding roughly scribbled words. One read:

You are a marked man. Prepare your coffin at once or leave this place. Your life is doomed, and you'll die like a dog if you stay here any longer as mine boss. By order of a stranger who knows you.

The second note said:

You have carried this as far as you can. You and the other mine bosses should be careful.

A third notice said:

If Hazard Flint don't stop, we will burn down his breaker and him in it.

Emma's mind raced. Who was behind this? Clayton? Nally? It didn't make sense. Clayton had told the miners to be good men. He would never threaten anyone like this, would he? Someone from last night's meeting must have gotten carried away.

"What do they mean?" she said, trying to sound naïve. "And who would do such a thing?"

"They're coffin notices," Percy said.

Aunt Ida held the handkerchief to her mouth, stifling a sob. "It's the Molly Maguires!"

Emma's skin prickled. *Was Mr. Flint right? Did Clayton bring in the Molly Maguires?*

"We don't know that," Percy said. "They haven't been around these parts for years. If they even exist. Somebody's just trying to scare us, that's all."

"They're probably nothing but empty threats," Uncle Otis said.

"But if a bunch of ignorant miners think they can scare Hazard Flint, they're damn fools."

"Do you think Clayton Nash is behind this?" Percy said.

"Of course he is," Uncle Otis said. "He's the only one smart enough to organize the miners. But Mr. Flint will take care of Nash and anyone else who's involved."

Emma felt light-headed. "What will Mr. Flint do to him?"

Uncle Otis stopped in the middle of pouring anther drink. He set down his glass and considered her for a long moment before speaking. Then he said, "What's it to you?"

"I was just—"

All of a sudden, Uncle Otis stormed over to the table and gripped the back of a dining chair, his knuckles turning white. "I thought I made it clear that you were to stay away from Clayton Nash. He's a murdering, no-good, son of a bitch."

"I am staying away from him," Emma said.

"You're lying," Uncle Otis said. His eyes blazed with fury. Then, before Emma knew what was happening, he flew around the table and yanked up on her braid, pulling her off her seat. "Tell me what you know!"

Aunt Ida jumped up, ran over to Percy, and buried her face in his shirt. Emma grimaced in pain and dug her fingers into the back of Uncle Otis's hand, trying to break free. "Let go of me!" she cried. Tears of pain stung her eyes. "I don't know anything!"

Uncle Otis spun her around, still gripping her by the hair. With his free hand, he grabbed her chin, pushing his bony fingers into her jaw. His whiskey-soured breath washed over her face. "Have you been seeing him?"

"No!" she cried.

He yanked her hair back and forth, rattling her head like a sack of potatoes. "Tell me the truth!"

"I am telling the truth!" she said. "I'm just worried about the orphans who live with him." As soon as the words were out of her mouth, she knew she'd made a mistake.

"How do you know he has orphans living with him?" Uncle Otis said. "Did you go to his house?"

Aunt Ida stormed across the room and stood beside Uncle Otis, a look of horror on her face. "Have you been having relations with that man?" she said.

"No!" Emma said.

Otis pulled harder on her braid, forcing her to her tiptoes. She cried out in pain.

"Let go of her!" Percy said. He came at his father, his face contorted in anger. "She doesn't have anything to do with this!"

Uncle Otis let go of Emma's hair, his nostrils flaring. He stood for a long moment, breathing hard and glaring at her. Then he took a swing at Percy. Percy ducked, and Otis stumbled and nearly fell. Then he found his footing, turned, and charged, grasping Percy around the waist and driving him into the china cabinet. The cabinet windows shattered and the shelves broke in two. Glasses and crystal bowls crashed to the floor. Aunt Ida screamed. Somehow Percy managed to stay upright. He leaned forward and pushed his father across the room, shoving him into the wall like a battering ram.

"Stop it!" Aunt Ida cried. "Stop it this very instant!"

Percy held his father against the wall, his arm thrust against his neck. "Leave Emma alone," he said. "She hasn't done anything wrong, and who cares what she's doing with Clayton? We've got bigger problems right now."

"Better let me go, boy," Uncle Otis said, his voice strangled and hoarse.

Aunt Ida pulled at Percy, slapping him about the neck and shoulders. "Stop it right now. You let your father go this very instant!"

Just as Emma opened her mouth to say something, someone pounded on the front door. Aunt Ida gasped and spun around, her face drained of color. She motioned for everyone to be quiet. The last thing she'd want is for anyone to hear them fighting. Percy let go of his father and stood there, panting. Uncle Otis slumped against the wall, trying to catch his breath. For a long moment, no one moved. Then the pounding came again, louder and more demanding with every blow.

"Otis Shawcross!" a male voice shouted. "I have a message from Hazard Flint!"

Uncle Otis straightened and gave Percy a withering look, then trudged toward the foyer, raking his hair out of his eyes and fixing his collar. Emma waited in the dining room with Percy and Aunt Ida while Uncle Otis spoke with the man at the door. Then the door closed. Heavy footsteps crossed the outside porch and went down the front steps. Percy hurried to the window and pulled aside the drape. Uncle Otis came back into the room, his forehead lined with frustration.

"As of noon tomorrow, the miners are going on strike," he said. "They've already derailed coal cars and left coffin notices on Mr. Flint's door too. They're going to walk off the job, and they won't come back until Mr. Flint gives in to their demands."

Emma couldn't believe what she was hearing. Clayton had said it would be two weeks before he called on the miners again. And not everyone was on board yet. There weren't enough men at the meeting to stage a real strike. What in the world was going on?

"What do they want?" Percy said.

"A twenty-percent pay raise, an eight-hour work day, and an end to enforced purchases at the Company Store," Uncle Otis said. "But don't worry. Mr. Flint will put a stop to it before it gets a foothold. He's making an announcement up at the breaker at one o'clock. Anyone who refuses to work will lose his job. And if there's trouble, he's not afraid to use force."

"What about the breaker boys?" Emma said.

"What about them?" Uncle Otis said.

"If the miners go on strike, they can't work. I don't want Mr. Flint to punish children for—"

"Breaker boys do what the miners tell them to do," Uncle Otis interrupted. "That means they'll go on strike too."

At one o'clock, the time of Mr. Flint's supposed announcement, Emma sat beside Aunt Ida in the horse-drawn wagon, scanning the crowd near the breaker for Clayton. But from where she and her aunt were parked, every hat and head looked the same.

Earlier, after Uncle Otis and Percy had left to go to the meeting, Aunt Ida ordered the driver to get her wagon ready, along with two loaded rifles in the wagon bed. When Emma realized her aunt was going up to the mine to hear what Mr. Flint was going to say, she asked to ride along. At first she thought Aunt Ida would refuse. After all, she would barely look at her. But then, to Emma's surprise, she said, "Only if you stay in the wagon and do as I say."

"I will," Emma said. "I promise."

"If Otis sees us, he won't be happy," Aunt Ida said. "But I have to know what's happening. It affects me too. If we stay far enough away and leave at the first sign of trouble, we'll be all right. But you better not be afraid to use a rifle if need be."

Emma had never used a gun in her life, but it wouldn't help to say that now. "I'm not," she said. For once she was grateful that her aunt had a burning desire to have her nose in the middle of everything. It would have been unbearable to sit at home and wait for news, and she had no idea how she could have gone up to the mine on her own without being seen.

Now, hundreds of miners and breaker boys filled the colliery yard. Wives and siblings waited around the far edges of the gathering, eager to find out what was going on. The breaker boys stood in groups scattered here and there, some with their arms crossed, or their hands in their pockets, trying to behave like men, while others laughed and played kick the can or catch. Emma wondered if the women and breaker boys had any idea of the significance of this meeting, or the danger surrounding it. She wanted to tell them to go home.

To Emma's surprise, a clear split ran down the center of the workers. She wondered if it was between those who wanted to strike and those who wanted to keep working. She had no idea which group was going to strike, but the numbers of miners on one side outnumbered the other at least four to one. A dozen Coal and Iron Police patrolled the two sections, pushing men back in place when they argued with one another. On one side, a miner carried an American flag on a pole, ducking the rocks being thrown at him, while the miners surrounding him sang patriotic songs.

At the top edge of a timber-lined embankment near the entrance to the breaker, six Coal and Iron Police stood with Mr. Flint, Levi, and Frank. The mine bosses, the foremen, and the supervisors, including Uncle Otis, surrounded them. Another row of grim-faced police stood along the railroad tracks at the bottom of the embankment, the iron rails like a line in the sand, daring the miners to cross it. Two more police stood on the lowest roof of the breaker, posed behind Gatling guns. Several more waited in open windows with rifles in their hands. *Would they really shoot a miner, right here in front of everyone, just for trying to make a better life for himself and his family?* Emma wondered. *What about a breaker boy? A woman?*

Mr. Flint stood with one hand in his jacket pocket, waiting for the crowd to settle. When everyone grew quiet, he started to speak. He had to shout to be heard.

"You have no leader!" he said. "Clayton Nash and the rest of the agitators who organized this upcoming strike are now in prison. They are members of the Molly Maguires, an illegal, secret society, and will be tried and hanged first thing in the morning!"

Emma gasped and put a hand over her mouth. Mr. Flint had no proof; how could he? And to hold a trial and hanging by morning? It seemed impossible. He had to be bluffing, trying to scare the strikers into standing down. The alternative was unthinkable. And yet Emma couldn't stop the trembling that worked its way up and down her limbs.

"Anyone thinking about going on strike had better show up for their shift on time and ready to do the work I pay them to do," Mr. Flint continued. "You have no union, and there's no possible way your strike will succeed. If you defy my rules and regulations, you will be fired, arrested, and your families will be evicted and sent packing. We've got plenty of firepower, and we're not afraid to use it. Men with repeating rifles will guard the mine and the breaker. To be clear, I have no quarrel with the honest, hardworking men of my company. The rights and interests of the laboring man will be protected and cared for, not by the labor agitators, but by the Christian men to whom God in His infinite wisdom has given control of these mines. It's my duty to protect the man who wants to work, to protect his wife and children. A coal famine is an ugly thing, and every man here well knows the disaster and the terrible suffering if the mines shut down."

The crowd of men and boys had been growing agitated through

all this, and now Mr. Flint's last arrogant comment brought angry cries.

"We don't need a leader!" a miner shouted. "We'll strike without one!" The miners around him roared in support, throwing their fists into the air.

"And we won't go back to work until you give us what we want!" another man shouted.

Several of the miners from the other group shouted too, but Emma couldn't understand what they were saying. Then one of the would-be strikers made it past a policeman and attacked another miner. A fistfight broke out. The line of police on the other side of the tracks rushed forward to break it up. Mr. Flint said something to Levi and Frank. Levi stepped back, and Frank took his pistol from its holster, raised his arm, and fired two shots in the air. In fits and starts, the men stopped fighting as the police dragged them apart and shoved them farther away from one another.

"I've said my piece!" Mr. Flint shouted. "Now you've all been warned! And in case you haven't heard about the situation down in Virginia, thirty thousand miners and their families are out of their homes and living in tents, with no money to feed their hungry families. All because of agitators and criminals like the ones who've been stirring up trouble in Coal River. It's a war zone down there, and people are dying! Nobody wants that here. Now go on home to your families and think about that. I expect, come tomorrow morning, you'll all do the right thing. If not, I'll be lowering your wages no matter which side you're on."

That final threat brought more yells and curses. The police lifted their rifles and pointed them into the crowd. Eventually the miners settled down and backed away. The crowd slowly dispersed. Aunt Ida snapped the reins and turned the wagon toward home, as if anxious to leave before Uncle Otis spotted them.

Emma gripped the edge of the wagon seat and tried to breath normally, thinking about Clayton in jail. Did he assume they were going to let him go again, or did he know they meant to hang him? If they let him go, would he give up, or did he still think he could get the better of Hazard Flint? And what had she been thinking? What gave her the idea that she could ever stand up to that kind of power? Maybe she should leave. If they were going to hang Clayton, she didn't want to know about it. Her already shattered heart couldn't bear it. Maybe she could steal enough money from Percy's dresser to buy a train ticket out of Coal River. Maybe she could get away and stop thinking about the breaker boys. She could stop thinking about Jack and Sawyer and Pearl and Francesca's dead sons. Stop thinking about Clayton and Albert. Put them all in a room inside her head, lock the door, and throw away the key. She wanted to believe it was possible. With all her heart. But she wasn't good at telling herself lies.

The wagon rounded a bend and merged onto the main road that led up to the miners' village in one direction and down the hill toward town in the other. A group of miners and breaker boys moved off the road to let them pass, talking excitedly amongst themselves. Several looked up at Ida and Emma. A few glared at them with contempt—the privileged women in the wagon who lived lavish lives because of their hard work. Amongst those who stopped was a breaker boy on crutches, his pant leg empty. It was Michael. Again. Staring at Emma with haunted eyes. Begging eyes. Emma searched his pale face, hoping for answers. It held her rapt. Staring into those eyes she knew only one thing: There was no getting away from Coal River.

CHAPTER 18

At half past midnight, in the shadow-filled kitchen of his shanty, Clayton was sitting on a wooden stool holding a basin full of blood-tinted water. Emma rinsed a rag in the basin and dabbed clotted blood from his hairline, careful to avoid the open gash in his forehead. Weak lantern light flickered along the shelves, glinting off mason jars and battered cooking utensils. She pressed too hard and he flinched.

"You need stitches," she said.

"I'll be fine," he said. "It will heal on its own."

She rinsed the rag again and examined the rest of his face. Along with the gash on his forehead, his upper lip was split in two places, and one eye was swelled shut, the surrounding skin colored black and purple. Earlier, she'd snuck up to check on the orphans and was shocked to find him there. "Why did they let you go?"

"I said I'd call off the strike," he said.

She wiped a smear of dried blood from his temple. "I thought you weren't striking yet?"

"We're not," he said. "But they don't know that. Like I said before, we need to keep them guessing while I get a few other things in place. That's why I told you to play along with Mr. Flint. I just never thought he would move that fast."

Emma stopped wiping. "I haven't told Mr. Flint anything. I thought he had you arrested because of the coffin notices you put on his door."

He looked at her, confusion furrowing his brow. "We didn't put coffin notices on anyone's door. That's not how I operate."

"Well, somebody did. This morning there were three notices on Uncle Otis's door, warning him to leave town or he was a dead man. There were notices on Mr. Flint's door too."

"Shit," Clayton said. Alarmed, he stood. "We didn't have anything to do with that. Someone else must be stirring up trouble." He took the rag from her and put it in the basin. "You better leave. I don't want you to get caught up in this."

Outside, a dog started barking. Clayton set the basin on the floor and went to a side window. He stood stock-still, listening, then rushed toward the front of the house. She picked up the lantern and followed.

"Blow that out!" Clayton said. He pulled the front curtains closed and moved to one side, peering out between the drapes. In the distance, galloping horses thundered along the slag road, drawing closer and closer.

Emma blew out the lantern and set it on the table, standing motionless and waiting for her eyes to adjust to the gloom. Moonlight seeped in through the faded ruby curtains, giving the air a strange, reddish glow. She strained to make out Clayton on the other side of the room, a dark, motionless shape next to the window. Outside, a horse whinnied, and a cacophony of hoofbeats rumbled past, pounding along the dirt path like a stampede. Then the horses slowed and stopped.

On the davenport, the youngest girl, Violet, stirred and started crying. Emma felt her way over to the couch and took the warm, sleepy child in her arms.

"Shhh," she whispered, rubbing Violet's thin back. "Go back to sleep."

Noises came from outside the shanty next door—horses snorting, saddles creaking, boots hitting the ground. Footsteps ran up wooden steps, a door splintered, and furniture crashed into walls. A woman screamed and children started crying. Two gunshots rang out. A child shrieked. Emma gasped and hugged Violet to her chest. Then footsteps pounded across the neighbor's porch and down the steps. Reins cracked, male voices urged horses forward, and a stampede of hoofbeats galloped away.

"Stay here and take care of the children!" Clayton hissed over his shoulder. Before she could protest, he opened the front door and slipped out.

Emma didn't know what to do. Violet was still upset, so she rocked the child back and forth to calm her while she gathered her own racing thoughts. What if Clayton didn't return? What if the men came back and broke into this house? When Violet finally grew quiet, Emma laid her down, tiptoed to the window, and drew back the edge of one curtain. Across the way, a gang of men on horseback dismounted in front of a two-story shack. Some of the men wore gunnysacks with dark eyeholes; others wore bandannas over their noses and mouths. The men drew pistols, broke down the door, and rushed into the house. A woman screamed, and three gunshots pierced the air. Emma let go of the curtain and leaned against the wall, her knees shaking to the point of near collapse.

"Clayton?" one of the children called out. It was Sawyer. He sat up in his bed.

Emma went over to the couch and scooped Violet into her arms. "Sawyer," she said as loudly as she dared. "Help me get everyone up. We've got to get out of here!"

"What's going on?" he said.

"Just do as I say!" Emma shook the other orphans awake, and Violet started whimpering again. Emma patted her back. "Get up but be quiet," she told the children. "Go into the storage room and wait for me!"

"I can't see," Edith said.

"Hang on to each other's hands," Emma said. "Sawyer will lead the way."

The children did as they were told, and Emma followed, Violet in her arms. In the storage room, grainy moonlight filtered in through a small window near the ceiling, illuminating the pale faces of the orphans but leaving the rest of the room in inky shadows. The children stood with their bare toes curling on the roughhewn floor, looking up at Emma with sleepy, confused eyes. She grabbed the handle to the back entrance, her heart booming in her chest.

"What's outside this door?" she asked Sawyer.

"Our backyard," he said. "And our backdoor neighbor's backyard."

"And Henny and Gus," Sadie whispered.

"Henny and Gus?" Emma said.

"Our chicken and mule," Sawyer said. "The stable boss was going to shoot Gus on account of he was sick, but Clayton brought him home. The stable boss thinks Gus got out and ran away. We're not supposed to tell anyone he's back there!"

"Is the backyard fenced in?" Emma said.

"Yeah, but there's a gate," Sawyer said. "Why? Are we leaving?"

"Just trust me, all right?" Emma directed her attention to the rest of the children, trying to keep her voice steady. "We're going to play a game of follow the leader. Sawyer is going out this door, and you're going to follow him, single file. But we can't make any noise, so you have to be really, really quiet. I'll come out last and close the door behind me."

Just then, the front entrance to the shanty opened and closed. Emma yanked open the back door and motioned the orphans outside. Sawyer went first and Jack followed.

"Emma?" Clayton called from inside the house.

"Wait!" she said. She gestured the confused children back up the steps and into the storage room again. "Stay right here!" With Violet on her hip, she hurried toward the kitchen. Clayton appeared in the doorway, breathing hard, with two young girls at his side. The girls' eyes were puffy and bloodshot, their cheeks wet with tears. Emma drew in a sharp breath. Drops of blood splattered their thin nightgowns and bare feet.

"My God!" she said. "What happened?"

Clayton herded the girls into the storage room. "Everyone, stay here until I tell you to come out. I'll be right back!"

"Where are you going?" Emma said louder than she intended.

"Just stay here and be quiet!" he said. Before Emma could protest, he turned and left again.

In the storage room, Emma put Violet down and coaxed everyone to sit on the floor. Then she sat too, pulling Violet into her lap, and tried to think of a way to keep the children still. The girls in the bloody nightgowns moved closer to her, sniffing and whimpering. The younger one clutched the older one's arm with both hands, her pinched face crumpled against her sister's blood-spotted sleeve.

Emma stroked the older girl's hand in a gentle, calming rhythm. "Everyone, be really quiet, and I'll sing a song for you," she whispered. "Clayton will be back before you know it."

"But we're not supposed to make any noise," Jack said.

"I'll sing very softly," Emma said. "I promise."

"Do you know 'Oh My Darling, Clementine'?" Sadie said.

"Yes," Emma said. Then she started singing, her voice just above a whisper, one hand petting Violet's head, the other stroking the older girl's hand. The children settled down, their frightened eyes locked on her face. When Emma finished the third round of the final verse, she heard men shouting outside. She stopped singing and told the children to stay silent. A few minutes later, the front door opened and closed. Emma put a finger to her lips, reminding the children not to make a sound. Then Clayton appeared in the hallway outside the storage room.

"They're gone," he said. "I saw them riding back down the hill into town. Emma, come with me."

Breathing a sigh of relief, Emma handed Violet to Sawyer. She stood and told the children to stay put.

"Don't leave us," the younger girl in a bloody nightgown cried. "It's too dark!"

"Hold on," Clayton said.

Emma stayed while Clayton disappeared into the kitchen and returned with a candle in a pewter holder. He lit the wick and set it on the floor in the short hallway between the kitchen and storage room. The flickering flame cast a yellow glow over the cluster of young anxious faces in the doorway.

"Is that better?" Clayton asked.

The girl nodded, pressing her lips together and trying not to cry.

Emma followed Clayton into the kitchen, where they moved to

the far side of the room so the children couldn't hear. She could barely see his face, his familiar features obscured by shadows. The candlelit doorway flickered in his somber eyes.

"What's going on?" she whispered.

"Hazard Flint's henchmen shot the people next door."

She gasped. "The girls' parents?"

He nodded. "There was nothing I could do."

"Why would they do that?"

"To prove Hazard Flint can get rid of us if we mess with him. And I can't be sure, but I have a feeling those murdering bastards went to the wrong house."

"What do you mean?"

"Either those bullets were meant for me, or they went to the wrong place on purpose to scare the miners and turn them against me."

She twisted a handful of her skirt in one fist, trying to stay calm. "They shot someone else across the way."

"I know."

"What are you going to do if they come back?"

He shrugged. "I'll stay and fight."

In the storage room, one of the newly orphaned girls began to sob, her wails like a siren in the close-walled shanty. Emma started down the hall to comfort her.

"Find those two something else to wear," Clayton called after her. "My wife's old clothes are in the bottom of the dresser in my room. I'll put the water on so you can get them cleaned up."

She stopped and looked him. "Are you going somewhere?"

"I've got to go get everyone settled down. They're all riled up. Can you stay for a while?"

She nodded and went to take care of the orphans.

CHAPTER 19

Two nights after Hazard Flint's henchmen murdered two miners and their wives in cold blood, a strong hand shook Emma awake in her bed. Before she became fully aware of her surroundings, she thought it was the doctor in the Manhattan hospital, waking her to break the news that her parents were dead, burned to ashes in a fire. Or maybe it was Michael, coming to deliver another message from Albert. Then moonlight streamed through her window and spilled across Percy's pale face, hovering above her like a wild-eyed ghoul. Startled, she pulled the blanket up to her chin and scooted toward the headboard.

"What are you doing in here?" she said.

Percy straightened. A man stood behind him wearing a burlap sack over his head. He was holding a pistol to Percy's back. Emma's heart did a hard double beat in her chest. The man waved his gun at her.

"Get up!" the man growled.

Emma scrambled out of bed and wrapped the bedspread around her shoulders. Her hands were shaking so bad, she nearly dropped it. The gunman motioned her and Percy out of the room and into the hall. She gaped at Percy, eyes wide, silently pleading with him not to let this happen, even though she knew there was nothing he could do. Percy shook his head, and they did as they were told, the gunman prodding them forward with his pistol. When they reached the stairs, Emma held on to the railing, certain she would trip or faint. Her heart was pounding so hard and fast that it seemed about to burst. Downstairs, the gunman forced them through the halls toward the front of the house.

Uncle Otis and Aunt Ida were in the dining room, still in their nightclothes, sitting back to back in chairs, their wrists tied to the armrests. The curtains were drawn and the room was dark except for a set of flickering hurricane lamps on the fireplace mantel. Two more gunmen stood near the sideboard, both with sacks over their heads. One of the sacks read POTATOES in blue letters. The gunman behind Percy and Emma joined the others. Two of the men were wearing hobnail boots, dark overcoats, and black trousers. The third wore cowboy boots and a deerskin jacket with a giant black cross on the back. The hair on Emma's arms stood up.

It was the shooter from the river. The man who'd murdered someone at Hazard Flint's command.

He slid Uncle Otis's whiskey bottle beneath the sack that hid his face and took a sip, while the other man pointed his gun at Uncle Otis's head. Aunt Ida stared at Emma and Percy with bulging eyes, her cheeks shiny with tears. Uncle Otis glared at the gunmen, his face red, his mouth contorted with fury. The whiskey-drinker set down the bottle and sauntered around Uncle Otis toward Emma and Percy. He drew his gun and pulled back the trigger with one thumb.

"Go stand by the wall," he said to Percy. With terror-filled eyes, Percy put his hands in the air, backed up until he ran into the fireplace mantel, then stepped sideways, wedging himself into a corner. The man in the potato sack kept his gun on him, while the one in burlap kept his pistol on Aunt Ida, who sat blubbering in her chair.

The whiskey-drinker yanked a dining room chair from beneath the table and ordered Emma to sit in it. She did as she was told, pulling the bedspread tighter around her shoulders. He stood in front of her.

"Do you know why we're here?" he asked.

She shook her head.

"Ida and I don't have anything to do with this!" Uncle Otis said.

"Shut up, Otis!" the man in the potato sack said.

Emma couldn't be sure, but he sounded like Frank. She looked in his direction. Every time she had seen Frank, he was in his police uniform, so the man's clothing gave no clue to his true identity. And like the others, he wore leather gloves, so she couldn't tell by his hands. The whiskey-drinker kicked the chair she was sitting in.

"Hey!" he said. "I'm talking to you!" He pushed the pistol against her neck.

She grimaced, her pulse throbbing in her temples. The barrel of the gun felt like ice against her skin. Despite her fear, she strained to see the gunman's eyes behind the mask. "What do you want?"

"Somebody's been cooking the books at the Company Store," he said.

Acid rose in the back of her throat and sweat broke out on her forehead. In a voice she hoped sounded bewildered, she said, "What does that have to do with me?"

"You been stealing from Hazard Flint?" he snarled.

"No!"

"So you don't know nothing about it?"

"I don't."

The whiskey-drinker straightened and withdrew his pistol. He strolled over to Percy. "Must be Percy messin' with the books then." He put the gun beneath Percy's jaw and pushed up his chin. "How about it, Percy? You been marking bills paid when they ain't? You been taking food and giving it to the miners?"

"Leave him alone!" Aunt Ida shrieked. "My boy would never steal from anybody!"

"She's right," Uncle Otis said. "He wouldn't steal from Mr. Flint because I'd kill him!"

The gunman in burlap put his pistol to Otis's temple. "Maybe it's you then!"

Uncle Otis winced, shrinking away from the barrel.

"You'd think a man with a nice house like this and a good job would be more grateful, wouldn't you?" the whiskey-drinker said.

"I sure would be," the gunman in burlap said. "I'd like a nice house like this."

"Come on now," Uncle Otis said. His voice was shaky. "It isn't me and you know it."

"Who is it then?" the whiskey-drinker said angrily. He grabbed Percy by the collar and pushed the pistol into his face, putting a dent in his cheek. "You better tell us who's been stealing from the Company Store or else you'll be bleeding all over this nice rug, and your old pa here will be out of a job by sunup."

"It's Emma!" Percy shouted, his voice breaking. "She knows how to mark the bills paid! She knows where I keep the books!"

"That's right!" Aunt Ida said. "She's the one causing all the trouble around here. She's been—"

Moving fast, the man in the potato sack tied a gag around Aunt Ida's mouth, stretching the corners of her lips toward her molars. She stomped her feet on the floor and shook her head back and forth in an attempt to break free.

"It's not true!" Emma cried.

"Half those miners never pay their bills on time," Percy said. "I knew something was up these past few weeks. I was just waiting to catch her!"

Emma shot him a withering look, fighting the urge to get out of her chair and punch him in the face.

The whiskey-drinker pulled the gun away from Percy's cheek and let go of his collar. "You don't say," he said.

Relieved, Percy sagged against the wall, his face running with sweat. Then he lurched forward and vomited on the floor.

The whiskey-drinker jumped out of the way just in time. "Jesus Christ!" he hollered. With a disgusted look on his face, he checked his boots. The other gunmen chuckled. The whiskey-drinker spun around and kicked Percy in the ribs, knocking him to the floor, then walked away. Percy grabbed his side and moaned.

"Well, Otis," the whiskey-drinker said. "Looks like you've got a bit of a problem on your hands. Hazard Flint isn't going to take kindly to your niece stealing from him. And those miners who accepted her help? I wouldn't want to be in their shoes. Come to think of it, I wouldn't want to be in your shoes either, especially when they find out why they were fired. Looks like everyone might be right after all. Your niece is bad luck all around. And you brought her here."

"Now just a minute," Uncle Otis said. "Let's talk about this. There's no need for the miners to find out why they were fired. You figure out how much Emma stole, Percy and I will pay the bill, and we'll fire her. I'm sure Mr. Flint will go along with that. No one else has to know anything about it."

Aunt Ida stomped her feet again, grunting and trying to get someone to pay attention. The gunman in burlap went over to her and pushed his mask in her face. "You got something to say, fatso?"

Aunt Ida mumbled behind the gag.

"No more screaming?" he said.

She nodded again and he untied the gag.

"Emma will never step foot in that store again," Aunt Ida said, breathing hard. "Please, we'll do whatever you want. Just don't hurt us. We had no idea what she was up to, but now we do. From now on, I'll keep her here, working for me. I swear, I'll lock her in her room, and we won't let her out of our sight! What else do you want? Money? We'll pay you. Just let us go!"

"My wife is right," Uncle Otis said. "We'll take care of Emma, I swear. And I've got a tidy sum of money tucked away in my dresser upstairs. It's yours if you leave us be. There's no need to get anyone else involved. What with the threat of a strike and all, Mr. Flint doesn't need another headache."

"There isn't going to be any strike," the gunman in the potato sack said. "We're making sure of that."

Hearing his voice a second time, Emma knew it was Frank. An image of the girls in blood-splattered nightgowns flashed in her mind, and anger shot through her like a lightning bolt. Suddenly, she forgot all about being terrified.

"How are you going to do that?" she said. "By breaking into miners' houses in the middle of the night and murdering them in their beds? By leaving behind a bunch of orphaned children? I thought the police captain was supposed to protect people?"

His head snapped in her direction.

"You're nothing but a bully, Frank Bannister," she said. "Always have been and always will be. The only difference between now and when you were young is now you're hiding behind a gun and a mask. I guess that makes you a coward too."

The man in the potato sack stormed across the room, put his gun against her forehead, and pulled back the hammer. "I'll show you a coward," he said.

She glared up at him, hate searing a hole through her chest. "I saw you shoot those men down by the river. You and Mr. Flint, and that one over there." She jerked her chin toward the whiskey-drinker. "What's one more murder? Go ahead and pull the trigger."

"I don't know who you think you're talking to," he said, his voice filled with anger, "but you've got the wrong man."

"Let her be," the whiskey-drinker demanded. "It won't do us any good to have the supervisor's niece show up dead. We got what we wanted. Mr. Flint will decide what to do next."

Frank stayed where he was, his breath coming fast and heavy, the burlap over his mouth billowing in and out. Emma gritted her teeth and closed her eyes, waiting for him to pull the trigger. Finally, he lowered the pistol and stepped back.

"Let's get out of here," the whiskey-drinker said.

"What about the money?" the man in burlap said.

"That's not what we came here for," the whiskey-drinker said. "We ain't crooks."

Taking their time, the gunmen holstered their weapons, then turned their backs and left the room. The whiskey-drinker glanced over his shoulder to look at Percy one more time, as if daring him to try something. Then, finally, the three men disappeared into the foyer. The front door opened and closed. Footsteps crossed the porch and pounded down the steps. Percy pushed himself up and stumbled over to untie his parents. Outside, horses galloped away. Emma stood and pulled the bedspread around her shoulders, trying to decide if she should help Percy, who was fumbling with the rope around his mother's wrists. Uncle Otis struggled to break free, his crimson face covered in sweat. Then he caught sight of Emma and stopped.

"That's right," he growled. "Just stand there and watch, you ungrateful little wench!"

Emma hesitated, then bit her lip and went over to lend a hand. Percy had untied one of his mother's wrists but was having a hard time with the other.

"Go help your father," Emma said. "I'll get this." She tugged on the rope around her aunt's wrist, releasing the tight knot.

"Get away from me!" Aunt Ida screeched. "I can't stand the sight of you!" Emma let go and took a step back.

"I was just trying to untie you," she said.

Aunt Ida leapt out of the chair and slapped Emma across the face. "You, shut up! We took you in out of the goodness of our hearts, and this is how you repay us? By almost getting us killed and nearly getting your uncle fired? Everyone is right. You *are* cursed. And I don't want you anywhere near me!"

Emma put a hand to her cheek, her eyes burning. "Keep telling yourself you took me in out of the goodness of your heart if it helps you sleep at night," she said. "But we both know that's not the truth. You wanted free help, and that's the *only* reason I'm here."

Aunt Ida gasped, as if she couldn't believe what she was hearing. Uncle Otis ripped his arm from the rope before Percy finished untying it, then stood and spun around to face Emma.

"I'll give you five minutes to pack your bags and get the hell out of my house!" he said, spittle flying from his lips. "We're done with you!"

"He's right," Aunt Ida said. "We've done all we can for you, but it was never enough. This will be the first time in my life that I've ever put myself first, but I need to take care of my family and myself. I can't do that with you around here, causing trouble every time we turn around."

A ripple of anger and fear quickened Emma's heart. *Where would she go?* Despite her apprehension, she squared her shoulders and looked her aunt in the eyes. "I'll be more than happy to leave," she said. "But if that's what you want, I'll need money for the train."

"You're not getting one more cent from us," Aunt Ida said, her voice quaking.

Emma turned her attention to Uncle Otis. "Well, if that's the case, perhaps I should leave you both with something to remember me by. I'm sure you remember the Fourth of July dance when—"

"We'll give you money for a ticket," her uncle interrupted. "After that, I don't give a damn what happens to you."

CHAPTER 20

At four o'clock the next morning, Emma sat on a peeling bench outside the train station, trying to figure out what to do. The ticket window wasn't set to open for another two hours, so she had plenty of time to think. Finally, she had money for a ticket out of Coal River. Her uncle and aunt had kicked her out, and she had nowhere to live. The decision had been made for her. Now she had to leave, and somehow she would need to find a way to survive. This was her chance to put this place behind her once and for all. And yet she didn't know if it was possible.

An image of Nicolas flashed in her mind. Then Francesca's beautiful twins, Pearl's son, the red tips, the boys with missing arms and legs, the line of small coffins. How could she just get up and leave when young boys were suffering and dying to make other men rich? Was she going to let the breaker boys down the same way she'd let Albert down?

But what if there was nothing she could do? It was terrifying to think of starting over somewhere new with no money or clear-cut plan, but the thought of staying in a place with so little regard for human beings that they put young boys to work in one of the most dangerous industries known to man was agonizing. Her life had already been filled with so much tragedy; why would she want to subject herself to any more? Maybe this time, she should give up. She was too tired to fight. Maybe it was time to admit that Hazard Flint held all the cards. He had won.

Not to mention the fact that, if she stayed, along with being homeless, she might get herself killed. Now that Mr. Flint and his henchmen knew she was stealing from the mining company, they might decide to do away with her. Even if her aunt and uncle had locked her up in their house, she never would have been safe. She had seen firsthand what Hazard Flint could do. She had to leave to protect herself, didn't she? And leaving was what she'd wanted since the day she'd stepped foot back in Coal River, wasn't it?

If she left, she could go back to Manhattan. Maybe the former theater owner would take pity on her. Maybe he had purchased a new building and would give her a job. Maybe her luck would change.

Of course the thought of never seeing Clayton again twisted in her chest like a knife, but she was used to misery. It was part of her now, just like her unruly hair and too-small fingernails. She would learn to live with it, wouldn't she? She would tuck it away, along with her grief for her parents and Albert, and all the children who were dead and dying in Coal River, and eventually it would turn to ice, making her heart beat a little slower, making it harder and harder to breathe.

Making it feel like I'm drowning.

She hung her head, her face growing red with shame. How could she be so selfish? Even if Mr. Flint's men shot her dead in the middle of the night, at least she would die standing up for what was right and true. It would be better than running away. She had already done so much for the miners' children, bringing them extra food and teaching some of them to read and write. She couldn't abandon them now. She looked at the dark edges of the woods, scanning the long shadows beside the train depot. For once, she wanted Michael to be there, watching her with his dark, haunted eyes. If she saw him, she would beckon him over and ask him what to do. And if what Simone said was true, and Albert really was trying to communicate with her, maybe he would have the answer. But then again, Emma didn't need a message from Michael or her dead brother to tell her anything. There really was no other choice. She had to stay.

By the time early dawn arrived in a faint, gray smear behind the hills east of town, Emma was trudging up the steep road leading to the miners' village, suitcase in hand. She stared up at the dark, hulking silhouette of the breaker. Devourer of children. The waning moon was coming and going among the clouds, blinking off the breaker windows as if someone were inside, sending her a coded message. A low white mist hung in steep angles above the pine forest that ran along the highest peak of the mountain, suspended in the air like frozen snowfall.

Cresting the last knoll, Emma rehearsed what she was going to say to Clayton. She had to convince him to take her in, to make him understand that she wanted to stay and help, no matter what. If he refused, she'd knock on other miners' doors and offer her uncle's money for room and board. Someone was bound to let her in. And yet, somehow, she knew Clayton wouldn't send her away. If nothing else, he needed a hand with the orphans. And God knew his house needed a woman's touch. The thought of moving in with a widower weighed heavy on her mind, but she would do it anyway, if he'd let her. Maybe she ought to start the conversation by showing him the money she had tucked into her brassiere instead of saying anything about the breaker boys. Maybe she should tell him how she felt about him. No. Admitting that she thought she was falling in love with him would only complicate things. Besides, that wasn't important right now.

She thought back to when she first saw Clayton at the Fourth of July celebration, how he had taken command of the situation between Frank and Nally, how he had looked rugged and handsome in his Sunday best. At the time, she only knew him as the troublemaker Percy and her uncle had talked about, but now she wondered if somehow, deep inside, she had known there was something special about him. Then he came to her rescue at the dance, made her feel safe on the Ferris wheel, and had enthralled a roomful of desperate miners. She couldn't put her finger on exactly when her feelings toward him had started to change, or when she stopped ignoring them; she only knew that they had. He wasn't anything like the boys in New York, the pale-faced actors in the theater who only cared about their careers, the dockworkers who drank beer and played poker next to the fish market, or the rich young men in fancy suits who never gave her a second glance. Clayton was a hard worker who took in orphans and believed in equality for all. She had never met anyone so sure of what he believed in and where he belonged. But that was another reason not to tell him how she felt. He would never leave Coal River, and she couldn't stay forever.

As she drew closer to the last bend in the road before the village, a cluster of yellow lights near the culm banks caught her eye. At first she thought they were fireflies, floating between the mounds of shale and clay and rock. Then she drew nearer and realized they were oil lanterns.

Emma put her head down, moved to the far side of the road, and walked faster, trying to stay on the compressed shoulder to lessen the crunching beneath her shoes. Then the rising sun bloomed behind the peak of Bleak Mountain, and in the thin light, she spotted a group of women and children picking through the mine waste. They were filling their buckets and wheelbarrows with bits and pieces of coal. Three women hunched over the tallest pile halfway up, their hands and shoes slipping on the rubble. They worked with their sleeves pushed up to their elbows, their long aprons stained black with coal dust. A boy of about eight was searching through the freshest culm near the crest of the bank, over fifty feet in the air. On the ground, a toddler in a filthy bonnet and torn tights sat on a burlap sack in one of the wheelbarrows, her sleepy face smeared with soot. A blond girl in a one-piece dress carried two buckets over to another wheelbarrow, her clothes and arms sullied up to her armpits, as if she'd been dunked in black mud. As if by signal, the women turned off their lanterns, took children, sacks, and wheelbarrows in hand, and began to disperse with the arrival of day.

Then one of the women saw Emma and froze, her face filled with fear. When she realized who Emma was, her shoulders dropped in relief. It was Pearl. She came out to the road.

"You makin' another food run?" she said, eyeing Emma's suitcase.

"No," Emma said.

"Runnin' away?"

"Something like that. I can't stay at my uncle's anymore." She set down her suitcase to rub her aching hand.

"I'd offer you a bed," Pearl said. "But we barely got enough to make ends meet as it is, 'specially without Tanner's pay." Her eyes filled, and she put a hand on her lower abdomen, rubbing her soot-covered fingers in small circles. "We can't take in another mouth to feed, what with me expecting and all."

"That's all right," Emma said. Then she hugged Pearl, a sudden flood of tears burning her eyes. "I'm so sorry about your son."

Pearl hugged her back, then drew away and ran a black hand beneath her nose. "Guess it was the good Lord's will to take my boy away," she said, sniffing. "And now He's blessed us with another child to heal our broken hearts."

Forcing a smile, Emma tried not to think about the poverty Pearl's new baby would be born into. "How are you feeling?" she said, because she couldn't think of anything else to say.

"I'm getting along all right," Pearl said. "You want me to ask one of the widows to take you in?"

"No, no," Emma said. "I got myself in trouble. I'll get myself out."

"Your uncle find out you been helping us?"

Emma nodded, then looked over Pearl's shoulder at the women and children still near the culm banks. "What are you doing out here?"

Pearl followed her gaze, her forehead furrowed. "We're cullin' coal," she said. "There's good pieces of anthracite mixed in with all that gravel and rock. Mr. Flint says we're supposed to buy our coal from the pluck me store, but it ain't right us having to pay for coal when our husbands are the ones who dug it from the earth. And some of us can't afford to anyway, even if it was right."

"Makes sense to me," Emma said.

"You won't tell?"

"Of course not. Haven't I proved myself to you yet?"

Pearl nodded. "I s'pose you have."

"But why are you out here so early?" Emma said. "Wouldn't it be easier to wait for more daylight?"

"Uh-uh," Pearl said. "Used to be the Coal and Iron Police would look the other way when they saw us cullin' for slag coal. But as of late they been patrolling this area, smashing our baskets and wheelbarrows if they caught us. Last time they said if they seen us again, they'd search our houses and charge us double for all the coal we had on hand, no matter if we bought it from the pluck me store or not."

Emma shook her head in disgust. How could anyone as rich as Hazard Flint be so greedy?

Just then, the thunder of galloping hooves traveled up the mountain road. Pearl didn't wait to see who it was. She raced over to the culm piles, gathered up the toddler from the burlap sack, and disappeared into a stand of scraggly pines. The rest of the women and children followed, leaving buckets and wheelbarrows behind. On the peak of the highest bank, a young boy started down, sliding on the loose culm. His mother waited at the bottom of the incline, urging him to hurry, her arms outstretched as if to catch him.

Four policemen rode up the hill behind Emma, floating like phantoms in a gray cloud of dust. Emma picked up her suitcase and ran toward the woods, her shoulders hunched. Then someone screamed, and she stopped and spun around. It was the mother waiting at the bottom of the culm pile. Her boy had slipped and fallen, starting an avalanche of shale and rubble. The culm was collapsing around him, swallowing him alive. It was already above his knees. Emma's blood went cold. She ran over, dropped her suitcase at the bottom of the pile, emptied one of the buckets, and lurched up the side of the bank with it. Trying to avoid the collapsing rubble, she climbed parallel to where the boy was disappearing. The culm shifted and rolled beneath her feet, and she was forced to get on her hands and knees. She had no idea what she was going to do, but she couldn't just stand by and watch the boy die. The mother screamed over and over, crying for someone to please save her son.

The boy was panicking and digging himself deeper with every

movement, clawing at the culm with bare hands. He twisted onto his side and reached toward the peak of the bank as if swimming in black quicksand, his fingers scratched and bloody.

"Stop moving!" Emma shouted. The boy did as he was told, his eyes wild and staring at her, his thin face ashen. Still, the culm kept shifting, slowly swallowing his waist, inching toward his narrow chest like a downward conveyor belt of rocks and dust. For a second, Emma froze. The mine waste had turned white, and she saw Albert falling through the ice. She shook her head to clear it, then lay down and stretched across the rubble, parallel to the ground and slightly above and to one side of the boy. The sharp shale stabbed her stomach and chest. She edged closer and closer, her legs splayed out behind her, and tossed the bucket toward the boy, keeping a grip on the handle.

"Grab hold!" she yelled.

The boy threw himself sideways and reached out, clamping onto the bucket for dear life. She pulled, but it was no use. He was in too deep. She edged closer, testing the firmness of the rubble as she went. When she thought she was close enough, she threw her body across the culm and latched on to the boy's elbows, pulling with every ounce of strength she could find. It wasn't enough. She let go and started digging around him with the bucket, hoping to free him enough so he could pull himself out. But the slag and gravel filled in faster and faster, and the boy kept sinking deeper and deeper. She tried to think, her pulse thrashing in her ears.

At the bottom of the culm pile, two policemen grabbed the screaming mother by the arms and started dragging her away while the other two kicked her wheelbarrow over and emptied her bucket on the ground. Then one of them stopped and looked up, as if noticing Emma and the boy for the first time. It was Frank.

"Hold on!" he shouted, and ambled up the side of the bank in wide, powerful strides.

He reached the boy within seconds and pulled on his arms, grimacing with the effort. Sweat broke out on his forehead. Emma tried to help. It was no use. They couldn't get enough leverage. While she held on to the boy, Frank took a step sideways, trying to get closer. Then the culm shifted beneath Frank's boots, and rock and clay and shale started sliding down the bank like a black river. Frank stumbled and fell. The culm gave way and swallowed his legs up to his knees, as if a sinkhole had opened up beneath him. He slid several feet down the pile, away from the boy. Then the ground shook and rumbled, as if the earth was caving in. And Frank started to sink. Fast.

Keeping a grip on the bucket handle with one hand and holding the boy's wrist with the other, Emma stretched out and extended the bucket in Frank's direction. But he was too panicked to notice. In what seemed like slow motion, the culm pulled him deeper and deeper. He tried grabbing hold of something, anything, to pull himself out. But there was nothing to grab on to, and his hands and arms slipped on the culm as if it were ice. Within seconds the gravel and shale were up to his waist. Unaware that he was making things worse, he kept reaching out again and again, clawing more and more culm toward himself. He was burying himself alive.

Emma shouted his name over and over and, finally, Frank came to his senses. He stopped struggling and reached for the bucket, his eyes bulging with fear. On the first try, he missed and let out a yell of terror. But instead of trying again, he dug more frantically at the shale, trying desperately to break free. The cords on his neck stood out, and his mouth opened in a silent scream. Inch by inch the culm kept swallowing him. Then he stopped struggling again and looked at Emma. He was breathing hard, his coal-dusted face slack-jawed with a strange mixture of shock and recognition. He knew he was going to die.

Emma stretched out as far as she could, inching the bucket a tiny bit closer. "Grab on!" she yelled. "You can reach it!"

After what seemed like forever, Frank tried again, and again, but he still couldn't reach it. Every time, his attempt grew weaker and weaker as panic and horror sapped his strength. He gasped and coughed as the culm started to crush his chest. Then he gave up and went limp, and Emma was certain it was the end. She shouted his name again and, to her surprise, he tried one more time. Finally he caught the rim of the bucket with one hand, and then the other. But the culm kept on pulling him.

Using every ounce of strength she had left, Emma held on to the bucket and the boy, her shoulders and arms screaming in pain, as if her muscles and bones were being ripped apart. Then she started sliding too, closer and closer to the black river of shifting culm.

Just when she thought she couldn't hold on another second and was going to be swallowed alive, a policeman grabbed her around the waist and pulled. The other two pushed a long beam beside Frank and the boy. The boy wrapped his arms around the lumber and held on. Frank let go of the bucket with one hand and caught the wood with the other. One of the policemen gripped Frank's wrist until Frank could latch on to the beam with both hands. With the policeman's help, Frank heaved himself out, then grasped the boy by the arms and pulled him free in turn. The other policeman yanked Emma backward and out of the way. They all fell back on the culm bank and scrambled away from the sinkhole.

But the sinkhole kept getting bigger, growing wider and wider. It moved toward them, its black edges falling away bit by bit. It swallowed the bucket and the wooden beam. Emma grabbed the boy's bloody hand and scrambled down the bank. Frank and the other policemen followed, trying to outrun the avalanche of shale and rubble. At the bottom of the bank, the policemen caught the horses and ran out from between the culm piles. Emma followed, dragging the boy toward the road, where his mother was on her knees, wailing.

Finally in the clear, everyone stopped. Behind them, the pile continued to rumble and shift. The boy ran to his mother and collapsed on the ground. She knelt, wrapped her arms around his head, and pressed him against her heaving bosom. Frank bent over and put his hands on his knees, struggling to catch his breath. Emma coughed and spit to get the dust out of her lungs. When she was finally able to breathe without choking, she went over to see if the boy was all right. His hands and forearms were scraped and bloody, his trousers ripped. One of his shoes was missing.

"I told you it was too high," his mother said. "Given the chance, that culm will swallow you whole."

"I know, Mama," the boy said. "I won't do it again."

Emma put a gentle hand on his back. "Are you all right?" she said. "Does anything hurt?"

The boy shook his head, his chin trembling.

"Can you stand?" Emma said.

The boy pushed himself off the ground and walked to prove he was okay, limping on the ball of one bare foot.

The woman touched Emma's arm, her eyes full of tears. "Thank you for saving him," she said. "I don't know what I—"

"We warned everyone to stay away from the culm," one of the policemen interrupted. "Now you're all under arrest for stealing." He made a move toward Emma. The other policeman started toward the boy and his mother.

Frank straightened and came over. "Let them be," he ordered the policemen. Rivulets of soot and sweat streaked his temples. He brushed black dust from his sleeves and trousers. The other men frowned.

"But Mr. Flint said—" one of the men started.

"I don't care what Mr. Flint said," Frank said. "Neither of you saw anyone stealing coal today! Is that clear?"

One of the policemen jerked his chin toward Emma. "I'm not going against the rules just because you're sweet on this one."

"Don't give me that shit!" Frank said. "I can throw you both in jail, and Mr. Flint won't even ask why. Now get back on those nags and get over to the mine shaft. This isn't why we came up here, and you know it!"

The men mumbled and spit on the ground, then started toward their horses. They climbed on and waited. Frank waved them away.

"Go on!" he shouted. The men turned their horses and rode off, their faces hard. When they were out of earshot, Frank directed his gaze at Emma.

"What are you doing up here?" he said.

Her mind raced. "I was—"

"Was that your suitcase?"

She tensed and glanced toward the culm piles. She had dropped her suitcase when she scrambled up to help the boy. Now the entire bank had shifted, and her suitcase was nowhere to be seen. The culm had swallowed everything she owned. Then it occurred to her that if she was going to stay and help the breaker boys, it would be easier if everyone thought she was gone, especially Frank Bannister and Hazard Flint. "I'm leaving Coal River. My aunt and uncle never want to see me again."

He frowned. "This have anything to do with Clayton Nash?"

Struggling to control herself, Emma bit down on the inside of her cheek. Frank knew perfectly well why her aunt and uncle never wanted to see her again. Less than twelve hours ago, he had been in their living room, holding a gun to her head. She opened her mouth to call him a liar, then stopped. It wouldn't help her situation to egg him on any further.

"We've had some horrible disagreements," she said. "So they ordered me out."

"That doesn't explain why you're up here," he said. "Unless you're lying."

The veins in her neck throbbed as if about to burst. She had just risked her life to save his, and now he was treating her like a criminal? Again? Maybe she should have let him die.

"My train doesn't leave for another two hours," she said. "I just came up to say good-bye to some of the miners' wives and children." She pressed her lips together, as if trying not to cry. "I know you and I have had our differences, but please don't tell anyone I was up here again. There have been so many bad rumors. And despite my quarrels with my uncle, I don't want to cause Aunt Ida anymore pain. She's my mother's sister, after all, and she's been good to me. I just want to put all this behind me and start over someplace new."

"I just need to know one thing," he said.

"What?"

"Why did you save me?"

She blinked, surprised by the question. "Because it was the right thing to," she said. "That's all. And besides, you're not worth the guilt I'd feel for letting you die." The words came out before she could stop them.

"That's it?" he said, searching her face. "No other reason?"

She shook her head, wondering what other reason he thought there might be. What did he think, that she wanted his protection?

That she had come to her senses and realized they were meant to be together? If so, he was out of his mind. "No other reason," she said.

"What about the fact that I didn't tell Mr. Flint you were down by the river that day?"

She gaped at him. "You mean right before you tried to get me in trouble for talking to the miners' wives and Clayton Nash? Or before you held a gun to my head for calling you a coward?"

He sighed heavily and crossed his arms. He had been caught. "So where's your train ticket?"

She placed her fingers above her bosom, patting the money folded inside her brassiere. "It's safe," she said. "Where no one will find it."

His eyes fell to her chest and he reached for her hand. She snatched it away.

"You're bleeding," he said.

She looked down. Her fingernails were torn and black, her skin and knuckles caked with coal dust and blood. A long, bloody scrape ran down the back of one hand.

"I'll be fine."

He gestured toward his horse. "Why don't you come with me?" he said. "You can't go anywhere looking like you just crawled out of a mine shaft. I'll take you down to my place, and you can get cleaned up. Afterward I'll escort you to the station."

"No," she said, a little louder than she'd intended. "I mean . . . one of the miners' wives will help me wash up."

He narrowed his eyes. "I'm not sure I should allow you to go over to the miners' village. You've caused enough trouble, and I get the feeling you're not telling me everything. Maybe I should take you down to the jailhouse for your own good."

"Maybe I should have let you die in that sinkhole."

He stared at her for a long time, then wiped the back of his wrist across his mouth and looked at the ground. For the first time ever, he looked ashamed. "I guess I owe you one."

"Yes," she said. "You do. And since I'll be gone before the day is over, you can forget all about me. It will be like I was never here."

"You don't have to leave," he said. "If you need a place to stay, my mother and I have a house down at the end of Susquehanna Avenue. Your aunt would approve, and you'd be safe there. It's not much, but I'm working on it. And it's more than you've got right now. I'll bet it's more than you'll have wherever you're going."

"No," she said. "I've made up my mind."

"I could take good care of you, Emma. You know that, right?"

She couldn't believe what she was hearing. Was he really that dim-witted? Or had he hit his head when he fell? She resisted the urge to tell him she'd rather die, or go to jail, than be with him. "I'm sorry. I can't stay. This place holds too many bad memories."

He sighed again and, after a long pause, said, "Good luck, then. I mean that."

"Thank you." She forced a smile.

"If you change your mind," he said, "you know where to find me."

"I do."

"I guess this is good-bye, then.

"It is."

He nodded once, then turned toward his horse. She watched in silence, her chest and shoulders loosening in relief. Now, for the first time since coming down from the culm pile, she felt pain in her stomach, arms, and back. Sulfur burned the cut on her hand. Her entire body ached as if she'd been hit by a runaway wagon and trampled by a hundred hooves. Frank put his foot in the stirrup and glanced over at her one last time. *Please, just go,* she thought. Finally he climbed on, kicked the horse, and galloped away. If he told Mr. Flint, or anyone else, that she was up here this morning, who knew what would happen? Maybe Uncle Otis would come looking for her. Maybe he would drag her home and lock her in a closet, or have her taken away. Maybe Mr. Flint would send someone to arrest or shoot her. She took a deep, shaky breath and made her way toward the miners' village, praying Frank would keep his word.

CHAPTER 21

At first, Clayton refused to let Emma move in, insisting she obey her uncle and take the next train out of Coal River. Things were getting too dangerous, and he didn't need any more trouble. Besides, it wasn't her fight. She had stood on his leaning porch in her filthy, soot-covered clothes, one hand covered in blood, and said she'd go to one of the widows' houses and offer to help them with their passel of children instead. Either way, she wasn't leaving. He stared at her then, thinking. Then she pulled the money out of her brassiere and, after a long moment, he let her in. They hid the money in a mason jar and sent the oldest girl, Edith, to buy cornmeal, a ham, potatoes, and five pounds of flour.

Clayton gave Emma some clothes from the bottom drawer of his dresser—a faded housedress with low pockets, a blue Sunday dress with a white collar, two aprons, a cotton skirt, and a button-up blouse with a high neck. Using a needle and thread from a sewing basket she found in the storage room, Emma took in the bodices and shortened the hems to fit her petite frame, then did her best to ignore Clayton's unsettled glances when she wore his late wife's clothes.

During the first week of her stay, Emma swept the walls and

floors, wiped down the table and chairs, and washed the windows a hundred times. Despite her efforts, coal dust clung to every crack and crevice and surface, inside and outside the shanty, as if they were living inside a giant water globe filled with anthracite powder instead of snow. By the third week, her hair had grown oily and limp, and no matter how often she rinsed her arms, neck, and face, a fine, gritty dust coated her skin. Like the rest of the women and children, she only bathed on Saturday nights, saving water for the miners and breaker boys.

To get water, she had to wait in line with the other women at a well pump near the end of the lane, then carry the heavy buckets home, her shoulders and hands aching. One well supplied water for twenty-five families, and when it went dry, they used buckets and tubs to scoop runoff from the brackish ponds near the culm banks.

With the help of Clayton and Edith, Emma slipped into the rhythms of village life. Monday was washday, Tuesday, ironing, Wednesday, baking—if they had the ingredients—Saturday, Edith and Sadie did the shopping, and Sunday was supposed to be a day of rest. Clayton usually spent it drumming up interest for the union and making repairs around the house. Emma had little experience growing vegetables and tending animals, but did what she could to clear the garden of weeds, and learned how to take an egg from beneath Henny without getting pecked. She went into the woods with the girls to search for nuts and berries, learned how to make dandelion salad, exchanged goods with the other women, and stuffed the holes in the shanty with rags to keep out the vermin and flies. In the evenings, she met with some of the miners' children in the living room to teach reading, writing, and basic math. She also held a weekend class for several of the immigrants' sons and daughters to teach them English.

While the women cleaned up after supper and tended to the children, a good number of the miners went down to the village tavern to bet on cockfights, play poker, and drink moonshine and beer. Clayton stayed home to wash dishes and work in the garden, picking cutworms off the struggling potato leaves and feeding them to Henny, or fixing the makeshift fence to keep out the neighbor's goat.

And while Emma was happy to have a purpose, she realized she was living like Clayton's wife without the benefit of his affection. At night she slept in the storage room on a pile of old blankets, aching to go into his bedroom and crawl beneath the covers with him. Every day she had to remind herself that having a relationship with him wasn't why she was there. She was there to help the miners' children and the breaker boys. When two of the village women asked if she and Clayton were betrothed, she shook her head and dropped her eyes. Luckily, the women had too many troubles of their own to pry further. But the question had made her uneasy, and filled her with a strange, yet familiar, sense of loss.

Because for some reason, despite the attention Clayton had paid her when they first met, he was all business now, skirting around her so they wouldn't bump into each other in the small kitchen, sitting on a stool if she was on the davenport, refusing to let her wash his soot-covered back after work. He seemed grateful and happy to have her help with the children and the household duties, but she couldn't figure out if he had lost interest in her, or if he was too preoccupied with organizing the strike and the next secret meeting to think about anything else. After sunset he was skittish, jumping up from his seat to look out the window if he heard the creak of an axle, or a barking dog.

Or maybe he didn't want to be unfaithful to his late wife.

After all, Pearl had told Emma that Clayton and Jennie were best friends at ten, and had gotten married at sixteen.

"When she died," Pearl said, "you could see it in his face that he could barely stand to keep on living."

Whatever the reason for Clayton's behavior, maybe it was for the best. They had more important things to worry about.

Then, yesterday, when the colliery whistle blew before noon, Emma went into a panic, fighting the urge to run over to the mine to make sure Clayton and Sawyer were all right. But she couldn't take the chance that Uncle Otis might see her, so she kept checking the main road for the Black Maria. When she saw it coming a few hours later, she stood trembling on the front porch, her heart pounding so hard, she thought it would burst. She gripped the railing to steady herself but had to sit on the stoop to wait and see where the hearse would stop. When it went by the last shanty at the end of the row and turned into the next lane, she hung her head, blinking back tears of relief.

Within minutes, the tortured screams of a new widow filled the hollow.

That night, Clayton told Emma that a vertical mine shaft had shifted and started to collapse. One miner was crushed while another fell four hundred feet to his death on the gangway below. Thinking about it afterward, Emma couldn't imagine living with that fear every day, wondering if her husband and son would come home from work alive. Then realization hit her, and she had to sit down in the nearest chair.

She was completely and hopelessly in love with a miner. And unless there was a change in the way the colliery was run, or a miraculous turnaround in their fortunes, Clayton would always be in danger. When she first moved in with him, she knew she had feelings for him. But after living here all these weeks, after working together to make a home for the orphans, after sharing meals and quiet evenings on the porch, drinking sweet tea and watching sunsets, those feelings had turned into something more. Now she was certain. Clayton was the love of her life.

What was she thinking? That she could convince him to leave Coal River? That a strike would change everything? That she would help the breaker boys, and life would be trouble free from that day on? Even if the strike gave the miners a fair wage, coal mining would always be dangerous work. And Clayton would never leave. Working in the mines was all he had ever known. Was she willing to live in constant fear to be with the man she loved? Or would she have to leave to stay sane? Overcome, she put a hand over her mouth and wept. She was so tired of feeling helpless and confused. What would she do if something happened to Clayton? And what if the townspeople were right, that she really was cursed? Maybe she would have to leave to protect him.

She allowed herself to wallow for a few minutes, then wiped her eyes and took a deep breath. To her relief, the gnawing stress had eased. She tried to be rational. Clayton wasn't interested in having a relationship with her. And no matter how badly she wanted him to return her feelings, perhaps he never would. Maybe the interest he had shown her earlier was his way of trying to heal after the loss of his wife. Maybe he thought the distraction of someone new would ease the horrible, wretched pain in his heart. But now that Emma was there, living under his roof, maybe he realized pursuing her had been a mistake. He would never love anyone as much as he loved Jennie, and he would never be unfaithful to her memory. Little did he know he didn't need to worry, because Emma was only staying until she could figure out how to help the breaker boys. That was it. After that she was leaving. Until then, she would get through every day as best she could. She had lost loved ones before. She would survive losing Clayton. And leaving him behind would be easier than seeing him killed in the mines.

Now, Emma stood in front of the hot coal stove in Clayton's kitchen, stirring water, lard, and flour in a cast-iron skillet with a battered wooden spoon—her first attempt at making bulldog gravy. It wasn't like any gravy she'd ever had, but Clayton said he'd made it a hundred times. It was one of his mother's old recipes. Besides, it was the closest thing to gravy they could afford. She wiped her brow with the back of one hand, and stirred fast to get rid of the lumps. In another skillet, she pushed thin slices of old cornbread and squaw biscuits around, hoping the lard would soak in and soften the stale edges. Other than the occasional egg from Henny and the scraggly carrots from Clayton's struggling garden, it seemed they'd been living on squaw biscuits and wild greens for weeks. She wondered what they'd eat come the cold weather in November, only a few weeks away. She couldn't believe it'd only been a little over three months since her return to Coal River. It felt like three years.

Now, it was nearing dinnertime, and Clayton and Sawyer would be coming home any minute, trudging in the back door, bone-tired and starving, their clothes heavy with mud and coal dust. Emma checked the kettles to see if the bath water was boiling, then went to the storage room to get the wooden tub. She dragged it into the kitchen and put it in its usual spot next to the coal stove, centered in the round sooty stain on the floorboards. The youngest girl, Violet, was napping, while Jack and the older girls, Sadie and Edith, played in the backyard.

Emma gave the bulldog gravy a good stir, and heard footsteps on the porch steps. At first she thought it was Clayton and Sawyer, but she hadn't yet heard the miners' boots crunching up the slag road. Besides, they always came in the back door so they wouldn't track dirt into the house. Then someone knocked. She went to the front window and peered around the curtain to see who was there. Two children waited on the porch. She opened the door to discover the neighbor boy, Jimmy Fitzpatrick, and his younger brother, Nelson.

"You wash your hands yet?" she said.

"Yes, ma'am," Jimmy said.

"Come get some supper then."

Jimmy was ten, the third boy in a family of six brothers and two sisters. He couldn't work in the breaker because of deformed fingers, and his father was dead, killed in a cave-in last year. His mother took in boarders to bring in a small income.

Jimmy came inside holding his younger brother by the hand. "I just brought Nelson," he said. "I already ate dinner."

Four-year-old Nelson was barefoot, his face and shirt covered with dirt and day-old snot. But his hands and lower arms were clean, as clean as Jimmy could get them anyway. Emma divided a slice of cornbread between two bowls, scooped a spoonful of gravy from the skillet, poured it over them, and set the bowls on the table. Despite his claim about already having eaten, Jimmy eyed the food as hungrily as his brother.

"You can share my portion," Emma said. "I'm not very hungry tonight."

Jimmy and Nelson climbed onto the chairs and sat down, waiting patiently as she got silverware.

"Go ahead and dig in," she said. The boys did as they were told. Within seconds they were done, licking crumbs off their forks.

"Does your momma have milk for the baby today?" she asked.

Jimmy nodded. "One of the boarders brought her a jug yesterday."

"You let me know if she ever runs out," she said. "And I'll figure out a way to get her more."

"Yes, ma'am," Jimmy said.

Just then, the crunching of a hundred footsteps on slag drifted in from outside.

"Best run along," Emma said.

The boys wiped their mouths, thanked her, and left. A few minutes later, Clayton and Sawyer came in through the back door after removing their jackets and boots outside. Their faces were black.

"Is that bulldog gravy I smell?" Clayton said.

"I hope so," Emma said. She wrapped a dishcloth around the handle of a boiling kettle, hefted it up with both hands, and poured hot water into the tub. Curls of steam swirled into the air. Clayton and Sawyer put their dinner pails and canteens next to the sink and took off their shirts. Every night the routine was the same—first they would get cleaned up enough to eat; then, while everyone was outside or upstairs, they would finish bathing in private. Emma handed Sawyer a bar of lye soap and took the shirts out into the back room, where they would be scrubbed on a washboard and hung up to dry. When she came back into the kitchen, Sawyer was on his knees bending over the tub, scrubbing the coal dust from his hands and the back of his neck. Clayton was at the stove, tasting the gravy, the end of the wooden spoon in his mouth. When he saw her watching, he grinned, his eyes wide and white in his black face.

"You caught me," he said.

"Well," she said. "How did I do?"

"It's gravy all right."

She crossed her arms and smiled. "What's that supposed to mean?"

"It's just like my mother used to make." He took another taste, then put the spoon on the edge of the skillet, his face suddenly serious. "Sawyer, finish washing up and go outside with the others. I need to talk to Emma." He went over to the sink and leaned his back against it, waiting.

With a hard slab of fear forming in her gut, Emma sat down at the table. This was it. He was going to tell her she had to leave. There was nothing they could do to stop Mr. Flint, so she might as well be on her way. He was going to say he was grateful for her help with the children and the housework, but her uncle's money was long gone, and he couldn't afford to keep her there any longer. Time slowed to a crawl as Sawyer finished washing up and dried his hands and face on a towel. After what seemed like forever, he went outside.

"What is it?" Emma asked Clayton. "Is something wrong?"

"You said you wanted to help, so I need you to do me a favor."

She exhaled, relief washing over her. "Anything."

He picked up his dinner pail, set it on the table, took off the lid, and pulled out a newspaper. It was a copy of the *Scranton Times.*

"I need you to write a letter," he said. "To this man, Johnny Mitchell." He pointed at a picture of a dark-haired man on the front page. "The person who gave me this paper said Mr. Mitchell could help us. He's the president of the United Mine Workers."

"I can do that," she said. "Just tell me what to say."

"We need to join the union before we strike, and we need him to talk to the miners, to convince them it's the right thing to do. Tell him what we're up against, and ask him to come to Coal River."

"Do you think he will?"

"I don't know, but it can't hurt to ask."

Together they looked at the picture of the man in a suit and tie, his hair slicked back from his clean-shaven face. Emma wondered if one man really had the power to bring about such change. If so, one woman surely had the power to help the breaker boys. A few paragraphs below Mr. Mitchell's picture, a grainy, black and white photo showed a group of miners gathered at the mouth of a mine shaft, their faces grim. The caption said: "Three miners killed by coal company guards on a picket line in Brackenridge, Pennsylvania." She could barely make out individual features, but the pain and hardship in their eyes was as plain as the coal dust caked on their skin.

Then she noticed Clayton was only holding the paper, not really looking at it. His eyes were darting over the page, but he wasn't reading the articles. She assumed he had asked her to write the letter for her penmanship, but now she wondered if he could read and write at all. Instead of asking, she reached for the newspaper.

He gave it to her, and she began to read out loud the article featuring Mr. Mitchell's picture. "Says here the soldiers of Company E of the Ninth Regiment stationed in Parson, Pennsylvania, lustfully cheered the name of 'Johnny' Mitchell as they marched by the headquarters of the United Mine Workers of America in Wilkes-Barre today. Most of the soldiers in the company are coal miners."

"See," Clayton said. "That's why we need him. We need the support of every worker, and we won't get it until we have someone who can take charge, someone the miners will listen to."

"They listen to you," she said. "And Nally."

"Some of them listen to me. But not all. And they still don't trust Nally."

"Do you think this Johnny Mitchell can help the breaker boys too?"

He shrugged. "I don't know."

"Maybe I'll write to this man too," she said, pointing to the name of the journalist who wrote the story. "Maybe he'd be willing to write an article about the breaker boys."

"That won't get you anywhere. Most folks in coal country grew up knowing about the breaker boys. It wouldn't be news to them. They'd just look the other way like they always have."

"Then maybe we need to tell someone outside this region." She skimmed the paper again, then gasped, wondering why she hadn't had the idea before now. "I should write to the *New York Times*! I bet they'd be interested in a powerful mine owner breaking the law."

He made a face. "You really think people in New York care? As long as they have their coal in the winter, it doesn't matter how it gets there."

"You're wrong," she said, thinking about the people she'd known in the city. "They care like anyone else. They have families, children. If they find out how little boys are dying and being maimed, they'll care. I know they will."

"They'll think you're a lunatic and throw the letter in the trash."

Then another idea came to her, sending a jolt of energy through her body. "What if they could see the breaker boys for themselves? Then they'd understand. They'd know."

He looked at her like she was crazy. "What are you going to do, invite the editor of the *New York Times* to Coal River?"

"No. The only way to show them is with pictures. All I need is a photographer."

"The *New York Times* isn't going to spend good money to send a photographer all the way out here to take pictures of a bunch of poor breaker boys."

"You don't know that," Emma said, breathing fast now. At last she had an answer. She just knew it. "If just one photo of those little breaker boys with their black faces gets put in the *Times,* someone will help."

Clayton had seemed dismissive, unable to understand why people in New York might care about the children working in the mines, but now his face softened. "You go ahead and write that letter. Maybe it will do some good, maybe not. But I need you to write to Johnny Mitchell first. That's where you can make a difference."

"I'll write your letter," she said. "I'll tell Mr. Mitchell that you're standing up to Hazard Flint. I'll tell him about the breaker boys, and that the mining company is taking shortcuts and breaking the law. Maybe he can bring someone here to take pictures. Or maybe he has he own—" Then an image flashed in her mind: Uncle Otis, Aunt Ida, and Percy on the front steps of their house, waiting to have their photo taken. "Or better yet, *we* can send pictures to the *New York Times*! They can't ignore the truth if it's staring them in the face!"

"Okay, but where are you going to get a camera? They don't even sell them at the Company Store."

"No," she said. "But I know where I can get one."

Clayton scratched the back of his neck and considered her, his face doubtful. "All right, let's say you get ahold of a camera somehow. How are you going to get inside the breaker? You think they're just going to let a woman walk in there and start taking pictures?"

"No," she said. "But they'll let a breaker boy in."

He frowned, his coal-dust–covered brow furrowing. "No," he said, shaking his head. "I won't ask Sawyer to take that risk. If they caught him, they'd beat the tar out of him, or worse."

"I wouldn't ask Sawyer to do it either."

"Then who?"

She tapped her chest. "Me."

CHAPTER 22

At one the next morning, Emma crept in her stocking feet along the dark hallway outside her aunt and uncle's bedroom, staying close to the walls. A fine layer of nervous sweat coated her skin, and her ears prickled, listening for any type of movement. It was hard not to imagine Uncle Otis yanking open his door, seeing her skulking outside his bedroom, and charging after her, his eyes wild with rage. What would he do if he found out she hadn't left Coal River? What would he do if he discovered that, instead of being out of his life for good, she was inside his house, breaking in to steal his things? He would probably throw her over the balcony or shove her down the stairs, then carry her down to the river and toss her in, where she would disappear beneath the churning waves and wash ashore downstream, where no one would find her corpse except the possums, raccoons, and deer. What was one more dead body in this Godforsaken place?

Before coming upstairs, she'd snuck into the pantry to fill a gunnysack with bread and canned goods, then went into the sewing room to steal needles, thread, and a few bolts of leftover material to make clothes for the children. She was pushing her luck, but couldn't pass up the opportunity. After setting the sack of food and the dress material outside the veranda door, she went back inside to look for the pocket camera.

Now, she stopped in front of her aunt and uncle's bedroom, saying a silent prayer that the camera was still in their closet. She put a trembling hand on the engraved brass handle, and slowly turned it. The latch clicked like a gunshot in the quiet hall, and she jumped. Holding her breath, she waited to hear the jingle of a lamp chain, or the creak of bedsprings. But the only sound was the deep-throated rumble of someone snoring, a low, rattling noise that vibrated through the wood-paneled door like a locomotive. She slowly pushed the door open and tiptoed into the dark bedroom.

Moonlight reflected off the round dresser mirror, illuminating the massive four-poster bed, the cherry armoire, and the red velvet chairs. Luckily, she knew her way around, having changed the linens on a regular basis. On this side of the bed, Aunt Ida lay snoring with her mouth open, and Frownies—skin patches used to prevent wrinkles—stuck to her forehead and the outer corners of her eyes. Uncle Otis lay on his back next to her, his hands crossed over his chest as if he were lying in his coffin. Even in sleep, his face was hard, the sides of his mouth pulled into an elongated frown, making him look like a bullfrog. Emma tiptoed around the foot of the bed and crept past her uncle, keeping her eyes on him in case he stirred.

When she reached the closet, she knelt and felt around on the floor, searching blindly between boots and shoes and slippers. Nothing felt like a camera. She stood and groped through hanging jackets, dresses, and trousers, until her fingers touched the back wall. Slowly and carefully, she felt her way through boxes and bags on the shelf above the clothes, trying not to knock anything over. She was just about to give up and search the floor again when she felt a thin container behind a hatbox. It was the right size for a camera. She pulled it out, moved to the window, and stood in a shaft of moonlight so she could see what she had in her hands. It was the camera case.

She opened the case to make sure the camera was inside. Along with the seal grain leather camera, there was a roll of film. A note fell out of the case and floated to her feet. She picked it up and opened it. The writing was hard to read in the weak light, but the signature was as clear as day: *With all my love, dear Otis. Kisses, Charlotte.*

Emma's stomach twisted. No wonder Uncle Otis was so protective of the camera. It was a gift from Charlotte Gable, the young woman he'd been playing hanky-panky with at the Fourth of July dance. The thought of them together made Emma nauseous and angry. She tiptoed around the end of the bed and left the note on Aunt Ida's nightstand, laying it open beneath her ivory brooch. Then, just as she turned to leave, Uncle Otis grunted and sat up. Emma dropped to the floor and rolled beneath the bed, her heart seizing in her chest. The bedsprings creaked and bulged down on one side. Her uncle got out of bed and stood next to it, his bare feet on the floor, his toenails like yellow claws in the moonlight. He shuffled over to the dresser and stood in front of it, his dry feet scratching like sandpaper on the wood.

"Emma," he said, his voice monotone.

Gooseflesh rose on Emma's arms.

"Be careful," he said.

Then, without another word, he turned away from the dresser and got back in bed. Within seconds, he started to snore. Emma lay on her stomach, the camera clutched to her chest. She had no idea her uncle walked in his sleep. And how bizarre that he was dreaming about her. Then another thought came to her, and tears burned her eyes. She recalled the medium's words: *The dead will use any means possible to be heard.* Could it have been Albert?

If that was you, she thought, *I wish you'd find a way to let me know for sure.*

After waiting another minute to make sure no one else was getting out of bed, Emma shimmied out from beneath the mattress and stood, her eyes fixed on the dresser. The moonlight was stronger now, as if the giant, glowing orb were right outside the window, shining into the room like a thousand lanterns. It reflected off the mirror, making it look like ice. She started toward the door, then froze, certain she saw Albert's face in the mirror. Then she blinked and he was gone. With a lump in her throat, she slipped out into the hall, glancing over her shoulder one last time. The mirror was dark.

CHAPTER 23

Before dawn the next morning, Emma stood in a nightgown in front of Clayton's dresser, weaving her hair into one long braid. She pulled each plait tighter and tighter to make sure the braid wouldn't come loose. When she was finished, she tied a piece of string around the top of the braid just below her earlobe, and another around the other end at her waist. Then she picked up the scissors and cut the whole thing off above the top string, the dull blades chewing through her hair like a beaver chewing on a tree. She put the braid in an old pillowcase and set it aside, remembering the ads she used to see in magazines touting "switches made of splendid quality-selected human hair." The switches were made to match any shade, and prices ranged from ninety-five cents up to twenty-five dollars for a customized style. Maybe Sawyer or Edith could sell her hair to one of the foremen's wives, or trade it for a bag of flour or sugar.

With the braid gone, she held handfuls of what remained of her hair straight out from her head and cut it off. Watching herself in the mirror, she tried to make it as even as possible. Then she trimmed around her ears and clipped her bangs. When she had finished, she wet her hands in the washbasin, ran her fingers through her short tresses to slick them back from her face, and looked in the mirror again. Albert's twin stared back at her, his eyes worried and wide.

Until now she hadn't realized how much they resembled each other. She studied her refection for a long time. *If you're really around,* she thought, *please, help me get through this if you can.*

She closed her eyes and tried to clear her mind. After a minute she pulled on a pair of Sawyer's knee-length cotton underdrawers and tied the drawstring tight around her waist. Then she slipped off her nightgown and pulled on a pair of wool trousers. Behind her, someone rapped lightly on the door.

"You almost ready?" Clayton's voice was muffled and low, and she imagined him out in the hall, leaning forward, his wide, work-worn hands on the doorframe.

"Not yet," she said. Earlier she'd cut a burlap sack into long, wide strips. Now, she picked the strips off Clayton's bed and laid one across her bare nipples, reaching around her back and winding it around front again, trying to bind her breasts. Chances were no one would notice her small bosom beneath a thick work shirt, but she wasn't going to take any chances. Except the strips kept slipping out of place, and she couldn't get them tight enough.

"I need help," she said over her shoulder.

"You want me to come in there?" he said. He sounded surprised and unsure.

"Well, you can't help me from out there."

The door creaked open, and she watched over her shoulder as he slowly came into the room, his eyes lowered. He closed the door behind him, then looked at her and gasped. "Your hair," he said.

"Never mind that," she said. "It barely fit beneath a cap, and I can't take the risk."

"What do you need help with?"

She was standing next to his bed, her naked back to him, holding the burlap over her breasts with one arm. "I can't pull this tight enough," she said. She reached back with her free hand to give him the end of one strip.

He cleared his throat and came up behind her. "This is suicide. If they catch you . . ."

"Did you tell the miners' wives I was sick and won't be doing lessons for a while?"

"Yes."

"What did you tell Sawyer and Edith?"

"That you're going to work because we need the money. They know better than to tell anybody our business. And the little ones don't understand that women don't belong in the mines."

"What if someone slips up?"

"I told them we'd all be in a heap of trouble if they squealed, most likely put out of our house and sent packing with nothing but the clothes on our backs. That scared them enough to keep quiet."

"I'm sorry," she said.

"For what?"

"That you had to lie to them because of me."

"You don't have to do this," he said. "We can tell everyone you chopped your hair off to get rid of lice."

"You should tell the little ones that anyway. And yes, I do have to do this. Now help me out, will you?"

"What do you want me to do?"

"Pull these tight, like you're lacing up a corset."

"Lacing up a corset?" He sounded bewildered.

"Tie them once in the back, tightly, then hand them round front again."

Clayton did as he was told, and she lifted her elbows, reaching down to take the burlap around front and hand it back again. His warm arms brushed against her bare skin, and the heat of desire flashed across her chest and belly. She fought the urge to turn around and kiss him, to let the burlap fall to the floor and press her bare breasts against his shirt, to feel his heart beating against hers. But this was not the time or place. This was the bedroom he had shared with his wife, and there were children in the other room. Besides, no matter how scared she was, making love to him wouldn't stop the inevitable. She needed to do this before she changed her mind. And they couldn't be late for work. She was here to help the breaker boys, not throw herself at Clayton. Besides, what would she do if he pushed her away?

He pulled the burlap tighter and tighter until her breasts were squished to her chest. "Am I doing it right?" he said. "Is it too tight?"

She inhaled, filling her lungs partway to make sure she could breathe, unaware until that moment that she had been close to hyperventilating. "It's fine."

When he finished, he tied the ends of the last strips together and tucked them into the waist of her trousers. "Now what?"

Emma pulled on a long-sleeved shirt, then turned to face him. "Well?"

"Well what?"

"Do I look like a boy?"

He stared at her, his eyes locked on her face. "I guess so, especially with your hair chopped off."

"That's not what I'm talking about," she said. "Look down here." She pointed to her chest.

He dropped his eyes to her bosom and quickly looked away. "Yup."

"What does that mean?"

"It worked," he said. "You can't tell you have . . . um . . ."

"Breasts?"

"Yes." His face went red.

She grinned. "Thanks. Now I just need a dinner pail and a canteen, and I'm ready."

"What about the camera?"

"I've been practicing with it, opening the locking lever and pulling out the lens panel as fast as I can. I'll have to wind the key to get to the next exposure, and I'm not sure how long that takes, but I'm going to take more than one picture, so I'll have to take my chances."

"That's not what I mean. How you going to sneak it into the breaker?"

"For now I just need to get inside," she said. "I want to learn my way around and figure out the best time and place to take pictures. Then, when I'm ready, I'll either hide it under my jacket or put it in my dinner pail."

He gaped at her. "You're going in the breaker more than once?"

"Yes. There's no sense in doing this if the photos don't turn out. And I want to take some pictures of the boys inside the mine too, the nippers and spraggers."

"How are you going to do that?" he said. "Breaker boys don't usually go into the mine. And I've been thinking. How are you going to get the pictures developed?"

"If I can't figure out how to get the film developed, I'll send it with the letter and convince the people at the *New York Times* that they need to see what's on it."

"All right. Do you have a flash for the camera? It's dark inside the breaker."

"The sun must come through the windows at some point, doesn't it?"

He paused, thinking. "Maybe for a few minutes, when it's high in the sky. But the windows are pretty dirty."

"The pictures don't have to be perfect. After the *Times* sees them, maybe they'll send a professional photographer out here to take better ones. And as far as getting inside the mine, we'll figure that out later."

"I don't know," Clayton said. "Maybe we should think this through a little more before we go off half-cocked."

"I'm not thinking about anything but helping the breaker boys."

"I know," he said. "But you're a . . ."

"I'm a what?" she said. "A woman?"

"Yes. What if something happens? What if there's an accident?"

Emma turned away from him, picked the belt up off his bed, and threaded it through the loops of her pants. "If something happens, at least I tried."

He came up behind her then and turned her around, his strong, gentle hands on her shoulders.

"Emma Malloy," he said. "I think you're the bravest woman I've ever known." Admiration flickered in his eyes, but there was something else too. It was the same look her mother had on her face when Emma collapsed next to Albert's casket. It was the fear of losing someone you loved more than yourself.

Emma started to tremble. If Clayton said he loved her, if there was the slightest chance that they could be together, she didn't know what she would do. She'd already lost so much. Would she be brave enough to go through with her plan and go inside the breaker? What kind of fool would risk her one chance at true love? And even if she survived going into the breaker, was she willing to live the rest of her life in constant fear of losing him to a mining accident? She took a deep breath and tried to pull herself together. This wasn't about her. It was about the breaker boys.

"Or maybe the most foolish," she said.

"Just be careful. I don't know what I'd do if something happened to you."

With that, despite her attempt at being rational, waves of elation washed through her. Finally she knew how he felt about her. Her heart swelled in her chest, overflowing with love and relief and fear. It was nearly more than she could bear. What was going to happen after they helped the breaker boys and miners? Could she stay in Coal River, knowing she'd be living in constant terror of losing Clayton? Or would she be able to convince him to leave, to find a safer job someplace else so they could grow old together? She tried to smile, to reassure them both, but it didn't work. Her eyes filled with tears. Then he was kissing her, and she forgot all about being afraid.

Emma stood beside Clayton inside the colliery office, a clapboard building near the mouth of the main shaft, between the engine house and the powder shop. Coal dust had seeped into every crack and crevice, staining the floors, ceilings, and walls, making the wooden planks look like slabs of gray granite. A chalkboard on one wall read:

Steam Coal: 4–6 inches. Broken Coal: 3–5 inches. Egg Coal: 2–2.5 inches. Stove Coal: 1–1.6 inches. Chestnut Coal: less than an inch. Pea Coal: less than a half inch. Culm: rock, slate, dirt, clay, ash.

Pulling Sawyer's cap low on her forehead, she stuffed her hands in her pockets to keep them from shaking. Along with one of Sawyer's heavy jackets, she was wearing hobnailed boots that were a size too big, and a wool scarf around her neck. Clayton had said she would need the scarf to put over her nose and mouth while working, and even though the inside of the breaker was hot as a furnace, she'd need the extra layers of clothing to protect her skin from the sulfur in the coal dust.

The pit boss stood on the other side of the counter, squinting at her over the top of his round glasses.

"This is my nephew," Clayton said. He put a strong hand on Emma's shoulder, shaking her to show how sturdy his nephew was. "Come over from Wilkes-Barre. He's staying with me now and needs work."

"You got a name, boy?" the pit boss said.

"He don't talk much," Clayton said. "Had the fever when he was small. Name's Emmet."

"How old?" the pit boss said, reaching below the counter for the necessary paperwork.

"Old enough," Clayton said.

"You got proof he is who you say he is?" the pit boss said. "Birth certificate or somethin'?"

"No, sir," Clayton said. He pulled a letter from his pocket and began to unfold it. "All I have is this note from my sister, written on her deathbed asking me to take good care of her boy."

The pit boss waved the letter away and started filling out Emma's working papers. "You ever work in a coal mine, Emmet?"

She shook her head.

"We lost a nipper yesterday," the pit boss said. "Idiot fell asleep and didn't hear the mine cars racing down the track until it was too late. He opened the door, but he weren't no match for a four-ton coal car. Think you can handle the job, Emmet? Of course you have to listen to the mountain while you're sitting there too, and warn the miners if you hear the gangway roof working."

"I don't think that's the best place for him," Clayton said. He tapped his ear. "Fever affected his hearing a bit too. Seems I recall there was always room in the breaker for another set of hands."

"All right," the pit boss said. "Take him over to the breaker. I'll let Walt know he's coming."

"Will do," Clayton said, and turned to leave

Emma followed Clayton out of the office and toward the breaker, rivers of sweat running down her back. The first coal cars of the day rumbled out of the mine and traveled up a set of steep, narrow tracks, pulled by heavy cables to the top of the breaker. Sawyer was waiting near the breaker steps, waving beside a gang of boys. Emma kept her head down, hoping no one would recognize her. When she and Clayton reached Sawyer, he pulled a folded bag out of his pocket, shoved a wad of chewing tobacco between his gum and cheek, and offered it to her.

She shook her head.

"If you want to keep the coal dust out of your throat," Sawyer said. "You better take a pinch."

She looked at Clayton.

"He's right," Clayton said.

Emma reached into the bag, pulled out a clump of the dried, red leaves, and pushed them inside her cheek. The sharp tang of tobacco juice seeped over her teeth and tongue, making her saliva run and filling her mouth with a bitter taste, like a mixture of dirt and prunes and rotten wood. She swallowed.

"Don't swallow!" Sawyer said.

She spit on the ground and wiped her lips, her stomach churning. "I can't do it," she whispered. "It tastes horrible."

"You'll get used to it," Clayton said. "It's better than having a mouthful of coal dust. Just keep spitting."

She spit again, trying not to gag. Then the boys started moving toward the stairs on the outside of the breaker. Sawyer motioned for her to follow.

"Just do what you're told," Clayton said. "Every time. And if Mr. Flint is making the rounds, keep your head down." He gave her a watery smile, squeezed her shoulder, and left.

Emma followed Sawyer up the steep, narrow steps on the outside of the breaker, cringing as the bone-dry staircase creaked beneath her boots. Gripping the iron railing with one hand, she hoped no one would see the terror in her eyes. The smell of wet timber and coal dust filled her nostrils. As she climbed higher and higher, the colliery opened up below her like a monochromatic painting where everything was various shades of gray and black—the culm piles and boiler house, the lamp house and carpenter shops, the silt ponds and mule yard.

She pictured the other boys working inside the mines, the nippers and spraggers and mule handlers. She wasn't sure which would be more terrifying: climbing up the side of this multistory building that looked ready to collapse in a pile of splinters and coal dust, or riding the trip cars deep into the belly of the mine, dropping thousands of feet into the earth. She imagined water dripping from the rocks, rats scurrying along the dark tunnels.

Then she swallowed and was instantly dizzy. For a second she thought she might throw up. She spit the wad of chewing tobacco out over the steps, wiped her chin, and pulled her scarf over her nose and mouth. The tobacco was too strong, and she wouldn't be able to work if she was nauseous.

When she reached the flight outside what she thought was the fifth floor, the machinery inside the breaker began to churn, giant belts screeching and whirring, colossal gears grinding. The monstrous building was beginning to wake. She held the railing tighter, certain the breaker was going to fall apart, or the stairs were going to collapse beneath her feet. The entire structure started shaking and moving, as if it were about to grow legs and climb up the mountain. It was all she could do not to turn around, fight her way past the others, and run back down the stairs. Her legs felt heavy as stone, but she gritted her teeth and kept going, trying to remind herself why she was there.

Finally, she reached the entrance and followed Sawyer inside. The grating roll of the crusher was deafening. Emma put her hands over her ears; the boys laughed and pointed. She dropped her arms and looked around, berating herself for drawing attention. Blackened beams held up the high walls, and a fine dust fell from the shaking rafters like black snow. Faint beams of sunlight filtered in through a soot-covered set of multipaned windows on the far wall, and pitted metal shades with grimy bulbs hung from the high ceiling, giving off a weak yellow light. Her heart dropped. Maybe Clayton was right. The inside of the breaker was darker than she'd imagined.

No, she told herself. *It's still early. The sun might get stronger as the day goes on. Besides, it's too late to turn back now.*

At the top of the breaker, the coal cars were tipped, and tons of coal tumbled into a wide iron channel, roaring into the building like a black avalanche. Before the coal went into the crusher, men and older boys picked out the largest pieces of slate. Some of the coal chunks were as big as a bull, heavy enough to crush a grown man. After being broken up by the great teeth of the crusher, the coal streamed into iron troughs lined by conveyor belts. The troughs ran side by side at steep angles down through the building like giant slides. Rivers of coal shook and rattled on the belts, filling the air with clouds of smoke and black dust. Each trough was flanked by smaller chutes on one side, and a set of wooden steps on the other. Across the tops of the troughs were wide planks set at regular intervals, like rungs on a ladder.

Between the black rivers of coal, three men with gray mustaches and bristled chins stood holding brooms on the steps. They watched the boys with pitiless eyes, their pallid faces weathered by hard labor and buried grief. A fourth man sat on the edge of a trough, grinning and tapping the iron with a long stick. Two of his front teeth were missing.

"Get to work!" he shouted. "I'll be checking the first run in ten minutes! And it better not be full of culm!"

The boys scurried up the steps and found their places on the planks. They sat down and straddled the troughs, five and six in a line, one above the other like passengers on a carnival ride. Sawyer motioned for Emma to follow, then climbed halfway up and sat on a wooden plank. She clambered up the steps behind him, pulling her scarf tightly over her face. Another boy sat on a plank above Sawyer, and another sat below. She stood on the steps, awaiting further instruction. Sawyer braced his boots against the coal-filled conveyor belt, using his feet to slow the flow.

"Pick out the slate, clay, and rock!" he shouted. "And throw it in the culm chute!" He picked up a piece of clay to show her, then tossed it into the narrower trough. "Then let the coal go by. Like this!" He lifted his feet and let the coal continue on to the boy below him.

"You there!" a breaker boss shouted. "At chute five!" Emma turned to look. It was the gap-toothed boss, pointing his long stick in her direction. She lifted her chin to let him know she heard him. "Get to work!"

Emma looked around for an empty seat. The only available plank was near the top of the breaker, right below the crusher. She climbed the steps, straddled the iron chute, and sat down, coal dust clogging her eyes, nose, and throat. The snarl and roar of the crusher was deafening, like dynamite repeatedly going off inside her ears. The breaker boss lumbered up the steps and stopped beside her, towering above her head.

"By the time that coal gets down to the final boy, it needs to be pure!" he shouted. "Pick fast and don't make their job harder, or you'll be seeing the end of my stick!"

She nodded and turned back to the trough. The breaker boss cracked his stick on the edge of the chute near her foot, then made his way back down the steps. She clenched her jaw and reached into the rushing river of black coal.

CHAPTER 24

That evening, Emma sat at Clayton's kitchen table in her work clothes, her coat and scarf in a dust-encrusted heap on the floor. She bit down on a leather strap, tears of agony streaming down her cheeks. After ten hours in the breaker spent sitting on a wooden plank and crouching over an iron chute, her back ached, and the bones in her buttocks screamed in pain, as if knives were being pushed into her muscles. Her shoulders and legs trembled and throbbed, and she felt as weak as the old women on widow's row. Her ears were ringing, and she could still see the black river of coal in her mind, rushing between her feet and legs, her filthy, blood-spattered hands reaching in over and over and over and over. But all of that was nothing compared to the pain in her fingers.

With a worried look on his face, Clayton took her hand and slowly lowered it into a basin of water on the table. She grimaced and tried to pull away, the sting of tar soap like needles in her fingertips. Clayton gently held on and forced her fingers below the surface. She let out a tortured moan, grateful for the leather strap that stifled her scream. Earlier, Clayton had instructed the children to go outside and told Sawyer to knock if they needed to come back in, but only if there was an emergency. Then he locked the doors.

"Still want to go through with this?" Clayton said.

Emma hung her head and closed her eyes, tears and sweat running off her face. She clenched her stomach, trying to hold on to consciousness. In spite of that, she managed a nod.

"Give me your other hand," he said. "Best get this over with as fast as possible."

She let him put her other hand into the basin, groaning as soon as her fingertips hit the water.

"Hold on for another minute," he said. "We've got to get the sulfur off your skin."

The burning was like nothing she'd ever felt before. If she didn't know better, she'd have sworn someone had cut off the tops of her fingers and rubbed the bloody stubs in a vat of vinegar and salt. How could anyone think it was acceptable to put young boys through such agony? How desperate did a mother have to be to see her child in so much pain, then send him back for more the next day? It was unimaginable.

After what seemed like an eternity, Clayton retrieved two clean rags from beneath the sink, spread them on the table, and gently lifted her fingers from the water. Fighting the instinct to yank her hands away, she let him place them on the rags. The water in the basin swirled red with blood.

"Don't move," he said. He pulled the curtains closed and filled the washtub on the floor with water from the stove, then he tenderly covered her hands with the clean rags until he had wrapped them up like mittens.

"Can you stand?" he said.

Emma nodded and pushed herself up on weak legs. The leather strap fell from her mouth. Clayton put his arm around her waist and led her over to the washtub.

"I'll help you get washed," he said. "But you've got to get out of those clothes."

With tears of pain still blurring her vision, she lifted her elbows so he could remove her shirt. He pulled the dust-covered shirt out of the waist of her pants, then held the ends of the sleeves while she pulled her arms free. Despite the rags around her hands, the slightest contact with the sleeve material felt like a hot iron searing her fingertips.

"Close your eyes," he said.

Emma squeezed her eyes shut, and Clayton pulled the shirt over her head. As the shirt came off, coal dust went into her mouth and nose. She sputtered and spit and, even though she was still wearing the burlap binding, instinctively covered her breasts with one arm. Clayton wet a rag and wiped her lips and eyelids, then put a bar of soap in the tub, swished it around to make suds, and gently finished washing her face, careful not to get soap and dust in her eyes. Then he told her to kneel on the floor and bend over the basin. Without a word, he knelt beside her and washed her short hair, scrubbing the grime from around her neck and shoulders, his strong hands massaging her sore muscles. When he had finished, he helped her stand again. Then he unbuckled her belt, pulled down her trousers, and instructed her to step out of them.

In too much pain to care that she would be half naked in front of him, Emma did as she was told. Even though she had been wearing two layers of clothes, a fine black powder coated her skin and underdrawers.

Clayton gestured toward the washtub. "Get in."

She stepped over the edge of the wooden tub and stood in the water. With gentle hands, Clayton washed her shoulders and arms. Gritty water cascaded down her body, making her feel like a porcelain statue in a muddy fountain. He ran the wet rag under the top and bottom edges of the burlap binding, his warm fingers touching her waist and the slight swell above her cleavage. She started to shiver.

"I'm nearly done," he said.

By the time he got to her legs, her cotton drawers were soaked though with water, and she worried he could see through the thin material. He ran the wet rag along the waist of the drawers, his fingers skimming just below her navel. Then he knelt and rolled the legs of the drawers up as far as they would go and washed her knees and thighs. Her face grew warm and she looked at the ceiling, trying to think of something else. Despite her throbbing fingers, a tingling sensation filled her pelvis, and all pain retreated from the forefront of her mind. It was as if her hands had disappeared or fallen asleep, and the only thing she could feel were his hands on her body. She struggled to breathe normally.

Clayton stopped. "Am I hurting you?"

"No, I'm fine."

He finished rinsing her legs and straightened. "I'm sorry," he said. "I'm afraid I can't do a proper job while you're still . . . when you still have your . . ."

"While I still have my drawers on?"

He nodded. "And the binding."

She bit down on her lip. She had imagined undressing in front of him numerous times, just not like this. But the coal dust felt like grit on her legs, and the sulfur was already burning the delicate skin around her nipples and the tender, inside creases of her thighs. It was bad enough that her fingers felt like they were on fire; the last thing she needed was burning skin anywhere else.

"Then I'll take them off," she said. "But you'll have to untie the burlap for me."

His face flushed, and he shook his head.

"It won't be the first time you've seen a woman naked, will it?"

"No, but I don't want you to think—"

"It doesn't matter," she said, stepping out of the washtub. "Please. My skin is burning. Just get fresh water, will you?"

"Are you sure?"

She nodded. "I'm sure."

Clayton untied the burlap, leaving it in place, then emptied the tub with a bucket, tossing the water out the back window until it was light enough to pick up. While he was busy, Emma turned her back to him and let the binding fall from her chest. Just as she suspected, black dust encrusted her nipples, and the skin was tender and sore everywhere the burlap had touched. When she turned around again, she crossed her arms over her breasts. Clayton glanced at her once, then quickly looked away.

Once the tub was empty, Clayton refilled it, his eyes downcast, his face serious. He dropped the washrag and bar of soap back in and swished them around to make new suds. When that was done, he straightened and turned away from her.

"Go on," he said. "Get in and sit."

"I'm still wearing drawers."

"You can't . . . take them off yourself?"

"No. You wrapped my fingers. I can't use my hands. Just untie them for me."

Clayton turned around and moved toward her, his eyes on the floor, her feet, anywhere but her face or bare chest. She lifted her arms and he closed his eyes and reached out, his big hands fumbling on her ribs, her hips, and finally her waist. With hesitant fingers, he felt his way around front to the drawstring, untied it, and pulled the waist open as far as it would go. Then he stepped back and turned around again. Using her wrists, Emma rolled the top edge of the underwear down. But the soggy material twisted and got caught on her wet skin.

"I can't do it," she said. "Just yank them off."

"Are you sure?"

"Please. I'm so tired."

"Turn around first."

She turned, and he came up behind her and tugged on the legs of the drawers. They slid to her ankles and she stepped out of them, trying not to picture her naked buttocks in his face. He spun around again and stood with his back to her. She got into the water and sat down Indian style, the warm, soapy water like liquid silk on her irritated skin. Her white knees stuck out of the suds, resting on the wooden tub walls.

"I can't wash my chest," she said.

"Can't you just sit forward and rinse yourself off?"

"The water isn't deep enough. Please, I just want to get this over with. Close your eyes if it makes you feel better."

He sighed, then came over and squatted next to the tub, keeping his face turned to one side. "Where's the washrag?"

"I'm sitting on it."

His shoulders dropped. "Lord in heaven."

"Listen to me," she said. "It doesn't matter. None of this matters. I trust you."

Clayton looked at her then, his eyes filled with affection. "I'm glad you trust me," he said. "But I never should have let you go through with this in the first place."

"It was my decision."

"But I hate seeing you in pain."

"I'll be fine. Really. Who am I to complain when little boys suffer like this every day?"

He kept his eyes locked on hers for a long moment, as if deciding whether to kiss her, then reached into the water and pulled the washrag out from beneath her thigh. Washing her shoulders again, he squeezed the rag and let the soapy water run down her chest. This time, he watched what he was doing, his jaw tense.

"You're going to have to do better than that," she said. "The coal dust is sticking to my skin."

He dunked the rag in the water again and swept it over her breasts. She held her breath and tried to think of something besides what he was doing. It was no use. She was mentally and physically exhausted, putting all senses on high alert. The gentleness of his touch and the soft, soapy rag against her skin took over all thought. Right now the only thing she wanted was to be in his arms, to feel his warm skin against hers, his strong hands keeping her safe. Unable to hold back any longer, she put her wrist behind his neck and pulled him close. His brows shot up in surprise, but then he dropped the washrag, stroked the back of her head, and leaned in to kiss her softly on the lips. She trembled and kissed him back, all pain disappearing into the pull of desire.

He groaned and kissed her harder, his mouth open and hungry. After a while, he pulled away and lifted her to her feet. Retrieving a towel from the back of a kitchen chair, he wrapped it around her shoulders. She stepped out of the washtub and stood near the coal stove to let him dry her off. Moving slowly, he gently rubbed the towel over her skin, softly caressing her arms and breasts through the thick material. She put her head back and sighed, her breath heavy and deep. He kissed her collarbone and neck, then wrapped the towel around her shoulders again, lifted her into his arms, and carried her into his bedroom. When he put her down next to his bed, he let the towel drop to the floor. He pulled back the blanket, guided her back on the sheets, and placed her hands above her head, where they rested on his pillow. Then he locked the door, took off his shirt, and unbuckled his belt, his eyes fixed on her face.

Emma shivered in anticipation as she watched him undress. She wished she could run her fingers through his thick hair, and touch his skin. He climbed in next to her, propping himself up on one elbow.

"Are you sure about this?" he said. "You're in pain and exhausted. I don't want to hurt you."

"I've never been more certain of anything in my life," she said.

He drew closer and gently moved above her, his warm body finally touching hers. He kissed her mouth, his heart pounding against her chest, then made his way down her throat toward her breasts. She shuddered and looped her arms around his head. He moved up to kiss her again, and their heads turned and rolled as their kissing became greedy. When he pulled away and stared into her eyes, she thought his look of uncertainty mirrored her own. She'd always believed she would lose her virginity to the man she married, but right now she wanted nothing more than to give herself to Clayton. There was no going back now. She pulled him to her, kissing his face.

Beyond all the books she had read, she had no experience at all. But it did not surprise her how clearly she knew what she wanted. They began to make love, the bed creaking with their movement. Even if they couldn't be together forever, at least she would have this moment. Right now that was all that mattered.

Later, Clayton went out to the kitchen to feed the children, then returned to sit on the edge of his bed and rub goose grease on Emma's fingertips. He undid the rags and started on her right hand. She gritted her teeth, trying not to cry out. It seemed like the pain was worse than ever.

"This will help them heal," Clayton said. "But the next few days are going to be even harder."

"I know. But I think I might be able to take pictures right before . . ."

He pressed too hard on one finger and she drew in a sharp breath.

"Sorry," he said. "Keep talking. Maybe it will help."

Emma tried to concentrate. "Right before the midday break. That's when the breaker bosses leave the steps, get their dinner pails, and wait by the door until the crusher stops. I'll do it when they're not looking."

He finished putting the goose grease on her fingers and stood. "Just do it soon, so you can get out of there."

"I've got to wait for the light to be just right," she said. "Besides, it might be a while before I can push the damn exposure level on the camera anyway." She held up her fingers and gave him a weak smile.

He kissed her forehead. "I'll bring you in some dinner, then you've got to get some sleep."

"I've got my own bed."

He shook his head. "You're not sleeping on a wooden floor anymore. And I hate to say it, but you need to rest so you can go back to work in the morning."

CHAPTER 25

Over the next few days, the sky was overcast. Then it rained for two days. Not only did the foul weather make it seem like the middle of the night inside the breaker, but it made it impossible for Emma to use the camera. The photos had to be taken on a bright, sunny day, when the inside of the building was filled with the most daylight possible.

Every day she wrapped her uncle's camera in a rag and took it to work tucked into the waist of her trousers and hidden beneath her jacket. Every day, she sat at the top of chute five, praying for the sky to clear so she could pull the camera out when the sun was at its highest in the windows, turn in her seat, and take pictures.

In the meantime, while sorting coal and trying to keep her hands and feet from being torn off by conveyor belts, she paid attention to the bosses' routines and noticed what sorts of things drew the boys' attention away from their job. When the bosses were distracted, she sent pieces of pure anthracite down the culm chute for the miners' wives to cull from the banks, and picked through the coal with one hand, switching back and forth to give her fingertips a chance to heal. Even with nightly applications of goose grease, she wondered if her burning, cracked skin would ever scab over and harden. At mealtime she could barely hold a fork or a piece of cornbread. How did young boys face this day after day?

While they were working, the breaker boys gestured with their hands behind the bosses' backs, fingers flying to make letters and communicate with one another. During the midday break, they ate their meager lunches with filthy hands, then smoked cigarettes, played baseball and tag when it wasn't raining, or ran into the machine shops to get nuts and pieces of iron to throw at the bosses when they weren't looking. They played pranks on one another, throwing balls made of grease and coal at the back of someone's head, nailing dinner pails to the floor, or tying a boy's jacket in knots when he removed it during lunch. Luckily, Sawyer had told them that "Emmet" was a new orphan and didn't talk much because he'd had the fever, and they left Emma alone.

She watched from the side, amazed that the boys had enough strength to do anything more than rest and eat. It seemed as though they had become like their fingertips, both cracked and bleeding, and hard and calloused at the same time.

Every day she looked for Michael, ready to turn away if she saw him. More than likely, he worked on a different floor in the breaker, but she worried he would recognize her if they got too close. Then one day she thought she saw him, eating his lunch on an empty dynamite box near the train tracks. His hat was off, his thick dark hair sticking up in all directions, and a pair of crutches lay next to him on the box. Plus, he was the only breaker boy eating alone. But his face was black like all the others, and she couldn't tell for sure. Still, there was something about the way he held his head that looked familiar. Luckily, he sat in the same spot every day, making it easy to keep her distance.

When the breaker bosses cracked whips and brooms across the boys' backs, it took all her effort not to stand up and push them down the steps. Daily, she had to fight the urge to scream at the gap-toothed boss when he rapped his long stick across a boy's knuckles. She was shocked and horrified to see that the boys were abused for not working fast enough, for turning their heads and talking, even for coughing too long. How was it possible that these men, who had worked in the breaker when they were young, showed no mercy for those who labored there now? Had they forgotten what it felt like to be afraid and in pain? Had they forgotten the need for sunshine and fresh air, the desire to swim and fish and do all the things young children were supposed to do? Had all those years in darkness turned their hearts to stone, like the pressure of the earth turned tree roots and fallen branches to coal? She knew the men needed their jobs, and Mr. Flint probably fired them if the coal wasn't pure, but working in the breaker was hard and dangerous enough. Was it necessary to cause more pain in the process? Or did they believe they were readying the boys for the hard life ahead? Every time one of the breaker boys cried out in agony, Emma blinked back tears. It had to end.

By Tuesday of her second week, she wondered if the sun would ever come out again. It rained all morning, and during the lunch break, the sky was still filled with high clouds. Then, an hour later, the sun finally slipped out from behind a thunderhead, shining in the highest corner of the grimy windows and filling the breaker with gray light. She touched the bulge beneath her jacket, wondering if she should get the camera out now or wait for a brighter day. Then one of the bosses shouted and she jumped.

"Wake up, you lazy shit!"

Emma glanced over her shoulder, her heart pounding in dread. It was the gap-toothed boss. But he wasn't talking to her. He was standing beside a young boy at the bottom of chute two who looked to be about seven or eight. The boy jerked awake and straightened, his eyes bloodshot and puffy.

"Yes, sir," he said.

"This is the third time I've caught you dozing today," the boss said.

"I'm feeling sick," the boy said. "Can't get warm and can't stay awake."

"I'll keep you awake," the boss said. "Put your hand right here." He tapped the step with his stick, parallel to where the boy was sitting.

"I won't doze off again," the boy said. "I promise."

The boss lifted his stick and cracked it across the boy's back.

The boy cried out in pain. Most of the breaker boys had turned to watch, while others kept working, their heads down. The other bosses and a foreman were on the floor of the room, leaning on brooms and talking. Emma unbuttoned her coat and fumbled to unwrap the camera, her hands shaking. She had waited long enough. She opened the locking level, pulled out the lens panel, and turned in her seat, the camera held close in her lap.

"Put your hand on the damn step!" the gap-toothed boss yelled.

The sick boy did as he was told, grimacing and knowing he had no choice. The gap-toothed boss lifted his hobnailed boot and stomped on the boy's fingers. The boy howled and hunched over, his face twisting in agony as the boss pressed his foot down harder and harder. Emma pointed the camera at them, struggling to hold it steady. She pushed the exposure level, waited for the shutter to close, then faced forward again and wound the key to get to the next picture, coughing over the winding noise, even though no one would hear it above the crusher and the boy's tormented wails. Then she twisted in her seat again and pointed the camera toward the far corner of the breaker, hoping to capture several boys and chutes at once. She took the picture, turned forward again, and wound the roll of film to the next exposure. She did this four more times, moving the camera right and left, her entire body quaking.

Finally, the gap-toothed boss took his boot off the boy's hand. The boy slumped forward and held his bleeding fingers in his lap, sooty tears streaming down his black face. Just then, a man in a top hat and three-piece suit entered the breaker through a side door. One of the bosses left his broom and hurried over to talk to him. It was Mr. Flint. Emma spun forward, pushed the camera closed, and shoved it back inside her jacket. She glanced around to make sure no one had seen her taking pictures. The gap-toothed boss was going down the steps while the rest of the boys went back to work. A few of the younger ones were weeping. Emma let out a trembling sigh, her teeth chattering with a mixture of anger and fear. It was all she could do not to get up and push the gap-toothed boss down the stairs. But for now she just had to get through the rest of the day.

She couldn't even think about what would happen if the photos didn't turn out. There were twelve exposures on the film, so counting the two of her aunt, uncle, and Percy on the Fourth of July, and the six she took today, she had four left. She just had to find a way to get inside the mine to take pictures of the nippers and spraggers so she could fill the roll. But instead of worrying, she went back to work.

All of a sudden, the crushers and shakers slowed and ground to a halt. The entire breaker shuddered, like a giant beast shaking off water after a swim. Coal dust drifted down from the rafters like black rain. The boys straightened and looked around, confusion lining their faces. Emma stayed hunched over, one arm over the camera inside her jacket. Panic exploded in her mind. Had someone seen her taking pictures? Is that why they'd shut down the breaker? Was she about to feel the end of a whip, or worse? Or had someone discovered her identity? Maybe Mr. Flint was here to take her to jail.

"Why are you shutting down?" Mr. Flint bellowed up from below.

"There's a boy in the crusher!" a man shouted above Emma's head. "He was oiling the machinery and fell in!"

Emma gasped, a jolt of horror rushing through her body. Several of the boys covered their ears and squeezed their eyes closed. Some cried out in alarm.

One of the boys stood, his eyes filled with fear. "Who was it?" he shouted.

"Jesus Christ!" Mr. Flint roared. He started toward the bottom of the coal chutes. "You boys, shut up and get back to work!" Then he yelled up to the man above Emma's head, "Start her back up and keep working! You can take care of the body at the end of the shift!"

Emma pushed her elbows into her sides, struggling to stay in her seat. She wanted to run down the steps and beat Hazard Flint with a stick until he bled. Maybe the breaker boys would help by holding him down. Then the giant gears above her started grinding again, the crusher turned, and she heard what sounded like ribs splintering. She hung her head and put a hand over her mouth, trying not to be sick. The conveyor belt between her legs started moving again. When she could breathe without gagging, she gritted her teeth and reached into the trough, tears stinging her eyes. She grabbed a piece of slate and immediately dropped it. The river of coal was streaked with bits of ragged flesh and glistening blood.

CHAPTER 26

A week after taking pictures inside the breaker, Emma made her way into the mouth of the Bleak Mountain Mine, trying to stay hidden between Nally and Clayton, her eyes on the ground. All around her, miners, nippers, spraggers, and mule drivers carried bar-down tools and tamping rods, cans of blasting powder and Davy lamps, drills and picks, sprags and bullwhips. Together they trudged into the dark shaft, talking and coughing, their dinner pails and tools and canteens clanging, their boots crunching on the loose slag. On one hand, she was relieved to be finished at the breaker. On the other, the thought of traveling hundreds of feet into the earth, moving beneath a massive mountain into long black tunnels of coal and rock, made her insides feel like they were being stirred in an iron kettle. She pressed her lips together and tried to breathe slowly, already feeling dizzy.

The previous night, when Clayton had said a roof collapse had crushed Nally's helper's leg while he was robbing the pillars—removing coal from support pillars in a spent shaft, sometimes supporting the roof again with lumber, sometimes letting the roof collapse—Emma knew it was the perfect opportunity to go inside the mine and take pictures of the spraggers and nippers. Clayton had already explained that miners often had "butties," or helpers, to carry their tools, fill lamps with oil, inspect work areas for poisonous gases and unstable roofs, and share in the miner's pay. Sometimes miners used their sons, who were only allowed to load their fathers' cars. That way, if the boy got injured or killed, the mining company could say he wasn't on the payroll and had no business being down there in the first place.

But when Emma suggested she could replace Nally's butty, Clayton was against it. Then she threatened to go to the Irishman's house and offer to be his "free" helper, and Clayton agreed to invite Nally over to discuss it. A few hours later, in the middle of the night, the three of them sat at the kitchen table, making plans over a growler of beer.

"Emma seems to think that if we get the attention of the newspapers," Clayton said, "Hazard Flint will be less likely to retaliate when we move forward with the strike."

"I like the way ye think," Nally said, his eyes shining with enthusiasm. "The old Irish try just doesn't seem to work around here."

"The new shaft, number six, will be the least crowded," Clayton said. "There's less chance of being caught there."

"The biggest problem will be having enough light to take pictures," Emma said. "Can we take in extra lanterns?"

"Don't worry about that, lassie," Nally said. "I'll make sure ye have all the light you need."

"You can't breathe a word of this," Clayton said to Nally. "You know how the miners feel about women in the mines. We have to use every caution."

"If I betray ye," Nally said, "may the curse of Mary Malone and her nine blind illegitimate children chase me so far over the hills of Damnation that the Lord himself can't find me with a telescope." He finished the rest of the beer and slammed the growler on the table.

Now, Emma lumbered along the railroad ties, jostled between men and boys funneling down the timber-lined gangway like rats entering a sewer. When they reached the first chamber, the miners stopped at the inside boss's desk to turn in their brass tags. The inside boss placed the numbered tags on a pegboard, to be picked up later when the miners left for the day. If a tag was still there at the end of the shift, the inside boss went looking for the missing man.

After the inside boss's desk, the miners went to the Dutch door of the fire boss's room to pick up the safety lamps used to check for dangerous gases. Beside the door, Uncle Otis stood talking to the fire boss, his arms crossed. Emma dropped her eyes and kept moving.

Clayton had told her that the inside of the mine was like a vast underground city, and the miners were extracting coal from numerous beds on different levels, like the floors of an apartment building. Shafts, chutes, and slopes, like a black labyrinth, connected everything. She imagined the noise would be deafening, but to her surprise, the mines were echoless, the tramp of boots and the clang of shovels and picks absorbed by the thick earth and layers of coal.

Farther in, they passed the mule stables and the emergency hospital, which was nothing more than a whitewashed timber room with a red cross over the doorframe. The door was open. A man lay moaning on a cot inside, his forehead wrapped in white gauze, his arm in a sling. A bald man wearing dirty white overalls dipped a wooden blade into a metal jar and applied a black tincture to an oozing wound on the moaning man's leg.

After the hospital, there were no more wall torches to light the way. The miners lit the oil wicks on their caps and slogged deeper and deeper into the tunnels, shuffling into the darkness like shadows into the night. The walls grew closer and closer, and the ceilings dropped lower and lower. Massive slabs of wet rock sloped left and right, mere inches above Nally's head. Sometimes he had to duck to get into the next chamber. The farther into the earth they walked, the colder it grew. Water dripped from the ceilings, and Emma couldn't shake the feeling that they were inside a giant grave. In a sense, they were. How many men had died down here? How many bodies remained entombed beneath cave-ins, buried forever beneath monstrous piles of earth and coal and shale?

She hunched her shoulders against the chill, struggling to push away images of the support timbers cracking and breaking, the roof collapsing, the mountain of rock and dirt burying them alive. After a while, she and Nally lagged behind the rest of the miners, letting them move ahead so she could get out the camera. When they were alone, they could only see as far as the fluttering circles of light from their head lamps. Behind them and in front of them, there was nothing but blackness.

They stopped to talk to one of the nippers, or door handlers. The boy worked by himself, opening and closing a wide wooden door to let the coal cars through. He looked to be about eight years old. Nally introduced "Emmet" and showed off "his" new camera, then asked the nipper if he wanted his picture taken, promising to show him the exposure after the film was developed. The nipper eagerly agreed and stood on the tracks with his arms crossed, grinning. Nally opened his powder can and pulled out three fat sticks, their ends wrapped in oil-soaked rags. He lit two of the homemade torches, laid them on the rock floor, and held up the third.

Torchlight lit up the tunnel, flickering off the jagged walls and sloping roof, illuminating initials carved in the heavy wooden door. The mine walls and ceilings were marbled with various colors— whites and greens, blacks and grays, and a strange yellowish orange that looked like veins of copper or rust. Every surface dripped with condensation. The thick timbers that held up the gangway were covered with white and black mold.

"Sit where you always do," Emma said to the nipper. "And don't look at the camera. I want you to look like you're working."

The nipper sat on a wooden box next to the door, the flame of his oil wick head lamp shooting up from the brim of his hat like the distant beacon of a ship. An extra jacket hung from an iron peg above his head on the black wall, next to the pipes used for pumping water out of the mines. Emma shivered, imagining the boy sitting in the dark chamber all alone, ten hours every day, opening the door when he heard a coal car coming, listening to the trickle of water and the groans and cracks of the mountain settling all around him. And what about the huge rats Clayton had told her about, watching the boy with hungry red eyes? She didn't think she could be that brave.

Nally stood to the side while Emma took two photos. When she was done, Nally stomped out the torches, then pulled a roll of Necco Wafers from his dinner pail and gave them to the nipper.

"Not sure how the boss would feel about us playing around with a camera instead of working," he said, winking. "But what he don't know won't hurt him, right?"

The boy smiled and took the wafers, stuffing them into his pants pocket and nodding. Then he pulled on the iron door handle with both hands and leaned back, using his weight to open the giant door. He waved Nally and Emma through, then started to whistle as he closed the door behind them. As they made their way farther into the shaft, Emma slipped the camera back into the waist of her pants and beneath her jacket. In low-ceilinged tunnels leading off both sides of the passageway, miners and their butties worked in water on their hands and knees, their clothes heavy with black mud. After she and Nally passed the workers, a low rumbling sound came from somewhere deep inside the mine, like distant thunder.

Emma stopped. "What was that?"

"It's just the mountain," Nally said. "Some days she likes to talk."

He smiled and motioned for her to keep going. She took a deep breath and started moving again, an icy trickle of fear crawling up her spine. A voice drifted around a bend in the passageway.

"Gee!" a boy yelled. "Wah-haw!"

Chains rattled up ahead, axles creaked, and hooves crunched on loose slag. Nally gestured wildly, telling Emma to get the camera out again. She did as she was told and a mule appeared around the bend, pulling an empty coal car driven by a teenage boy. Two younger boys sat in the car bed behind him, holding wooden sprags. Nally pulled a bag of chewing tobacco from his jacket pocket, stepped between the tracks in front of the plodding mule, and held the bag in the air.

"Interested in some fresh chew?" he said.

"Whoa," the mule driver said, and brought the animal to a halt. He jumped to the ground, and the other boys climbed out of the car.

"What do you want for it?" the mule handler said, his hands on his hips. "You want us to play a prank on somebody?"

Nally shook his head. "Nay," he said. "We just want to take a picture of ye and your fine mule."

"What for?" one of the boys said. He was still holding a wooden sprag, resting it on one shoulder like a baseball bat. "This have anything to do with the upcoming strike?"

"My friend is trying out his new camera, 'tis all," Nally said. "There're two bags of tobacco in it for ye if ye can keep your mouths shut about it."

"Why do we have to kept our mouths shut about it?" the mule driver said.

"Because if ye don't, I'll tell the foreman it was you lads prodding those boys to ride the empty cars down the slope the day that new spragger got run over and killed. Ye'd be in a sad state if the foreman found out, ye having to tell your mums why ye lost your jobs and all."

"I ain't got no reason for telling anybody about you and your stupid camera anyhow," the mule driver said. He reached for the tobacco, but Nally held it higher, well out of his reach.

"Stand for the picture first," Nally said. "Next to the animal."

Then there was a loud crack, like a boulder breaking in two. It sounded like it came from deep in the shaft, behind the mule and coal car.

Emma stiffened, fighting the urge to turn and run.

The mule put his ears back and started moving forward, his eyes wide with panic. The driver grabbed the mule's bridle to stay him. "There's lots of noise in shaft six this morning," he said. "We was just coming back out to let 'em know it needs checking."

"Yeah," one of the spraggers said. "Somethin' ain't right in there."

"Let's get this picture taken right quick then," Nally said.

The driver held on to the mule, and the spraggers stood next to him. Nally relit the torches. Emma took two pictures of the boys, trying not to shake as she pushed the exposure level and wound the key. More than anything, she wanted to get out of the mine as soon as possible. Once the film was used up, she needed to leave. Maybe Nally could tell the bosses she was deathly ill and couldn't work. Then again, the bosses probably wouldn't care. She was probably going to be stuck in here the rest of the day. Nally gave the boys their reward, and they climbed back on the coal car and rode away.

Emma closed the camera and began to put it in the waist of her pants while Nally stomped on one of the torches to put out the flames.

Just then a high-pitched squeaking drifted up from the depths of the shaft, like a thousand wheels turning on dry axles. Nally picked up one of the still-burning torches and held it high, peering into the mine. Hundreds of rats came scurrying around the bend toward them, zigzagging back and forth, hopping over rocks and rail ties like a brown wave, their long tails scratching along the slag. Then there was a thunderous crash of rocks and timber, and a powerful gust of soot-filled air knocked Emma off her feet. Nally dropped the torch, yanked her up, and started running, dragging her with him.

"Cave-in!" he shouted.

She stumbled beside him, coughing and gagging on the thick dust, terror rising in her throat like bile. She felt for the camera beneath her jacket. It wasn't there.

"Where's the camera?" she yelled.

"Ye must have dropped it!" he shouted.

She stopped and raced back to where she fell, ignoring Nally's cries to leave the camera there. The still-burning torches glowed on the rock floor, orange flames flickering in the dust-filled air. She pulled her scarf over her nose and searched the floor for the camera. But the coal dust was getting thicker and thicker, and she could barely take a breath without gagging. Panicked voices traveled up the shaft, shouting and yelling. Then a silver glint caught her eye and she knelt, searching blindly through the slag with her fingers. Finally she felt something hard and square. She grabbed the camera and straightened. But now she was turned around. Which way was out? One of Nally's torches set a support beam on fire. It burst into flames. The timber hissed and spit.

Every instinct told her that the exit was behind her. But the blinding dust and smoke left her disoriented. She heard Nally calling for her, but the direction of his voice was lost in the cacophony of shouting men, snapping timber, and crackling fire. If she ran the wrong way, she would die.

Emma closed her eyes and tried to remember which side of the tracks she was on when she fell. She kicked the ground until her boot hit a railroad tie. Had she been on the right? She turned around and hurried toward what she hoped was the exit, squinting and spitting, trying to see. For what seemed like forever, she stumbled along the tunnel, one hand pressing the camera to her chest, the other on the cold, hard wall, feeling her way. Then someone grabbed her wrist. It was Nally. He pulled her forward. Other men surrounded them, miners who had stumbled up in the dark.

"Everyone, out!" Nally yelled. "Run! Get out!"

An explosion shook the shaft behind them. A blast of hot air roared past, nearly knocking Emma to her knees. Nally held her up, and they staggered through the nipper's door, then made their way toward the slope leading up to the main shaft. Men stumbled and fell all around them. They were shouting and pushing. Mules brayed and whips cracked. The smell of burning wood mixed with the sulfuric odor of coal dust and rock, stinging Emma's eyes and nose.

"Where's Clayton?" she shouted.

"I don't know!" Nally said.

"Did he come down the same shaft?"

"No!"

She gripped the back of Nally's jacket, hanging on for dear life. Her teeth rattled as she pounded along the passageway. Nally pushed past the other miners, moving faster than she thought possible. After what seemed like an eternity, they came out into the main gangway. At the inside stables, Uncle Otis was yelling at the stable hands to unlock the stalls and let the mules free.

"Damn the men, save the mules!" he shouted over and over.

A thunderous roar rumbled deep in the earth below. Hot air filled the mine like a living, breathing thing. Nally and Emma ran up the slope toward the exit. The timber roof of the gangway creaked and shifted above their heads, like a great ship being tossed at sea. Finally they burst into the sunlight and kept running. Debris and smoke spewed out of the mine's yawning mouth.

When Nally and Emma were far enough away, they stopped. Dozens of other miners did the same, staggering and limping, taking inventory of who made it out and who didn't. The mine whistle was screaming, announcing the disaster. Men fell to their knees, coughing and spitting and wiping their burning eyes. Emma could hardly see. She fumbled with the camera, struggling to put it back beneath her coat. At last she slipped it into the waist of her trousers and pulled the edge of her jacket over it. Someone put her hands in a bucket, and she rinsed her face with gritty water. She stood and looked desperately for Clayton, her head spinning. She didn't see him anywhere. Was he still in the mine?

No, God. Please. Not Clayton.

A dark pillar of smoke poured out of the mine, rising in the sky until it obscured the sun. Fire crawled up the trestle leading to the top of the breaker, the dry lumber bursting into orange and yellow flames. Bits and pieces of timber broke away from the trestle and fell to the ground like burning leaves. Then an entire top section of the track gave way, and two coal cars tipped over and fell hundreds of feet through the air, hitting the earth with a thunderous crash.

A stream of boys poured out of the breaker, gripping the iron railing and scrambling down the rickety steps. They glanced over their shoulders at the mine and the fire crawling up the trestle, their eyes wide with terror, trying to watch their step at the same time. One fell halfway down, and others helped him up, struggling to keep their balance while being crowded from behind. The boys at the top of the stairs hollered and cursed until the line started moving again. Another boy slipped below the railing, hung on for a moment, and dropped to the ground below. His feet hit hard and he stumbled forward. Then he got up and scurried away, his hand on his cap. Several others followed suit. One boy slipped, tumbled beneath the railing, and fell. He lay in the dirt for a moment, rolling in pain, then got up and limped away. When the rest of the boys hit the last step, they immediately started running to get away from the building.

Emma spotted Uncle Otis a few feet away. He stood panting and looking back at the mine, his thin face dripping with soot and sweat. It was only then that she realized she'd lost her mining cap. If her uncle looked in her direction, he'd recognize her. She turned away and tried to disappear in the crowd. Then she stopped in her tracks. Mr. Flint and Levi were headed straight for her, hurrying toward the mine. Before she could run or hide, they shoved past, bumping into her shoulders. Frank followed directly behind them, oblivious to the fact that she was mere inches away. Mr. Flint and Levi stormed over to Uncle Otis, Frank on their heels.

"What the hell happened?" Mr. Flint shouted.

"Damn if I know!" Uncle Otis said. "Near as I can tell, it was in shaft number six."

"The new one?" Mr. Flint said.

Uncle Otis nodded.

"Did everyone get out?" Levi said. While his father and Otis looked angry, Levi's face was filled with worry and dread.

Uncle Otis shook his head.

"Are the mules safe?" Mr. Flint asked him.

"Half of them were already in the mine," Uncle Otis said. "So I'm not sure."

"Damn it all to hell!" Mr. Flint said. His jowls trembled with fury.

The top half of the breaker was on fire now, and the roof was starting to collapse.

"You, there," Levi yelled to a group of miners. He pointed at the breaker. "Get over there and put that fire out! Form a bucket brigade at the pumping station!"

"Get the coal car and engines away from it first!" Mr. Flint said. Several of the men followed Mr. Flint's orders while the rest went over to the pumping station to get buckets.

"They need to put the fire out first," Levi said. "There are still boys inside!"

"We can rebuild the breaker," Mr. Flint said.

From the direction of the miners' village, groups of women came running up the road, their long skirts bunched in their fists, their faces contorted with terror. They ran as fast as they could, as if being chased by a monstrous beast. Some held toddlers or babies in their arms, while others ran ahead of crying children. One woman was in nothing but a nightgown and bare feet. Several others still had dishcloths hanging over their shoulders, or flour on their faces and hands.

Within seconds, a crowd of frantic miners' wives surrounded

Otis, Mr. Flint, and Levi, clamoring with questions about the fate of their men. They gathered in swarms, crying hysterically and asking about their husbands and sons in English, Polish, German, and Italian. When Uncle Otis shook his head and shooed them away, they moaned in anguish or screamed. Some stood rigid and stared at the smoking pit, while others covered their eyes and sank to their knees, sobbing and praying. Frank herded the women away from Mr. Flint, beating them back with his truncheon at times.

Unlike the other men, Levi seemed to understand the women's anguish. "I'm sorry," he said over and over, trying to comfort them. "I'm so sorry. We'll do everything we can to save your husbands and sons."

"Go home!" Mr. Flint shouted. "There's nothing you can do! There's nothing anybody can do! Now go away!"

"There's something I can do!" someone shouted above the fray.

All of a sudden, Nally appeared in the midst of the women, a pistol in his hand. A woman screamed, and the rest retreated. Everyone's eyes went wide, and they moved out of the way. In what seemed like slow motion, Nally cocked the hammer and pointed the gun at Mr. Flint.

"Now ye'll die, ye son of a bitch!" he yelled.

Unable to move fast, Mr. Flint turned and tried to run, ducking behind his son and Uncle Otis. Nally pulled the trigger, and the bullet hit Levi instead. It entered his chest, kicking him off his feet and spraying blood over the left side of his face. Levi collapsed backward, head down and arms thrust out, and hit the dirt hard. The women screamed. Emma recoiled in shock, her hands over her open mouth. Mr. Flint rushed to his son's side, his face ravaged with horror. He fell to his knees and took Levi's head in his hands, shouting his name over and over. One of the foremen and Uncle Otis tried pulling Mr. Flint to his feet to get him away from Nally, but Mr. Flint refused, thrashing like a trapped animal to free himself from their grasp.

The rest of the miners moved farther away, except a few who looked like they were either going to jump Nally or try to reason with him. Nally stood in place, seemingly stunned by the violence, as if he couldn't believe he had pulled the trigger. He looked uncertain of what to do next. Then, in the next instant, he seemed to regain his senses. He fired again, shooting Mr. Flint in the upper arm. Mr. Flint fell sideways, kicking up a cloud of black dust. As if suddenly hypnotized by the power of bullets, Nally shot one of the foremen in the head. Then he aimed the gun at Uncle Otis. Behind him, Frank drew his pistol and pointed it at Nally.

"Drop your weapon!" Frank shouted.

Nally spun around and aimed his pistol at Frank.

Emma shoved her way through the retreating crowd, her heart hammering in her chest. She broke into the clearing and stepped between Nally and Frank, facing Nally. "What are you doing?" she cried. "Put that gun away!"

"Move, Emma," Nally said. "This isn't yer fight."

She shook her head. "No!" she said. "This wasn't part of the plan! You're not shooting anyone else!"

"Guess I'll just have to shoot around ye then," Nally said. He closed one eye and pulled the trigger.

A bullet ripped through Emma's bicep like a hot poker through butter. At first it felt like she had been hit hard with a board. Then her arm started to burn, as if someone had set her muscle on fire. She crumpled to her knees and grabbed the wound, her hand filling with sticky blood. Two more shots rang out in quick succession, and she cringed, waiting to feel a bullet shatter her skull. When nothing happened, she looked up. Nally was on the ground, his lips slack, his stomach bleeding. She turned to look at Frank, who stood with his gun still aimed at Nally, the barrel smoking. A few feet behind Frank, Clayton lay on his back, his eyes closed, blood trickling out of his mouth. Emma cried out and crawled over to Clayton, the slag stabbing her knees and hands, her body vibrating. A black, jagged hole darkened his jacket just below his collarbone, and blood oozed from its center. Emma put a trembling hand on Clayton's face. He felt cold and clammy. She put an ear to his chest, holding her breath to hear a heartbeat. The only thing she could hear was Hazard Flint, howling in agony.

She shook Clayton by the shoulders. "Say something!" she screamed. "Please, Clayton! Say something!"

He didn't respond.

"We need a doctor!" she shouted, a sob bursting from her throat. "Please, somebody help!"

All around her, more members of the Coal and Iron Police appeared, trying to get the crowd under control. One held a gun on Nally, who was lying motionless on the ground, while two others knelt over Mr. Flint and Levi. Frank moved toward Emma, aiming his pistol at her with both hands, his face twisted in anger and confusion.

"What the hell is going on, Emma?" he said.

"I don't know!" she said.

"You were in cahoots with Clayton and Nally!"

"No," she said. "That's not what—"

"I told you Clayton was trouble!"

"Clayton? Nally just shot him!" She shook her head, tears streaming down her face. "I have no idea what just happened, but it's my fault, not Clayton's. We didn't know Nally was going to shoot anyone!" All of sudden she felt dizzy and weak. She swayed and closed her eyes.

"Arrest her!" Frank shouted.

Two policemen hurried over, yanked Emma up, and handcuffed her wrists behind her back. A jolt of pain shot up her shoulder and into her chest, like someone was ripping off her arm.

"I just took a bullet for you," she said to Frank. "And now you're going to arrest me?" Then she felt herself falling. And the world went black.

CHAPTER 27

Beneath a coal black sky, Emma stood on a frozen river surrounded by a circle of boys—Albert, Michael, Nicolas and his twin brothers, and Pearl's son, Tanner. For reasons she didn't understand, they were shouting at her, telling her to run. Then a shot rang out and the boys broke through the ice, screaming her name. She fell to her knees and spun around, reaching for them, but it was too late. One by one, they disappeared beneath the dark water. The only thing that remained was one of Michael's small crutches, splintered and lying at her feet. She was alone. All around her, the ice thumped and groaned, echoing like the bottomless moans of a subterranean creature. She put her face in her hands and wept. Then she heard Clayton calling her name. She looked up and saw him on a train trestle, high above her head. Then the ice cracked and splintered beneath her, and she dropped into the icy river.

Emma jumped, jerking herself awake. Slowly, she became aware of two things: a stabbing ache in her upper arm, and the acidic stench of old urine. Then she realized she was shivering, despite the fact that she was fully dressed. She was lying on something hard, on top of what felt like a scratchy blanket, and her chest felt heavy. Her head felt full of molasses. She blinked and opened her eyes. The high, curved ceiling above her was the color of stone, pockmarked and river gray. She looked down and saw she was wearing dirty trousers, boots, and a shirt with one sleeve ripped off. A cluster of flies buzzed around a cloth bandage on her arm, gathering at the dark smudges of blood seeping through the white material. Wincing, she sat up and swung her legs over the side of a metal cot. Then she started to cough, a dry, burning bark, deep in her chest. At first she couldn't catch her breath, and she wondered if her lungs were full of water. Maybe she had nearly drowned. But that didn't explain the wound on her arm, or the black, sooty stains on her hands. When she could finally inhale without coughing, she looked around, trying to remember where she was and what happened.

The room was about the size of a root cellar, with stone walls and a plank floor stained black by mold. Thin sunlight filtered in through two tiny, recessed windows several feet above her head, just below the arch of the ceiling. The only exit was a narrow door covered with thick iron mesh. Then it all came back to her, and she knew where she was. She was in a cell inside the stone jailhouse, and there had been an explosion at the mine. *Then Nally started shooting people.*

A rush of panic ignited her chest. *Clayton.* Emma stood too fast, nearly fell, and sat back down. She gripped the edge of the cot and took slow, deep breaths, trying to calm herself. Then she put a hand to her waist, feeling for the pocket camera. It was gone. When she thought she could trust herself to stand, she staggered over to the door and hooked her fingers through the mesh. Just outside the door, thick stone walls blocked her line of vision, making it impossible to look left or right. The only thing she could see was another cell across a wide hall.

"Is there anyone out there?" she called. She rattled the iron mesh. "Please! You have to let me out of here!" Her voice was raspy and hoarse, and her wounded arm began to throb in time with her rapid pulse.

"Sorry, lass," a voice said from somewhere nearby, echoing in the stone building. "No one is going to listen to ye."

"Nally?" she said. "What the hell did you do? And where is Clayton? Is he alive?"

"I don't know," he said.

"Why did you shoot him?" she cried.

"Sorry. I was aiming for Frank."

Her legs went weak, and the floor rolled beneath her. She leaned against the door, waiting for the dizziness to pass. If Clayton was dead because she had insisted on going inside the mine, she'd never forgive herself. The orphans' faces flashed in her mind: Sawyer, Jack, Sadie, Violet, and Edith. Would she be responsible for destroying their lives too? She swallowed the burning lump in her throat and tried to find her voice.

"Why did you have a gun?" she said. "Shooting people wasn't part of the plan!"

"Ye won't get anywhere in Coal River with strikes and taking pictures," Nally said. "The only thing a man like Hazard Flint understands is violence."

"Well, we won't get anywhere from in here!" she said, her words rattled by fury.

Nally didn't reply.

She kicked the wall, anger and frustration and fear churning in her mind. She had to get out of there, had to find out if Clayton was dead or alive. And she had to find the camera. She rattled the door again.

"Hello?" she shouted. "Is anyone out there?" Then she had another thought and froze, afraid to ask Nally what he knew. "What's happening at the mine? Did everyone get out?"

"I don't know," Nally said. "It's not likely."

She clutched the mesh with her fingers, pressing her forehead against the cold iron. "Damn it all!"

It wasn't enough to take pictures of the breaker boys; she had to insist on getting pictures of the nippers and spraggers too. Not to mention she had trusted Nally, a man she barely knew. The cave-in wasn't her fault, but she and Nally were the ones who had brought in the torches that started the fire. For the second time in her life, someone might be dead because she'd felt the need to make things right. It had been her decision to chase Percy and his friends down to the river the day Albert drowned, and it had been her decision to go inside the mine. Who did she think she was anyway? She blinked back tears, hating herself for messing up everything. "Do you know where the camera is?"

"Frank took it."

She groaned and hung her head. How would she ever get the camera back now? And what if Frank had the film developed, or worse, destroyed it? Somewhere on the block, a heavy door creaked open on rusty hinges, then slammed, echoing like a shot in the stone hall. Footsteps banged along the floor. Keys jangled. Frank came into view and stopped in front of her cell.

"Frank!" she cried. "Where's Clayton? Is he all right?"

Frank jerked his chin to one side, indicating the next cell over. "They patched him up as best they could," he said. "Which don't make a whole hell of a lot of sense to me since he'll be hanging from a noose by the end of the week."

Ice-cold terror seized Emma's heart. "What are you talking about?"

"Clayton has been charged with conspiracy to commit murder."

"But he didn't have anything to do with that!" she said. "He was shot too, for Christ's sake!"

"That bullet was meant for me, and you know it," Frank said

" 'Tis true," Nally said. "I'm a lousy shot."

"We didn't know Nally had a gun!" Emma said.

"I only fired in self-defense," Nally said.

"Shut your pie hole, you Irish thug!" Frank barked. He raised his arm, signaling someone for help. "Move this prisoner to the other end of the block!"

From somewhere above, footsteps marched along a stone floor and rattled down iron steps. Frank pulled a key from a metal ring on his belt and disappeared from Emma's view. The door to Nally's cell screeched open, and the corridor filled with the sounds of men wrestling—heavy breathing, grunting, the smack of fists meeting muscle and bone. For a hopeful second she thought Nally had managed to overpower the police and would appear at her door, panting and disheveled, to let her out. Yes, he was a criminal, and he had shot Clayton, but unless she got out of this cell, she couldn't help anyone. Then a policeman appeared, gripping Nally by the arm, his mouth knotted in anger. Nally's face was bruised and bloody, his hands cuffed behind him. The policeman dragged him away. Frank reappeared in front of her cell. He put his hat back on, straightened his jacket, and watched Nally being taken across the block.

"Whatever happens, Emma," Nally shouted, "don't forget, they're wrong and we're right!"

Frank glared at her.

Emma shook her head. "No, he doesn't mean—"

"Save it for the trial," Frank said, and started to walk away.

She rattled the door. "Wait!"

He came back and crossed his arms over his chest, his brows knitted.

"Please, just tell me," she said. "What happened at the mine? Was anyone killed?"

"Over forty men and boys are missing. And they're still trying to put the fire out. Won't know anything until they can do that."

"Oh no," she said, her eyes filling. "What about the breaker boys? Are they all safe?"

"As far as we know. Yes."

"Do you think the men and boys inside the mine are all right?"

"No one knows how many were killed by the explosion, or how many were trapped behind the cave-in. If any were trapped, they've probably suffocated in the afterdamp by now. More than likely, a good number will be going home in the Black Maria."

"Oh my God." Emma put a hand over her mouth and sagged to the floor, leaning against the stone doorframe.

"What were you doing in the mine, Emma?" Frank said. His voice was hard. He uncrossed his arms and took a step closer. "And why were you with Nally? Did he and Clayton talk you into something? Did they make you cut your hair?"

She swallowed and looked up at him, her vision blurred by tears. "I . . ." she said. Then she hesitated, her shoulders dropping. Was it possible that Clayton had known all along what Nally was going to do? It was one thing to plan secret meetings and fight for the rights of miners; it was quite another to commit murder. Then she shook her head to clear it. No. Clayton wasn't like that. He was working toward peaceful opposition. It was her idea to go inside the breaker and the mine, not his. She'd practically had to beg him to let her be Nally's butty. Then, when Nally came face-to-face with Mr. Flint, he took the opportunity to carry out his own plan. Maybe Nally thought he'd get away with it during the chaos.

Emma pulled herself to her feet and locked eyes with Frank. "I wasn't with Nally. I went into the mine on my own."

"I don't believe you."

"I don't care if you believe me or not."

"Do you have any idea how much trouble you're in? They're ready to hang all three of you."

The blood drained from her face, and her stomach turned over. "Why?"

"They said you caused the explosion. And you brought Nally to Coal River to shoot Mr. Flint and the others."

"That's not true!" she said. "There was a cave-in, and the torches started a fire. After that I—"

"Levi Flint is dead!" Frank said. "One of the foremen too!"

Emma's heart turned to lead. Why Levi and not his father? Levi would have changed things if given the chance. He was the one who wanted to replace old equipment because it was a danger to the miners. He was the one who worried about the boys inside the burning breaker. The only thing Mr. Flint worried about was money.

"I'm so sorry to hear about Levi," she said. "I mean that with all my heart. He didn't deserve to die. But I—"

"Don't say another word," Frank said. He put a key in the lock, opened the cell door, and waited for her to come out.

Bewildered, she stepped out into the cellblock. Was he letting her go? Before Frank could stop her, she darted over to the next cell. On the other side of the iron mesh, Clayton was lying on his back on a cot, his eyes closed. She rattled the door.

"Clayton!" she cried. "Wake up!"

He didn't move.

Frank grabbed her by the arm and pulled her away. "Let's go," he said.

"Please, just let me talk to him for a minute!"

Ignoring her pleas, Frank dragged her across the jailhouse, his plank-thick fingers digging into her skin. The cavernous cellblock was cold and damp, and smelled like wet stone. At the far end, a set of iron stairs led two stories up to a walkway with an oak railing. The walls along the second level were lined with more cells. Five guards stood around the perimeter of the upper walkway, rifles in hand. A vaulted ceiling soared two more stories above their heads.

Frank noticed her looking up. "Our jailhouse was built to have indoor hangings."

Emma shivered. No wonder this place had always made her uneasy. And now that she was inside, the oppressive shroud of misery was a thousand times worse. The air was thick with the memories of human suffering, as if every square inch was filled with the ghosts of past prisoners. It made her anxious and nauseous. Frank took her through a locked metal door and down a short hallway into an office. He ordered her to sit in a chair, closed the door behind him, then stood over her, his arms crossed. He wasn't letting her go.

"I'm going to give you one more chance to tell me the truth," he said. "If you admit Nally and Clayton talked you into this, I might be able to protect you. Otherwise, I'm done asking questions. What were you doing in the mine? And where have you been staying? You told me you were leaving Coal River."

"Will you let me go if I tell you?"

His face went dark. "You know I can't do that."

Emma's mind raced. Why did he bring her into an office where no one else could hear? Did he really think she would point the finger at Clayton to save herself? And what if she did? What then? Did he hope she would feel obligated to him for helping her? Was he still trying to prove he could protect her? Frank knew her well enough to know she didn't have anything to do with shooting Mr. Flint and Levi, didn't he? Regardless of his motives, this could be her last chance to get him to listen. He wouldn't go against Mr. Flint and release her, and he might not be able to save her from the hangman's noose, but at the very least, maybe she could get him to help her another way. If she was going to be punished for a crime she didn't commit, she might as well try to finish what she'd started. She refused to believe it had all been for nothing.

"Where's the camera?" she said.

"Jesus Christ, Emma," he said. "You've got bigger problems than losing a camera! Haven't you heard a word I said?"

She clenched her fists in her lap until her knuckles turned white. "It was you."

He frowned, confused. "What was me?"

"You were the one who threw my locket out on the ice."

"What are you talking about?"

"I'm talking about my brother, Albert. You remember him, don't you?"

Frank unfolded his arms. "What does your brother have to do with this? And why in the world are you bringing that up now?"

"You owe me."

"You want an apology? Now?"

"That would be a good place to start," she said.

"Emma..." he said, shaking his head. "That was the past. You're in trouble here. Now. Today. You need to—"

"No," she said. "It's not the past. I live with it every day. And I wouldn't be sitting here right now if my brother were still alive."

Frank sat on the edge of the desk, and his eyes dropped to the floor. "I was just a boy."

"Albert was just a boy too. Two or three years younger than you as I recall. You knew that river ice was dangerous because you grew up here. Albert didn't. He thought it was safe."

"I'm sorry. I didn't know he would go after the locket. I thought ...I don't know what you want me to say. If I could go back and change things, I would. It was an accident."

"No," she said. "It was your fault. And still, even after what you did to Albert. Even after everything you've put me and my family through, I risked my life to save yours, twice. I even took a bullet for you."

"I know," he said, his brow furrowed. He went around the other side of the desk and sat down. "All I can do is offer to help you now, if I can. What more do you want?"

"You know I didn't do anything illegal."

"Maybe," he said. "But that's not going to get you very far during a trial. Nally is a member of the Molly Maguires. He'll hang without a formal trial. There were a lot of witnesses, so there's no way he'll get off. And I've never seen Mr. Flint like this. He's so broken up over losing Levi, I thought he was going to need to be sedated. He's lost everyone now. First the nursemaid kidnapped his second son, then his wife committed suicide, and now Levi has been murdered."

"Don't ask me to feel sorry for him."

"I'm not, but Mr. Flint wants someone to pay. And unless you want to be hanging from a rope next to Nally, you better tell me what you were doing in the mine. The only way I can help is if you tell me the truth."

"I'll tell you the truth if you promise to do something for me."

He looked doubtful. "What?"

"Promise me first."

"I'm not promising anything until I know what you're asking."

"I just need you to mail something for me, that's all."

"That's it?"

She nodded.

He stared at her for a long time, clenching and unclenching his jaw, his temples working in and out. Then he leaned back in the chair, eyeing her suspiciously. "All right. I'll do that for you. Now tell me what happened."

"I was in the mine taking pictures," she said. "There was a cave-in, and Nally dropped the torch I was using for light. I didn't know he had a gun, or that he was planning on shooting anyone. I just used him to get into the mine. Clayton knew I was going into the mine, but he didn't know Nally had a gun either. That's the truth. I swear on Albert's soul."

"So you cut off your hair and dressed like a miner just to take pictures?" he said. "And I'm supposed to believe that?"

"Yes."

"What were you taking pictures of?"

She chewed on the inside of her cheek, unsure of how to continue. She couldn't think of a lie that sounded believable. It wasn't likely that she'd cut off her hair and risk her life for a photography hobby.

"It's Uncle Otis's camera," she said. "I stole it so I could take pictures of the breaker boys and the nippers and spraggers."

"Why?"

She moved to the edge of the chair. "Please, I just need you to mail the film for me. That's all."

He shook his head. "Not until you tell me the rest."

"It's for a good cause, I promise," she said. "And we had a deal, remember? Just do the right thing for once, will you?"

"What did you think? That you could help the miners get what they want by sending pictures to your friends in New York?"

She kept a straight face, despite the fact that he'd figured everything out so quickly. "No," she said.

"You're being naïve if you think anything is going to change around here."

"Then it won't matter if you help me."

"Where have you been staying?"

"Why does it matter?"

"You said you'd tell me the truth."

"With Clayton."

He swore under his breath, and red blotches bloomed on his face.

"Please," she said. "Just mail the film for me. No one has to know."

He exhaled heavily. "To who?"

She dropped her eyes and picked at the blackened skin around her thumbnail.

Frank sat forward. "Quit pussyfooting around and just tell me what the hell you're up to. You might not believe this, but I don't want to see you strung up by the neck any more than you do."

Outside the office door, the front entrance to the jailhouse opened and closed. Heavy footsteps tromped across the wooden floor.

"Captain Bannister?" a man called out. It was Hazard Flint.

Moving fast, Frank yanked open the desk drawer and pulled out a sheet of stationery with the jail letterhead. He dipped a pen in an inkpot and poised it over the paper, ready to write. "Where do you want me to send the film?" he said.

"To the editor of the *New York Times*."

He hesitated, scowling. "Why?"

"You said you'd help me."

"What's the address?" he said impatiently.

"One Times Square," she said, starting to shake. "New York, New York."

Before Frank could write the information down, the door handle turned and the door started to open. He dropped the pen, hurried around the desk, and stood over Emma. Mr. Flint entered and closed the door behind him, leaning hard on his cane, his left arm in a sling. He looked shriveled and sick.

"What the hell is going on in here?" he snarled. "Why is she out of her cell?"

"I'm questioning her," Frank said. "She was just getting ready to tell me what she was doing in the mine."

Mr. Flint made his way into the room and stood at the end of the desk, his face drawn with anger and misery. "You're not a lawyer!"

"I've had previous run-ins with this prisoner," Frank said. "I'll get the truth out of her. Just let me do my job."

"Do whatever you want to her then," Mr. Flint said. "Just make sure she's alive when it comes time to string a rope around her neck." He squeezed his eyes shut as if he were in pain, pinching the bridge of his nose between his thumb and finger. "What a hellacious mess we've got on our hands."

"Any progress at the mine?" Frank said.

Mr. Flint shook his head. "Twenty-four men escaped with minor injuries, but we can't get the fire out to reach the others."

Emma took a deep breath and tried to stay calm, overwhelmed by a strange mixture of relief and despair. Twenty-four were now safe, but how many more were going to die?

"Miss Malloy knows how it started," Frank said. "And she was just getting ready to tell me what she knows about Nally."

"Save it for the trial, if there is one," Mr. Flint said. "You don't want to give her any ideas on how to change her story!"

"But she could lead me to other Mollies through Nally's cohorts," Frank said.

Mr. Flint stood silent, as if trying to decide what to do. "All right, but write down every damn word she says!" Then he swayed and grabbed the edge of the desk. Frank pulled the chair around and helped him into it.

"You all right, boss?" Frank said.

Mr. Flint leaned back in the seat, breathing hard. "I'll be . . ." he started. But then his lip trembled and he shook his head, unable to speak.

Despite her hatred for the man, Emma's throat tightened. She knew the agony of grief all too well, and seeing it break down this tyrant only proved its power.

"I know you don't believe me, Mr. Flint," she said. "But I'm truly sorry about Levi. His death was a tragedy. He seemed like a good man."

Mr. Flint blinked at her with crusty, bloodshot eyes. He looked as though he might scream, or yank out a gun and shoot her dead on the spot. But to her surprise, his face crumpled in on itself. He took a handkerchief out of his vest pocket, his shoulders convulsing.

"Yes," he said. "My son was a good man. A better man than I'll ever be. And I never told him. . . ." His voice caught, and he couldn't go on.

Emma swallowed. Now that Mr. Flint had lost his son, maybe she could reason with him. If there was one thing she knew for sure, grief had a way of changing people. Maybe he would finally see that putting other people's sons in danger was wrong. "I know it's not the same as losing your child," she said. "But I have some idea how much pain you're in. I lost my brother. And my parents. That's why it's so hard for me to understand what's happening in Coal River."

As if suddenly coming to his senses, Mr. Flint shook his head. He wiped his cheeks and pushed himself to his feet. "You should have thought about that before you brought in a radical mine striker," he snarled. Then he stuffed his handkerchief back in his pocket, brushed past her, and started toward the door.

Emma clenched her jaw, berating herself. What was she thinking? A heart made of stone could never be changed. She turned in her chair. "Now you know what the parents of dead breaker boys suffer," she said. "You're feeling the same pain. The same grief."

Mr. Flint froze midstride and spun around. "Was that your plan? To teach me a lesson?"

"No," she said. "I would never wish the death of a loved one on anyone, not even someone as greedy and vile as you."

"How dare you?" he yelled. "My boy is dead because of you!"

"Have you ever asked yourself how many mothers and fathers have lost their boys because of you?" she said.

With that, Mr. Flint stormed toward her, his face wild. She leapt to her feet and backed away, her heart kicking in her chest. He herded her into a corner and raised his cane to strike her, his lips pulled back, his teeth bared. She lifted an arm to protect herself, cowering between the wall and a wooden cabinet.

"Stop!" Frank yelled.

Mr. Flint brought down the cane, aiming for Emma's head. Frank grabbed the cane and stopped it in midair.

"She's not the reason Levi is dead," Frank said. "And that won't help us find out the truth."

Lowering the cane and breathing hard, Mr. Flint glared at Frank for a long time. Then he grunted and staggered across the office, grabbing the desk and chair to steady himself as he went. Finally he disappeared through the door and Emma breathed a sigh of relief.

Frank gaped at her. "Are you out of your mind? That man can hang you without a trial! Do you understand that?"

On wobbly legs, Emma left the corner and went back to the chair. "Then I don't have much time. Give me a piece of paper. I need to write a letter to send with the film."

Frank gave a frustrated shake of his head. "It's not going to do any good."

She sat down and looked up at him. "Are you going to help me or not?"

He swore under his breath and fetched a piece of paper from the drawer. Emma calmed her trembling hands and wrote as fast as she could without smudging the ink as Frank watched from the other side of the desk. In the letter, she explained where the pictures were taken, and that Hazard Flint was breaking Pennsylvania child labor laws. She said he was taking shortcuts in the mine and murdering anyone who opposed him. She described how she had gone undercover as a breaker boy and miner's butty. Then she paused for a second, remembering that Levi was trying to change things. She added that to the letter, not wanting to sully his name. But Hazard Flint wasn't the only guilty one. Some of the other bosses, including her uncle, had broken the law too. She signed her name at the bottom, picked up the letter, blew on the ink to dry it, and folded it in thirds.

"I need an envelope," she said.

Frank reached for the letter. "Let me read it."

"No," she said. "You're doing the right thing this time, remember?"

For a moment it looked like Frank would refuse, but then he dropped his arm with a grimace, and searched in the desk for an envelope.

CHAPTER 28

At dawn the next morning, the rattle of a key in a lock startled Emma awake in her cell. She sat up and looked toward the door. No one was there. The cellblock was dark except for a thin, yellow glow coming from a single ceiling lamp at the far end of the corridor. Briefly, she wondered if she was dreaming. She had been dosing in fits and starts all night, alternating between furious nightmares and dreams of her parents and Albert. At times she felt like she was drifting in and out of consciousness, not sure where the dreams ended and the all-too-real nightmares began. Then she realized the sound of keys was coming from the next cell. *Clayton's cell.* She swung her legs over the cot and rushed to the door. The only thing she could see was the back of a guard from one side. An iron door screeched open, and the guard disappeared into the cell.

"Is that you, Frank?" she called.

No one answered.

Heavy footsteps crossed the cell floor, a metal cot creaked, and it sounded like a body was being moved and lifted. Then the guard reappeared, a man's bloody arm draped over his shoulders. Boots scraped across the floor, and a man groaned. Two guards half carried, half dragged Clayton past Emma's door. Neither of them were Frank.

"Clayton!" she cried.

He didn't answer. The cold fingers of fear clutched Emma's throat.

"Where are you taking him?" she shouted.

Then Frank appeared in front of her cell, making her jump. "Mr. Flint wants him moved to the infirmary."

"How come?" she said.

"He wants the satisfaction of seeing him hang at the end of a rope."

"Are you saying there's a chance he might die from the gunshot?"

"Hard to tell," Frank said. He sounded deflated. "Depends on how hard he's willing to fight, I guess." He started to walk away.

"Wait!"

He came back. "Now what?"

"Did you mail the film?" she whispered.

"I don't know what you're talking about," he said, and disappeared from view.

Frank's footsteps echoed across the stone block, then a heavy door screeched open and slammed closed. Emma turned back into the cell, fell onto the cot, and put her face in her hands. Clayton had to survive the gunshot. The alternative was unthinkable. Then again, what was the point of surviving if he was just going to be hanged? She closed her flooding eyes and tried to quiet her racing thoughts. But once her tears started, she was helpless to stop. She pictured Albert and her parents, and sobbed out loud. She wept for the orphans, for the mothers and fathers who had lost children, for the miners still trapped in the mine, for the dead and maimed breaker boys, and for all the others suffering in this town to satisfy Hazard Flint's greed.

She prayed for exhaustion to overtake her, to release her into sleep. But it was no use.

Over the next few days, the pounding of hammers and the scraping of saws filled the stone jailhouse. Carpenters walked back and forth in front of Emma's cell, carrying timber, tools, rope, and carriage bolts. They laughed and joked, milling about during dinner breaks, asking the guards if they'd be allowed to witness the executions. Frank stopped outside her cell door to tell her the carpenters were building a gallows in the center of the block, and to give her updates about the mine. Every day, she sat on her cot and leaned against the wall, hugging her knees and alternating between crushing sorrow, pulse-pounding fury, and panic. Every so often the wound on her arm started bleeding again, but any pain was eclipsed by terror.

The news from the mine was horrific. Seventeen men and boys were still missing. Rescuers had found two dead mules in the shaft, and the overwhelming presence of lethal levels of black damp left little hope for any trapped miners. A fan powered by a steam donkey engine arrived a few hours after the accident to ventilate the tunnels, and they had sent a canvas hose into the mouth of the mine to pump down air and establish fresh air bases. But by late afternoon the day after the explosion, rescue crews had only succeeded in advancing seventy-five feet down the gangway, despite the ventilation. They found the ventilation furnace and an adjacent pile of coal blazing, which stalled efforts to circulate air deeper into the mine. Since debris in the shaft had blocked normal ventilation, black damp continued to be produced at lethal levels. Water piped from the surface finally extinguished the fire and, eventually, with the help of downcast fan ventilation, successive fresh air bases were established. By four a.m. the next day, workers were able to move down the shaft, several hundred feet inward. There, the first two victims were discovered, their bodies bloated, blood oozing from their mouths. It was the inside foreman and a young mule driver.

By the fourth day, rescuers arrived at the east gangway, a crosscut off the passageway where the cave-in occurred. A hundred feet in, they encountered a makeshift barrier of coal, rock, scrap wood, mud, and canvas. The trapped miners had apparently constructed the barrier in an attempt to stop the infiltration of black damp. But when the rescuers pierced the barrier, they found the bodies of nine men and boys who appeared to be asleep. A father was found embracing his son, some men held hands in prayer, and others leaned against gangway walls. Some seemed to have struggled for a final breath, their faces buried in the coal dust of the floor or wrapped in shirts, their eyeballs protruding, blood dried around their mouths and noses. There was little hope that the remaining six missing miners would be found alive.

With every report, Emma wished she had died in the mine. All those miners, all those boys, dead, in part because of her. Maybe she deserved to be hanged.

When the carpenters finished building the gallows, guards set up chairs in the cellblock, lining them across the floor in straight rows. Watching through her cell door, Emma struggled against the writhing coil of panic that threatened to cut off her air. What about the trial? Frank would have told her if all three of them were going straight to the gallows, wouldn't he? And if there wasn't going to be a trial, who were they going to hang first? Nally? Or Clayton, before he died from his wounds? After all, he was the connection between her and Nally. Maybe they blamed him for everything. Or maybe they were going to hang her first because she had snuck into the mine, and obviously had something to hide. She went back to her cot and waited, trying not to be sick.

Three hours later, the jailhouse was filled to standing-room only with men in suits, women dressed in their Sunday best, and the entire regiment of the Coal and Iron Police in full uniform. They talked and chattered and gossiped in rising and falling waves, filling the stone space with an electric current of tense expectation, nervous excitement, and a droning murmur, like a million bees buzzing inside a giant hive. Emma watched from her cell door, trembling in the grip of impending doom.

Then Frank appeared in front of her cell, unlocked the door, and ordered her to step out. She did as she was told, every beat of her heart like an explosion beneath her rib cage. She was shocked to see Nally already on the gallows platform, high above the cellblock floor. They'd cuffed his hands behind his back and tied his feet together. His brow was bloody and bruised, his lip split, and one of his eyes was swollen shut. Two Coal and Iron Police stood beside him looking out over the crowd, their faces void of emotion. Armed guards stood on either side of the scaffold.

Two other guards dragged Clayton up the aisle toward the front row. His skin was gray, his face pinched in pain. He was wearing a shirt, but it was only buttoned at the collar, and the left sleeve was empty. His arm was bandaged tight to his body beneath the shirt, and his chest was wrapped in white cloth. He looked like he was struggling to stay awake. Emma's bowels turned to water and she gasped for air, fighting the flood of terror rising in her throat. *They're going to hang us all!*

Frank handcuffed her and led her toward the gallows. She stumbled beside him on rubbery legs.

"What about the trial?" she cried.

"They held a quick trial this morning," he said. "This is what Mr. Flint would have wanted."

"What do you mean, what he would have wanted? Where is he?" Emma scanned the crowd for Mr. Flint but didn't see him.

"Mr. Flint is unwell right now. The Coal and Iron Police, the mine supervisors, and the foremen made the final decision in his place."

"But you can't let them do this! You can't just..." Emma gagged on her words, unable to continue.

"Be quiet," Frank said, his voice hard.

Above her, spectators filled the second-floor walkway, looking down with curious eyes. *This can't be happening,* she thought. *Maybe I'm having a nightmare. Maybe I'm asleep.* She tried to think of something she could do, some action she could still take to save them. But she couldn't think of anything. Frank pushed her into a wooden chair at the end of the first row and stood beside her, his face set, his arms behind his back. The other guards put Clayton in a seat on the other end of the row, propping him against the backrest as if he were a rag doll. Clayton's head kept dropping to his chest. A guard stood beside him, nudging him to stay upright.

The wooden gallows soared above the floor at the end of the cellblock. Two front beams of the scaffold formed a cross that faced the audience, and thick wooden stairs led up to the platform. Above it, three beams formed the hanging frame that reached above the second level of the jail, like a swing set built for giants. A thick brown rope hung from the horizontal crossbeam. At the end of the rope was a noose.

Emma felt like she was going mad. *Who are they going to hang after Nally?* she thought. *Clayton? Me?* The crowd murmured and pointed at the gallows. At Clayton. At Emma.

She looked up at Frank. "Clayton and I didn't do anything," she said, her teeth chattering.

Frank ignored her.

Standing in front of the gallows, a gray-bearded policeman read from an official-looking book, but Emma heard only phrases: "Guilty of murder in the first degree . . . inciting rebellion . . . fearful deeds . . . criminal organization . . . death by hanging." When the man finished reading, one of the policemen on the platform put a black hood over Nally's head, covering his face. A second policeman put the noose around Nally's neck and pulled it tight below his left ear. They both stepped back and put their hands on a thick lever coming out of the floor.

Emma got to her feet, ready to run, or yell in protest, but Frank pushed her back down. "I said, be quiet," he hissed.

The crowd grew silent. The gray-bearded policeman turned and gave a nod. The policemen on the platform pulled the lever and the trapdoor beneath Nally's feet dropped open. Nally fell through. The trapdoor swung back on its hinges and hit him in the head, knocking him sideways. The hood over his head darkened with blood. Nally jerked to a halt at the end of the rope and immediately started flailing. Blood gushed from beneath the hood along his neck and torso, running down his trousers in red rivers and dripping onto the floor. He wheezed and whistled, trying to get air. Emma closed her eyes and dropped her chin, bile rising in the back of her throat. Women gasped. There was a heavy thump on the other side of the room, as if someone had fainted. Wood and rope creaked in protest against the heavy weight of Nally's writhing body until, little by little, the only sounds were women softly crying and sniffing.

Emma looked up, tears burning her eyes. Nally hung limp at the end of the noose, his blood-covered boots just inches from the stone floor. Frank put a hand beneath Emma's arm and pulled her to her feet. She struggled to tear herself from his grasp, unwilling to go to her death without a fight.

"We didn't know he had a gun!" she cried. "Clayton and I don't deserve to die!"

Everyone looked at her and started talking at once. Men pointed and women turned to one another, putting gloved hands over their open mouths. Frank tightened his grip on Emma's arm, yanking her closer.

"Shut up," he said. "You're just here to bear witness."

Overcome with relief, Emma sagged halfway to the floor, every muscle and bone going loose. If it weren't for Frank holding her up, she would have fallen. Her vision began to close in and, for a second, she thought she was going to pass out. For the last few days she hadn't cared if she lived or died, would have almost welcomed her demise to ease her guilty mind. But then, when faced with the hangman's noose, she fought against death with everything she had. Either she was coward, or she had an incredible will to live. Which one, she wasn't sure.

Frank pulled her upright and held her there, and the room swam back into focus. The crowd was beginning to disperse. The guards had pulled Clayton out of his seat and were dragging him out of the room. Emma watched him go, wondering helplessly if the next execution would be his.

CHAPTER 29

The exterior of the Carbon County Courthouse looked more like a castle or a church, with turrets, four-story walls built from sandstone quarried in the northern part of the county, and a corner bell tower with a four-sided clock surrounded by an ornamental iron frame. After Nally's hanging, a dozen journalists had descended on Coal River to cover the mining accident and the shootings. Now they waited with the townspeople on the court steps, anxious to hear the results of the trial. Inside the courthouse, imported Minton tiles graced the imposing hallways, and oak wainscoting lined the courtroom walls. Gas chandeliers provided lighting, and a stained-glass portrait of the Goddess of Justice looked down from the vaulted ceiling.

Emma sat in the witness box in the main courtroom, her hands clasped in her lap while she waited for the prosecution to ask the next question. Her defense attorney, Jacques Bonnet, a thin, gray-haired man with liver-spotted hands, watched from a narrow table in front of the audience. Since the mining accident nine days ago, a jury had been assembled of mostly Welsh and German miners who barely spoke English and didn't get along with their native-born American and Irish neighbors. The judge, who happened to be an old family friend of Hazard Flint's, had come in from Scranton.

Now he sat hunched over the bench like an aged mountain man, heavy bags under his eyes, his long, white sideburns hanging past his double chin. He had allowed only two reporters inside the courtroom, and they sat in the front row, taking notes and making sketches.

Next to the defense attorney, Clayton watched with his arm in a sling, his face the color of ash. His eyes were bleary and he looked like he wanted nothing more than to put his head on the table and go to sleep. On her way to the witness stand earlier, Emma had walked behind him. She brushed her fingers along the back of his shoulders, and felt the heat of fever burning through his shirt. She couldn't believe they were making him stand trial. Clearly, he was unwell and in pain. Then again, why would they care? They only meant to hang him anyway.

In the second row, Uncle Otis sat next to Aunt Ida, his expressionless gaze locked on the judge and jury, as if refusing to acknowledge Emma's existence with so much as a glance. Aunt Ida fidgeted in her seat, fingering her brooch and chewing on her lip. Every now and then, she glanced down the row of spectators and scanned the audience behind her, no doubt worried what people were going to think. Beside her, Percy sat with a worried look on his face.

With shaking fingers, Emma combed her short bangs away from her forehead, trying to ignore the burning stares of the dead foreman's widow and a good number of miners and their families. She imagined Sawyer, Jack, Edith, Sadie, and Violet were somewhere in the crowd, but she couldn't bring herself to search for their small, heartbroken faces. Her body felt limp as a dishrag, the sharp claws of guilt tearing at her insides. Not only were the orphans possibly on the verge of losing Clayton, but six miners were still missing.

According to Frank, Mr. Flint had collapsed in his driveway the day after he attacked Emma in the jailhouse, and he had been confined to bed ever since. The doctor suspected a weak heart and a mental breakdown. Mr. Flint refused to eat or speak, but in his dreams, he cried out for Viviane and Levi. Over the last few days he had rallied somewhat, but the doctor had advised him not to attend the trial, claiming him too weak to relive the day his son was shot.

But Mr. Flint had insisted on getting out of bed and being driven down to the courthouse. Now he sat in the front row, his gray hands gripping his cane as if it were the only thing keeping him upright. His face was thin, his skin the color of clotted cream. He looked like he had aged ten years. Every now and then he fixed his weary eyes on Clayton and frowned, as if trying to remember what was going on, or who he was. Then he dropped his gaze to the floor, took out a handkerchief, and wiped his forehead and cheeks.

"On the morning of Friday, October twenty-fifth, 1912, were you aware that Nally O'Brian was carrying a firearm?" the prosecutor asked Emma.

"No, sir," Emma said.

"Did you know he was a member of the Molly Maguires?"

"Objection!" the defense attorney said. "There is no proof the Mollies exist. How would my client know if Nally was a member of a made-up, secret society?"

"Overruled," the judge said. "Answer the question, Miss Malloy."

"I'd never heard of the Molly Maguires until my uncle told me who they were," she said. "Uncle Otis seemed to know a lot about them." In truth, she couldn't remember if it was Otis or Mr. Flint who told her about the Mollies. And right now, she didn't care.

Aunt Ida's mouth dropped open, and she glared at Emma with withering eyes. Everyone directed their attention to Uncle Otis, who sat with his arms crossed, his face straight ahead, no change in his expression.

"Your uncle is not the one on trial for causing an explosion at the mine, murdering Levi Flint, and conspiring to kill Hazard Flint," the prosecutor said. He turned and strolled past the jury, his chin high, fingering the watch chain hanging from his vest.

Emma took a deep breath. It was now or never. "Speaking of trials, Your Honor," she said. "Did you know the Coal and Iron Police and the mine supervisors hanged Nally O'Brian without a proper hearing?"

"Strike that last statement!" the judge bellowed. "Miss Malloy, refrain from speaking unless you're asked a direct question by me or one of the lawyers present."

"But that's not the way it's supposed to work!" she said. "In this country—"

The judge banged his gavel on the bench. "Miss Malloy!" he said. "You will either do as I say or be held in contempt of court! Now refrain from speaking and try to remember you're on trial for your life!"

She gritted her teeth. "Yes, Your Honor," she said.

"Miss Malloy," the prosecutor continued, "please tell the jury where you were living before going into the mine on that fateful day."

"In the mining village."

The prosecutor turned. "Where in the mining village?" he said. "In whose house?"

"Hazard Flint's," she said.

The prosecutor furrowed his brow, looking confused. "Hazard Flint's?"

"Hazard Flint owns all the houses in the miners' village," she said.

A murmur passed through the audience. Just then, four men slipped into the courtroom and stood at the back wall. One was in a suit and tie, and the other was in a black uniform and bobby helmet. The other two wore state police uniforms. Emma had never seen any of them before. The judge noticed them too. He started to open his mouth as if to ask who they were. But the men stood quietly, and the judge said nothing.

The prosecutor sighed and moved toward the witness box. "All right, but who was paying rent on the house you lived in, Miss Malloy?"

Emma looked down at her hands. Telling the truth would only reinforce their theory that she and Clayton had planned the whole thing.

"Please sit up and speak clearly," the prosecutor said.

She put her shoulders back, lifted her chin, and looked at Clayton. He gave her a weak smile, but his eyes were sad. "Clayton Nash," she said.

Aunt Ida put a lace hankie to her mouth, shaking her head.

"Were you aware that Mr. Nash had brought in a member of the

Molly Maguires to conspire against Hazard Flint and the Bleak Mountain Mining Company?"

"That's not what happened," Emma said.

"Isn't it true that you and Nally O'Brian arrived in Coal River on the same day? Not only on the same day, but on the same train?"

"Yes," she said. "But I didn't know Nally then. It was just a co-incidence that we were on the same train."

"Was it also a coincidence that you were living with Clayton Nash, the very man who hired Nally O'Brian to murder Levi and Hazard Flint?"

"No," she said. "I mean, yes! My uncle kicked me out and . . . Clayton didn't hire anyone!"

"Did you, along with the help of Nally O'Brian and Clayton Nash, put coffin notices on Hazard Flint's door the night of September second?"

"No!" she said. "We were as surprised by them as everyone else!"

"Did you cause the explosion in the mine?"

She shook her head. "It was an accident. There was a cave-in, and Nally dropped a torch."

"The torch he used to start the fire?"

"No," she said. "I mean, yes, the torch started the fire, but we didn't mean for it to happen. Nally only had the torch because I needed the light to take pictures."

The prosecutor gripped the railing in front of her. "You expect us to believe that Nally had a torch because you were taking pictures inside the mine?"

"Yes, sir."

The prosecutor chuckled. "Then where is the camera? Why hasn't it been entered into evidence?"

She nodded once toward Frank, who was standing at one end of the judge's bench. "Frank Bannister has it," she said. "He was supposed to—"

Just then, the man in the suit and tie started up the center aisle, a newspaper in his hand. The trio of police followed. "Your Honor," the man said. "If I may address the court, please!"

The judge scowled, the corners of his mouth pulling down his fleshy cheeks. "What's the meaning of this intrusion?"

The man held up a copy of the *New York Times,* its front page filled with grainy black and white photos. "I'm Lewis Hine, a photographer with the National Child Labor Committee," he said. "I'm looking for the woman who took these pictures of boys working inside the coal breaker. Emma Malloy?"

All eyes turned toward Emma.

CHAPTER 30

The judge banged his gavel on the desk. "I insist you leave my courtroom this instant!" he said. "Miss Malloy won't be speaking with reporters until after the trial."

"Let's hear what Mr. Hines has to say!" one of the reporters in the front row shouted. He stood and went over to Mr. Hines, his note pad ready. "You said Miss Malloy took pictures of breaker boys and they were printed in the *New York Times*?"

"That's right," Mr. Hines said. "She also sent the *Times* a letter. The people outside on the courthouse steps said we could find Miss Malloy and Hazard Flint in here. We'd like to speak to them and find out what's going on in this town."

The judge pounded his gavel again, harder this time. "Do as I say, or I'll hold you in contempt!"

The man in the black uniform and bobby helmet moved past Mr. Hines and stopped between the lawyers' tables in the center of the room. The state policemen followed and stood beside him, one at each shoulder. The man in the black uniform pulled out a badge.

"I'm the state constable with the Pennsylvania Office of Factory Inspection," he said, addressing the judge. "Miss Malloy has brought it to our attention that Hazard Flint and the Bleak Mountain Mining Company have violated the state child labor law, which states no child under the age of twelve is allowed to work in the breaker, and no child under the age of fourteen is allowed to work inside the mines. We've also been informed that the mine owner is not following mining laws, and has covered up several deaths."

The judge glanced nervously at Mr. Flint, then stood. "Mr. Flint is not on trial today," he said. "Now exit my courtroom at once, or I'll have you all arrested for obstruction of justice!"

Everyone started talking at once. The judge beat his gravel on his desk again, demanding order in the courtroom. No one listened. The judge motioned the bailiff forward, his face boiling red.

In the front row, Mr. Flint shifted forward in his seat and pushed himself to his feet, using his cane for leverage. His face and hands shook as he steadied himself and gripped the railing in front of him. He sighed heavily, then looked around, his lips pinched as if to keep them from trembling. Several people noticed him standing and, one by one, they stopped talking. They nudged their neighbors and pointed at him. Little by little, the crowd settled and stared at Mr. Flint, wondering what he was going to do. The judge banged his gavel two more times, then noticed Mr. Flint looking at him and sat back down. He instructed the bailiff to hold back. The room grew quiet.

"Your Honor," Mr. Flint said, "if I may, I'd like the opportunity to speak. I've got something important to say. A good story for all the reporters here."

The judge lowered his bushy eyebrows. "What's this all about, Mr. Flint? We're nearly finished with today's proceedings and—"

"I'm the one who hired Nally O'Brian," Mr. Flint said.

The crowd went wild, gasping and talking and yelling, and the judge picked up his gavel again. But the audience went silent before he had to use it, eager to see what would happen next.

"You're not on trial here, Mr. Flint," the judge said. "And if you insist on being a witness at this point, I'll have to declare a mistrial." He pointed his gavel at Emma and Clayton. "Are you one hundred percent sure you want to risk letting those two go free?"

"You'd better let the man finish speaking," the state constable said. "We all heard what he said."

"That's right," Mr. Hines said. He jerked his chin toward the other reporters. "And it's all being recorded. You don't want it to look like you were obstructing justice, do you?"

The judge opened his mouth to reply when someone in the audience shouted, "Let him talk!"

Others joined in with demands to hear out Hazard Flint. The judge held up a hand to quiet them, then directed his attention to Mr. Flint. "Go ahead."

"I need to do this, Your Honor," Mr. Flint said. "It's my fault Levi is dead." He hesitated, his chin trembling. Then he took a deep breath and gazed at the miners and their families, tears glazing his eyes. "And now that I know what it's like to lose a son, I want to apologize to the parents of the deceased breaker boys, and any other boys who have died in the mine. I now know the horrible agony you've been living with, and I can't say how sorry I am that my greed was the cause." He looked at the judge. "I have to set things right, once and for all."

"I understand," the judge said. "But are you sure you don't want to save it for your Sunday morning confessional?"

Mr. Flint shook his head, then shuffled out of the row of seats, and, leaning hard on his cane, made his way to the front of the courtroom. He picked up the Bible, handed it to the defense attorney, put one trembling hand on it, and raised the other. The defense attorney recited the oath.

"This is not proper procedure!" the prosecutor shouted.

The judge waved a hand to silence him, and leaned back in his chair, his arms crossed. "The man's son is dead," he said. "Let him speak."

Mr. Flint took his hand from the Bible, cleared his throat, and began to talk in a gravelly voice.

"Several months ago, I hired Nally O'Brian to go undercover and infiltrate the miners. I paid him to uncover murder plots and possible strikes, and pass along the information to me so I could have the troublemakers arrested. I had no idea he was a member of the Molly Maguires."

The judge sat forward. "That's all well and good," he said. "But Nally O'Brian has already been tried and hanged for the murder of your son. How does this information change anything for the two defendants? I insist you cease and desist with this public incrimination of yourself. You're the owner of the mining company that employs nearly every citizen in this village. It will be a social and economic calamity if your company shuts down!"

"I'm not the rightful owner any longer, Your Honor," Mr. Flint said. "My late wife's family owned the Bleak Mountain Mining Company, not mine. Viviane's son is the rightful owner."

The judge's brows shot up. "What on God's green Earth are you talking about, man?" he said. "I'm sorry to remind you of your loss, but Viviane's son Levi is dead. That's why we're here!"

The audience mumbled and whispered behind their hands, shaking their heads in pity and disbelief.

Mr. Flint held up a shaky hand, waiting for the crowd to go silent. "I know this is going to sound like an old man who's gone off his rocker, but hear me out. I'm not talking about Levi. I'm talking about Viviane's other son. You've all heard the story about the kidnapping of our second born. How my sweet Viviane was so distraught over losing her baby, she hung herself in the cupola." He paused, his mouth twisting as if holding back a sob. "And now I understand why she ended her life when she lost that boy. Forgive me, Lord, I surely do. The pain of losing a child is unbearable. Except, I'm here to tell you it was all a lie. My beautiful Viviane died for nothing because the kidnapping never happened."

Gasps and shocked murmurs rippled through the courtroom.

"And what, pray tell, does this have to do with what's going on here today?" the judge said.

"Have patience with me, please," Mr. Flint said. He pulled a handkerchief from his pocket and wiped his eyes. "You see, I found out all those years ago that Viviane was having an affair. When she grew heavy with child a second time, I knew right well the baby wasn't mine. So I ordered my hired man to do away with the newborn. Then I blamed the kidnapping on the nursemaid and used the ransom money to pay her off so she would disappear."

More murmurs and gasps came from the audience. The judge's face went dark. "Hazard Flint, are you confessing to murder right here in my courtroom?"

Mr. Flint shook his head. "No, Your Honor," he said. "God

knows, I'm guilty of a lot of terrible things, and I have to live with every one of them. You can arrest me for breaking laws, taking shortcuts, and covering up the deaths of breaker boys, because that's what I deserve. Miss Malloy was right about that. But I never murdered an innocent baby or paid anyone to do it either. I instructed my hired man to drop the infant off in the miners' village on the porch of the most honest, hardworking miner I knew at the time, Charlie Nash."

A collective gasp filled the room. Emma gaped at Clayton, gooseflesh rising on her arms. Clayton's eyes were locked on Mr. Flint, his lips slightly parted, his eyebrows raised.

"Viviane's son Clayton Nash is now the rightful owner of Bleak Mountain Mining Company," Mr. Flint said. "And I'm passing the company over to him, hoping he'll do a better job than I did."

Just then, the courtroom door flew open, and a young boy rushed in, breathing hard. "They found the rest of the miners alive!" he shouted.

In a noisy flurry, the miners and their families stood and fought their way toward the door. They flooded out while the upper class of Coal River stayed in their seats, whispering behind their hands, their shocked eyes darting back and forth between Clayton and Hazard Flint.

The judge banged his gavel on his desk one last time. "Case dismissed!" he shouted.

Emma hung her head, tears of relief flooding her eyes.

CHAPTER 31

When Emma looked up from the witness stand, Clayton was on his feet, making his way toward her. The lawyers were discussing what had just happened, hands gesturing wildly, heads shaking in disbelief. Frank was helping Mr. Flint out of his seat and trying to protect him from one of the reporters. The other reporter was asking Lewis Hine and the state constable questions, quickly scribbling notes and keeping an eye on Clayton. Clearly, he planned on questioning him next. Some of the audience members had gotten up and moved closer to the main floor to hear what was being said, while others watched from the gallery. Emma stood on trembling legs and stepped down from the stand. Not wanting to draw any further attention to herself, she fought the urge to run into Clayton's arms. In what seemed like slow motion, he drew nearer until, finally, they were face-to-face. For several seconds they stared at each other, and neither spoke. His eyes were still glassy with fever and something that looked like shock.

Finally he said, "Are you all right?"

She nodded and took his hand. "Are you?"

Before he could answer, Emma saw the second reporter making his way toward them. More journalists were filing in through the main entrance and hurrying down the aisle. She scanned the room, looking for an escape. The judge was disappearing through the door behind the bench. A few feet away another door had a sign that read: Witness Holding Room. She pulled Clayton toward it.

"No, come this way," someone said, tugging on Emma's arm. She turned, ready for a struggle. It was Percy. "Use the exit beside the jury box," he said. "Follow the hall to the end and you'll find a door that leads outside."

Emma gave Percy a quick smile of gratitude and rushed toward the exit with Clayton. Together they raced down the hall and slipped outside, where they stopped on the landing to get their bearings. To their right, a set of flagstone steps led down to a walkway that followed along the side of the building, then turned right across the front of the courthouse. Beside the walkway, the land gradually sloped downhill to a slow-moving brook, then climbed back up to a granite cliff. From the top of the cliff, a waterfall cascaded down the rocks, filling the air with the soothing sound of falling water. Above the waterfall, a pine-covered swath of Bleak Mountain soared into the blue sky. A breeze had come up, temporarily clearing the smog from the valley. Emma felt as if she were seeing the natural beauty of Coal River for the first time. Her breathing slowed, and she turned toward Clayton, who looked like he was waking from a nightmare.

"I can't believe what just happened," she said. "I thought we were both going to . . ."

He wrapped his good arm around her, crushing her to his chest. "Shhh, I know. But it's over now. We're going to be all right." Afraid she was dreaming, she pressed herself into him, to feel his heart pounding against hers. He kissed the top of her head. At last, the long days of fear and grief melted away beneath his strong embrace. He held her tighter. She smiled up at him, tears in her eyes, and then his lips were on hers, kissing her long and hard. After a few moments, she pulled back and gazed up at him.

"I'm so sorry Nally shot you," she said. "Are you still in a lot of pain?"

"I'm fine," he said. "Getting better every day."

"Thank God."

"What about you?" he said. "How's your arm?"

"It's practically healed." She reached up to caress his face. "I'm so glad you're all right. I never would have forgiven myself if something had happened to you."

"It wasn't your fault."

"But if I hadn't insisted on going inside the mine. If I hadn't—"

"If you hadn't insisted, Hazard Flint would still be in charge, and everything would have stayed the same."

"But the other miners would still be alive if . . ."

He put a finger over her lips to quiet her. "There was a cave-in," he said. "That wasn't your fault either. Things are going to get better around here, and it's because of what you did. If you hadn't sent those pictures to the *Times,* Hazard Flint never would have confessed to anything. He knew he was cornered. Every man who died would be grateful to you for that."

She laid her head against his chest, her throat tight, praying what he said was true. After a long moment, she straightened and searched his face. "Did you have any idea you were Viviane Flint's son?"

He shook his head. "No. I thought my mother and father were . . . my parents."

"I'm sorry," she said. "I can't imagine what you must be feeling. But the people who raised you *were* your parents. They're the ones who loved you and taught you right from wrong. They're the ones who made you the man you are today. That's all that matters, and nothing will ever change that."

He smiled and put a gentle hand on her cheek, his eyes filled with love and gratitude. "I love you, Emma Malloy."

With gentle fingers, she combed his hair back from his forehead. He was by far the most striking man she had ever known. Even now, pale and feverish, he was beautiful to her. While every contour of muscle and bone was purely masculine, his face was so sensitive, his eyes so caring. "I love you too."

"I just have one question," he said. "Are you going to stay in Coal River and finish what you started?"

She gazed up at him, pondering her previous determination to leave after helping the breaker boys. So much had happened since then, and so much was about to change. Maybe she should stay and see how things turned out. Clayton might need her help. Besides, how could she leave the man she loved? She nodded and he grinned.

But the moment was ruined when a group of journalists came around the corner of the courthouse and sprinted toward them.

"What does it feel like to find out you're Viviane Flint's missing son?" one of them shouted.

"How soon will you take over the Bleak Mountain Mining Company?" another one said.

Clayton and Emma kissed again, then sighed and turned to face the questions.

CHAPTER 32

Emma stood at the ballroom window of Nash Mansion, formerly known as the Flint Mansion, holding back the red velvet curtain. It was early May, nearly a year since her return to Coal River, and the snow in the high forests was finally gone. From here, she could see the river, a silvery gray ribbon cutting through the land between the surrounding mountains and the east edge of town. Now when she looked at the roiling water, she was no longer overwhelmed by a sense of grief and dread. The river was nothing more than a powerful waterway, surrounded by rocks and wildlife and trees, their branches filling with buds. It was just part of the earth, as vulnerable to the will of man as any human. Coal River wasn't to blame for the death of her brother, any more than the surrounding mountains or this village. It was the people who lived and worked here who were the forces behind what had happened in the past, and they would be responsible for what would happen in the future.

After Mr. Flint's confession at the trial, the state constable had arrested him and his henchmen, including Frank, and taken them to a Scranton jail. The honest mine bosses and miners had run Uncle Otis, Aunt Ida, and the other crooked bosses out of town.

Clayton had taken over the Bleak Mountain Mining Company, and after a few months of repairs, the mine opened up again. The majority of Hazard Flint's money was in the company's name, so Clayton used it to replace dangerous equipment, build emergency exits, and install proper ventilation systems. He handpicked the new supervisors and foremen, gave all the miners a fair wage, and replaced the breaker boys with men. He gave money to the miners to raise barns, and brought in livestock to help them become more self-sufficient. He renamed the Company Store Albert & Michael's General Store, lowered the prices, and gave the miners the choice to shop where they wanted.

Before moving into the mansion, Clayton sold the paintings, rugs, and furniture at a Scranton auction to raise money for the miners' families and the orphans of Coal River. Now simple furniture and handmade rugs—purchased from the miners' wives and other poor Pennsylvania craftsmen—filled the house. Everything was going better than Emma could have dreamed.

She let the curtain drop, her stomach filled with nervous butterflies. What if today didn't work out the way she'd hoped?

The double ballroom doors opened, and Clayton entered, wringing his hands.

"Do we have enough desks?" he said.

She made her way toward him, moving between the rows of wooden benches and desks. "I hope so!"

"What about the chalkboard?" he said. "Is it big enough?"

She turned to look at the freestanding chalkboard he had ordered. "Yes, it's perfect."

"Is there anything else you need?" he said. "Do you have enough chalk? Enough books? Enough rulers?"

"Yes!" she said. "Yes! Stop worrying, will you? You've gotten more than enough supplies for us." She bit the edge of her lip. "I just wonder how many will show up. I mean, I know Sawyer, Jack, Edith, Sadie, and Violet will be here. After all, they live right upstairs, but . . ."

Clayton took her in his arms. "Don't worry, Mrs. Nash. You've earned the trust of so many of the miners and their families. The rest will catch on when they see the other children doing so well. Besides, how could all those boys not come to school when they're going to have such a beautiful teacher?" He kissed her long and hard on the mouth.

Someone knocked on the open door. It was her cousin, Percy.

"Emma?" he said. "There's someone here to see you."

"Oh," she said. She lifted the hem of her skirt and made her way toward him.

"No," Percy said. He pointed to the doors that led out to the balcony. "They're waiting for you out there."

Puzzled, she turned toward the balcony. Her mind raced, going over the speech she had prepared to welcome the students to their new school. She rehearsed the rules and how she was going to get the kids excited about learning. She hadn't decided if she should begin by reading a story or asking everyone to stand and introduce themselves. More than anything, she wanted the students to like her so they would come back. She grabbed the balcony door handles and hesitated, suddenly afraid the miners' wives had come to tell her they didn't want their children attending school when they could be helping out at home.

Taking a deep breath, Emma swung open the double doors and stepped out onto the sun-filled terrace. She stopped short and put her fingers over her trembling lips. Her eyes grew misty. Clayton came out and stood beside her, grinning as he looked out over the railing. Before them, filling the manicured lawn, stood dozens of young girls and former breaker boys, waiting to attend their first day of school in Coal River. Behind the children, near the wading pool in the center of the front lawn, Michael stood with one hand raised. For the first time ever, he was smiling. Emma never found out how he knew about Albert, or if her brother really was trying to communicate from beyond the grave. But for now she would have to accept that maybe there was no answer. Today, she was looking toward the future.

AUTHOR'S NOTE

During the writing of *Coal River* I relied on the following books: *Early Coal Mining in the Anthracite Region,* by John Stuart Richards; *Growing Up in Coal Country,* by Susan Campbell Bartoletti; and *Historical Account of the Mollie Maguires,* by A. Monroe Aurand Jr. It is important to note that for the purpose of plot, the date of the article in the *Scranton Times* was changed from 1902 to 1912. By the time of my story, Johnny Mitchell had retired as president of the United Mine Workers of America (UMWA). It is also important to note that Lewis Hines was a real person who, through his photography, exposed child labor in coal mines, cotton mills, factories, the newspaper industry, seafood ports, agriculture, and retail sales. The town of Coal River, Pennsylvania, is fictitious, and should not be confused with any actual place.

Please turn the page
for a very special Q&A
with Ellen Marie Wiseman!

What was the inspiration for _Coal River_?
I've always been fascinated by coal mining, and the fact that men risked their lives every day to make a living by going deep in the earth despite the danger of cave-ins and explosions. I can't imagine how difficult it must have been. When I found out young boys were used to sort coal until their fingers bled, and realized other people hadn't heard of the breaker boys either, I knew it was a story that needed to be told. I also wanted to write about the boys who worked as nippers, spraggers, and mule drivers.

How did researching the breaker boys make you feel?
It was heartbreaking to read about young boys working ten hours a day in extremely dangerous conditions, knowing they never really had a childhood, and that there were so many injured and killed. Although public disapproval of the employment of children as breaker boys existed by the mid-1880s, the practice did not end until the 1920s. For ten hours a day, six days a week, breaker boys sat on wooden seats, perched over the chutes and conveyor belts, picking slate and other impurities out of the coal. They would stop the coal by pushing their boots into the stream of coal flowing beneath them, pick out the impurities, and then let the coal pass on to the next breaker boy for further processing.

As if sorting coal wasn't hard enough, the breaker boys were forced to work without gloves so that they could better handle the slick coal. The slate, however, was sharp, and boys would often leave work with their fingers cut and bleeding. Not only that, but coal was often washed to remove impurities, which created sulfuric acid and burned the breaker boys' hands. Sometimes they had their fingers amputated by the rapidly moving conveyor belts. Others lost feet, hands, arms, and legs as they moved among the equipment and became caught under conveyor belts or in gears. Many were crushed to death, their bodies retrieved from the machinery only at the end of the working day. Others were caught in the rush of coal, and crushed or smothered. Dry coal would kick up so much dust that breaker boys sometimes wore lamps on their heads to see, and asthma and black lung disease were common.

Did you do any on-site research for this book?
Yes, I went inside the Pioneer Tunnel Coal Mine in Ashland, Pennsylvania, and visited Jim Thorpe, Pennsylvania, to see the Asa Packer Mansion Museum and the Old Jail Museum, where seven accused Molly Maguires met their death on the gallows inside the cellblock. Ironically, being deep inside the mine didn't bother me, but being inside the jail was very disturbing. I couldn't wait to leave!

Your first two novels, *The Plum Tree* and *What She Left Behind*, feature young women who refuse to give up hope and are determined to do the right thing. In *Coal River*, Emma wants to help the breaker boys no matter what it takes. Why do you think you're drawn to write about strong women?
Probably because I'd like to think that I would strive to do the right thing in those kinds of situations too. I think most people can relate to that.

This is your third novel. Does writing books get any easier?
I wish! For me, it seems to get harder every time. Partially because I'm not clever enough to come up with new ways of saying things, and partially because every story comes out differently, meaning bits and pieces come to you as you write, and you're not sure if it's making sense, if it's in order, or if what you're writing is even important to the book. When that happens, it can be scary because it feels like you have no idea what you're doing! Hopefully, by around the third draft, you find your way and finally see that, thank goodness, there really is a story there. A wise author friend once told me that one thing to remember and accept is that we're all learning, and that each novel we write will teach us something. I try to remember that, but sometimes it can be hard. The other thing that makes it difficult for me is that I wish I had more time to polish my prose. It's what I'd like most to improve on.

COAL RIVER

Ellen Marie Wiseman

ABOUT THIS GUIDE

The suggested questions are included
to enhance your group's reading of
Ellen Marie Wiseman's *Coal River*.

Discussion Questions

1. The use of breaker boys began in the mid-1860s. Their job was to separate impurities from coal by hand inside the coal breaker, ten hours a day, six days a week. Not only were they forced to work without gloves, but the working conditions inside the breaker were extremely dangerous. Had you ever heard of the breaker boys before reading *Coal River*? Were you surprised to learn that young boys were used in coal mining?

2. Many of the miners' wives allowed their underage sons to work in the breaker to bring in an extra income, especially if they had other children to feed, or their husbands had been injured or killed. Sometimes parents even lied about their son's age so he would be hired. If you had been in the same situation, living in poverty and unable to feed your children, what would you have done?

3. Orphaned and penniless, Emma is forced to choose between the poorhouse and going back to Coal River where her brother drowned and her uncle mistreated her. Considering the times, what do you think would have happened to Emma if she had chosen the poorhouse? What would you have done?

4. To help the miners, Emma steals food from her aunt and marks bills paid at the Company Store. She knows stealing is wrong but does it anyway. Why do you think she felt it was okay in this situation? Would you have done the same thing? Why or why not?

5. In the early days of mining, there was a lot of tension between the mine owners, the Coal and Iron Police, and the miners. There was a lot of violence, and sometimes it was hard to tell the good guys from the bad guys. In *Coal River,*

did you know right away who was good and bad? Why or why not?

6. How do you think Emma changed over the course of the novel? What were the most important events that facilitated those changes? Why do you think she was so determined to help the breaker boys?

7. How did you feel about Clayton when you first met him? Did you trust him? What about Nally? How were Clayton and Nally the same? How were they different?

8. Emma is doubtful that her dead brother is speaking to her through Michael. In the end she is still not sure. What do you think? Do you believe in channeling and mediums?

9. When Emma and Uncle Otis are arguing up at the mine, they both have different memories of the time her parents were staying in Coal River. Otis thinks they were freeloading, while Emma remembers them helping Aunt Ida by fixing the roof and doing housework. It's said that people remember history differently, even if it's a conversation or argument from the day before. Has that ever happened to you? Have you had conflict in your life because someone remembered an incident differently than you did?

10. How did you feel about Percy when you first met him? How about Frank? Did you end up feeling differently about them by the end of the book? Why?

11. What do you think Frank's motives were when he told Hazard Flint that Emma was becoming friendly with the miners' wives and children? Why did it backfire?

12. Twice, Emma risked her life to save Frank. Why do you think she did it? Would you risk your life to save someone who had harmed or mistreated you?

13. Even though Pennsylvania child labor laws came into effect in the late 1800s, many mine owners got away with putting underage boys to work in the breakers and mines until the 1920s. Why do you think it was allowed to continue for so long? What could have been done to stop it?

14. At the time of the story, unions were important for helping miners stand up for their rights against powerful mine owners. Why do you think that was? Do you think unions are a good thing or a bad thing? What do you think of unions today?

15. At the end of *Coal River*, secrets were revealed that changed everything. Which ones surprised you the most? Did you see any of them coming?